The Songwriter Gets His Girl

JANE POLLER

BOOKS

Dedicated to my husband, who tells me to pull my head out of my ass and listen to my intuition on these stories. Thanks for telling me I'm a good writer and for building me up when I'm freaking out over little things. You're my Happily Ever After, and I'm forever grateful for you.

Vinci Books

vinci-books.com

Published by Vinci Books Ltd in 2026

1

Copyright © Jane Poller 2022

The author has asserted their moral right to be identified as the author of this work in accordance with the Copyright, Designs and Patents Act 1988. This work is a work of fiction. Names, characters, places and incidents are the product of the author's imagination or are used fictitiously. Any resemblance to actual persons, living or dead, places and incidents is entirely coincidental.

All rights reserved. No part of this publication may be copied, reproduced, distributed, stored in any retrieval system, or transmitted in any form or by any means, including photocopying, recording, or other electronic or mechanical methods, nor used as a source for any form of machine learning including AI datasets, without the prior written permission of the publisher.

The publisher and the author have made every effort to obtain permissions for any third party material used in this book and to comply with copyright law. Any queries in this respect should be brought to the attention of the publisher and any omissions will be corrected in future editions.

A CIP catalogue record for this book is available from the British Library.

Paperback ISBN: 9781036707958

By Jane Poller

Crimson Creek

The Soldier Gets His Girl
The Sheriff Gets His Girl
The Songwriter Gets His Girl
The Surgeon Gets His Girl
The Mechanic Gets His Girl
The Ranger Gets His Girl
The Cowboy Gets His Girl
The Convict Gets His Girl

Prologue

I'd say it's the perfect day, but it fades to gray without your face. In the sunlight, can't you see? It's not the same without you here with me.
undefined.

Five years ago

"Who knew Tennessee was so beautiful?" Landry Williams glanced out the window of his childhood best friend's truck. The trees were turning colors, and the sun reflected oranges and reds as it began to set. There was a nip in the air that didn't happen in Texas this early in fall, and he was damn glad to get out of the state.

"Getting sentimental in your old age?" Andy smirked, making Landry laugh.

"Twenty-four is hardly old, but if it was, what does that make you, Grandpa?"

Andy chuckled and shook his head, making Landry

grin. Andy may have been a few years than him, but the two had been best friends while growing up. He was one of the few who'd left Crimson Creek that Landry kept in contact with.

"So, what made you decide to come up for the weekend?" Andy pulled away from the Nashville traffic and onto the road leading north to Fort Campbell.

"Parker has a rare weekend off from soccer at his university. His roommate, Mike, is from Nashville, so they flew up to go to some party with Mike's parents. They're apparently big names in the music business."

"You didn't want to go with them to the party?"

Landry turned from the window and grinned at Andy. "It's been almost a year since you've been home. I'd rather catch up with you. Besides, Pops would've killed me if I was this close to your base and didn't come see you. What have you been doing?"

Andy laughed. "How's your grandpa doing after losing your grandma?"

Landry shrugged and looked back out the window. "He's ok, mostly. He hasn't been alone at the shop since and is feeling smothered by Mom. He practically pushed me out the door, said he could handle all the jobs by himself this weekend."

Landry loved working with his grandpa as the town's handyman and general contractor. They stayed busy, and Landry had been working since high school to take over the business. His grandparents had semi-retired a few years ago, but his grandpa had thrown himself back into it after his grandma passed.

"I'm sorry I missed her funeral."

Landry shrugged off the tightness in his chest. "You

were deployed, dude. Don't worry about it. I hear you got a promotion too. How's that going?"

Andy talked about his last deployment and his promotion, then asked about news from their hometown.

Landry snorted. "As if your Aunt Suzie doesn't keep you updated on all the latest gossip."

But like any loyal friend, he launched into the latest drama at the church, whose family was moving out, who had moved in, and what school friends were married now.

"So, what's the plan for the weekend? What kind of trouble are we gonna cause?"

Andy turned off the highway and into Clarksville. "Pool party tonight with my Army buddies. Remember Kendall, the guy from basic training years ago? It's his house. Tomorrow, we're going fishin' and campin' at Land Between the Lakes."

He parked the truck, and they hopped out. The little house was in a small neighborhood, and vehicles already lined the street.

They walked up the sidewalk to the front porch just as the door flew open. The last of the sun's rays landed on a gorgeous, petite blond, her hair spilling in waves around her shoulders.

Her thin green sweater hung off one shoulder, her top the same forest green as her eyes. She glanced at them as she walked out the door.

Landry was mesmerized by the flecks of gold in her eyes that shone in the light, glimpses into heaven that he couldn't quite grab but wanted to reach for.

She blew a bubble with her gum and popped it right as she passed him on the stairs, her pink lips causing his cock to twitch. He turned to watch her bounce down the stairs and to a little white car.

Her hips were distracting in those skintight blue jeans. So much so that he stumbled on the stairs, his arms flinging out and catching Andy.

Andy grunted. "What the hell, man?"

"My bad. Got distracted." Landry hadn't even turned to look at Andy; he was still watching the woman get into her car and drive away.

Andy chuckled. "Yeah, I see that, but she's off limits. That's Kendall's sister."

The door opened again, drawing his attention. A tall blond shook Andy's hand, his green eyes warm and smiling.

"Andy, you made it. Perfect timing, man. Come on in. A few guys from my platoon are here. Did you invite yours?"

"You know it. This is Landry, a childhood friend. He's up visiting for the weekend. Landry, this is Kendall."

Landry stepped up to shake the man's hand. "It's nice to finally meet you. Thanks for letting me crash your party."

"Hey, the more the merrier. You just missed my sister, but the rest of the guests are inside. I'll show you around, and you can tell me about Andy and Crimson Creek. Is the town really that great?"

Landry was led inside as they talked. Music played softly on a karaoke machine in the corner. He lost track of the names of those he met and how many snacks he ate. An hour later, he was slightly tipsy when the bubble gum angel from earlier returned.

He tracked her as she drifted across the floor to her brother, who stood making cocktails at the wet bar. Landry guzzled the last of his drink and walked over for a refill, eager to meet her.

"I don't care, Holly. He's not welcome, and you shouldn't be drinking." Kendall's frown could rival Andy's

The Songwriter Gets His Girl

scowl, and Landry wondered if they taught that expression to every Army recruit.

"Kendall, I'm twenty-one. I can drink if I want to, just like everything else. It's my life, remember? Not yours." Her voice was soft and lilting, like honey draping across his tongue and making his mouth water.

"I'm just looking out for you, you know this. It's what big brothers are for."

"Well, back off a little and let me be me. First order of business? A drink."

Landry slid his drink across the bar's countertop. "I'd like one too, while you're at it. Hello, Miss. You must be Kendall's sister?"

He held out a hand to shake and barely heard Kendall growl. Her eyes narrowed, her lips tipping on one side in a mischievous smirk.

"Well, hello to yourself. Name's Holly, but you're the only one here who will talk to me tonight. He's warned every other person away."

Their hands met, and Landry felt his tremble, not from her grip but from the electricity that ran down his arm at the contact.

He cleared his throat. "Landry. I'm a friend of Andy's from Texas, which might be why Kendall didn't warn me away. I'm not a military guy like all these fine gents."

Holly grabbed their drinks and handed his over before looping her arm in his and dragging him away from the bar and Kendall's murderous gaze. "Excellent, I'm about fed up with military guys. Tell me, Landry, what do you do if you're not military?"

"I co-own a handyman business with my grandfather. If he didn't need me so much, I would've joined the military, but it hasn't worked out that way."

She led him to the front porch where a swing sat empty in the corner. He sat and took a long drink of his beer, his mouth parched in her presence.

She pulled a leg up and turned to face him, her back to the arm of the swing, and set it to rocking softly with her other leg.

"That's very admirable of you, to stick around for him. What's he like?"

Landry opened up like never before, perhaps from the alcohol or perhaps she just had that effect on him. He didn't even talk with his mom so freely. He talked about losing his grandma last year and how his grandfather's health had declined steadily, how he'd wanted to go off to college and had a full ride music scholarship but had given it up.

"So if you could do anything in the world, what would you do?" Her eyes glowed in the soft porch lights. He could happily get lost in those eyes every day of his life.

His heart raced at the thought. Maybe she was the one. Maybe she would complete him and make life worth living, the way his grandma had made life worth living for his grandpa.

He took a drink to settle his nerves. "I'd make music that brings happiness to others. I like to make people laugh and see them have a good time. My brothers and I play on weekends at the local bar, and it's so fun. They aren't there to see us, of course, but we make them smile and help them relax after a hard week. So it's worth it to me. I don't want to play at a bar forever, but I... well, it's fun."

She tilted her head to the side. "Fun is good. My brother loses sight of that, but it helps balance all the bad that's happened."

"I'd hate to think anything bad happened to you."

Her blush made his pants a little tighter, and that coy

glance away slayed him. Her voice was soft, floating on the breeze and barely discernible.

"You're sweet, but life isn't all sunshine and rainbows."

The sadness in her eyes speared his heart, making him nearly gasp from the suddenness of it. He wanted nothing more than to see her laugh and smile and be happy. He finished his drink, then turned to face her more.

"So, what happened?"

She shook her head and glanced to the parking lot. "Mom had cancer and my aunt died in a house fire right after I graduated high school. That was when I moved in with Kendall, and he isn't the easiest to live with."

"Yeah, he seems pretty protective, but I imagine I'd be the same way if I had a sister."

She rolled her eyes. "Yeah, but I started dating an Army guy while he was deployed. Then my boyfriend deployed right before Kendall came home. But now Eric's back, and Kendall's not happy about it."

She looked out at the driveway, as if she were waiting for someone.

He frowned and looked down, picking at the label on his beer bottle. "Are you still dating him?"

She sighed and sank against the back of the swing. "I don't even know anymore. He went to the field last week, and right before he left, we had a big fight about Kendall and the meaning of family. We broke up, but he texted me earlier about how he needed to talk to me. I didn't answer."

She took a sip of her drink, and the crickets sang to them in the cool night. His heart jumped to hear she was single, but she was clearly still hung up on this other guy. He couldn't stand to see her so sad. The sadness that hung around her ate at him, driving his need to fix it, to cheer her up and change the subject.

"So I hear this is supposed to be a pool party? Is that music I hear in the backyard?"

She brightened and nodded. "Yep, pool's out back. Did you bring a swimsuit? You can borrow one of Kendall's if not."

"I brought one. It's in Andy's truck." They walked to the truck, talking about everything and nothing at once. By the time she led him to the bathroom to change, he knew her favorite food, drink, color, and preferred music. And best of all, she was smiling and laughing again.

When he shut the bathroom door and changed, he realized it hurt to be away from her. He wanted to spend the entire night with her, just talking and seeing how her mind worked.

Well, to be honest he wanted to fuck her, but that was just part of it. A knock sounded on the door.

Her face lit up when he opened it, then her mouth formed an O as her gaze drifted over his arms and across his pecs. He wasn't ripped like a bodybuilder, but being a handyman kept him in good shape. Of course, he flexed a little as he reached for the towel on the shelf by the door.

She shook her head, then sucked in a breath, pushing her breasts against the thin fabric of her hot pink bikini, visible in the see-through swim cover she wore. She'd reapplied her lipstick, and his swim trunks were not doing a good job of keeping his erection down. She popped another bubble, the pink rivaling her lipstick and swimsuit.

"Ready?" Was it just him or was her voice breathier, higher? Was that what she'd sound like when he fucked her? God, he hoped so.

He nodded, and she spun on her bare heel and led the way out the back door. The party was in full swing now, with a few dozen people lounging or swimming in the pool.

The Songwriter Gets His Girl

Some guy did a cannonball right as they walked past, splashing them both. Holly squealed and Landry laughed, ushering her to the end of the pool and a quieter corner of the back yard.

His hand tingled where it settled on the small of her back.

She waved to the side of the house. "Pool or hot tub?"

It was well lit, but only a few people were in the hot tub, hidden from the rowdier guys in the pool.

"Hot tub." He wasn't sure he could survive the heat combined with her next to him, but he didn't want the guys in the pool staring at her in the bikini. The urge to keep her from prying eyes and all to himself was too strong.

He climbed into the hot tub, quickly sinking down to hide his erection. She took off her swimsuit cover, and he sucked in a quick breath. She was lean and toned but not really curvy. He immediately wanted to pick her up and feel her wrap her legs around him. She was small enough to balance easily.

A tall, dark-haired soldier came up behind her. Before Landry could open his mouth to warn her or jump out of the hot tub, the man had wrapped his arm around her waist from behind. She gasped and turned around.

She squealed a laugh as he picked her up and spun her in circles before setting her down. Her bikini-clad body smashed against the man, still in most of his uniform, and he leaned down to kiss her. Landry's breath whooshed out like someone had punched him in the gut.

She pushed against him and broke the kiss. Landry gripped the edge of the hot tub, ready to leap out and punch him if he didn't let her go.

"What the hell, Eric?"

The man grabbed her hands and pleaded with her.

"Look, I'm sorry about last weekend. This was the hardest week of my life. The deployment wasn't even as bad as this week, because then I could still talk to you. But this week without you? Knowing you were mad and disappointed in me? Holly, I can't be without you again. Please forgive me."

She sighed, and he kissed her again. Landry felt like he was going to be sick. His fists clenched and sweat broke out on his forehead. What the hell was going on?

When they ended the kiss, the man hugged her tight. "Damn, that was a long week in the field. I came straight here."

"I can tell." Her laughter rang softly through the night, the voices of the others in the hot tub drowned out by her joy. "You didn't even shower, Eric."

"No time. I can always just jump in the pool." The man's lopsided grin was sickening because Landry knew that look. It was the same look his dad gave his mom and his grandpa had given his grandma.

His head spun as he looked at Holly, because she was giving the man the same love-sick look. Shit. Of course, she was taken. They might have been broken up, but her face said it all. She loved him.

And that guy was the luckiest son of a bitch at the party. She was gorgeous, sweet, kind, and sassy.

Landry's eyes landed on Kendall when he stormed outside and glanced around. Catching sight of Holly, he hustled across the yard, dodging people as he strode through with a scowl. But before he reached them, the soldier dropped to one knee. Landry and Kendall both froze, jaws dropped in surprise.

She pulled away with a gasp, but he kept hold of her hand.

"Holly, you're the reason I get up every morning and

why I try to be the best man I can be. You're my future, my joy, my entire world. I can't stand to be apart from you, not talk to you before going to bed. Will you marry me?"

Holly started jumping up and down, pulling his eyes. Landry's body reacted with a jerk and tucked away the memory to analyze later.

But right now, his heart was being drug through the fire, hardening him as once again he was left on the outside of happiness. Throughout high school, he'd been the third wheel, the geeky band nerd little brother.

After high school, he'd learned the business, taken handyman certification classes, and watched as friend after friend found their special person and got married. He'd slipped into a pattern of one-night stands and girlfriends who only lasted a few weeks before they realized he would never move out of his hometown or get a different job.

This gorgeous woman had given him hope. But it was a pipe dream meant for everyone else but him.

The man slipped a ring onto her finger and then swept her up into a hug. The whole crowd cheered. Except for Kendall, who strode forward, a fake smile on his face as he held out his hand to shake his soon to be brother-in-law.

Chapter One

I'd say it's the perfect day, blue skies and golden rays, but it's missing something sweet, since you're not here next to me.

April, 2 years ago

Leaning her head against the passenger side window of Kendall's car, Holly stared at the man on the ladder fixing the Diner's sign. It was spring in Crimson Creek, Texas, and the trees on Main Street were blooming beautiful lilac-colored flowers, but inside Holly was still cold and frozen.

She'd felt like that since August when her entire world fell apart. Her mind shied away from that night, and she focused on regulating her breathing like the therapist said as Kendall parked on the street and cut the engine.

"Come on, sis. Let's get some lunch. I don't have groceries, but we can eat before getting you moved in. Then I can get groceries later."

"Still living on military grub?" Even her voice sounded hollow to her own ears. Catching sight of her reflection in the window before she opened her door, she sighed at the bags under her eyes and the wan, lost expression on her face.

They reached the sidewalk, and Holly frowned as she pulled her sweater around her. The man on the ladder seemed familiar somehow. He was a typical small-town hunk with his dirty work boots, faded jeans, and a green Henley. He was beefy too, rather than tall and lanky like her brother. Covered in a fine layer of dust, he used his cordless power drill to fix something behind the sign.

As they walked closer, he glanced down. A smile broke out on his face, and she stumbled to a halt. It was the guy from the pool party, from when she'd gotten engaged to Eric years ago.

He stepped down the ladder, his movements hurried and causing his foot to miss a rung. She gasped and stepped aside as he fell the last two feet, wincing as he landed wrong.

"Whoa, you ok, Landry?" Kendall reached out a hand to grab the man by the shoulder so he wouldn't fall all the way to the ground.

His name was Landry. She'd forgotten that, in the excitement of the engagement.

Landry grimaced, putting pressure on his foot with a hiss. "Yep, just fine. Probably sprained it, but nothing an ice pack won't fix. I see you convinced her to move to town after all."

He nodded at Holly, his hazel eyes bright in the spring sun. His light hair was almost brown, with natural blond streaks any girl would kill for. She nervously touched the end of her long braid, now dyed silver. Her hair used to be more blond than his.

Kendall nodded, clapping Landry on the back. "Come inside with us and prop that ankle up. We'll get some ice on it. If you're hungry, then by the time we're done eating, you'll probably be ok to get back to work."

"Aye aye, Doc." Landry winked at her brother, who just rolled his eyes and moved the ladder out of the way on the sidewalk, laying it on its side.

Holly blinked, unsure of this side of her brother. Admittedly, they hadn't seen a lot of each other in the three years since she'd married Eric, but with his death last August, Kendall had been... nicer wasn't the right word. Deferential?

Three years ago, there's no way that Kendall would've invited anyone to eat with them. He'd always tried to keep her away from guys, which was why he and Eric hadn't gotten along very well.

She took a deep, shuttered breath as Landry hobbled closer.

"Hello again." She nodded her head and held her hand out, but the man didn't stop to shake her hand. Instead, he wrapped her in a warm hug.

She froze in his arms, her hands automatically going to his waist. Her heart stopped, her breathing stopped. Everything froze.

There hadn't been anyone to hug for a while now. Her in-laws were cruel, and all her friends had sort of just stopped coming around, not knowing how to be around her when she was so broken. This was... nice. She swallowed hard as her eyes teared up.

"I'm sorry about your husband and baby." His voice

was low, raspy from emotion that only came from someone who'd experienced significant loss and was still dealing with it. It choked her up, a knot forming in her throat as she blinked back tears.

The hug lasted longer than it should have, but she didn't mind for once. It was the warmest she'd felt in months, like she was protected and nothing could hurt her again while she was in the safety of his arms.

God, she was a mess. She sucked in a ragged breath, breathing in the comforting smell of leather and mint, and whispered, "Thank you."

He chuckled awkwardly and pulled away to look down at her, his hazel eyes bright in the spring sunshine. "Sorry, I'm a hugger. And we've already met, so it's not as awkward as hugging a stranger, right?"

His grin was infectious. She didn't even realize she was smiling softly back at him until Kendall froze, looking at her with surprise. Then she caught sight of her reflection in the windows of the Diner. She shook her head, surprised by the normalcy of her smile.

Landry continued. "Don't think that your brother is the only friendly face you have in town. Anytime he's at work and you need something, just call me. You hungry? I can introduce you to everyone in the Diner."

She nodded, swallowing hard and wrapping her sweater around her again as they walked the last few feet to the Diner's door. Kendall opened it, and she stepped inside. With red and white checkered floors and red booths along the wall, it was a classic all-American place that smelled of fried food and home. A counter with bar seating right led to the kitchen. It was country cute and reminded her of her aunt with its homeliness.

She'd grown up in Dallas and then had moved to military bases with Kendall and then Eric. This small-town thing was going to be an adventure, and Kendall said she needed it. God knew she needed something to get her out of the hell loop she'd been in with Eric's parents.

She walked to the booth where Kendall now sat and slid in next to him, but he frowned. "No, you sit over there with Landry, so he can prop his foot up. I've already asked Dot to bring him a pack of ice."

Holly sighed and stood to take the opposite bench, the red leather smooth under her black yoga pants.

"Thanks for this, Kendall, but you know I'm fine, right? Nothing to worry about, although I'm not one to turn down a meal." Landry chuckled as the waitress brought a bag of ice.

"You must be the Doc's sister. It's nice to meet you, honey, and really hope you like living here. You need anything at all, just pop your pretty head in here and holler, okay?" The woman's smile was genuine, surprising Holly.

Landry laughed as he took the bag of ice and slid in beside her. "I just told her the same thing outside."

Holly just nodded back at the waitress and picked up her menu, hugging the wall and putting as much space between her and Landry as possible. His body heat was still radiating toward her like some kind of furnace.

Maybe he was a lava god or something. Except he kind of looked like the actor in that new King Arthur movie that had just come out. Maybe a Viking, but with shorter hair, his hair cropped close on the sides but longer on top. Not quite the military hair cut she was used to, but long enough to run fingers through.

"You ready to order?" the waitress asked.

Holly glanced up, shaken out of her musings to see

Kendall frowning, his brow wrinkled in worry. Landry was smiling patiently, his eyes seeing too much.

They must have already ordered, and she'd missed it, lost in thought again. She turned the menu over.

"Just a loaded baked potato is fine, no bacon. Thanks."

They handed the menus over, and Kendall turned to Landry. "She's a vegetarian. Don't know how, since we grew up in Texas eating lots of barbecue."

Landry grinned and met her eyes, his mischievous and making her lean away. He was too full of joy, his face ready to burst into laughter at any moment. It must be exhausting to be that happy.

"Really? That's kind of cool, but don't you miss it? Come on, what was your favorite meat?"

She shrugged. "Don't miss it, no."

Kendall jumped in, raising his brow at her. "She used to love when I'd smoke ribs and pulled pork, but when she moved in with me after high school, she decided it was vegetarian for her. I thought it was just another little rebellion at being uprooted, but I guess I was wrong."

Holly smirked and crossed her arms. "Let me get out my phone to video that. I need it on record."

Landry laughed, the sound somehow making her feel lighter. He pulled Kendall into a conversation about the different things he'd done around town, since Kendall had only been living here about a year. They were apparently in a weekly poker game at Landry's house.

That was good because her brother had been lost after he'd retired from the Army. He hadn't been happy at the big city hospital but coming to this little town of Crimson Creek had been good for him. He seemed less stressed and more rested.

The Songwriter Gets His Girl

When a lull in conversation came, Holly interrupted. "Are you still doing handyman stuff, Landry?"

His eyes met hers in surprise. "You remembered?" He cleared his throat and glanced away as pink tinged his cheeks. "Um, yeah, I own the company, now that my grandpa passed away too."

She laid a hand on his arm, feeling sparks up her arm and jerking it back. "I'm sorry for your loss. What happened?"

Landry shrugged, his eyes sad as he fiddled with the straw in his water. "Broken heart. He hung around for a few years after grandma passed, but never got his energy and drive back. Ended up having a heart attack, which took him fast."

She swallowed hard and focused on breathing evenly. Before she could reply, the waitress arrived with their food.

"Here ya go, folks. Doc was telling me last week you were a yoga instructor. Are you going to open up a yoga studio? We sure could use it. There's nothing here. No gym, no workout space, nothing. Only way people are active is if they play in the softball league or go to the city pool."

Holly's eyebrows rose in surprise. "I hadn't thought about it, to be honest, but I suppose I could."

Landry swallowed a drink of his water before saying, "There's a few places on Main Street that could easily be remodeled into a yoga studio. I'm more than happy to help you look at them and decide, analyze the renovation budget, and all that."

"That'd be great, since I wouldn't even know where to start."

The waitress nodded. "Oh, you're in good hands. Landry's the best handyman in town."

Landry laughed. "I'm the *only* one in town."

The little brunette grinned, placing her hand on his shoulder and making Holly's stomach drop. She didn't know what this feeling was, but she didn't like the waitress touching him. "Doesn't make it any less true."

Landry waggled his eyebrows. "Make sure you tell my brothers I'm the best when they come in next."

She laughed before seeing if they needed anything else and leaving them to eat their lunch.

Chapter Two

Why'd you have to go? Why'd you have to leave? I'd give anything just to see you again.

A week after moving to town, Holly was a bundle of restless energy. Her brother, Kendall, had said to give it a few days to settle into his house, but she couldn't take the silence anymore. She didn't like staying home, watching movies, and wallowing. Thinking and feeling. That's what she'd done since August, mostly because she hadn't had the energy.

Kendall had said her body was still healing, but it was more than that. It was like she was in this limbo state or stuck in a vat of molasses with no way out. Her entire life's plan was gone, buried beside her husband and daughter.

Her throat started to close as she pictured her premature baby girl, born a few hours after the wreck that killed Eric. She'd been barely the size of her hand and had only taken a few breaths before she passed.

Holly wiped her eyes and turned from the window to grab her sneakers. Kendall was working the night shift tonight at the hospital, but it wasn't even dark yet. She could go for a bike ride. Surely the fresh air would do her good.

When she sat on the bike and kicked off, the wind seemed to blow her pent-up feelings away. She rode toward the center of town, turning onto Main and passing the grocery store.

Two kids were getting into a car as their mom loaded groceries into the trunk. Holly almost bit her tongue. How long would it take before she could see something like that and not feel such a stabbing pain in her heart? She was already fucking tired of it, so very tired.

She turned down a side street, admiring the trees that lined the road, their purple buds just starting to bloom. A few deep breaths and her heartbeat evened, feeling less like the weight of a thousand bricks pressing on it.

She approached a winding stream and slowed her bike, glancing around. A sidewalk led along the creek to an old mill, which appeared to be a business. After checking her phone's GPS map, she turned onto the sidewalk and biked along the path.

As she pedaled closer to the old mill, the faint sound of shattering glass shattered the quiet of the twilight. The parking lot was desolate, with no cars in sight and the business already closed for the day. She halted her bike, scanning her surroundings for the source of the noise and unsure whether to continue down the path to the creek or go back to the town to her right.

The echoes of smashing glass came from the creek. If it was kids, she didn't want them to get in trouble with the law or anything. She'd just go check and make sure everyone was safe.

She hopped off and walked through the grass to a tree, leaning the bike against it. She walked down the dirt path as the shadows lengthened. If it wasn't such a small town, she might have been afraid.

She shook her head. Who was she kidding? She had felt nothing but fear when riding in a car for months. Fear paralyzed her until she'd become numb. She'd cut off those emotions when the grief had gotten too hard to bear. Now she was just cold all the time. It was probably safer this way too, to not feel all the pain.

The path opened to a larger portion of the stream. A wide pipe ran across the creek, and on the other side was a small, old brick building, run-down now with the roof partially caved in. Two women had a fire going in a pit. The petite brunette cheered as the tall red head wound up and threw something against the side of the building.

Smash. The glass bottle shattered, and the women howled before high fiving. The dark-haired one turned to get another bottle and saw Holly.

"Hey, are you friend or foe?" Her low voice echoed in the near darkness.

The tall one spun around to see who she was talking to and put her hands on her hips to glare at Holly. "You better not tell Gunner we're here. We're not hurting anything."

Holly shook her head and frowned. "Who's Gunner? Never mind. I was just making sure it wasn't kids causing trouble or getting hurt. I'll leave y'all alone."

She turned to leave, but the dark-haired one called out, "Wait, are you the new girl in town? Lola, I think that's Kendall's sister."

The auburn-haired one scowled and crossed her arms. "If she's anything like her brother, then she can move right along. He's a dickhead."

Holly was so surprised by the comment that laughter burst out of her mouth. Then she couldn't stop it. The laughter just kept coming until tears ran down her face.

No one ever talked about her brother like that. Not even when they were growing up. Everyone loved him.

She finally wiped away the tears as her laughter slowed. The dark-haired woman stepped off the pipe on Holly's side of the creek and walked closer.

She was shorter than Holly and curvy in all the places guys liked. With a red streak in her hair that made her edgy and lipstick to match, she was a bombshell. Her eyes were red-rimmed, like she'd been crying too, but they were clear and welcoming.

She stuck out her hand.

"Hi, I'm Maryanne. I just moved here a few months ago, but my grandma lived here my whole life. So I've spent every summer here. That's Lola. She grew up here too."

Holly shook the woman's hand. "Holly, and yes, Kendall is my brother."

Maryanne waved. "Do you want to join us for a bit? There are plenty of bottles to go around."

Holly shrugged and glanced around as the night settled around them. "As long as you guys can show me the way home after this, I can stay."

Maryanne pumped her fist in the air. "Hooray! Lola, she's staying." Then she lightly ran along the pipe to the other side.

Holly glanced at the water underneath. It didn't appear deep, and the pipe was only about a foot wide, reminding her of the balance beam in dance class all those years ago.

She took a deep breath and followed Maryanne slowly across to the other side. They had two camping chairs

The Songwriter Gets His Girl

around the firepit and a box of different glass bottles and jars.

Lola reluctantly reached her hand out, and Holly shook it. "Nice to meet you, Holly. Sorry about your brother being a dickhead."

Holly laughed, surprising herself once more, but with these two by her side, it felt safe and natural. For a moment, it felt like the weight of the world had been lifted off her shoulders. As they laughed together, Holly felt a sense of camaraderie and comfort in their shared sarcasm and honesty. The small glimpse of normalcy gave her hope that maybe things were going to be alright after all.

"That's okay; he can be a dickhead sometimes. We fought like cats and dogs when he was in the Army, and I lived with him. He's much better to live with now, though."

Lola snorted. "If this is better, I can't imagine what worse looked like. The man is insufferable."

Maryanne held up a wine cooler. "Do you want a drink? We're not fancy wine people, so all we have are beers and wine coolers."

Holly smiled and took the drink. "I'd love one, thanks. What are y'all doing here anyway?"

Maryanne and Lola shared a look before Lola shrugged and picked up an empty glass spaghetti jar.

She tossed it in the air and caught it. "We're angry, so we're relieving a little stress."

Maryanne rolled her eyes as she sat in one of the camping chairs, waving Holly into the other. "Lola's grandpa just died, and she's hit the angry stage. I read this article about how the sound of shattering glass can help reset some stuff in your brain. So, we gathered all the glass jars we could find to try it."

"Took us a few weeks to save up enough to do it all at

once." Lola now tossed the jar from hand to hand, staring intently at it and refusing to meet anyone's eyes.

Maryanne turned to Holly. "When did you hit the angry phase?"

Holly frowned and tilted her head. "What?"

"You know, the angry grief phase. Everyone in town knows you lost your husband in that car accident, which is why you moved here last week."

Maryanne paused, catching Lola's eye, before looking back at Holly and clearing her throat. "Um, sorry about that. My filter doesn't work well when I'm grieving, and I say things without thinking. I should have asked in a better way. And like, sorry for your loss and all that."

Holly chuckled, surprising herself again as she looked into the fire. She took a deep breath and shook her head. "It's fine. Everyone back home was so... well, it was like they were walking on eggshells, afraid of saying the wrong thing. So, they just said nothing at all, and then they just sort of disappeared."

Maryanne's eyebrows rose. "Leaving you to process your grief alone? That sucks. No wonder you moved here."

"I wasn't entirely alone, but I wish I was." Holly took a few deep breaths but neither of the women said anything more. It was a comfortable silence, like they were letting her take all the time she needed, and they'd be there when she was ready.

She cleared her throat and looked at her drink. "My in-laws blame me for the wreck."

Lola growled, making Holly jump in her chair. "What? How could they blame you?"

Holly rubbed her forehead, pushing her newly dyed silver hair out of her face. "Because I drove that night. Doesn't matter that it started to rain or that someone else

The Songwriter Gets His Girl

t-boned us, which sent us into a tree. I was the one driving."

The only sound was the crickets and frogs, the fire crackling in the pit at her feet. Lola walked a few feet away, her auburn hair swishing along her back in her ponytail. She reared back and threw her jar at the side of the building. Glass shattered, breaking the silence.

Lola slammed her hands onto her hips. "Fuck that shit, Holly. You weren't at fault. It was just an accident, and accidents happen. Sometimes bad things happen to good people, and there's nothing you can do about it. Nothing—"

Her voice choked up, and Maryanne hopped up to pull her into a hug. Maryanne's smooth voice floated on the breeze as she comforted Lola. Holly felt empty, loneliness clawing at her and threatening to suffocate her.

Lola spun out of Maryanne's embrace and grabbed another clear jar. But instead of throwing it like Holly expected, she held it out, her hands shaking from emotion.

Holly blinked at the little spaghetti jar, the label long gone, her heart racing. "For me?"

Lola nodded, frowning. "Pretend you're throwing it at your in-laws."

Holly sat her drink in the dirt and took the offered jar. She walked to where the other two had stood and stared at the brick wall.

She hadn't actually reached an angry phase, probably because she had been so numb, cutting herself off from the pain. But as she stared at the small pile of glass at the base of the wall, she felt part of the ice around her heart crack.

"This is for making me feel like I could have prevented it, like it was my fault." She reared back and threw the glass. *Smash.*

Clear shards exploded in every direction, faint light

from the fire reflecting off them like little fireflies. When it shattered, she felt a piece of the frozen wall around her heart break along with it.

Maryanne clapped, and Lola handed her another. She glanced down and her jaw dropped. "This is a baby food jar."

Her throat closed, but no one said anything. She glanced at the two women, her head swiveling back and forth. "Did you know about the baby?"

Both frowned and shook their heads, with Lola asking, "What baby?"

Holly looked at the jar and felt tears run down her cheeks. "The car accident put me into early labor. They couldn't save her."

She glanced at them, fire licking through her veins as she thought back to that night. "They couldn't save her."

She glanced at the tiny jar, the pressure increasing on her chest until she threw it against the wall. *Smash.*

Small pieces shattered against the wall, and part of her heart smashed with it. But who was she kidding? Her heart had been devastated last year when she held her tiny little girl in her hand.

"They should have saved her. He should have been there with me. After losing so much, I'd finally found where I belonged and then it was all ripped away. Why me?"

Maryanne handed her another colorful jar, and she threw that one too. *Smash.*

The glass shimmered in the light, and her jaw firmed as Lola handed another baby food jar.

"Why us?" She reared back and threw it harder than before. *Smash.*

Tinier pieces flew in every direction, but Holly barely saw them through the pain in her heart. Another jar appeared in front of her, and she gripped it so hard her knuckles turned white.

"Why does everyone always die and leave me alone?"

Smash. The glass was piling up at the base of the wall, and Holly stared at it as she panted.

Lola picked up a jar and stepped up beside her. "How dare he leave me to run the farm? I'm not fucking prepared for this." Then she threw her jar. *Smash.*

Maryanne grabbed one for herself and stepped up beside them. "She didn't tell any of us she was in hospice and sick. She should have told us, so we could savor our time with her, so we could help more, be there more." She threw it hard, and it joined the rest of the broken pile on the ground.

Holly drained her drink and walked back to the throwing spot. "He shouldn't have left me. He'd said he'd never leave, but he did." *Smash.*

Their grief piled up, pieces atop pieces. They threw jar after jar until the box was empty and their faces tear stained.

Lola was right. Fuck that shit. She had years and years ahead of her, and she might not ever love again. But she could laugh, have friends and a life worth living.

She looked at the two women around her as they passed a joint and smiled. Moving here was the best decision she'd made in a long time.

Chapter Three

A peaceful summer afternoon, birds are chirping, sun in bloom.
Everything's right, yet feels so wrong, 'cause I'm here waiting all alone.

June, last year

Landry sat on his front porch swing with his guitar and worked on his latest song while he waited for Parker. He hummed the tune and strummed, watching two butterflies dance around each other in his flower bed.

The roses were transplants of his grandmother's and reminded him of going to their house when he was a kid. This time of year, he'd be sitting on the front porch with his grandpa, eating watermelon and having a spitting contest to see who could send a seed the furthest.

He glanced at the porch, remembering when he'd helped Pops renovate it. Landry had first purchased the house as a flip project to take Pops' mind off his grief. It had

The Songwriter Gets His Girl

helped get his grandpa up and out of the house when his grandma had just died.

He hadn't intended to live in it, but it was a good house. The moving truck pulled into the driveway with a little red sports car behind it. Parker hopped out of the car with a big grin on his face, his aviator sunglasses reflecting the waning light.

In his tan golf shorts, bright red sneakers, and white polo, Parker sure didn't look like he belonged in Crimson Creek anymore. Their other brothers, Gunner and Hunter, climbed out of the moving truck and went to roll up the back, both in jeans and t-shirts.

Landry felt some of the heaviness pressing on him lift to see his brothers, and he set his guitar on the swing. Walking down the sidewalk, he rounded the back of the moving truck.

He slapped Parker on the back. "Took y'all long enough to get here."

Parker shrugged. "Had to stop for gas and lunch."

Hunter snorted and handed Landry a box. "Princess Parker had to go inside to eat because there's a no food in the car rule."

Landry laughed as they started to walk boxes inside the house to Parker's room. A few hours later, they'd reassembled the bed, dresser, and other furniture. Parker was still fussing about his clothes in the closet when Landry went into the living room.

Gunner and Hunter sat on the couch already, their feet propped on the coffee table, so Landry went to the kitchen and grabbed them all beers. After distributing them, he opened his own.

Landry finally sank onto the recliner. "Thanks for helping get him moved in."

Gunner grunted. "You sure you want to put up with him? There's plenty of room at the bunkhouse with us."

Landry raised his brows. "Can you imagine Parker living in the bunkhouse?"

"I know, I know. He's too particular about his stuff. Do you think he still spends an hour working on his hair?"

Landry shrugged. "Doesn't matter to me. I'm not the one that has to get up early and go to work."

Parker came into the living room and flopped onto the love seat across from Landry. The furniture made a U shape and faced a large screen tv on the wall. A handmade wooden entertainment center sat under it, a housewarming present from Pops and the last major woodworking project he'd done.

"What are we talking about?" Parker asked, grabbing the lone unopened beer off the coffee table and sitting back.

Hunter raised an eyebrow. "You, hot shot. We were wondering how you were going to handle getting up early to go to school, now that you're coaching."

Parker shrugged and smiled, his mouth slightly pinched. "Eh, I'll be ok. It's never been an issue for me to wake up early. That's Landry's job. Don't y'all remember dragging him onto the bus for school?"

Hunter laughed and slapped his leg. "I remember throwing him over my shoulder one morning and walking to the bus stop with him still asleep."

Landry rolled his eyes. "Do you remember how much trouble you got in when I ended up at the bus depot with the driver because I never really woke up?"

Gunner grinned. "Yeah, we got grounded, but you got your butt busted. You never fell asleep on the bus again, did you?"

The Songwriter Gets His Girl

Landry shook his head. "Nope, certainly did not. Thankfully, I have a job that lets me set my own hours, so I don't have to wake up to an alarm clock. That would've been terrible."

"Speaking of jobs, we have to get going. Sunrise is going to come early." Hunter set his now empty beer on the coffee table and stood up.

Gunner followed. "I have the morning shift tomorrow too. Welcome home, Parker. Mom expects you at dinner after church on Sunday. And we're playing at the Electric Cowboy tomorrow night. You got the group text of the song list, right?"

Parker rolled his eyes and waved. "Yeah, yeah, I got it, and I'll be there with bells on."

Gunner groaned, mumbling with Hunter as they let themselves out. Landry's phone buzzed, and he pulled it out of his pocket.

You're not going to write a song about Parker moving in are you?

Landry chuckled as he read the message from Mike in Nashville. He'd been writing songs for him for three years now, a few of them hitting it big with two country stars.

"That your girlfriend?" Parker asked before he took another drink of his beer.

Landry shook his head. "No, it's Mike. He's asking if you got moved in okay."

"Well, tell him I said hi. How's the songwriting going?"

Parker was the only one in town who knew of Landry's work with Mike. Parker had been on that road trip years ago when Landry and Mike had worked on their first song together. That trip was life changing in more than one way.

"It's going good. He wants me to write more emotional stuff, though."

Parker chuckled. "Less small-town back roads? What's he expect, love songs?"

Landry winced. "Something like that. Sex sells, and the songs I normally send aren't that. I'm not one to kiss and tell."

Parker nodded, but smirked. "I could give you plenty of stories to work off of, if you need some inspiration. This one time after a soccer game down in Austin, I—"

A knock sounded at the door, and they looked at each other before Landry got up to answer it.

He opened the door and sucked in a breath. Maryanne, Lola, and Holly stood in the fading light of the sunset. His eyes took in Holly's bright smile, her pink tank top and jean shorts, her cute matching pink toenails in little sandals. His stomach flipped as he held the door open for them to come inside.

He grinned wide and lifted his eyebrows. "Well, hello ladies. What brings you over this fine evening?"

Maryanne held up a box with Half Baked's logo on top. "Welcoming committee from the church is striking early. I brought a few days' worth of breakfast."

Lola smiled and held up a covered casserole dish as she walked inside. "Granny and I wanted to welcome Parker back to town, so we brought dinner. Have y'all eaten yet?"

Holly held up another casserole dish with a box on top. "I made food for tomorrow too."

Landry took Holly's dish and the box of breadsticks from her hands, feeling the shock that raced up his arm at the touch of their fingers.

He cleared his throat and glanced at the dish. "What is it exactly?"

The Songwriter Gets His Girl

"Fettuccine Alfredo and cheesy breadsticks. Just stick the bread in the oven for seven minutes."

He grinned and winked at her. "Perfect, I'll just put it in the fridge for tonight." He turned to follow Maryanne into the kitchen but stopped to nod at Parker, now standing in front of the couch.

"Holly, this is one of my brothers you haven't met yet, Parker. Parker, this is Holly. She's opening a yoga studio in town."

Holly reached out a hand to shake before Landry dipped into the kitchen and put the casserole into the fridge. Lola had set hers down on the island and was opening drawers.

"Where's your serving dishes? Granny didn't let me have any of this, and I've had to smell it the whole way here."

Landry chuckled and opened the right drawer then pulled plates down from the cabinet. Laughter rang out from the living room, making his ears perk up. Holly's laugh was like the first warm day of spring after a cold winter.

Lola and Maryanne plated up dinner, and he opened the fridge again to offer them all drinks. Holly and Parker slipped into the kitchen on their way to the table.

"Got it all ready, so grab a plate. It's still warm from the oven, but if you want it hotter, there's the microwave." Landry nodded and grabbed a plate and fork for himself before leading the charge to the kitchen table.

He sat at the head of the table, and Maryanne and Lola sat in the two chairs to his right. Holly sat on his left, then Parker sat beside her.

"Thanks for bringing this over, ladies. I appreciate the welcome home." Parker smiled that smooth Williams grin that had given the brothers an edge up with the ladies.

Lola was immune though, having grown up with them. And Maryanne was more likely to sweet talk Parker and himself into doing some stupid than the other way around. She was always getting them into trouble growing up.

Holly though... she seemed to perk up at Parker's smile, a little dimple popping out on the left cheek as she smiled back at him. Landry's stomach twisted, and he frowned, glancing at his food. Maybe he wasn't as hungry as he thought.

Dinner conversation turned to the yoga studio and Parker's new coaching job at the school. When Parker started bragging about his soccer career, Landry rolled his eyes. But when they started making plans together to open a community gym in town and for Holly to start offering classes to the teenagers after school, he narrowed his eyes.

He was almost finished eating when Parker laughed at something Holly said and laid his hand on her forearm where it rested on the table. Landry sucked in a breath and jumped up, making his chair scrape along the hardwood floors.

All eyes turned to him, and he smiled tightly. "Anyone ready for ice cream? I have three types of Blue Bell."

Lola grinned and Maryanne whooped. He breathed deeply before gathering his plate and taking it to the sink. After washing it off, Maryanne brought the rest of the plates while Lola grabbed the ice cream out of the freezer.

Maryanne helped wash up the plates and bumped him on the shoulder. "When are you going to admit you like her?"

Landry scoffed and nearly dropped the fork in his hand. "Psh, I don't know what you're talking about."

"You think I haven't seen the way you look at her? Just ask her out, Lan."

The Songwriter Gets His Girl

"When are you going to ask Gunner out?"

She crossed her arms and jutted out her chin. "You think I haven't been asking him everyday he comes into the bakery?"

He let the comment go and stacked the last of the dishes on the drying rack before turning to meet her brown eyes. He sighed, opened and closed his mouth before finally just shaking his head. "She's not ready." Then he grabbed bowls and turned to the pair still sitting at the kitchen table, talking. "How about we go eat this on the front porch? It's a beautiful night."

Landry led them to the front porch, where Maryanne and Lola took the two rocking chairs while he sat in his spot on the swing. He moved his guitar, and Parker waved Holly to the open seat on the porch swing. Parker then leaned against the railing of the porch. Sitting next to Holly on the porch swing reminded him of that first night they met, the night he'd found what he'd been searching for his whole life only to realize she would never be his. An idea for a song began to percolate in his brain.

The conversation was now light and airy. Maryanne started telling stories of all the trouble she, Parker, and Landry would get into in the summers, with Lola interjecting some sarcastic comment here or there.

It eased the tension in Landry to hear Holly laugh. It didn't even matter that she was laughing at him. When he finished his bowl and set it on the side table, he picked up his guitar and began to strum.

The same three chords kept floating through his mind, the ones that molded with Holly's melodious laugh. He was happy while they talked, at peace, the loneliness lifting as he enjoyed the warm summer night with his friends.

When the ladies left, Parker helped bring in the bowls and spoons so Landry could bring his guitar in.

"That was more fun than I thought it'd be. I thought the only fun social interaction I'd have would be at the Electric Cowboy on the weekends. But here I am, first night back in town, and three sexy ladies show up. This small town thing is going to be better than I thought."

Landry shook his head and smiled. "It's good to have you home, Parker."

Parker set the dishes in the sink and leaned his hip against the counter, crossing his arms. "Is Holly seeing anyone?"

Landry frowned and went to the sink to wash up the dishes. He couldn't stand leaving dirty dishes in the sink overnight. "No, but she's a widow, and I don't recommend you going for it."

"Why not? When did she lose her husband?"

Landry paused in scrubbing and frowned. "Almost two years ago come August."

"Well, that's ok then. She might be ready to date again."

Landry snorted. "Doubtful. But even if she's not, there's still her brother to contend with. He's very protective of his little sister. You'll meet him next week at poker. He's the new town doctor, and the reason they both moved here. Oh, and he's a friend of Andy's from the Army. Andy's supposed to move back here permanently next year, did you hear?"

Landry tried to distract Parker with talk of their childhood friend. But Parker got that faraway look in his eye, the one that said there was a challenge, and he was going to win it. Landry felt the bottom drop out of his stomach, and he rubbed his forehead.

"Oh no, I know that look."

"What look?"

"That's the look you get before a soccer game, or before you enter any kind of challenge, really. Holly isn't something to win."

Parker rolled his eyes and walked out of the kitchen. Landry wiped his hands off on the dish towel and followed him.

"I'm serious, Parker. She's not fling material. You live here now, so you can't go around crapping where you eat. You have to think about these things if you're going to date someone from town."

"So I should just do like you and find a chick to hook-up with from the bar on the weekends? One-night-stands aren't really my thing."

Landry crossed his arms and squared up to Parker. "Not mine either. Most of them stick around for multiple weekends, but none of them want to settle in this little town."

"Well, there ya go. Holly is already settled in this town."

Landry shook his head. "No, you can't date her. She's someone to be treasured, not someone you win. You've always gone for the forbidden fruit, Parker, and I'm telling you. Leave this one alone."

Parker snorted and turned to his room. "Whatever. We'll just have to see how it goes, won't we?"

Landry ran a hand over his face and glanced at the kitchen, satisfied that everything was in its place. But he was frustrated now, worried that Parker was going to hurt Holly when she'd already been hurt enough. He went to his room and changed into his running clothes. The only way to burn away some of this tension was to escape it and running was the best.

Chapter Four

Wish upon the clouds above, that you'd really see me, my summer love. With you, the world's complete, but every day's just bittersweet. One day, you'll see the real me. One day, you'll be beside me. One day, you'll love me.

October

Landry hopped in the truck with Hunter, Nick, and Parker as they followed Andy and Kendall across town to Kendall's house. They'd been having a grand time welcoming Andy home at poker night, when they'd found out the girls were preparing for a bake sale at Kendall's.

Landry laughed at Nick's slightly slurred singing and car dancing to the song on the radio. The former Marine was always down to party and a regular at poker night and the Electric Cowboy on the weekends. Nick had called on him to help with the equipment rental business when he'd first moved to town a few years ago, and now he was a good friend.

Landry felt light, partly because poker nights were always guaranteed fun that he needed to unwind. Deep inside, he knew he was also feeling excited at the idea of seeing Holly.

They'd not run into each other very much the past few months, since he'd finished the remodel of the upstairs studio apartment. But her business was doing well, judging by the amount of after school classes and the new Saturday sunrise yoga in the park.

They parked behind Andy and followed Kendall to the door, where he promptly stopped.

"Hey man, let us in." Parker poked him in the back, then they crowded into the kitchen. Landry winced at the mess, because there was water dripping everywhere, even from the ceiling. Dirty pans and bowls were on the counters. Cindy and Holly were on either side of Lola, holding her arms. Were they fighting for control of the water faucet?

He felt his eyes widen as Kendall yelled, "What the hell is going on here?"

Lola shook off Cindy's hands and crossed her arms. "What's it look like, Ken doll? We were just washing up."

Oh no, shit was about to go down. Kendall and Lola had been dancing around each other almost from the moment he stepped foot in town. Landry eased around the group of guys to the counter where Holly now stood with a rag.

Lola and Kendall squared up to each other and started whispering furiously, pointing fingers and waving their arms. Andy went to Cindy while Maryanne and Gunner disappeared. Parker caught Nick as he stumbled to the dining table, which was covered in pies and cookies.

Landry grabbed a cloth to help Holly wipe the counters, getting just close enough to smell the lavender of her shampoo. Then Parker fucking ruined it.

"Holly, can we help clean up? Will work for cookies." Parker took the dish towel from Holly and winked. She just beamed at him like he'd hung the moon. No matter that Landry was *already* cleaning up and not just flirting about cleaning up.

"Of course." She practically batted her eyelashes at him. *Good God, have some pride, woman.*

You hush, you've no right to talk about her like that.

You're jealous but still defending her? Shit, this is worse than I thought. You've got it bad.

He paused, looking around now that the counter was clean. Holly sat at the kitchen table with Parker and Nick on either side of her, but Andy and Cindy were sitting opposite them.

Landry grabbed the dirty bowls and utensils, then shoved his hands into the soapy dishwater. He scrubbed a pie pan hard, frowning. He wasn't jealous. It was Parker, what was there to be jealous about? He glanced over, seeing Holly bump shoulders with both Parker and Nick.

Nick was a veteran and business owner. He might get drunk more often than Landry liked, but he wasn't going to judge. Landry couldn't really fault Holly if she chose to date Nick.

But she shouldn't be flirting like that. He paused again, frowning. Had *he* ever tried flirting with her like that? Maybe if he let loose the reins a little, she'd respond to him like she was with Parker and Nick? She was definitely flirting with them, giving little touches here and there.

Hunter leaned against the counter and peered into his

face. "You ok, man? You look like you're about to swallow a bug."

Landry breathed deep and pasted on a smile. "Yeah, just tired, I guess. Big project at work."

"Anything I can help with?"

Landry shook his head and glanced at Holly while he wiped his hands off on the clean dish towel. "Not unless you want to give me a ride home?"

"Sure, I can do that." They walked over to the others and said goodbye. Lola and Kendall were still arguing in the hallway, so they just waved and left.

Landry breathed easier once he was outside, but that sense of dread remained in the pit of his stomach. What if Parker or Nick stayed the night here tonight?

You're such a dweeb. They're not going to stay the night with her. That's Kendall's house. There's no way he'd let anything happen under his roof. He's even more protective of her than you are.

Shut up.

Just relax, because you know I'm right.

He pursed his lips and buckled up for the ride back to his house while Hunter turned up the radio and began to sing softly. His conscience might be right, but it didn't make him feel any better about the fact that Parker was still flirting with her.

Middle of December

Holly parked her bicycle in front of the grocery store and kicked the stand down. She couldn't stay in the house any longer, and she wanted to make Maryanne, her best friend, a few freezer meals now that she was going through the nausea and tiredness of early pregnancy.

Not that anyone else in town knew about it yet. Holly was excellent at keeping secrets, but this was hard, considering all she'd gone through the past few years.

She'd tried to stay away from most people her first year here, but Lola and Maryanne hadn't let her. They'd kept dragging her to town functions, had instituted a weekly girl's night, and had been there when she'd needed someone to cry on.

They'd not let her get lost in the pit of sadness when it tried to tug her under. Instead, they'd encouraged her to open the yoga studio and had even helped her pick a location, since Maryanne had just gone through the same process a few months before with her bakery, Half Baked.

And now Maryanne was going to be a mom. Holly ignored the jealous green monster pushing on her chest and grabbed a basket. She walked to the produce section, but when she rounded the corner, she saw Landry standing with his cart.

He was wearing dirty jeans and a green t-shirt covered in dust. She smiled, his clothes reminding her of her first day in town. When she'd first moved here two years ago, she'd been surprised to see a familiar face.

They'd become friends, although not nearly as good of friends as Maryanne and Lola. Still, he'd helped her inspect the yoga studio before she'd signed the paperwork, then he'd helped her remodel it.

She remembered that first day when the studio had officially become hers. She'd only been in town a few months, but she'd wanted to get the yoga studio up and running. Her mind couldn't handle the slow days with too much thinking time. She needed to be busy.

The Songwriter Gets His Girl

The realtor had met her at the front door on Main, unlocking it before dropping the keys into Holly's hand. When the weight of the keys had settled in her palm, her heart had raced and her breathing had grown shallow. The woman had said something, then hopped into her car before Holly could even comprehend this monumental event in her life.

This was the first step toward a future without Eric, a future on her own. She'd never been independent before, and she was so afraid to be alone. If this business didn't work out, it was all because of her own inefficiencies. The weight of it pressed onto her shoulders, much like the weight that had been on her chest for months now, ever since that night her life had changed beyond repair.

She was staring down at her keys, emotions and thoughts flying through her mind, when scuffed boots stopped in front of her. She couldn't look up, look away from this symbol of her future.

A calloused finger reached out and tipped her chin up, bringing her gaze up to hazel eyes that saw too much. Landry stood there, staring curiously at her. He was always so warm, welcoming, and light-hearted, quick to joke and laugh. But right now, it was like he could see all the pain that she tried to keep hidden when she was in public.

She felt raw, exposed on the sidewalk. And when his smooth, deep voice floated to her on the summer breeze, she'd shivered in anticipation.

"What's going on, Holly? Why are you just standing here?"

She opened and closed her mouth, unable to talk past the knot in her throat. Her eyes had teared up, and his had softened before he'd pulled her into his arms.

She stiffened, not liking the physical contact—and yet, she needed it, needing those muscular arms wrapping around her.

"Shh, it's going to be okay. Just let it all out. I got you."

People had said that before. When her mom had died, then her aunt, and again with Eric and the baby. But with Landry, she actually believed him. He spun them through the door of the studio and off the sidewalk and prying eyes.

Then she'd sobbed on his shoulder. It hadn't been pretty, quite the opposite, actually. It was loud with her wailing, messy with tears and snot collecting on his t-shirt, and he just held her through it all.

It was probably ten minutes before the tears had slowed. One hand was on her lower back, drawing circles, and the other was cupping the back of her head. And he was swaying them back and forth, which was so soothing.

She pulled back, only to see his own tear stains running down his cheeks and into the short, scruffy beard he now wore. Her fingers itched to wipe those tears away, but she just cleared her throat instead and stepped away.

"Um, thank you for that. You okay?"

He nodded with a sigh and wiped his own face with the hem of his t-shirt. She caught sight of washboard abs covered in ink before he pulled it back down. Dear Lord, the man was hotter than a Texas July picnic. And the ink was new. She didn't remember any tattoos when they'd met at that party years ago.

He looked around, avoiding her eyes and settling his thumbs on top of his tool belt. "Yeah, I'm good. Just came by to take some measurements and talk about the renovations you have planned. Is now still a good time?"

She nodded slowly and began to walk around the large open room. If he wanted to ignore it for now, that was fine. They could focus on business instead. "That wall is going to be floor to ceiling mirrors. Back here, I need a little office and bathrooms on this side and locker rooms on this side."

He was writing furiously in the little notebook while following her around. She walked to the side where the rickety stairs began and pointed to the front door. "To the right of the front door, I want a counter with a register. Behind it, I want shelves for different products like essential oils, lotions, muscle rubs, and stuff."

She began to walk up the stairs, gently placing each foot and testing the step before putting her full weight on it. Then she explained where she wanted the massage room and the bathroom at the top of the stairs before turning to the windows at the end of the long room.

"I love these windows. Is there a way to make them one way only, though? I don't want a ton of people on Main looking into my bedroom."

"Bedroom?" He bent to measure the hole in the floor in the middle of the room and made notes.

She turned from the window and looked at the empty room, dust particles sparkling with the sun shining through and making it look magical. Hope blossomed in her heart, and she sighed.

"Yeah, I want this to be an open loft style. Bed here by the windows with a floor to ceiling closet, then the living room right where you are, followed by a kitchen. I'd like an island and a table. Oh, and a pantry, I'll need a walk-in pantry."

"We could put in a long skinny pantry here, from the wall to the back of the massage room and bathroom that we're going to install. It could go all the way to the back, so at least ten feet by four feet."

She clapped and grabbed his bicep, leaning toward him. "Could you? That would be so cool. Yes, that's exactly what I want. It could double as the storage space too."

He looked down at her and shifted closer, causing her breast to brush against his arm. She gasped and stepped back, glancing around and launching onto the first topic to distract them both.

"Why were you crying? Downstairs, when I was a blubbering mess."

He stiffened, then shrugged, his eyes suddenly sad. "Just thinking of my grandpa. Missing him, wishing he were here to help on this renovation. He loved seeing old things given new life."

"Is that why you drive that old truck?" She'd seen him driving it around town while she biked to the park. It was a classic, and although it was restored to pristine condition, she'd seen him actually using it to

haul construction equipment. Yet it was always washed and shone bright baby blue.

He grinned, that twinkle in his eye again. "Yep, my buddy, Jake, restored it a few years ago before Grandpa passed. It was his seventieth birthday present from me and my brothers. He'd driven it for decades until it'd just stopped working around the time I was ten."

"You miss him a lot."

Landry nodded before he said softly, "Like you miss Eric a lot. Is that why you were crying?"

Holly stiffened and looked away, shaking her head. "Not really. It's just, this is a big step, opening a yoga studio. It's like this is the first step to a new chapter of my life, and I'm not sure I'm ready to close the last chapter yet."

"Letting go is never easy."

She snorted. "Got that right."

He grinned and walked closer, grabbing her hands and breaking out into song, "Let it go, let it go."

She laughed as he spun her around the room, careful to avoid the hole in the floor and the weak spots. He sang the entire song and danced her back toward the stairs while she laughed.

Somehow, he'd turned a scary day into a memory that made her smile. And it wasn't the last time he'd done something like that in the past two years, either. He just had a way of making her laugh every time they hung out.

He reached for a watermelon and lifted it into his cart, his biceps bulging. She realized her heart was racing again, like it had every time they were in the same room.

She jerked, spinning in the other direction, but accidentally hit a display of cantaloupes sending several rolling. She jumped back, almost rolling her ankle on one before she froze to wait for them to stop tumbling around.

Holly knew her cheeks were as red as the peppers on the

shelf next to her when she glanced up and met Landry's surprised green eyes. Then he grinned, and it felt like she was on a roller coaster, her stomach twisting and turning.

Chapter Five

Your smile lights up my heart. When I'm with you, I'm finally out of the dark.

Damn that smile. It told her there was fun to be had, that he had the perfect plan to cause some mischief. It told her to leave her worries behind and just trust him.

But that path was frivolous. No matter how hot he was or how her hand always tingled when he touched it, she refused to be a romantic again. Her heart couldn't take another beating.

She'd told herself that so often over the past two years since she'd moved here. It was practically part of her daily affirmations now.

Today will be a good day. You will laugh, find peace, and be happy in your work because the pain isn't worth trying to find someone to share life with. This is your life now, and it is wonderful. You have friends who love you, and that's enough. You are enough.

The Songwriter Gets His Girl

She may or may not have written that on a note on her bathroom mirror to read every morning.

"Need a hand with your melons?"

His voice made the hair on the back of her neck stand up. It was deep and smooth, like the best whiskey. If she took a sip, would he leave her choking or craving more of that smooth burn?

She giggled, then felt her cheeks heat even more. *Oh God, what's with the giggling? Turn it off, turn it off!*

"I'll handle my own melons, thank you very much."

Sweet Jesus, what was wrong with her? This wasn't the first time she'd ran into him around town, but she always seemed to make a fool of herself where he was concerned.

He tilted his head, making his dark blond hair shine like spun gold in the bright lights as he laughed. He slid around his cart, stepping into her space. The action made her jerk out of whatever spell he'd cast on her.

She glanced away and dropped to her knees to pick up the cantaloupes.

He cleared his throat, then knelt beside her and reached for a melon. "I know you can handle yourself, but if it's all the same to you, I'll still help pick these up. You okay?"

His dirty, calloused hand picked up a melon so gently. Would his hands be rough on her skin? Shit, he'd asked something. What was it?

"Oh yeah, I'm fine. Sorry, I was just thinking of what I could make Maryanne for dinner tonight."

"It's not a tofu something, is it? Because you know that didn't go over well at the last get together, even though it was delicious."

She'd taken a tofu casserole to a potluck at his parent's house a few months ago, when everyone was there to celebrate his mom's fiftieth birthday. Only she and Landry had eaten it, but he'd had such a pained look on his face while he swallowed every bite.

She giggled at the horrified expression on his face as he knelt and picked up the last of the melons, placing them back on the display. When his fingers brushed hers, she pulled away to tuck her hair behind her ear.

"Your face that day said it was definitely not delicious."

He propped a hand on his hip and tipped his chin up. "Tofu is apparently an acquired taste, but give a guy a break, will ya? It was the first time I'd tried it." He laughed, his eyes twinkling.

She grinned. "Don't worry, it's not tofu. I was thinking macaroni, cornbread, and beans. I know Maryanne wanted Southern comfort food. Think that's ok?"

He leaned on the handle of his cart and nodded. "Yep. Only thing that'd be better would be to add some fried chicken and maybe a pie."

Holly rolled her eyes. "I'm not making fried chicken."

"Hey, not everyone can handle being a vegetarian. Personally, I can last about half a week before I give in."

"Wait, you've tried being a vegetarian?"

He nodded. "Still trying. I call it being a half-a-tarian."

She laughed. "When did you start that?"

He shrugged and glanced away, a tinge of pink on his whiskered cheeks.

"A year or two. Don't remember exactly, but I've been vegetarian a few days a week for a while now. You have nothing in your basket yet. What do you need to grab?"

He grabbed her basket and put it in his cart, moving his food out of the way.

She grinned and mouthed off. "I just said macaroni, cornbread, and beans. Geez, Lan, do you need to clean your ears?"

He threw his head back and laughed, making her breath hitch in her throat. He was taller than her, beefy because he had to do so much heavy lifting at his handyman jobs. His chest was broader than it'd been five years ago when they'd first met.

She wanted to look away, but was captivated. Her palms began to sweat at being close to him again, like they did when they'd painted the apartment and his scent had filled her nose.

"So, how have you been the past few weeks? Haven't seen you much since we finished remodeling the apartment above your yoga studio. When do you move in? I can swing by and give you a hand, if you like."

She shrugged as they walked to the canned goods. The remodel on the studio itself had been completed last year, but they'd waited until this summer to remodel the upstairs apartment. Partly because she'd wanted to focus on getting the business up and running and in the black. Partly because she could only handle so much time with Landry before she wanted to throw caution to the wind and jump him.

She cleared her throat and looked away, searching the shelves for the food she needed. "I don't know when I'll move in exactly. I've tried talking to Kendall about it, but you know him."

Landry snorted while she grabbed the beans off the shelf. "Yeah, overprotective doesn't even begin to cover it. But you can't really blame him. I think if I had a sister, I'd be like that too."

"Kendall's always been more of a father figure, to be honest. He was thirteen when I was born and babysat me while our mom worked."

They reached the baked goods section, and she grabbed

cornbread mix and pie shells before holding up two different boxes for pie filling.

Landry pointed to one. "The chocolate. It was Maryanne's favorite growing up. Speaking of growing up, where was your dad, if Kendall was your father figure?"

She put back the other box. "Oh, he took off a few months after I was born. Kendall's dad had died in combat, my mom had remarried. But Kendall always said my dad was a bit of a jerk."

There were no memories of her dad, and her mom hadn't talked about him much. It was only Kendall who'd had anything to say about him, about how he didn't deserve to be in our family and that's why he'd left. It was one of her earliest memories, arguing with him about her dad. As an adult, she'd let the argument go, since he was obviously right.

"Well, good riddance, then. Maybe you're better off without him."

Her breath caught as she caught his leathery scent. It helped clear her head, but her stomach was rolling. This was the first time since moving to town that she'd opened up to someone other than Maryanne and Lola. Why him and why now?

This was something she needed to talk to her new therapist about.

She smiled at him, ignoring the butterflies in her stomach. "Maybe. Probably. Are you helping Andy with the wedding?"

He grinned and pushed the cart. "Yeah, it's pretty funny to see him trying to juggle the wedding and figuring out how to be a father all at the same time. I'll be over with the rest of the guys on Thursday to help set up the studio for the ceremony. It's nice of you to offer the space for it."

She shrugged. "It's the perfect place for it, and inside which was important for middle of December. I hear you'll be in charge of music for the reception?"

"Yeah, any special requests?"

She shook her head and smiled. "Nope, as long as you sing something, I'll be happy. I love hearing you sing."

They grabbed a few boxes of macaroni before turning to the checkout, Landry's cheeks now tinged pink again.

She bit her lip and waved back the way they'd come. "Actually, I didn't get the produce, so if we can go back that direction?"

He nodded, and they meandered to the fruit.

"I don't remember Kendall or you ever talking about your mom before. Where is she now?"

Holly kept her face averted while she picked out the bananas, then went to the spinach and lettuce.

She sucked in a quick breath before saying in a rush, "She's gone. This is all I need for now, I think. What projects are you working on this week?"

He raised a brow at the subject change but she just shook her head. He sighed, then launched into a description of his work this week while they walked to the checkout.

The cashier was a freckle-faced pimply girl and couldn't stop stealing glances at Landry, who seemed oblivious as he loaded the conveyor belt with their food, adding a divider to separate them.

"So no expected date to move in to the studio apartment?"

"Not yet. Probably won't be until after the holidays. Kendall wasn't really on board with it, and I didn't want to fight him. It wasn't worth it. I'm going to stay there when he works overnight once a week to get used to it. It's clean and bright and airy. I'm excited about the new bed I had delivered a few weeks ago. It's so comfy."

Her cheeks tinged at the thought of her bed with him in it. Her bed at Kendall's was the same one she'd had since she'd first moved in with him a decade ago, right around high school graduation.

He cleared his throat. "So you're happy with my work?"

The uncertainty in his voice melted her heart. He was the best handyman in a thirty-minute radius, surely he knew that.

"I'm thrilled with the remodel. Actually, Kendall and I have been talking about updating his bathrooms in the house. Think we could get you to come out and look at them?"

His face lit up like a boy coming downstairs on Christmas morning.

"Oh yeah? Why don't I load up your bike and take you home in my truck? Then I can look at the bathrooms and take some notes. What time will Kendall be home so I can ask what he wants to do with them?"

Holly laughed as she paid for her groceries, his excitement infectious.

"Sure, we can do that. He'll be home later, but you can text him."

They walked out into the chilly overcast parking lot, Landry pushing the cart with all their groceries to his truck. She grabbed her bicycle, rolled it over to him, and he put it in the back of his truck. His muscles rippled at the motion, but she glanced away and hopped into the passenger side.

He was just a friend, helping her out with the bathroom remodel. He was just a friend.

The radio started playing a Michael Buble song when

The Songwriter Gets His Girl

he started up the truck, making her smile when Landry started singing softly under his breath as he drove.

His voice was smooth as honey and just as sweet. When it was over, she said, "I miss hearing you sing in the studio while working on the remodel."

He grinned and met her eyes before winking. "Well, you'll just have to come to the Electric Cowboy more often and hear it."

Another song came on, and he started to sing it too, his voice louder and filling the cab. Several times when he was working on the studio, she'd walk in the back door to find him already upstairs, singing to the radio. His voice always soothed her soul and relaxed her body, setting her mind at ease when the thoughts and emotions swirled. She knew it was going to be a good day when she heard him singing.

He turned the truck and pulled into Kendall's driveway. She hopped out, and they sorted through the bags to bring in the right ones. She unlocked the door, and winced as she took in the living room and kitchen, looking at it from his eyes.

It was rather messy, something that drove Kendall up the wall. Pillows were strewn on the couch with a few throw blankets. Shoes were by the door, a pair was by the hallway, and another under the dining table. Opened and unopened mail was on the counter, and the island still had bowls on it from breakfast.

"Sorry for the mess."

He arched a brow and glanced around, his charming smile firmly in place. "What mess? This isn't picture perfect, but it's an actual lived-in home, Holly. I'll just put these bags on the table. Which bathroom do you want to look at first?"

She led the way to the main bathroom in the hallway and pushed open the door. It was the one she used, so makeup, vitamin bottles, and various toiletries were completely covering the counter top. A dirty towel sat on top of the hamper and a hot pink lacy bra hung over the side of it.

She hastily shoved them inside and shut the lid as Landry chuckled.

"Pink, eh? I bet you look delicious in it. Tell me there are matching panties."

He wiggled his eyebrows, making her laugh even as she felt her cheeks heat. She crossed her arms and shuffled her feet, trying to maintain her distance. He was always teasing her, trying to make her laugh. Maybe she could make him laugh too. She suddenly yearned to hear his deep laugh.

She glanced up at him through her lashes. "Sorry to burst your bubble, but no matching panties." She paused, unable to hold back her smirk while she lowered her voice to a whisper. "Just a matching thong."

She swallowed hard, unable to believe she'd actually said that out loud. Yeah, she'd flirted with others in the past few months, but with Landry there was always something holding her back. Flirting with him exhilarated her, and she wanted to get a rise out of him.

Landry threw his head back and groaned, shoving his hands in his front pockets and turning away from her. She saw him adjust himself in his pants, and her eyes were drawn to the hard ridge of his jeans.

Dear God, was that his—

"You're killing me, Smalls. Quick, change the subject. What do you guys want done in here?"

She smiled, enjoying his misery, and leaned against the counter. Hugging her waist and looking at her feet, she tried to take her mind off his hard-on and all the dirty thoughts running through her head. She could not let her mind go there, could not analyze why he'd been flirting more with her than he had before.

With a deep breath, she glanced away. Not looking at him would help her shake this hum of desire coursing through her.

"Obviously, I need more storage space. There's nowhere to store towels or anything except the one cabinet under the sink. Also, the tub is pretty old and starting to look weird. Look."

She pulled the shower curtain back to show the iron stain near the drain.

He pulled out a notebook from his back pocket and scribbled something on it.

"It looks like you might need to add water softeners to your tank. I'll check the age of the house, but it's normally something you want to do every few years to keep those iron stains from starting up. We can add some cabinets above the toilet, but you have this dead space here by the tub that can have a little floor to ceiling cabinet added too."

God, he was so sexy when he talked shop like that. He knew exactly what to do in here, and the excitement in his voice helped her visualize what he was saying. He tapped his mini pen to his luscious lips, the pink of them standing out among the scruff on his face.

"It's pretty dark in here too. Extra lights? Maybe a lighter paint color? And what's the theme in here exactly?"

Holly laughed. "Yeah, that's all Kendall. I have changed none of it since I moved in. It'd be nice to have one theme instead of all this chaos, don't you think?"

She glanced at the dark brown cabinets, forest green walls with some kind of leafy patterned peeling wallpaper, and the tan shower curtain with an Army logo. The soap dispenser and small trash can were navy blue with seashells.

Landry grinned, making her heart skip a beat. "Yeah, definitely need one theme. Is the other bathroom this way too?"

She waved him to back up, her hand accidentally hitting his arm and sending a shock through her body. But he moved and followed her through Kendall's spotless bedroom to the master bathroom.

All the toiletries were lined up along the back counter nice and neat, but the side was peeling off. She showed him the wobbly toilet and the shower that was too short for her brother.

He made more notes in his notebook and talked through his ideas for it. Her phone chirped, and she read the message from Maryanne, asking what time she'd be coming over.

"I need to start in on that dinner for Maryanne. Do you have enough to draw up some quotes to talk to Kendall about?"

He nodded and slid the pen and notebook back into his pocket. Then they walked back to the front of the house, her eyes drawn to his ass in his jeans. She glanced around, looking for a distraction from the way her heart raced when she was near him. Her eyes landed on the groceries, so she began to take them out.

He shifted on his feet, spinning his keyring on his finger.

"I'll text Kendall to ask about the bathrooms later."

She nodded, her mind conflicted over the way her body reacted when she was near him. "Will do."

He paused, then caught his keys and turned to the door.

"Well, I better be going. Tell Maryanne I'll swing by the bakery later this week."

She saw him to the door and watched him walk to his truck, her eyes once again on his fabulous ass, her mouth suddenly dry. He pulled her bike out of the back and set it inside the fence, waved, and then got into his baby blue old truck.

Part of her wanted him to stay, just to talk while she made dinner for her bestie. She had loved hanging out with him the past few months while he remodeled the apartment. She'd been less lonely when he'd been around.

And now Maryanne was having a baby. Holly swallowed past the lump in her throat and started making dinner for Maryanne. She texted Lola to see if she could give her a ride, since Kendall would be working until later.

It sucked that she didn't have a car, but what sucked more was why she refused to drive. She sighed, her mind shying away from the past as she flipped over to her music app, turned up a Shakira song, and started singing at the top of her lungs, shaking her hips while she cooked.

Chapter Six

Life is a circle, and no one wins. Life kicks my ass, and I get back up again.

Landry fidgeted with his best friend's tie and chuckled. "Come on, Andy, don't tell me you're nervous. Cindy is perfect for you."

Andy glanced around at the wedding decorations. They were standing under a flower arch in the yoga studio, the wall of mirrors now draped with lace. The preacher stood talking a few feet away, and everyone else sat at round tables around the space. It was open seating, except for the family tables.

"It's not nerves exactly. I just never thought I'd marry someone after barely three months together."

Before Andy had moved here, he'd been all alone like Landry. Sure, surrounded by family, but they had both gone to sleep in cold beds at night. Now his friend had found his

The Songwriter Gets His Girl

soul mate. Landry was happy for him, but it left something unsettled in the pit of his stomach.

Landry grinned and bumped his friend with his shoulder. "It's funny how life can change so quickly. But you're marrying the woman of your dreams, and it's going to be worth all the lonely nights to spend the rest of your lives together."

Andy rolled his eyes. "You're so cheesy. How you're still single, I'll never know. When are you going to settle down?"

Landry froze, his eyes flicking across the crowd, looking for the one woman whom he could never have. He breathed easier when he couldn't see her and pasted on a smile.

"Eh, if it happens, it happens. Someday, I'd love to wake up next to a beautiful woman, maybe make breakfast and bring it to her in bed."

Andy grinned. "You? Breakfast? That would require waking up before noon."

They laughed just before Lola, one of Cindy's best friend's, gave him the thumbs up sign from the bottom of the stairs. He pulled out his phone and changed the instrumental music playing through the speakers to the processional music.

When the bridal march began, Andy seemed to stand taller beside him, his grin bigger than ever before. It made Landry yearn for what he didn't have. Love to last the ages. His own family to make dinners chaotic and loud like the ones he'd grown up with.

An hour later, he'd eaten, mingled, and was playing guitar for the couples dancing on the little dance area, his melancholy seeping deeper. His eyes shifted to Lola and Holly sitting at a table.

Holly took his breath away, like always. She was a beacon of light in his lonely world, the one who got away five years ago, the one who could never be his. He'd thought she needed time to grieve, but he was coming to realize she'd never be ready to date again.

She was stunning in her mint green lace dress. It reminded him a bit of a Greek goddess, the way it was draped over her sweet little body.

Her dyed silver hair was piled up high on her head and had some sort of red lace twisted in. He wanted to pull out all the pins and run his hands through it.

An hour later, he set his guitar in its case and followed everyone outside to say goodbye to the newlyweds.

He only had eyes for Holly, though, weaving on her feet in front of him. A commotion had him looking around until Cindy's bouquet came flying. Holly reached up and caught it, but it threw her off balance.

He lunged just in time to catch her, curling her face into his shoulder as she laughed.

"Holly, are you ok?"

God, why did she have to feel so good in his arms? She glanced up at him, her face open and trusting. He just basked in her joy and held her steady.

"I caught it, I caught it! Oh wait, I can't. This is terrible. Here, someone else take it." She tried to stand up again but stumbled as she thrust the flowers to the woman beside her.

Maryanne scowled from behind her. "Nope, you can't do that. If you give those flowers to anyone else, you'll curse that woman to never find her groom. You have to keep it."

"Oh." Holly looked so crestfallen as she looked at the flowers, so he wrapped his arm around her shoulders and pulled her back into the warmth of the building. In the two years she'd been living in Crimson Creek, he'd hugged her only a handful of times, not trusting himself. If this allowed him just a few more minutes of touching her, he'd take it.

He cleared his throat past the lump suddenly lodged there. Holly stumbled again, and he moved his arm to her waist to hold her upright.

Maryanne laughed. "Looks like Holly's not going to make it. Can you take her home, Landry, so she's safe and out of the way?"

"Hey, I'm always safe, and I'm never in the way. I'm too short to be in anyone's way." Holly's voice was soft and lilting, her eyes unfocused in the twinkle lights from the ceiling.

He grinned. "Yeah, I can help."

Maryanne shooed him off, and he started helping Holly to the door.

Her slurred words tickled his ear. "I can just crash upstairs. I had a bed delivered, remember? Hey, I still need you to come put in all the cabinets and paint the walls."

His body hummed at the thought of her and a bed. There was nothing that'd come of it, though. She just wasn't ready, no matter how much he dreamed otherwise.

He turned to the stairs. If Kendall was around, he'd probably just take her home, but he was nowhere to be seen.

Holly leaned her head on his chest more with each step. He squeezed her closer against him, the smell of lavender enveloping him. When they got to the top of the stairs, Landry frowned and slowed his steps.

His eyes widened in surprise as the sounds registered in his brain. "Um, we should go back down."

Holly perked up and lurched out of his arms. "Wait, is someone having sex up here? Who is it? Let me see."

"Holly, no," he whispered, jerking her back into his arms. "We all have to live in this town and see each other nearly every day. Let's go."

She looked up at him and arched an eyebrow. "Yet you're not leaving."

His jaw dropped, and she giggled softly. He clapped a hand over her mouth and slipped behind her, wrapping his other arm around her waist to hold her against him back to front. He groaned, feeling her tight little ass wiggling against his now hard cock.

"Sh, if you stay quiet, we'll take a peek." He walked them slowly forward, Holly's feet shuffling in front of his as she tried to stay upright. They peered around the sliding barn door that separated the massage room and bathroom from the rest of the apartment.

She had a kitchen table up here now, and the bed all the way on the other end, but no other furniture yet. And there on the bed was a half-dressed Kendall. A flash of pale skin and red hair made Holly gasp under his hand and jerk back.

He walked them quickly back into the bathroom. Softly shutting the door, Holly was now bouncing on her feet.

"Oh my God, oh my God, oh my God. That was my brother! Ugh, why haven't I put in washcloths up here yet? I need to wash my eyes out."

He chuckled, keeping his voice low. "Yeah, but did you see who he was with? That red hair can only be Lola's."

She gasped and stared at him. "Are you serious? I didn't look that hard, too shocked. Thank God he had his pants still covering his ass, because ew."

He laughed, and this time it was she who slapped a hand over his mouth.

"Sh, we have to get out of here. Do you have your truck downstairs?"

He nodded under her hand, then stuck his tongue out and licked her palm. It tasted like sweat and chocolate from

The Songwriter Gets His Girl

the chocolate wedding cake. She gasped and jerked her hand back. He wanted to make her gasp in other ways.

"Yeah, think you can walk that far? I can carry you if you need me to."

She shook her head and cracked the door to peek out. "Seeing Kendall kind of sobered me up, so I'll be okay. The coast is clear. Let's go."

She half crouched and then tripped on the hem of her dress, so he wrapped an arm around her waist and helped her down the stairs.

He glanced around, not seeing anyone else. They went out the back door to his 1957 powder blue Ford.

"Oh, it's so cold. Doesn't this truck have a heater?" He got her settled on the seat and slid his guitar in beside her before shutting the door and jogging to the driver's side.

He shut the door and answered her. "It does, but it takes a long time to warm up. Here, I keep a blanket under the seat." He pulled out the patchwork quilt his grandma had given him when he'd turned fifteen.

After he started the truck and backed out, he glanced at her still shaking. "You can slide over here if you want to share body heat."

She glanced at him with a raised brow and narrowed eyes, but he just shrugged and continued driving. Then she sighed and slid along the bench seat beside him to lean her head on his shoulder.

He felt a surge of victory. She hadn't let herself get close to anyone in the two years she'd lived here. She'd kept him firmly in the friend zone, but somehow the lines were blurred tonight.

She tucked the blanket around their waists, and he pulled his right arm behind her so she could snuggle deeper. Something seemed to shift in his chest because this felt natural and right. It felt like this was exactly where he was meant to be in this exact moment.

He pulled up to Kendall's house and glanced down to find her asleep. He looked around and didn't see her purse. With a frown, he realized the door was going to be locked. She and Kendall had both grown up in the city and always locked it.

He put the truck into reverse. If he took her to his house, Parker would see her in the morning and talk shit. Why had he thought sharing a house with his baby brother was a good idea? He groaned, picturing Parker and her dancing tonight. Nope, not taking her home. He wanted to keep her as far from him as possible.

Lost in thought, he didn't realize where he was driving until he pulled up to his parent's barn. Not the one by the house but the one that was on the back of their land and only used for storage, stock sales, and holiday parties.

The hunting cabin was just over the hill, out of sight, but he knew Andy and Cindy were spending the weekend there. His parents were in the house. There was a room that Hunter hid out in at the back of the barn, but that would require Holly going up the ladder.

No, the barn was the only place that would be warm enough tonight and would keep her from prying eyes. He turned off the engine and slid out of the truck, slowly pulling her with him. He wrapped her in the blanket and picked her up, one arm under her legs and the other under her shoulders.

"What?" She stirred, snuggling her head onto his chest.

"Sh, we're going to sleep this off. It's going to be okay."

He carried her inside, and soon they were laying on a pile of hay. But his heart was beating too fast for sleep.

He'd dreamed of this moment for so long, but the

The Songwriter Gets His Girl

reality was so much better. He moved his arm under her, so she laid her head on his chest. He kissed the top of her head, smelling the lavender shampoo and forcing his tense body to relax.

He knew this wasn't going to last. Tomorrow she'd go home, and they'd go back to friends like normal.

But for now, for tonight, he could pretend that she was his, sleeping in his arms and filling his heart with peace and joy.

This wasn't how he'd intended to spend his night. But maybe it was what his soul needed. This was confirmation that he was meant to take care of someone, meant to love someone and provide no matter the situation.

Maybe there was hope for him yet, that the love of his life was out there, and he just needed to be patient. He just needed to let go of this fascination with Holly, his bubble gum angel, because she was still and always would be out of reach.

He breathed in the deep scent of hay and her lavender shampoo and let his mind wander, part of him wishing she could be his other half.

If only she hadn't already found hers years ago. If only she could love again after losing it. If only he'd asked her out five years ago when they first met.

Chapter Seven

You'll never know how much you mean to me. You'll never know how I watch you smile. Your laugh carries me through the lonely miles. Smile for me, smile for me, smile for me.

Grass tickled her nose, the smell of dirt and earth making her not want to wake up and lose the peace. It was such a flaky thing, and not one that she'd experienced a lot of in the past two years.

Her nose still itched, and she pawed at the offending nub. Her eyes flew open as she grasped a piece of straw off her face. Where was she?

She raised her head. This was the Williams' barn where they held the annual Halloween party. A snore startled her, and she jerked. Landry lay asleep underneath her.

His head was turned toward her, his hair appearing golden in the soft light. The stubble on his jaw seemed fuller. He was wearing his button-down dress shirt and pants from Cindy and Andy's wedding last night.

The Songwriter Gets His Girl

She glanced at herself and heaved a sigh of relief that her dress was just twisted up around her thighs. She was warm under the blankets and—were those tablecloths? Her bare leg was outside the covers, but inside the cocoon with his body heat, she was toasty.

She tried to ease away from him, but her other arm was stuck under his. When she moved, he wrapped her tighter in his arms, making her lay her head back on his chest. The rise and fall of it was even, lulling her into a false peace.

False because this was all kinds of wrong. Eric would be so disappointed to find that she'd spent the night in a barn with him. Except, Landry was a friend, and nothing happened.

Dear God, she hoped nothing happened. She remembered going upstairs to her apartment last night and seeing Kendall and Lola doing it like bunnies. Gag. She remembered being cold in his truck, but nothing after that.

She laid her free hand on his chest, feeling the even pace of his breathing soothe her confused thoughts. He raised his other hand and engulfed her fingers with his. He took a deep breath and turned his head slightly.

Her heart raced because he was waking up. What would she say to him? She glanced up and saw him open those gorgeous hazel eyes. He blinked a few times before looking down at her.

Then he smiled.

Not his entertain the people smile, but the real Landry smile, the one that curled her toes and made her stomach quiver. Desire coursed through her at that look, but when he spoke, she about whimpered.

"Mornin,' angel." His voice was rough in the morning, his lips pale and inviting. She could tip her head and kiss him easily. Her body said yes, but reality hit her like a bolt of lightning. She couldn't just move on from Eric's death with a simple kiss.

She jerked back, causing his arm fell away from her as she sat up. Breathing raggedly, she looked at him, her emotions warring within her. Landry had always been open, accepting, and comfortable, but how could she betray Eric's memory?

He rolled over to face her, pulling a makeshift pillow under him.

"Do we have to get up and head home now?" He grumbled like a bear waking from hibernation, and it made her smile and relax a little. He wasn't trying to replace someone who was irreplaceable. He was just a friend, a good man who apparently wasn't a morning person.

"Looks like someone needs coffee to function in the morning."

He grunted and pulled a blanket up higher on his shoulders. She smiled and reached out to push the hair out of his eyes. It felt so natural to touch him, but she stopped herself, pulling her hand back. What was she doing? He was a friend. Just a friend.

He'd welcomed her to town two years ago with open arms. He'd helped her remodel the yoga studio and the apartment above it, singing and dancing and making her laugh everyday he was there. But that was just because he was a good friend, a good listener. Sometimes he even listened as she talked about her husband, since he had met Eric five years ago.

Landry had been cute when they'd first met, but the past years had made him more toned, and every day she hung around him left her salivating a little more and kicking herself for her treacherous thoughts.

She shook her head, sadness making her body weighted

down. "Come on. If you drop me off at home, I'll make you a cup of coffee. I even have some leftovers from the bakery."

He opened one eye and looked at her. "I'm listening."

She chuckled and rolled out of the hay. "Is this your parents' barn from the Halloween parties?"

He grunted again, so she grabbed the first blanket on top of him and began to fold it up. There was a tub nearby that said tablecloths on it, so she began to stack them inside. She finally had all of them folded except the two he was lying on and the blanket from his truck.

She pulled the blanket off him, tugging, but he grabbed it and held on tight, grunting. She laughed. "Wakey, wakey." He yanked on it again, and she stumbled forward.

He wrapped his arm around her waist to catch her, but it just made her fall the rest of the way on top of him.

Her hands were trapped between them, the blanket somehow covering them both. His arms circled her waist, pulling her flush against him. Their faces were inches apart, and his heartbeat was fast and steady under her palms. Too overwhelmed by the intensity of their embrace, shivers sped down her spine as she glanced into his deep hazel eyes in the dim light.

"Landry," she sighed his name and glanced at his lips, her body, mind, heart, and soul arguing within her.

"Kiss me awake, angel." His rough voice hushed her own inner voices, but he didn't force her head to his. His command made her want to obey, that underlying pleading tone making her feel like he desperately needed the kiss as much as she did.

Her lips moved closer to his as if in slow motion. Her brain was scrambled, unable to think of reasons to stop. She knew there were plenty, but all her brain said was everyone should wake up like this.

When their lips touched, her body melted in his arms. Soft and gentle, his tongue swept against hers. Once, twice, and then he deepened the kiss until her toes curled.

He rolled them, pinning her under him, his knee sliding between her legs. She ground on him and grabbed his shirt to pull him closer, gasping at how good and right it felt. He kissed like a god, and she was damn lucky to be on the receiving end of it.

He leaned on one elbow and pushed her hair out of their faces with the other, trailing his fingers down the side of her neck to her collarbone. She arched up to get closer, to draw him deeper into the kiss.

But his hand on her breast was like a bucket of water to the face. She gasped and turned away, quickly glancing at him when he pulled his head back to meet her gaze.

Her mouth gaped, and she sucked ragged breaths. They just stared at each other, neither moving. A myriad of emotions flew across his face too fast to identify. He rolled onto his back and sat, pulling his knees up and putting his face in his hands.

She sat up slowly and adjusted her dress, making sure everything was covered properly. How could she have been so foolish as to kiss him? He was just a friend, and she wasn't ready to erase the memory of Eric's lips and replace them with Landry's. She froze, trying to remember what Eric's felt like.

This was wrong. It was against the rules. She'd promised to love Eric forever, and Landry was her friend. Just a friend. Right?

Frowning, she shook herself as panic filled her. She wasn't ready to move on or even get close to someone else.

The Songwriter Gets His Girl

It was too soon, too intense. A peek at his face, and her heart hurt at how dejected he seemed.

"Landry, I—"

"I know. I shouldn't have done that, no matter how much I've been wanting to. I'm sorry. Think you can forgive and forget?" He sucked in a breath and turned to her, his face carefully neutral except for his soft, entertaining smile.

The pressure built on her chest. She didn't like that smile, the one that said he was hiding the real him, the real thoughts and feelings. And what did he mean, he'd been wanting to kiss her? She slowly nodded, too confused to argue with him when she wasn't even sure what she wanted.

She reached out a hand to touch his back. But he jumped up at the contact and dusted the hay off his suit pants, avoiding her eyes.

She frowned. "Landry, I'm the one who should be sorry. It's not you, it's—"

"I swear to God, if you say it's not you, it's me, I will scream." He looked at her, his eyes raw, hurt, bitter.

It surprised her enough that her jaw dropped. "No, it's just against the rules. You're my friend, and if we cross that line, I might lose you forever. I—I value your friendship too much to risk it, Lan."

He stared at her, his eyes hard and empty, then he pasted on a fake grin and bent to grab the blanket and fold it up.

"I value you too, so let's just forget about it, okay?"

She wanted to. Desperately. But the tingle still on her lips said that would be easier said than done.

New Year's Eve

A few weeks later, Holly put on the finishing touches to her makeup and stepped out of her hideous bathroom at Kendall's house. She hadn't been able to fully move into the new apartment yet, although she'd washed all the sheets and blankets from the wedding night.

She kept waiting for Lola to say something about it, but she and Kendall were still bickering every chance they got. It was like nothing had changed between them at all.

She wished she could say the same for her and Landry. She hadn't seen him at all in the past few weeks. Not at the grocery store, at Half Baked, anywhere. It was like he'd disappeared, even though others had talked with him.

"There you are. Are you finally ready?" Kendall stood up from the couch and looked her up and down, making her feel like a teenager with a too-short skirt. She tipped her chin up and nodded, walking to the coat rack to grab her jacket and purse.

"Yep, I'm ready. If you'd wanted to get there earlier, you should have told me. I could've had Lola pick me up." They locked up the house and climbed into his Audi car. Music played softly in the background.

"Can you believe this is their last night playing at the Electric Cowboy?" she asked her brother to fill the silence. They'd never really had festive holidays, and New Year's typically pulled them both out of their seasonal loneliness.

Christmas had been quiet this year. The two of them had watched Christmas cartoons and movies for two days straight, surviving on pizza, popcorn, a frozen pot pie, and ice cream. They'd spoken maybe ten minutes total in that time too, each lost in their own thoughts and feelings about the holiday.

The Songwriter Gets His Girl

"It's been a long time coming, though. Apparently, Landry, Hunter, and Gunner have been playing nearly every single weekend for the past six years. That's a long time."

She nodded, staring out the passenger side window at the darkness. "It's good though, because it shows Maryanne that Gunner is really in it with this baby thing."

"Yeah, but he's the most responsible man I know. Of course, he's going to do everything he can to take care of them."

The silence stretched, and Holly felt the pressure increase on her chest. She was cold, even though the heater was blasting and she was wearing her jacket.

She cleared her throat and said softly, "Why didn't you see that in Eric?"

Kendall gripped the steering wheel hard and minutes passed. She didn't think he'd answer at all, but she kept her face turned to the window away from him.

Finally, he sighed. "It wasn't about Eric, not really. I felt like you were my responsibility, and when he came into the picture it seemed like you were saying I wasn't doing a good enough job at taking care of you. Like you didn't want me anymore."

She turned to face him. "And that's why you were always mad."

"Yeah." He sighed and shifted in his seat. "I thought you'd started dating him while I was deployed because I wasn't there. Then when I was there to take care of you, he didn't go away like I expected him to."

Holly laughed bitterly. "Well, he's gone away now, hasn't he?"

He glanced at her and frowned. "I never wanted that, Holly. He was a good man, a good husband, and I wish every day that I'd treated him better, thanked him for loving you and taking care of you."

She leaned her head against the window and crossed her arms over her seatbelt. "I wish y'all would've gotten along too. You were both so similar, like the pot calling the kettle black." She smiled, remembering how protective Eric was, just like her brother.

They pulled up to the Electric Cowboy and got out of car, her heart heavy. Once they made their way inside to the back room where they normally hung out, Kendall went to order their drinks, leaving Holly to walk across the room to Lola.

She smiled and slid into the booth across from her. "Hey, how's it been so far? The guys sound good, even if they are just warming up now. Can you believe Kendall was worried we'd be late?"

Lola nodded and rolled her eyes. "Your brother is a control freak. Don't let it get to you. They're doing really well. Just waiting on Gunner before they officially start for the night."

Holly grinned and leaned forward on the table. "Maryanne's probably getting some right now, which is why they're not here yet."

Lola threw her head back and laughed. "Lucky girl, but hey, at least one of us is, right?"

Holly raised her eyebrow and waited, hoping now was the moment Lola admitted to sleeping with Kendall.

But Lola just looked around the room and grimaced. "There's a ton of people here tonight."

"Yeah, because it's a holiday." The loud music and bright lights were already getting to her, but she needed to be here, needed to let the past stay in the past. What better time to do that than New Year's?

"True, but I was hoping to celebrate our friends on their last official night here. I'm going to miss their singing."

Kendall came back with a pitcher of margaritas and a stack of cups. He slid into the booth next to Holly and poured them drinks.

"What are we talking about?"

Lola raised an eyebrow and crossed her arms, leaning back in her chair. "Wondering why Gunner's late and how sad we are that this is their last night playing here."

Holly sipped her drink to hide her smirk, because Kendall couldn't take his eyes off Lola's cleavage in that blue party dress. It matched her eyes and made them really pop.

After Maryanne and Gunner finally arrived, blushing and disheveled, Holly glanced at Lola and they both winked at each other, then burst into laughter. Apparently, they were right on why their friends were late.

Toward the end of the evening after midnight, Gunner took a break singing to check on Maryanne. Holly had just come back from the bathroom and was making her way around the dance floor to the back room where their friends were.

"Wanna dance?" Some cowboy slid up beside her and grabbed her hand. His eyes sparkled with mischief and promised harmless fun, so she shrugged and nodded. Honestly, dancing across the dance floor was going to be faster to get back to her friends anyway.

They danced, but her eyes kept going to Landry, now singing in the spotlight after taking Gunner's place. He looked like he was having fun and was a natural on stage, his charm and smile infecting all who listened and watched. She felt herself start to have relax, dancing with this random guy just because she could hear the joy in Landry's voice.

Then Landry's eyes found hers. The cowboy swung her closer, and Landry's eyes narrowed. He sped up the tempo on the song, and she raised her brow at him. He shrugged and deliberately looked away.

It hurt, that he wasn't really acknowledging her. But she didn't really blame him, after the way they'd ended that kiss a few weeks ago. She didn't want to get his hopes up, though. Landry still needed to find his happily ever after, and Holly wasn't it. She'd already had hers, and nothing could ever live up to that love, the joy she had for those short years with him.

Landry deserved happiness too, but if she'd continued that kiss, it might have distracted him from finding his true love. And she wasn't going to stand in the way of anyone's path to happiness, much less his.

Chapter Eight

Your kiss takes me up to the stars, where dreams are close and fears are far. In your arms, I'm safe and sound. In the quiet, love's the loudest sound.

February

"Give me an hour, Mrs. Helen, and I'll be out of your hair."

Landry took off his tool belt and knelt beside the kitchen sink. Helen was a friend of his mom's and had been his English teacher in high school, but by that time he'd been calling her Mrs. Helen for years.

"You're in luck that the hardware store had the part in stock, otherwise I would've driven to Denton and taken another day."

He moved the last items from under the sink and began removing the busted pipe.

"I'm so glad you're able to get it done today. The strawberries and grapefruits are near bursting already, and I wanted to start canning today."

"You'll be making some of that famous jam? Think you can save me a jar or two?"

She chuckled and slid onto one of the wooden kitchen chairs to chat more.

"Absolutely, Landry. How's your mama doing?"

They settled into an easy conversation about his parents, then his brothers and others around town.

"How are Maryanne and Gunner doing with the baby prep? That was quite the surprise to the town."

Landry grunted as he wrenched off the pipe. Maryanne had always gotten him into trouble when they were kids. When they were eleven, she'd had the brilliant idea to tube down the river. She'd quickly convinced Landry and Parker to join, and they'd all gotten in trouble when Gunner had to fish them out hours later way off in another county.

Gunner was always bailing them out, but for once Gunner had gotten into trouble with Maryanne. Well, if one considers getting pregnant trouble. Personally, Landry was slightly envious.

They were a perfect fit, and Landry was glad that Gunner was finally realizing that Maryanne loved him. He'd seen that look in her eye before they were even teenagers, the same look that his grandparents had shared. The look that he craved.

He shook his head, focusing on the task and conversation at hand.

"They're doing good. You heard they got married last weekend while up in Colorado, didn't you?"

Helen chuckled. "Yeah, that bit of news spread through

Crimson Creek faster than a wildfire. The showers are tonight, right?"

"Yep. As soon as I'm done here, I'm heading over to help Mrs. Williams and Ma get everything set up."

"You're a good kid, Landry."

Landry snorted. "I'm almost thirty, Mrs. Helen. Not such a kid anymore."

"Well, when are you going to find a lady of your own then, hm?"

Landry slid the bolt off, then grabbed the new replacement pipe and pieces. He grinned at Mrs. Helen and winked. "Oh, you know me. Always a bridesmaid, never a bride."

She laughed and it made Landry happy to hear. He always wanted those around him to be carefree and enjoy life.

"More like always a flirt. Your grandpa was like that, God bless his soul. He had all the ladies in town chasing him, but when your grandma rolled through? Well, it was like no one else existed after that."

"They really loved each other, didn't they?" Landry's voice was soft as he focused on fitting the part. His grandparents had been inseparable. His grandpa had been the town's handyman, construction guru, and town inspector for years, and his grandma went on most jobs with him, lending a hand here and there.

"Most definitely. We were all heartbroken when she got sick and your grandpa's singing on the job turned so sorrowful. It was only when you started going on jobs with him in high school that his songs turned around."

"I miss his voice." Landry felt his throat closing up as he tightened the wrench.

"Will you sing me something, Landry? Something like your grandpa used to sing?"

Landry cleared his throat, swallowing past the lump as he remembered the good times with his grandpa. He began singing *Can't Smile Without You* by Barry Manilow, remembering a time when it was the only song his grandpa would sing.

His voice was low and smooth as molasses, practiced and refined from years of singing with his grandpa. When he'd hit puberty, his voice had become nearly identical to his grandpa's, like a merger between Frank Sinatra and Michael Buble.

Then he moved on to *Fly Me to the Moon* by Dean Martin. By the time he was done with the sink, Helen was smiling, staring into space, and probably remembering the good times. He hoped so, at least.

He turned on the water, then tested the sink before cleaning up his mess and replacing all her under cabinet cleaning supplies.

"That's it, Mrs. Helen. I have to get going if I'm going to get myself decent for the party tonight. Will we see you there?"

"Of course, my dear. I'm going to wrap her present, then make a casserole for Lola's mama. Vonda said Carla hasn't been doing very well this winter."

"I'm glad you're there to help them. The church ladies wouldn't be nearly as organized without you leading the helm, Mrs. Helen. If you feel like making an extra casserole, I know of two men who would eat it up before you know it."

He winked as she opened her arms for a hug.

"You and Parker both need to find some women to take

The Songwriter Gets His Girl

over that job. Keep your eyes open because she could blow into town like your grandma."

He grinned. "Then it'll be game over for me. I'll see you later."

He whistled on his way out the door, his mind wandering to all the women in town that he'd dated over the past ten years. He'd never tell Mrs. Helen or anyone that he'd found a girl five years ago, only for her to be out of reach. Their pity wouldn't help the situation, and they already tried to set him up with everyone under the age of forty.

He'd dated every eligible girl years ago, and it hadn't worked out. He'd started meeting girls at the Electric Cowboy on the weekends, but most of them were looking for a one-night stand or a weekend fling.

Then, when Gunner had found out he was going to become a dad and sheriff, the brothers had all decided it was time to stop playing at the Electric Cowboy. Landry hadn't been fond of the idea, but Mike had hooked him up with some gigs down in Dallas and Fort Worth on the weekends.

He had plenty of opportunities to meet women there, but none of them were meaningful connections. He'd dated a few, but most of them had just wanted the thrill of dating a singer. It'd only been six weeks, and he'd already given up on all the groupie girls, which meant it'd been months since he'd last been with a woman.

And he didn't really feel a need to correct the situation. His mind was still stuck on Holly no matter how hard he tried to set her aside and let her go.

The old Ford took two tries to turn over the engine. He whistled more Sinatra and parked at home, hopped out, and went to take a shower. When he stepped out and wrapped a towel around his waist, he saw a missed message from Mike in Nashville.

When will you have the next song ready?

I plan on finishing it tomorrow after church.
Family party tonight.

Tell Parker I said hi. Actually, I'll text him.
Maybe he can convince your ass to get out here.

Good luck. lol
I told you, work is busy here.

Yeah, yeah. We both know you can retire and just write songs for me, with what I pay you.

And I appreciate it. I like $ lol
But I like helping people here.
You know that.

I know, I know. You're such a damn good guy.

lol I try.

Parker pushed his partially open bedroom door and groaned.

"God, put some clothes on, man. What are you doing? You're not sending a dick pic are you, because that's so cheesy and never works."

Landry laughed and tossed his phone on the bed before grabbing clean clothes.

"I was talking with Mike. He says hi, by the way."

The Songwriter Gets His Girl

Parker leaned against the door frame and crossed his ankles.

"He convince you to go to Nashville yet?"

Landry raised his brows and glanced at his brother. His blond-brown hair was falling in his eyes, but was shorter on the sides in what Landry jokingly called the classic soccer player hipster haircut.

Landry pulled on his jeans and turned to the mirror above his dresser to run a hand through his own short cropped, dark blond hair. He needed to shave, but he always looked like that. He liked the scruffy two-day shadow that barely classified as a beard, as he kept it trimmed and neat.

"Of course I'm not going to Nashville. I have things to do here, between work and playing around Dallas on the weekends."

Parker grimaced and sniffed. "I'm glad you can take time out of your busy schedule to help pull off this baby shower, wedding shower, bachelor and bachelor party conglomeration."

Landry pulled on his long-sleeve pearl-snap green plaid shirt that matched his eyes and winked at Parker.

"You know I can't resist a party. The guys are *still* talking about Andy's bachelor party."

Parker rolled his eyes. "Yeah, because you won't let them forget it."

They both chuckled while Landry slid on his socks and cowboy boots, but Landry couldn't stop the worry that seeped into his head at his brother's comments.

"Did you find out if Gunner wanted a traditional bachelor party? Do you think tonight will be okay to wrap it all into one or should we plan something separate for him?"

His brother shook his head and turned to walk into the

hallway, Landry following on his heels. Parker raked his hand through his hair.

"I've told you, this is fine. You're the only one who insists on all the parties. Most of us are much more low key than what you typically have in mind. I'm not even sure when you started getting so fussy about parties, but it's damn annoying sometimes."

"Hey, I'm not fussy. I just like planning something that brings a smile to people's faces, you know?"

Landry frowned because fussy was definitely not a term he wanted associated with himself. He grabbed his light jacket and the two presents he'd gotten Gunner and Maryanne.

"Where are your presents?"

Parker shrugged into his own jacket and patted his pocket as he replied, "I got them a gift card and a diaper subscription."

Landry laughed. Of course, Parker would go the route of least resistance and most practical. They walked down the street and around the corner as they talked about their family and the town.

When they turned up the walk to Gunner's new house, Landry was glad that he'd remodeled the kitchen a few years ago for the previous owners. He had a sense of pride at seeing his handy work being so loved by someone he cared about. With Gunner just down the street, it made living in town away from the rest of his family more bearable.

The door wasn't locked, so he walked in to the sound of women's voices coming from the kitchen. He set down his presents on the dining table before glancing through the doorway.

Lola, Maryanne's best friend from childhood, stood

drying the clean dishes. But Holly... Holly took his breath away. Again. You'd think he'd be used to it by now, but no.

Holly stood at the kitchen sink, the sun bouncing light off her silver hair, dyed to match her grief.

It was like a physical barrier between her and any guy who wanted to ask her out, himself included. When her husband had died and she'd moved in with Kendall, Landry had wanted nothing more than to sweep her into his arms and hold her while she cried.

He shoved his hands in his pockets to keep from reaching for her. Maybe Mrs. Helen was onto something when she said a woman would blow into town and knock him out of his boots. If only Holly would open herself up for love.

She was still gorgeous, still a pixie-sized bubble gum angel. His hands twitched to wrap her in his arms, but like always, he ignored it. She'd never be his, no matter how much he wished otherwise.

Chapter Nine

To you, I give my all. With you, I don't fear the rise, don't fear the fall. With every touch, my soul takes flight. You're my day, my heart, my night, my shining light.

May

Holly threw open the front door and kicked off her sneakers haphazardly into the living room. She needed a nice, long, hot shower after today. The kids in yoga kept making googly eyes at each other, which was cute but annoying when she was trying to lead a class. The sunrise yoga session was good, but those little old ladies from church just kept talking about Maryanne's baby.

Then she'd found out that both Cindy, Maryanne's sister, and Dot, the waitress from the Diner, were pregnant too, both just a few weeks along. And damn it, it made her mad.

The Songwriter Gets His Girl

She slammed the front door closed and pulled her shirt over her head as she stomped down the hall.

She was a mom without her baby and tomorrow was Mother's Day. Her arms felt more and more empty as time went on. The people who said that time heals all wounds were full of shit and had obviously never lost a baby before.

Why couldn't she just have a baby on her own? She paused in the middle of the hall, her fingers in her yoga pants with them slid halfway down her thighs. Now, there's a thought. She *could* have a baby on her own. People did it all the time with in vitro and artificial insemination and sperm banks. Why not her?

She shook her head and shimmied out of her pants, leaving them in the hallway as she stepped into the bathroom and turned on the shower to full blast. Kendall would kill her, but he wasn't the one who would raise the baby.

She'd need to move into the yoga studio apartment, prove she could live on her own. She'd only lived on her own for two years of her life, during Kendall's deployment when she first moved in with him after her aunt died, and that first year after Eric died when she still lived at Fort Hood.

With a deep breath, she stepped into the shower and let the hot water wash her frustration away. Maybe she could do this. If others could, then she could too. She felt hope bloom in her chest as she pictured herself in the yoga studio, teaching a class with a sleeping baby in a play pen next to her.

Thunk.

She spun around and got a face full of suddenly ice cold water. She screamed, throwing her hands up to grab the shower head and move it, only to find that there was no shower head. Through the water, she saw it laying in the shower's floor. Moving to the side and glancing up, the water was now gushing through the metal pipe above her.

She twisted the knob to turn the water off, only to have it pop off into her hand. The sudden move caused her to lose her footing, and she screamed as she fell into the bottom of the shower.

A shout was outside the door, then a voice yelled, "Holly? What the fuck?"

Holly stumbled to her feet, but the shower curtain flew back. She screamed once more, jerking her hands to cover her body and falling out of the tub and onto Landry.

"Oomph."

She gasped and jerked her head back, staring into his wide hazel eyes. The shower curtain had come down around them, cocooning them on the bathroom floor.

This day just kept getting better and better.

Landry lay there, staring at the goddess on top of him. He'd imagined his bubble gum angel naked thousands of times over the years, but his imagination didn't measure up to *this*.

He'd just gotten a peek, but damn. She straddled him and gasped, the sound raking down his spine and making the hair on the back of his neck stand on end. His hands were out of his control, naturally settling on the smooth skin of her hips.

He hissed, "Be still, Holly, or I won't be responsible for my actions. Are you ok? What happened?"

She sat up, shaking, and wrapped the shower curtain around her gorgeous shoulders. The movement brought her warm core down on his hard cock, making him groan.

The Songwriter Gets His Girl

"Today is the fucking worst day ever. And now this!"

Oh no, she started crying. He couldn't stand seeing the tears pool on her lower lashes and roll down her cheeks. She looked away and started to climb off him with a sob, but he grabbed her around the waist and sat up with her on his lap, straddling him.

She stiffened in his arms until he said, "Sh, it's okay. Don't worry about this. Tell me why today is the worst day ever, angel."

He pulled her head to his chest, his shirt already soaked from her wet hair, and rubbed circles on her back until she melted in his arms. Her head on his chest felt right, not to mention the heat from where their bodies were touching could burn the whole house down.

She whimpered and wrapped her arms around his back.

"It's just—tomorrow is Mother's Day, and Maryanne, Dot, and Cindy are all pregnant. It's hard because I miss her, Landry. I miss her so much. I only got to hold her for an hour, and my arms hurt from missing her. Why do they get a baby but mine was taken from me? Wh—why?"

Her sobs broke her words, and her body shook with pain and grief. He started to rock her, but quickly stopped, the friction just distracting him too much. He needed to focus and help, not be some randy teenager who could only think with his cock. Instead, he just drew circles on her back through the shower curtain and let her cry. It felt like his heart was going to break at her pain.

When her sobs slowed to soft shutters and hiccups, she said, "I want a baby, Lan."

His heart skipped a beat, and his arms tightened around her. "Well, angel, that would require a man, don't you think?"

She sighed and shrugged. "I guess I'll have to start dating again."

This was his chance! His heart raced and his hand on her back stilled, while his other hand snuck around to tip her chin up. Her green eyes shone like brilliant emeralds in the bathroom's light, tears still clinging to her lashes.

His heart raced and he growled, "You could always date me. I'd gladly put a baby in you, angel."

Her eyes widened in surprise, and he panicked. Afraid that she would laugh in his face or friend zone him again, he crashed his lips down to hers. When she gasped, he swept his tongue inside and groaned. She was hesitant, but he couldn't stop tasting the sweet candy that was her mouth. It was more addicting than sugar, and he'd craved more since that kiss in the barn.

Her tongue dueled with his, slowly and then more boldly. Soon, she was grinding on him, her hands fisting his shirt. His hands gripped her hips for dear life. He held on, afraid if he let go she would disappear like all the dreams he'd had of her over the years.

He couldn't live in fear though, so he sucked in a breath, deepened the kiss, and slid a hand to the back of her head. The fingers of his other hand trailed down to where their bodies met and plunged into her short-cropped blond hair to find the hidden jewel.

His thumb grazed it, and she jerked in his arms. Holding her head to his, their tongues still dancing in their kiss, he strummed her like a guitar, long and slow, back and forth, pressing gently in until she was grinding to meet him.

Her mewl of need made his racing heart skip a beat, and he turned his hand to slide a finger inside her warm, wet center. His mouth watered at the thought of tasting her, but first he needed to feel her come.

He hooked his finger and rubbed his thumb on her clit, causing her to moan and rock against him. Their kiss became frantic as she rode his hand. She gasped and bit his lip when she came. He'd wanted to see her face, but this was totally worth it. The feel of her squeezing his fingers, the pulsing and shaking of her body.

It was what he'd been craving for years. No other woman had ever measured up to her.

She started to pull away, and he kissed her lips softly one more time. His mind told him to savor it because it might be the only time she would do this. He prayed for his mind to be wrong.

Her eyes slowly cleared of the post-orgasm glaze, and she glanced around nervously before rolling off him. He caught a flash of her breasts before she wrapped the shower curtain around her and stood up, backing up to the wall where she avoided his gaze.

She looked at the still spurting shower and nodded to it. "What the hell is going on with that? Why did my shower fall apart, and why are you here?"

Landry grimaced at her avoidance and stood up, turning away from her and adjusting himself before shoving his hands in his pockets to keep his hard-on from being too visible. He shook his head, trying to clear the horny haze on his own brain.

"That would be my fault, I'm afraid. I'm remodeling the bathrooms this weekend, remember? I started Kendall's this morning and it's almost finished, but I had to remove the knobs here to go get new hardware. I'm sorry, Holly. I didn't know you'd be home this early or that I didn't tighten the knobs all the way before I left. Are you ok?"

She glanced up at him, her long lashes partially hiding her emerald green eyes, her mouth frowning. He wanted to kiss her swollen lips again and wipe that frown off her sweet face. He forced himself back a step and bumped into the doorjamb.

She glanced at the running shower, then back at him, still avoiding his eyes, her shoulders tense as she hugged herself. "Well, for fuck's sake, turn the water off." Her pouty grumble was adorable and made him want to jump to please her.

"Sure." He turned to escape to the garage but stopped before leaving the bathroom completely. He needed to diffuse the awkwardness fast, or she'd never give him another chance.

"And my offer stands. Anytime you need someone to *fix your pipes* or give you a baby, I'm here." He wiggled his eyebrows suggestively.

She groaned at the cheesy joke, which made him grin as he walked away. That should help reset their friendship while she thought about his offer.

When he found the breaker box, he flipped the switch before walking back into the house. The bag from the store was in front of the doorway where he'd dropped it when she'd screamed.

Numbly, he picked up the bag and walked quickly to Kendall's room, refusing to look into the hall bath, water no longer gushing out of the shower, or toward her room. Where she must be changing. He wondered if she'd be wearing that pink lacy bra he'd seen back in December when he'd first come to look at the bathrooms.

Shit, he couldn't do this. He had to get her out of his head. It'd just been too long since he'd been with a woman, that's all. And he'd made his offer to date her and give her that baby. When he reached Kendall's bathroom, he checked the grout he'd set earlier, then stepped across to the shower. As he worked to replace the hardware, he focused on slowing his racing heart.

She'd avoided him since February's paintball party. He'd not seen her around town, not even at Gunner and Maryanne's house, which he'd been painting one room at a time as they settled on colors. Did she feel this spark between them, or was it all in his head?

Despite what they'd just done, he doubted she'd ever take him up on his offer. She just didn't see him like that, as evidenced by their first meeting five years ago. When they'd first met, he'd just been a nice guy whom she could talk to. He was the one who'd thought they had something special when obviously they didn't because she'd still been pining for her ex-boyfriend.

Just like now. He couldn't blame her for still being in love with her husband, even though he'd been gone a few years now. That was the love he wanted someday.

He sucked in a breath, trying to get his mind off of imagining her svelte body, glistening with water, her eyes wide and innocent looking up at him with her mouth open in a perfect O. Would she look like that before an orgasm? Or before he shoved his cock in her mouth?

He groaned, adjusted himself in his pants, and kept trying to redirect his mind to something else. Soon, he was humming songs to get her out of his head. It didn't work.

Dear God, what had just happened? She tiptoed to the dresser in her room and quickly grabbed underwear. A glance in her mirror showed her entire face was blushing in mortification. But she paused, standing there naked.

Her eyes were wild, her lips swollen from their kiss. Had

he seen anything before she'd fallen on top of him? She wasn't buxom like Maryanne or tall and leggy like Lola. She was just short and petite, with few curves to speak of. If she had a baby, she would get more curves, more boobs, stretch marks. The idea of finally getting a decent rack was appealing.

I wonder if Landry would like my boobs bigger. She frowned at her reflection and gave herself the stink eye. Who cared what he thought because he wasn't going anywhere near them again.

She shook her hands and turned to the side, glimpsing her ass. It had always been her best feature but Landry hadn't even seen it.

Shit, had she *wanted* him to check out her ass? What the hell was wrong with her? This wasn't right, regardless of how good it had felt to be with him. That orgasm had been... earth shattering. She still had goose bumps, and her legs felt like jelly.

She glanced at the dresser across from her bed. A large picture collage hung above it, and she met Eric's eyes in the one they'd taken on their honeymoon to the beach.

"Eric, what do I do now?"

He didn't answer, of course, but she realized she didn't feel a stabbing pain in her chest when talking with him today. In fact, she hadn't felt it in a while, in months, maybe.

Her mind shied away from what that meant, and she jerked her underwear on before pulling out a drawer to find a shirt. She dressed quickly and jerked a brush through her hair, avoiding her own eyes in the mirror.

"Holly, I'm home." Kendall's voice rang out through the house as she was braiding her hair. She walked into the

The Songwriter Gets His Girl

living room to meet him as he was taking his shoes off from work.

"Hey, how was work today?"

"Not bad. How about yours?"

She shrugged, pasting on a smile as she turned into the kitchen and pulled out the dinner makings. "Feeling like fried rice and spring rolls tonight. Want to give me a hand?"

He nodded, then tipped his head as they both heard Landry singing from down the hall. "Is Landry still here? Let me go say hi, then I'll help with dinner."

Holly took a deep breath, practicing her meditative breathing techniques to slow her racing heart. Surely Landry wouldn't say anything. He wasn't one to kiss and tell, or she would've heard about all his conquests from him over the past few years. Right?

She distracted herself by making the spring rolls. Ok, so not that difficult, since it was all box made stuff. She was crap at making things from scratch, but someday she'd learn.

Maybe when she was a mom, she could prepare from scratch nutritious meals for them. She smiled, thinking of a little light brown haired boy running in from outside with hazel eyes.

She stilled, her finger hovering over the oven start button as she realized who that little boy reminded her of. No, no, absolutely not. She would go to the sperm bank and request a donor with black hair, or her own blond.

If she could request that sort of thing. On the Friends show, they could pick out sperm donors, so surely that's how it worked. She smiled, her shoulders relaxing as she pulled out the frozen cream cheese wontons.

"Hey, Holly, set an extra plate. Landry's going to stay for dinner, since he's still got a few hours left in here."

So much for relaxed shoulders. Her posture snapped to attention, and she sucked in a breath before yelling back, "Ok, it'll be ready in about thirty or forty-five minutes."

Her mind whirled, and the time flew by. Her thoughts were jumbled, constantly going back and forth between thinking about having a baby and Landry. Every time she started to relive his lips on hers, she'd start to think of moving out and her yoga studio, but each distraction lasted mere minutes before she started thinking about him again.

Before she was ready to face him, dinner was ready and on the table. She squared her shoulders and took a deep breath.

"All right, boys, dinner's ready."

She sat in her usual seat and made her plate, setting it aside to begin eating her Miso soup. They walked in and washed their hands, Landry having turned the water back on at some point. She avoided his gaze as they joined her at the table.

"This looks delicious, Holly. Thank you." Landry's voice reverberated through her, making her shiver and her face overheat.

"You're welcome. It's not much, but it's filling."

"Don't sell yourself short, Holly," Kendall said before taking a bite of his soup. "This is a wonderful meal, and honestly I'm not sure where you learned to cook like this. It certainly wasn't Mom who taught you."

Holly smiled tightly and shrugged. "It's all box directions, Kendall. You know this."

"Yeah, but you're doing so good. Her New Year's was to learn to make something new every other week, and she's actually kept up with it."

She felt Landry's gaze, but didn't look up from her food as he said, "Wow. Congratulations. Consider me impressed. I don't know anyone who's actually followed through with their resolution this long."

Kendall asked, "What was yours?"

Landry drained his soup before replying. "You know how my brother's and I have stopped playing at the Electric Cowboy every weekend?"

Holly kept quiet as Kendall answered. "Yeah, New Year's Eve was your last big gig."

"Exactly. My New Year's Resolution was to get out of my routine and play for the fun of it. So that's what I've been doing on the weekends, going into Dallas and Fort Worth to play. It's been a lot of fun, and I've met some pretty cool people so far."

"I miss hearing you sing." She cleared her throat and set her now empty bowl aside to slide her plate closer. "And Kendall wasn't being completely honest about mine. My resolution was actually to step out of my comfort zone with food. I can follow box directions, but making things from scratch is completely beyond me. And a lot of the vegetarian recipes I just haven't been able to master because of it."

"Like making pasta from scratch?"

She nodded, finally meeting his gaze. She sucked in a breath and felt her shoulders relax to see his face open and friendly, smiling like normal as he ate.

"Yeah, and breads. I know a lot of people stay away from pastas and breads, but I love them so much. And it's not like it impacts my weight or anything, because I'm still a stick."

"A gorgeous stick." His mischievous smile made her heart skip a beat before she glanced away again.

Kendall cleared his throat, and Landry turned to him to ask, "What was your resolution?"

Her brother grinned. "It was actually to take a vacation, since I haven't had one in quite a while. I think I've only taken off maybe a long weekend, three or four days in a row, in the past two years of living here."

Landry laughed. "Oh, yeah, I'd say you're due for one."

The rest of dinner seemed to go better, with Landry and Kendall sharing stories of Andy, who'd introduced them all those years ago, and the townsfolk. When he'd laugh, she'd sneak a look to see his face light up. The joy soothed her, and eventually she joined the conversation more and laughed right along with them.

Chapter Ten

You can't run from your destiny. You can't run from your soul mate. I'll chase you to the ends of the earth, I'll never stop searching, never stop searching.

July 4th

Holly glanced around nervously before ducking into the Psychic booth at the carnival. There were games set up along the gravel walkway on the Square in the center of town. Thankfully, the trees kept some shade from the blistering Texas summer sun.

But that wasn't what made her panic. No, it was seeing Landry walking toward her, laughing with one of his brothers. Her heart had raced, and she'd needed an escape.

She didn't even care that she was such a coward to avoid him now. She'd done a pretty good job of it over the past few months, ever since that first kiss in December. It hadn't been that big a deal before the paint mess in March and the Mother's Day incident, as she had named it.

But after he'd left, she'd fallen asleep with a smile on her face... only to wake up hours later to soaked dreams about him. And the dreams weren't going away. Every single night, she'd wake up around three like clockwork, sweating and overheated.

She spun around and saw her therapist, Tasha, dressed up in exotic, colorful clothing, sitting at a little cloth covered table with a glowing ball in the center.

Her shoulders immediately relaxed as Tasha raised a heavily shadowed eyebrow and waved to the chair opposite, her bracelets twinkling in the light.

"Escaping your destiny again, my dear?"

Holly jumped at Tasha's changed voice, deeper and more lyrical than normal. Slowly, she slid onto the chair and tilted her head.

"What do you mean by that?"

"Give me your hand, and I'll tell you."

Holly rolled her eyes and smiled as she relaxed. Tasha was just doing a bit, playing a part. She knew nothing more than what Holly had told her in their counseling sessions the past few months.

Still, she was curious to see how this would play out. She held out her hand, and Tasha's henna covered hand held hers. Holly was surprised at the coldness of it because there wasn't a fan in the room.

She looked around, trying to find why the entire room was cold now, but Tasha's voice pulled her back.

"This is your head line. It keeps interfering with your fate line, which is this one and why they intersect. You will need to make a choice soon, between the head and the fate."

Holly frowned and leaned forward despite of herself.

"Your life line is long, with energy and enthusiasm for life. But see this part here?"

Holly nodded, so Tasha kept going.

"This means that your ability to live life to the fullest has been dammed up, blocked, or stalled."

Holly nodded her head. Of course, it had been. She'd been grieving for a while now, and the pain never went away. What did living life to the fullest even mean?

"And finally, we have your heart line. See how it has two diverging lines, and this one is short? That's the one you loved deeply but lost too soon. See this one? It's long, deep, and true, but the fact that it crosses your fate line means he's the one you're truly made for, the one who will bring your life back into fullness of joy and love."

Holly's breath caught in her chest, glancing over her shoulder as she heard Landry laugh outside the tent. It couldn't be him. No, she didn't want to love again. Not now, not anytime soon. It was too painful to lose something so precious.

"Hm, see this? Now this is interesting. The second love line starts here. See how both lines are present but diverge? That normally means that your second love started before the first ended, but since you're widowed, that's probably not what happened. Dang it, I knew I needed to study up on this a bit more before today. Sorry, Holly."

Tasha set her hand back on the table and patted it twice before leaning back in her chair and crossing her arms. Holly glanced away and fiddled with the hem of her blue tank top.

She'd met Landry the night she'd gotten engaged to Eric, but she didn't *love* Landry. He was just a good friend. *A good friend who you'd kissed.*

She frowned and twisted her hem. Landry'd been a rock in the storm of the past two years after losing Eric and her baby girl. He'd been a shoulder to cry on, and he always had a joke to pick her up and make her smile.

She hadn't told Tasha that she'd met Landry years ago when Eric had proposed. She hadn't told Tasha about the kisses with him or about her research into artificial insemination.

"Um, that's alright. I appreciate the reading anyway. But what if I don't want the second love? I'm not ready; you know this, Tasha. We've talked about it in counseling for months."

"And you've made tremendous progress on processing the past. I'm very proud of your work. You even went on a few dates! But you can't keep ignoring the future, Holly. The past, present, and future are going to converge soon, and you'll need to decide how you want to handle it."

Holly snorted. "Any way to tell when this will all happen? I'm not a big fan of surprises."

Tasha shrugged and smiled. "Not really. I mean, Mercury will enter retrograde next weekend, so expect things you haven't fully dealt with to come back and stare you in the face for a while. Life gets extra challenging, miscommunication abounds, and life gets pretty hectic and chaotic."

"Great, and I was already expecting Maryanne's baby to bring some of those feelings up. But you're saying it's basically going to be ten times worse than I thought, huh?"

"More like one hundred times worse." Tasha chuckled, which made Holly shake her head and rub her forehead.

"We are still on for next Tuesday?"

Holly nodded and glanced behind her as they heard a group stop outside the tent flap.

The Songwriter Gets His Girl

"Looks like my time is up. What do I owe you?" Holly paid before sliding out the door and glancing left down the gravel path.

A few hours later, Holly felt more and more unsettled as she watched Landry sing on stage with his brothers and waited for the fireworks to start. Fully dark now, she got up to throw her water bottle away, unable to sit still any longer. Maryanne waddled around the edge of the crowd, so Holly joined her, her heart aching at the way Maryanne and Gunner had sang together.

"Hey Maryanne, that was a beautiful moment between you two. Do you two sing together a lot at home?"

Maryanne smiled and nodded but avoided her eyes, making Holly winced. She'd been avoiding Landry and that had led to her inadvertently ignoring Maryanne too. Tasha thought it was because she didn't want to see Maryanne while pregnant, but that was only part of it.

Her heart hurt to see Maryanne so big and ready to pop. Her own baby girl had passed because of the car crash that killed Eric. She'd been twenty weeks along and went into a premature delivery. They'd tried to save her baby, but it hadn't worked. She'd sobbed in that hospital room and held her tiny baby in her hands, alone.

Maryanne asked about her dates over the past few weeks, and Holly shrugged. "I have two more dates scheduled for next week, but I don't know if I want to go through with them."

Maryanne frowned. "Why not? You're not looking for love or to replace Eric. You're just getting back out there and having fun, right?"

Holly sighed, her chest tight. "Yeah, but I really just want a baby, a family. The whole dating scene is a lot of stress."

Maryanne snorted. "Yeah, but sex usually makes the stress of a date worth it."

Holly scrunched her nose. "Ew, no. I mean, the two dates I've been on have been cute, but not *that* cute."

Maryanne laughed, and Holly's mind drifted to the only man she'd found even remotely sexy in the past few years. But Landry wasn't ever far from her mind, really, especially not after their three steamy make-out sessions.

They were halfway to the bathroom when Maryanne stopped abruptly, gripping her stomach and breathing deeply. Maryanne told her they were just Braxton Hicks contractions because she'd been having them pretty regularly the past few days, but maybe this was more.

"You sure you're not going into labor?"

Holly twisted her hands and shifted on her feet, but Maryanne laughed, her dark hair pulled back into a high bun on the top of her head, a streak of red down one side and blue on the other.

"Doubtful. Peanut has been doing somersaults in there all day long. It settled down while I was sitting, listening to Gunner. But dancing on stage was probably not the best idea."

They laughed again and continued walking to the porta potties near the parking lot.

Holly looped her arm through Maryanne's. "Well, you better tell me if they are real contractions. Kendall is right over there and can check."

"Yeah, that wouldn't be weird at all. He's your brother, and I see him all the time." They laughed at Maryanne's over the top sarcastic tone.

When they reached the porta potties, Holly held out her hand. "You want me to hold your phone?"

"How'd you know?"

The Songwriter Gets His Girl

Holly rolled her eyes. "You told me last year that you only make that mistake once."

Maryanne winced and handed over her little purse before going into the little restroom. Holly pulled out the hand sanitizer from her own purse and had it ready for when she returned. Then they switched, and Maryanne held their stuff.

Holly wondered what she would have done if Maryanne hadn't come with her. There weren't any hooks in there for her purse. She heard voices and finished up quickly before pushing open the door.

"Who are you talking to, Maryanne? Oh, hello."

The tall, lanky man leapt away and pulled his hand from behind his back, leveling a gun at Maryanne. "Don't move. Who are you? Shit, it doesn't matter. Mary, come on, and whoever you are, you'll have to come with us."

Holly's hands shook as she jumped in front of Maryanne, who turned her belly away from the man.

He waved the gun at her belly. "Nah, huh, huh. None of that now, Mary. We have unfinished business, and we're going to pull that little baby daddy of yours into it too. Come on. What's your name?"

Holly froze, then slid closer to Maryanne who grabbed her hand. The squeeze was sharp and made Holly speak up.

"Hol—Holly. Who are you?"

"This is Barry," Maryanne hissed, squeezing her hand again.

Holly's blood ran cold as all the stories of Maryanne's evil ex flooded her mind. Barry flanked them, pressing the gun into Maryanne's back and pushing them forward into the parking lot.

"Where are we going?" Holly asked, her voice raised to

catch someone's attention. Anyone, she didn't care. Someone had to be close to the bathrooms.

Barry barked at them. "Hush. Keep it down, or I'll be forced to use this thing too soon, and that's not my plan. Remember that barn from Halloween, Mary? That's where we're going. Out in the middle of nowhere."

They stopped at a black BMW that had seen better days. It was scratched up and missing a taillight. Barry had been arrested months ago, with the taillight being why Gunner had pulled him over.

Maryanne taunted Barry. "Still haven't gotten that taillight fixed, Barry? That's not like you."

Holly gasped as Barry pushed Maryanne against the car with the butt of the gun under her chin.

"Shut up. I've been in jail because of you, Mary. It's your fault the whole thing toppled over, and you're gonna pay. Now, get in and drive."

He waved to the driver's seat, but Maryanne snorted. "Yeah, I'm not going anywhere with you. I can't drive, dip shit. I'm too big."

He frowned, then waved at Holly. "You drive then. And I'll keep the gun on Mary."

Holly felt the blood leave her face, and her whole body trembled. The last time she'd driven, she'd almost ran over Andy and he'd ended up in the hospital. And before that... was the wreck that cost her everything.

Maryanne stepped in front of her. "No, she's not driven in years. She can't. You'll have to be a man and drive."

Barry snapped, twisting Maryanne's arm behind her back and throwing open the passenger side door. He waved the gun at Holly.

"Holly, is it? You're driving. Now."

Holly stumbled around to the driver's side and threw

The Songwriter Gets His Girl

open the door while Maryanne and Barry slid into the passenger side. She could do this, she could do this, she could do this.

She had to, if she was going to save Maryanne and the baby. She couldn't save her own baby girl, but she wasn't going to let anything happen to Maryanne's. The scent of cheap cologne filled the interior, nauseating Holly and making her palms sweat.

Maryanne said, "Holly, start the car and roll down the windows. Quick, I'm going to be sick."

Her hands shook as she pushed the button to start it. She turned on the air conditioner and rolled down the windows. She fiddled with the seat, moving it forward, and adjusted the mirrors. Maybe if she stalled—

"For crying out loud, put it in reverse and go already," Barry yelled in the small space, making both Maryanne and Holly jump. "You know the barn I'm talking about?"

Holly nodded. It was Landry's parent's barn, and she'd been to every Halloween party for the past two years. She slowly backed up and crept through the parking lot, looking for pedestrians.

Fool her once, shame on her. Fool her twice and hit two people in a parking lot, and she'd never get back to driving. She turned out of the parking lot and breathed a sigh of relief.

When she made it to the road that would take her to the Williams' ranch, she crept up to thirty miles per hour. Barry began to rant, which just made her sweat more. Her knuckles turned white on the steering wheel, but she breathed deeply and turned onto the dirt road.

Just as they pulled up to the barn, Holly hit a bump and squealed, slamming on the brakes. Maryanne turned slightly and threw up all over Barry's legs. Holly gasped and parked it, turning off the engine while Barry started foaming at the mouth.

"Holy fuck! You little bitch. You did that on purpose."

He threw open the door and pulled Maryanne out by an arm. She fell on the ground, and Holly cried out, jumping out of the car and rushing around to help.

"Maryanne, are you ok?"

Holly helped her sit up while Barry paced behind them, waving the gun frantically. Maryanne gripped her arm and squeezed, pulling her closer. Holly's heart was racing, but she could still hear Maryanne's whisper.

"Holly, my water broke."

Chapter Eleven

Together we're strong, hand in hand, Side by side, we'll always stand, My heart, my soul, my everything, yours forever, I'll make your heart sing.

Landry unplugged his guitar and helped his brothers, Hunter and Parker, pack up their equipment while the fireworks started. Out of the corner of his eye, he saw his other brother, Gunner, yell at Andy, hands waving wildly.

Shit, what would make his brother and his best friend argue like that? A sense of dread settled in his stomach, and he ran down the steps while Andy yelled back.

Gunner had backed down by the time Landry reached their side. Cindy came up beside them, waving her phone to say, "I texted Kendall. He's on his way. Gunner, who would do this?"

Gunner's legs gave out, and Landry caught him under one arm while Andy caught him under the other.

Landry looked at Andy over his brother's head and growled, "What the fuck is going on?"

"I took Mandy to the bathroom and saw a man take Maryanne and Holly at gunpoint."

Landry's arms felt weak and shaky as Gunner shook him off, but his mind was even more chaotic. No, this didn't make sense. There had to be some other explanation.

"Like, a kidnapping? Of two grown-ass women?"

Andy nodded at Landry while Gunner pulled his phone out to open the tracking app on Maryanne's phone. Looking over his shoulder, Landry said, "That's Mom and Dad's barn."

Kendall and another half dozen guys from their weekly poker group joined them, and Cindy quickly filled them in while Gunner called for his deputies. Landry just stood there, frozen in terror of something happening to Holly before he could tell her how he felt.

How *did* he feel about her? It was undefinable, all-consuming, entwined with his soul and unable to be separated.

His brother was amazing though, launching into action even though his hands shook and his lips were pinched with worry. Then they raced to the parking lot, Landry's heart beating hard. Maryanne was his childhood summer best friend, and Holly...

His mind refused to identify what Holly was, but neither of them deserved to be held at gunpoint. God, they must be so scared. He just wanted to wrap her in his arms and keep her safe. When they reached the sheriff's SUV, Gunner raised his hands and barked orders to the group.

When he finished, Andy scowled. "He made Holly drive."

Landry's stomach twisted in knots. She couldn't drive,

especially in the dark. She was too scared. They all knew the car accident that had killed her husband and baby had been when she was driving.

Gunner threw open the door to his SUV, and most of them piled in, but Landry ran to his truck with his other two brothers and a former Marine friend, Nick. They squeezed into the truck, but they were all practically in each other's laps in the crowded cab.

Landry gripped the steering wheel until his knuckles turned white, trying to get his heart rate under control. He'd never been so scared in his life.

Nick held the dashboard in front of him. "Landry, my guns are at my house. We're going to need them."

Landry cursed and did a U-turn on the highway, tires squealing. "We need to be at Mom and Dad's in fifteen minutes. Otherwise, they're going to surround the barn without us. We have to be there."

He heard his voice crack on the last word, and Parker glanced at him as he pulled up to Nick's house.

"I'm timing you. Two minutes. Hurry the hell up." Landry couldn't keep the frustration out of his voice.

Hunter slid out behind Nick, and they raced into the house. Landry watched the clock the entire time, his mind spinning at the idea that he'd never get to tell Holly how beautiful she was, how strong, how smart, how resilient. The list went on and on until Parker cleared his throat.

"They're going to be fine. Maryanne isn't gonna take any shit from that fucker, you know that. She can hold her own."

Landry's hands twisted on the steering wheel, unable to let go as he stared at the clock. "It's not her I'm worried about."

He could feel Parker's gaze boring into the side of his

head. "Holly will be okay too. She's more resilient than any of us think. She's had to be, to survive all she's gone through."

"And now this? Parker, she deserves so much more. She deserves someone to protect her from things like this, to be there at her side, to—"

He broke off and swallowed hard while Nick and Hunter burst through the front door with a duffel bag.

"To love her?" Parker asked quietly into the stillness before Hunter threw open the passenger door, and they piled back in.

Two minutes. He'd need to make up nearly three minutes of time by the time he backed up and hit the road again. The rest of the drive to Mom and Dad's was a blur as Hunter and Nick checked over the pistols and guns in the duffel, loading and checking safeties.

By the time they pulled up the drive, his jaw was aching from clenching it so tightly. He breathed a sigh of relief to see his brother's SUV turning down the dirt road to the barn.

They'd made it. Surely, they'd be in time to save them. They parked a half-mile away and tumbled out of the truck, leaving the doors slightly open. Nick handed over a gun, a 9mm, and he checked the safety as they jogged behind Gunner down the road.

Gunner motioned for them to split up, so Landry, Parker, and Nick went left while Kendall, Hunter, and Andy went right. Nick led their group, as he was prior military. With all their paintball experience, Parker and Landry knew exactly how to stack up on the wall.

Nick took high, and Landry crouched low as they both peered around the corner of the barn. Nick motioned them forward, and they followed, Parker sweeping the rear.

The Songwriter Gets His Girl

Fear raced up her spine as she met Maryanne's wild eyes while Barry screamed at them to get up and get in the barn. Holly helped Maryanne get on her knees, but Holly saw their purses lying on the car's floorboard.

Her pulse pounding in her ears, she slipped her phone out of her purse with shaking hands and and dialed 911 by the time Maryanne made it to standing. This wasn't happening. It was just a nightmare. She'd wake up any moment now.

She shoved it into the back pocket of her jean shorts and pulled Maryanne's arm around her shoulder. They slowly made their way to the barn door where Barry stood yelling at them. Her mind had tuned him out, but her heart still raced. She glanced at Maryanne as they walked a few steps, then stopped while a contraction hit.

"Breathe, Maryanne. It's going to be okay. We'll get through this, and the baby will be fine. You'll be fine. Everyone will be healthy and safe."

Maryanne nodded as they walked sideways through the door, the gun quickly shoving into Maryanne's back again. Holly frowned and practically growled at him. "You don't have to keep waving that gun around, you know. We're here at the Williams' barn. What's the next step of your grand plan?"

Barry waved them to the end of the bales of hay, closer to the middle of the barn. "Over here, away from the door. We're going to lure your cop out here, then I'm going to take you all out. The mother fucker is going to watch you die before I put him down like the dog he is."

Maryanne moaned as another contraction hit. Holly glanced around and nodded to the hay. "Let's sit down and lean against the hay, Maryanne. You can't stay on your feet."

"Yes, she can. She's my prisoner, not yours, and the bitch has to suffer."

Holly's head snapped to the deranged bastard. "I don't fucking care what you think. She's about to have her baby, thanks to you throwing her in and out of the car like that. Do *you* want to catch the baby?"

His face blanched, and he spun around, ranting about babies, Maryanne, and her cop baby daddy. Her whole body broke out in a sweat as he waved the gun toward them again. She'd never talked to anyone like that before. It was just like her to wait until she was held at gunpoint to grow a pair and stand up for something.

Maryanne moaned, and Holly ignored the dumb fucker who thought he'd get away with this. They were going to be saved. Between Gunner and her brother, she knew they would be. She just had to buy them time until the guys got here.

As the crazed man waved his gun around, Holly struggled to maintain a calm demeanor and focus on Maryanne. Memories of her own traumatic experience with childbirth flooded her mind, and her hands shook. Maryanne shifted on the floor, curling her body around the pain as she groaned. Barry still paced, muttering under his breath.

Maryanne whimpered. "Holly, this isn't going to work. I don't want to have her like this. Gunner's not here, and if he does show up, Barry's going to—"

"No, he won't. They're going to come to the William's ranch and find us, then they're going to stop the lunatic waving the gun at us. Here, lean back against the hay."

Holly used the movement to move her phone, making sure the call to 911 was still active, then placed it so that

The Songwriter Gets His Girl

Barry couldn't see. They couldn't get Maryanne in a comfortable position, so Holly got in the coaching position. When Maryanne leaned back, the back of her her head on Holly's chest, Holly wrapped her arms around Maryanne.

Maryanne was in labor, and it jerked Holly out of her own issues. The numbness that had wrapped around her when the bastard had first pulled his gun on them floated away. She needed to be strong for her friend, but every muscle in her body wanted to run away from the danger. Maryanne's pained moans filled the vast room, and Holly's heart ached at her friend's suffering, rooting her to the spot.

She could do this. She had to do this, for Maryanne. One of her best friends needed her. The baby needed her, and she refused to let another baby die on her watch.

She whispered to her friend, both their hands on Maryanne's stomach as they felt the contractions. "I have my phone and have called 911. Help is on the way, Maryanne. Just hold on. Let's practice the breathing techniques, ok?"

Barry walked to them with a lantern, swinging it wildly as he placed it at their feet.

"Okay, time to call your baby daddy. The town fireworks will be over, and he's had a good time to worry. Now he'll answer his phone and get his ass out here. Alone."

Maryanne moaned. "I don't have my phone. Are you going to go get it from the car? Because no one remembers phone numbers these days. Have you always been this dumb?"

"Shut up, bitch. We're going to call your little baby daddy. Then when he gets here, you'll all die a fiery death."

Maryanne gasped before grinding her teeth. "Don't have the balls to shoot us all? Figures."

"Shut up, bitch," he snarled.

Maryanne tensed through a contraction, yelling, "How are you going to start a fire, Barry? Your plan is flawed. The lantern is battery operated. You don't even know how to light a fireplace, or have you forgotten that I was always the one who did that?"

Holly leaned forward and whispered to Maryanne, "Good. Keep him talking. That will give them time to get here."

She slid her hands to Maryanne's stomach, feeling the contraction. Maryanne groaned, gripping Holly's knees, her nails digging into the skin and drawing blood. Holly didn't care, she was solely focused on the contraction.

When it passed, Barry was back to pacing in front of them. A ding sounded in the darkness, making Barry swing away. "What was that?"

It happened again and again, Maryanne digging at Barry, poking holes in his plan while he talked about some drug lord in Dallas. Soon, Barry was walking toward the tapping sound to investigate. He'd gotten a few feet away at the end of the bales of hay when two figures blurred as they rushed him.

They tackled Maryanne's ex, their punches landing with satisfying thuds. Relief coursed through her, making her body shake. The guys had made it!

A shadow to the right drew her eye. In dirty jeans and a t-shirt, Landry strode toward them with singular focus, glancing back and forth from the three men wrestling on the ground to Holly and Maryanne. Gun pointed to the ground and the men, he quickly got between them and the bastard that had kidnapped them.

He was like a beacon in the darkness, his blond hair darker in the dim light. The scruff on his chin cast more shadows, making him leaner and more intense. His hazel eyes were hard as he met her own before raking over them both, searching for injuries.

He panted, "Are you alright?"

With the fierceness of his expression, the barely controlled voice, and the way he crouched between them and danger, she knew without a doubt that he would protect them. Instead of making her relax at being rescued, she grew more tense. Someone was going to get hurt.

Time seemed to slow down, and fear and uncertainty swirled in her stomach. The numbness of earlier faded, leaving only fear of losing him. She opened her mouth to warn Landry to get away from the danger. She couldn't lose him too. She nodded, the knot in her throat and tears in her eyes preventing her from saying anything more.

A gunshot rang through the barn, making her ears ring and her heart stop before galloping away with her emotions. She screamed, and Landry threw himself in front of them, using his own body as a shield. His arms wide and hands settling on Holly's knees, he glanced behind him at the men. He'd just jumped between them and a bullet. She could lose him in an instant like she had Eric, and her heart stuttered with fear, guilt for him being here, and another emotion she didn't want to name.

With Maryanne between them, it should've been awkward, but when his gaze found hers, she felt like they were the only two in the room. Fear and fierce protectiveness radiated from him, wrapping around her. She somehow drew strength from his solid form in front of her, from his touch on her knees. She wasn't alone anymore, his presence giving her renewed hope and determination.

Shouts sounded outside, and the barn door on the opposite side of the wall opened before several figures swept inside, military style. Holly swept her hands along

Maryanne's stomach as another contraction hit, her own breathing coming easier now that Landry was in front of her, his touch anchoring her.

Holly's voice shook as she asked Maryanne, "You weren't hit, were you? Are you ok?" Her eyes searched Landry's and he shook his head, telling her without words that he wasn't hit either.

Maryanne nodded, gritting her teeth as another contraction rippled, and she moaned. "I'm okayyyyyy."

Holly recognized the men striding to them and breathed a sigh of relief. "It's going to be alright. Kendall's here, Maryanne. Kendall's here."

Tears prickled her eyes as her brother came into the light of the lantern along with several others behind him. Kendall knelt beside them and took over touching Maryanne's stomach.

"Her contractions are super close, Kendall. Parker, take my phone and talk to the 911 people." Holly slid her phone out and across the floor to Landry's brother.

Kendall frowned. "Maryanne, I need to check you, okay?"

Holly sucked in a breath and looked at all the men crowding around. "For the love of God, the rest of y'all go away. You can't see this part."

Maryanne moaned while Kendall flipped up her stained and dirty skirt. Holly didn't ask Landry to go, but he turned and ushered the rest of the men to the side where they watched the still wrestling men on the ground. No doubt they were all eager to jump in and help, but some of the peace and safety left with him.

Kendall let out a whoosh of breath. "Holy shit. Maryanne, you're crowning. You have to push. Where's the ambulance?"

Holly went numb and cold. Maryanne was going to give birth *here*? In her arms? She didn't know if she could do this, see another baby being born like this. Panic set in, but Maryanne moaned.

"Breathe, Maryanne." She told her friend, but it was for her own benefit too. She had to breathe. She had to help her friend.

Chapter Twelve

You're worth fighting for. You're worth dying for. But I'm not going anywhere, baby. I'm here to stay, here to protect, here to love.

The baby arrived in a flurry of activity, and Holly sat there through it all, tears streaming down her cheeks. Even as Maryanne and Gunner proclaimed their love for each other, Holly bit her tongue and kept quiet, just trying to process all the emotions.

Maryanne and the baby were loaded into an ambulance to go the hospital, and her ex was hauled into the other one, unconscious from a bullet wound but cuffed to the gurney. The guys who rescued them swaggered outside as Holly finally stood to her feet, blinking as a wave of dizziness washed through her. Her hands were cold and clammy and the barn walls were closing in on her, the air stuffy and filled with blood.

It reminded her of the wreck that cost her everything, and she glanced around and followed the others outside slowly, her legs weighed down with bricks. When they left the barn, she slid along the wall in the shadows, watching the ambulances pull away.

Her body trembled and her heart raced. She knew she was in shock because the cold was back. She'd been so cold for almost three years now, and it was stupid to be cold in a Texas July.

Kendall went to the kidnapper's car to get her purse, but as tears poured down her cheeks, a man stepped out of the door to her right. She gasped and jerked back, but Landry just held up his hands.

"Easy there. It's okay. It's just me. You're okay, Holly. He's not going to hurt you again."

Tears filled her eyes, because her head knew he was talking about Maryanne's ex, but her heart thought he was talking about Eric. Eric was gone, and he wasn't going to hurt her again by leaving. But he wasn't going to love her again, either.

He wasn't going to wake her up with kisses on the nose and pancakes. He wasn't going to sweep her into a twirly hug when he came home from work or leave post-its on the mirror.

He really was gone forever.

Landry reached out slowly and tipped her head up, his fingertips below her chin. "Hey, come here. Holly, look at me."

She'd not heard that tone of voice from Landry before. Her body trembled, and he swept her into his arms. Holding her tight, her body jerked before it melted against his sweaty chest.

The scent of leather and dirt rose around her, grounding her in the present and pushing thoughts of Eric to the back of her head. Maybe this was okay, maybe Eric had sent him so she could finally be warm and comforted in this chaos.

She felt safe in his arms—

Arms that were suddenly jerked away from her. Kendall spun Landry away and shoved him into the barn wall. Holly stumbled, but Kendall pulled her to his side.

"She's just been traumatized, Landry. Back off. She doesn't need some jackass putting a move on her right now."

Holly snorted and pulled away, jerking her purse from his hand. Yeah, Kendall was trying to protect her, like always, but this was fucking ridiculous.

She stepped in between them, shaking off Kendall's arm. "He was just comforting me, Kendall. You need to apologize right now."

"Holly, I'm not going to—"

"Yes, you fucking are." Holly tipped her chin and stared at her brother. She crossed her arms and pursed her lips. "Yes, I've been traumatized. Yes, I was crying, and he hugged me. Why do you always have to be so overbearing? This is neither the time nor the place, but it *is* time for you to leave me alone to live my life, Kendall. I needed comfort, and Landry offered it. There was nothing *sexual* about it. Now, apologize."

Kendall's jaw audibly ground together before he snapped, "Sorry, Landry. Thanks for comforting her." Then he stomped away to the truck.

Landry rubbed his tatted shoulder where it had hit the barn. "Uh, thanks for that. Seriously though, are you okay? I'm going to drive you and Kendall home, if you're ready. You'll have to go to the station tomorrow to give your statement."

She nodded and walked quietly beside him, very aware

The Songwriter Gets His Girl

of the body heat radiating off him and the scent of leather still filling her nose and settling her nerves.

She sighed when Landry settled his hand on her back and opened the truck door for her. She slid to the middle, Kendall already by the passenger side door, arms crossed and staring straight ahead.

Landry shut his door, and she rubbed her forehead. Her body began to shake, and Kendall settled his arm along her back, pulling her close.

She cried, wails that filled the cab. She cried for her empty arms, missing her baby. She cried for her missing husband. She cried for what could have been. She even cried because it was Kendall holding her and not Landry. Then she cried some more because she didn't realize she wanted Landry's arms until tonight.

Landry began to croon softly, singing a song that she'd never heard before.

The lemonade is sweeter with thoughts of you.
You're my sugar and the water that gives life.
Every drop is a memory. Every drop of my tears.
Every drop a reverie. Every drop another year.
Another day without you in my arms, threatens to break me.
If life gives you lemons, make lemonade.
But if life gave me you, sunshine, I'd have life made.

It soothed her brittle soul, and soon she was hiccupping, her tears slowing to a trickle. They pulled up to the house, and Kendall released her to open the door and walk away.

Before she slid out of the truck, she looked at Landry. Their eyes met in the dim porch lights, his so full of worry, fear, relief, and something else.

He licked his lips and swallowed. "Let me know if you need anything, angel. I'm here." His voice was soft and deep, too low for Kendall to hear where he stood waiting on the front porch, having gone to unlock it.

His phone rang, breaking the spell between them.

She nodded, taking a deep shuttering breath of that calming leathery scent before sliding along the bench seat to the passenger door and climbing out. This night wasn't what she'd thought it'd be. It was supposed to be an ordinary 4th of July night, not an earth shattering one.

The phone rang again, the sound echoing and growing louder and louder as the sky shimmered and the stars flew closer. Her head spun.

She gasped, sitting straight up in her bed as the dream memories of last night faded. She was at Kendall's in her old bed. She groaned, her throat dry and scratchy from crying last night and being awake almost all night thinking, planning, and researching. Anything to keep the traumatic kidnapping out of her head.

Her hands clenched the sheets, remembering the steering wheel under her hands. Shakily, she reached for the phone.

"Hello?"

"Hey, you're alive! I didn't get a text or anything after that shit show last night, and I've tried calling you like four times already this morning. What the hell happened?" Lola's voice came through, bringing her awake.

Holly grunted, laying back on the bed and rubbing her eyes. What had happened was her entire life shifting underneath her. She had to forget the dreams, the memories of Landry, because her life plans had completely changed because of last night.

After briefing Lola and planning to meet at the hospital to check on Maryanne and the baby, she got up and went to the bathroom.

She closed the bathroom door and quickly turned on

the water in the shower. A glance in the mirror showed her entire face was blushing. She paused, not used to seeing that look of freedom and excitement on her face.

Her eyes were wild and haunted, though. What had Landry meant by that? Did he mean *anything*?

He made her head spin even more. Between the kidnapping and the memory of their kisses swirling around, she felt shaky on her feet.

She turned on the water to the shower and tried to scrub the thoughts out of her head. She wasn't buxom like Maryanne or tall and leggy like Lola. She was just short and petite, with few curves to speak of.

Although, that would change if she went through with her new plan to have another baby. She'd get more curves, bigger boobs, and stretch marks. She took her pajamas off.

I wonder if Landry would like my boobs bigger.

She frowned at her reflection and gave herself the stink eye. Who cared what he thought because he wasn't going to get anywhere near them. This wasn't about him. It was about her finally becoming the mom she'd always dreamed of being.

She shook her hands and turned to the side, glimpsing her ass. It had always been her best feature but did Landry like it?

Shit. Stop. Stop. Stop. She didn't want him checking out her ass. What the hell was wrong with her? She'd just been kidnapped at gunpoint, and she was fantasizing about Landry?

This wasn't right, regardless of how good it had felt to be with him, how his kisses were so earth shattering, how thoughts of him kept her up at night.

Last night had changed everything, and Landry wasn't part of that. She had to let that go and focus on the future.

And she finally knew what that future was going to be. Goose bumps spread on arms and her legs felt like jelly. She really was going to do it.

She glanced at the large picture collage hanging beside the sink, and she met Eric's eyes in the one they'd taken on their honeymoon to the beach.

"Eric, can I do this?"

He didn't answer, of course, but she realized she didn't feel a stabbing pain in her chest when talking with him today. In fact, she hadn't felt it in a while, in months, maybe.

Her mind shied away from what that meant.

Last night, she'd watched as a healthy baby girl was born into this crazy world. By sitting as she was from right behind Maryanne's head, it was like she was giving birth again.

She felt tears flowing down her face, her heart opening up and yearning for what was lost. The woman in the mirror stared back at her, her eyes red rimmed. She thought she'd cried out all the tears last night.

But watching Maryanne bring her baby into this world... it changed everything.

She wanted that too. She wanted to be a mom. She could finally admit to herself that she'd never stopped wanting to be a mom. Life was a miracle, and her arms ached for the little girl she'd lost.

Holly's tears overflowed, and she stepped into the shower, sinking to the floor while she finally let out all the pain. It was cathartic, and after ten minutes, she really was out of tears.

When she stepped out of the shower, she felt like a new woman. Slightly shaky on her feet but determined to change her life. Determined to take charge and move forward. Ready to enjoy every moment life offered.

The Songwriter Gets His Girl

She wrapped the towel around herself and opened the bathroom door. A knock sounded on the front door, but she ignored it until a muffled voice came through.

"Holly? Are you okay? It's me, Landry."

She rubbed her temple and walked to the door, opening it. The sun shone behind him, casting a halo around him like some Greek god. He stepped inside and kicked the door shut.

She blinked, now able to see his face. He was frowning, worried, as his eyes searched her face.

"I brought coffee and your favorite donut holes, fresh from the bakery. Zarrel is so upset about last night that he's been baking for hours already."

His eyes widened and his voice tapered off as he looked her up and down. She glanced down and gasped, adjusting the towel and shifting from one foot to the other.

"Um, thanks. I appreciate it. I'm about to head to the hospital to check on Maryanne."

He set the coffee and the bag on the side table by the couch and stepped closer. She backed up, and he stopped advancing, his arms falling to his side.

She wanted nothing more than for him to hold her, but if he did, she'd crack. She needed to stand on her own two feet if she was going to move forward with her plan.

He shoved his hands into his pockets and frowned. "But are *you* okay?"

Their eyes met, his promising the entire world. If she'd just reach out, it'd be hers. She took another step back and nodded.

He held her eyes, and she swallowed past the lump. "Yes, I'm fine. Better than ever. Remember Mother's Day weekend?"

His brows rose and desire pooled in his eyes. "Do I?"

She rolled hers and looked away, her cheeks overheated. "Remember what we were *talking* about, about wanting to be a mom? I think, after last night, I'm ready."

Silence descended, and she looked back at him. A flurry of emotions were sparking over his face as he sucked in a deep, shaky breath. "That's amazing, Holly. That's a huge step forward with life. Have you thought about—"

Her phone rang in her bedroom, cutting him off.

He shifted and looked around. "If you want a lift to the hospital, I'll wait for you to get ready."

She nodded and strode to her room, answering the phone as one of her yoga students checked on her.

Chapter Thirteen

In the darkest of night, I lay myself before you. In the brightest of day, I hide nothing from you.

Holly knocked on the hospital door, juggling the diaper cake she'd made weeks ago. "Knock knock, special delivery."

"Oh, thank God, you're here. I need to run to the station, but Maryanne's mom won't be here for another hour. Can you stay with her? I don't want her to be alone after all that happened last night." Gunner rushed over and helped set the diapers on the counter in the room.

Holly nodded, still surprised that Gunner talked so much around Maryanne. The past two years, he'd barely said two words while in the same room as his now wife. It was bittersweet to have seen their relationship developing over the past nine months.

A soft cry came from the tiny roll-away baby crib, and Gunner picked up little Connie. He kissed her forehead before handing her to Maryanne, who began to breastfeed.

Maryanne moved her hospital gown down and turned the baby's head. Holly watched in awe as she latched on. What would that feel like? She wanted to know, wanted to cuddle her own little bundle of joy.

Holly cleared her throat, the knot of emotion hard to talk around. "I can stay. It's not a problem."

Gunner kissed Maryanne before walking out the door, closing it softly behind him. When he was gone, Maryanne's big brown eyes swung to Holly's, and she reached out a hand.

"Oh my God, am I glad to see you. I've been worried sick about you since I woke up this morning. Are you okay?"

Holly sank onto the edge of the bed on wobbly legs and squeezed her friend's hand, remembering last night. Fear had flowed through her veins like ice as she panicked, feeling alone and scared yet again. And Landry's arms thawed her out and made her feel safe. Why did it have to be his arms she craved?

"Holly? Holly, are you with me?" Maryanne's voice came through like she was in a tunnel, pulling Holly out of the memory.

Holly wiped the tears off her cheeks and nodded, clearing her throat. "Yeah, yeah, I'm fine. Just remembering last night. Are *you* okay? My God, Maryanne, he could've killed you. Or Connie."

"But he didn't. And you! Holly, you were so brave, driving us there, taking care of me."

Holly shifted on the bed, letting go of her friend's hand as Maryanne moved the squirming baby to the other breast.

"I can't quite believe it myself. I haven't driven in two years, not since—since—"

"I know, Holly. I know. This was a big step for you."

A knock sounded at the door, and Lola walked in. Her

auburn ponytail flipped behind her as she walked to the other side of the bed. "Are you up for a visit?"

Maryanne nodded with a smile. "Yeah, have a seat. We were just talking about how crazy last night was. Did you hear?"

Lola frowned and crossed her arms, pulling her tank top tight. "Yeah, it's the talk of the town. Your crazy ex kidnapped you both. Here, in Crimson Creek. Not just one kidnapping but two." She paused, scowling and uncomfortable with the high emotions. "You guys okay?"

Holly shrugged, and Maryanne smiled before answering. "Yeah, we're fine, thanks to Holly."

Holly shook her head. "No, I didn't do much but sit there, scared out of my mind."

Maryanne snorted, her brows raised in disbelief. "Are you fucking kidding me? Holly, you saved us all. You called 911, without letting him see you. You even mouthed off to him, remember?"

Lola's brows rose. "She mouthed off? Seriously? Sweet little miss usually keeps her snark to just us."

Holly chuckled, wincing. "Yeah, not my finest moment, to back talk the guy holding a gun to our heads."

"But there's no way I could've stood in that corner like he wanted us to. You got us to sit down, lean against the hay. You got him started on that rant, distracting him away from wanting to hurt me."

Her friend's brown eyes flooded, and her voice caught as they remembered. Holly reached for her hand again.

Lola cleared her throat. "Wow, I didn't know you had it in ya. Good job, kid."

Maryanne sighed, adjusting her top. "Me neither. I thought I was going to pass out when you had to drive."

"Shit, Holly drove to the barn too?" Lola sat up straight. Holly tucked her hair behind her ear and nodded.

Maryanne burped the baby. "You've come a long way in two years. I was worried your past trauma was going to stop you, but you didn't let it. You pushed through."

Holly felt the pressure in her chest increase, and she tried to turn the conversation again before she said anything she'd regret. "And you pushed out a baby."

Lola snorted, her green eyes laughing. "Ugh, push it. Push it real good."

They laughed at the song, startling the baby into a loud burp.

When their laughter slowed, Holly nodded to the baby. "But look what you have at the end of it all. She's here, and she's perfect, Maryanne."

Another set of tears rolled down her cheeks, and she wiped them away. Lola hopped up and held out the tissue box from the counter. She took one and patted her face. "I'm sorry. I know I'm an emotional wreck."

"It's to be expected. We had a traumatic event." Maryanne leaned back on the bed, baby Connie now asleep on her chest.

Holly leaned forward and propped a pillow under her friend's arms. "I know, but I think it's more than that. This whole thing has made me wake up and realize exactly what I want out of life."

"And what's that?" Lola asked.

Holly met first brown eyes then blue. She took a deep breath, gathering courage to say what she'd already been thinking about for months. "I want a baby."

Lola and Maryanne frowned, their expressions nearly identical. Then Lola crossed her arms and cocked a hip. "What do you mean, you want a baby?"

Holly looked at Connie and felt her face soften. "Just that. I want a baby. And I think I'll have one by the end of next year."

Maryanne gasped, her hand relaxed on Connie's back.

Lola shook her head, rubbing her forehead. "Holly, it's July. That only gives you seventeen months to find a guy and get pregnant. What are you going to do? Trap a man into giving you a baby?"

Holly shook her head and stood, turning to the window and looking out at the blossoming trees outside. It was a beautiful day, and after last night's events, she was seeing it in a new light. It was time to seize life by the horns and create her own destiny, her own future.

"I'm not going to trap a guy. I've gone on two dates in the past few months, remember?"

Maryanne interrupted. "Oh my God, are you already pregnant? Was it one of them?"

Holly scowled and turned. "No, neither worked out that well, remember? The dates were a disaster."

Holly laughed, remembering the dates. Garrett had taken her to the Old Mill for a perfectly lovely dinner. He had made her laugh with stories of his childhood, stories of his family. But when they'd walked to her door, the kiss goodnight had been beyond awkward.

The date with Nick had ended up at Sonic for ice cream. He was emotional about losing a military squad mate, and they'd both ended the night crying their eyes out.

Lola groaned. "You can't take the date with Garrett seriously. He's just a man-child."

Maryanne's forehead was wrinkled in confusion. "We know, but that's no reason to give up on meeting someone, developing a relationship, and having a baby the natural way."

Lola broke in. "Didn't you say Garrett kissed your nose and bumped your head?"

Holly nodded, sliding her hands into her pockets. "Yep, and Nick's wasn't any better. You'd think two guys as suave as them would have better moves, but nope. So why waste more time trying to find someone who's willing to become a dad within a few years?"

"You can't judge all the guys by just those two." Maryanne closed her eyes.

Holly shook her head. "It's not like I want to fall in love, although I'm not opposed to it. I mean, Eric was amazing, but I doubt anyone could ever top him. Not that I want anyone to."

She rubbed her temples and took a deep breath, refusing to think of Landry's kisses, his arms keeping her safe. She had to focus on the goal.

"I just want a baby. I've actually been thinking of this for months and have researched sperm donors and in vitro fertilization. This is what I want, what I need to finally move on."

Lola and Maryanne glanced at each other, seeming to communicate without words.

Then Lola shrugged her shoulders. "If this is what you want, we'll support you however we can. Just take your time thinking about it, okay? If it's a trauma response, I don't want you to later regret it. Can you do that for me? Just wait a few weeks and think about it?"

Holly nodded. She wouldn't change her mind. This had been floating around in her head since Maryanne announced her pregnancy. And with Cindy and Dot announcing their own pregnancies just before Mother's Day, she'd been thinking about having a baby of her own.

Oh, that weekend was something else. Maryanne's eyes

closed once more, and Lola sat in the recliner and pulled out her phone. So Holly turned back to the window and let the memory flow, heat spreading along her cheeks.

She couldn't believe she'd done that. And with Landry! He was just a friend. No matter that they'd had that kiss in Dec or the second one in March with the paint mess. No matter that they'd done so much more than kiss in the bathroom at her house in May. She sighed, staring out the window, not really seeing anything but the past and trying to figure out how to move into the future by herself.

Chapter Fourteen

A beacon of light in the lonely world, the one who got away, the one who could never be his.

Mid-July

Holly parked her bicycle in front of the grocery store and kicked the stand down. She couldn't stay in the house any longer, but she still didn't have a car to drive. She might have decided to have a baby via in-vitro, but that didn't mean she was quite ready to start driving all the time again. The bicycle was perfectly fine for now. It was safe and easy.

At home, the walls had started to close in on her, and she wanted to make Maryanne a few freezer meals now that she was home with baby Connie.

Holly ignored the jealous green monster pushing on her chest and grabbed a basket. She really was going to do the

The Songwriter Gets His Girl

in vitro thing. She'd made the consultation appointment just that morning. It was scary but exciting. She wanted to share it with someone, but no one else knew about it yet.

She walked to the produce section, but when she rounded the corner, she saw Landry standing with his cart, typing on his phone. Her heart stuttered, then raced.

He was wearing dirty jeans and a green t-shirt covered in dust, like what he wore when they'd painted her new apartment, which she still hadn't officially moved into.

She blushed, remembering that sunny March day. It played through her mind like it was yesterday, probably because she'd been reliving it in her dreams almost every night for months.

Landry's voice had echoed in the apartment above, singing at the top of his lungs. His voice always soothed her soul and relaxed her body, setting her mind at ease when the thoughts and emotions swirled.

And the more pregnant Maryanne became, her belly growing every day, the more emotional Holly felt. Holly kicked her shoes off by the back door and walked to the stairs, nervous to be alone with him since that kiss in December, since the almost kiss at the baby shower.

But he was just a friend. They'd been fine alone before, and this was just like all the other times they'd hung out. Nothing had changed. Nothing.

Just as she reached the landing, Landry's phone rang, and she paused as he answered.

"Hello?"

"Hey, Landry, what's up?" The phone was on speaker, so Holly heard every word.

"Not much, just installing a kitchen."

"Cool, I won't take up too much of your time, but wanted to go over a few things. The contract with the studio needs renewed. Check your email for the electronic copy, sign it, and send it back."

"Sure thing, I'll do that tonight."

Holly paused in the doorway, admiring Landry's backside as he lifted the cabinet door and ran the drill. When the sound died away, the man on the phone continued.

"Next, we really need you to come out to Nashville to record this new song you sent in January. It's going to be a big hit, Landry. I can feel it in my bones."

Landry laughed, the sound sending a shiver up her spine. "I don't know when I can get out there, Mike, but I sure hope it's a hit."

"Returns are still rolling in steady for the other three, but this one... Landry, I think you should sing it yourself."

Holly frowned, trying to make sense of the conversation.

Landry paused, setting the drill down. "Mike, I don't know about that."

"Just think about it, please?"

Landry sighed and ran a hand through his hair. "Yeah, okay. Anything else?"

"Yeah, the Pavilion in Dallas loved your performance in January. They want to make it a weekly occurrence. You up for it? It's great publicity, and the pay isn't bad for a few hours work."

Landry picked up a rag and wiped his face. "I can do that. Since we stopped playing local on New Year's Eve, I've just been picking up more handyman jobs on the weekend. But I miss playing live. Send me the details in the email?"

"You know it. Tell Parker I said hi, okay?"

"Will do. Bye now."

He hung up and turned, spying her leaning on the wall. His cheeks tinged pink, and she tilted her head.

"Who was that?"

He rubbed the back of his neck and glanced away. "That was, um... well, Mike."

"And who's Mike?"

He closed the now finished cabinets and opened the paint can, stirring the pale blue with the stick and avoiding her eyes. "He's my manager and producer. He owns a record label in Nashville."

She gasped, straightening and grabbing a paint roller. "And he wants you to go and record your own song? Landry, that's amazing! You have to do it. Wait, your own song?"

She knew how important music was to Landry, and she was glad he was still doing something with it, even if he wasn't playing weekends with his brothers at the bar.

He sighed, grabbing his own roller and starting on the wall. "Yeah, I write songs on the side. I've sold a few to other artists, and they've brought in some good royalties."

Her mind blanked with surprise. Most people would shout this kind of thing from the rooftops, and she'd known Landry for a long time. No one had ever said anything about this.

"How long have you been doing this?"

He shrugged, leaning down for more paint. "A few years."

"Years!"

He shrugged again, as if throwing off the attention. "Yep. Now that I'm not playing with my brothers, Mike is pushing me to do more solo work, go record my own songs, that kind of stuff."

She laid a hand on his arm, and his hazel eyes sparkled in the light. She squeezed, ignoring the tingles racing down her arm.

"You absolutely should, Landry. Remember what you said the night we first met? You said you wanted to make people happy. And your singing does that. It always makes me happy because I can hear the joy in your voice. Why not share it with the world?"

His eyes shone, intense as he stepped closer to her. She gasped as he crowded her space, cupping her cheek with one hand.

"Holly, why do you say things like that? It makes me think I'm special when we both know I'm not."

Her eyelashes fluttered, the tightness increasing in her chest. "You—you *are* special. You're fucking fantastic."

He chuckled, the sound pooling in her stomach and lighting a fire in her core. "I'm not, but when I'm around you... you make me want to reach for the stars. You make me want to try all the scary shit and see what I can accomplish."

She licked her lips, the paint roller clattering to the ground as her hands settled on his hips. Were they doing this? They'd never crossed the friend boundary before December, and she was frozen, unsure on if she wanted it again or not.

It was against the rules. He was friends with her brother. He was *her* friend.

He stepped closer but slipped on the wet paint. His hands left her cheeks and spun in the air.

She reached for him, trying to steady him, but they both tumbled to the ground, landing on the paint can and sending it flying in the air. Large globs of blue fell on them both, cold enough to make her shriek.

When she opened her eyes, she was half on top of Landry, paint covering his face as he gasped, trying not to

The Songwriter Gets His Girl

breathe it in, his face scrunched up. She scrambled off him, whipping her shirt off and wiping his face.

He sat up, taking the cloth from her and finishing the job. Paint dripped down the back of her head and along her spine. The cool air on her skin made her nipples stand erect, or maybe it was being so close to him in just her shorts and lacy bra.

What had she been thinking, to give him her shirt?

Just then, he opened his eyes, paint still stuck on his eyebrows and in his hair. He blinked rapidly, his eyes focusing on her kneeling beside him. Then his jaw dropped, and his eyes widened.

She cupped her breasts, trying not to let him see through the lace, feeling vulnerable and frustrated. Sexually frustrated, which was ridiculous. She was just trying to help a friend. They were just friends, right?

She scowled. "You done with my shirt?"

Her tone was shrill, and he arched a brow, his eyes slowly caressing her exposed skin.

"Pink, eh? You look delicious in it. Tell me there are matching panties."

He wiggled his eyebrows, making her laugh even as she felt her cheeks heat. She crossed her arms, trying to maintain her distance. He was always teasing her, trying to make her laugh. Maybe she could give a little payback. She suddenly yearned to hear his deep rumble, see him lose his cool.

She glanced up at him through her lashes. "Sorry to burst your bubble, but no matching panties." She paused, unable to hold back her smirk. She lowered her voice to a whisper and dropped her hands to her sides, her breasts on display in her thin barely there bra. "Just a matching thong."

Time seemed to stand still around them, the only sound her rapidly beating heart echoing in her ears.

She swallowed hard, unable to believe she'd said that out loud. Yeah, she'd flirted with other guys in the past few years, but with Landry there was always something holding her back. Perhaps because she'd always known with him, it'd lead to more.

Still, flirting with him exhilarated her beyond anything she'd ever known before, and she wanted to get a rise out of him.

Landry threw his head back and groaned, getting to his knees and turning away from her slightly. She saw him adjust himself in his pants, and her eyes were drawn to the hard ridge of his jeans.

Dear God, was that his—

"You're killing me, Smalls. Quick, change the subject. How are we going to clean this mess up?"

She sucked in a deep breath, pulling his gaze back to her. She leaned back on her hands, arching slightly.

His reaction was immediate. His spine snapped straight, and his growl ripped through the silence.

He began to crawl toward her, and she panicked. She backed up, slipping and landing on her back in the wet paint with a hiss. His knee settled between her legs, and his hands caged her in. A shiver of anticipation ran up her spine.

His eyes swept from her blue covered skin, over her bra, and up to her face. "Holly, Holly, Holly. Don't tempt me, angel. Your sweetness is going to get you in trouble. You literally gave up the shirt off your back and look where it's gotten you."

"Where's that?" Her voice was unrecognizable to her own ears, breathy and excited.

His eyes flared at the sound. "Exactly where I've been dreaming for years."

His hips connected with hers, grinding to her at the same time his mouth made contact. This kiss wasn't like the one in the barn. No, this one didn't start off sweet and savoring. It went straight from a match to an inferno.

The passion burned her. Somehow, her hands found their way to his biceps, slick with paint. But she didn't care about the mess. She didn't care about the cold wetness she was lying in.

No, all that mattered was the burning fire raging within, threatening to eat her alive if she didn't kiss him back. She needed to kiss him, tangle her tongue with his. He was like a life-saving drug, and she'd gone months without it.

The phone rang again, cutting through the lust like a knife. She broke the kiss with a gasp.

He rested his forehead in the crook of her neck, panting and making goosebumps flirt along her skin.

Dear God, what had just happened? What was she doing? This was Landry. She couldn't risk their friendship over some mind-blowing kisses. He pulled back, his eyes searching hers.

Then a glob of paint fell from his hair onto her forehead. She squeezed her eyes shut and laughed awkwardly. He sighed and chuckled, easing off her and giving her the shirt back. She wiped her forehead and sat up.

He stood, hands on hips and looked at the mess with a frown. "Shit, this is going to take forever to clean."

She grinned, hopping to her feet, hands waving as she slipped and righted herself. "Yeah, but it was fun, wasn't it?"

His eyes met hers, his soft and still full of passion as his hand settled on her elbow to steady her. "Yep, totally worth it."

She blushed and glanced away. "I'm—I'm going to the bathroom to clean this off. Good thing we went with the hardwood floors, huh? Easily washable."

He just nodded and watched her walk away, his gaze causing the tingles up her spine to linger.

Chapter Fifteen

It rolls through like a summer storm, sudden, intense. Catches me by surprise every time, overwhelming, immense.

Mid-July

She blinked, bringing herself back to the present as he reached for a sack of potatoes. His muscles bunched, and she frowned. She'd done a good job of ignoring whatever was between them for the past two years. Until that kiss in December at the barn, that is. Ever since, she'd felt off-kilter. A tide had shifted, and while he'd said he wanted to just forgive and forget, she wasn't sure she could.

And then there was the painting the studio mess in March and the Mother's Day incident when the shower collapsed. Her cheeks flushed as all the memories bombarded her at once.

She'd seen him around town but had avoided him as

much as possible. After the kidnapping last week... she was done hiding. She tilted her chin up and tried to regulate her shallow breathing.

He lifted the potatoes into his cart, his biceps bulging. Her heart was racing again, like it had every time they were in the same room. She was done avoiding him, but with her hormones raging, she was afraid of what she'd say if she talked to him right now. Hot and bothered, she might do something completely reckless like invite him over to her apartment.

She jerked, spinning in the other direction. Her elbow hit a display of cantaloupes and several went rolling. She jumped back, almost twisting her ankle on one before she froze to wait for them to stop tumbling around.

Holly knew her cheeks were as red as the peppers on the shelf next to her when she glanced up and met Landry's surprised green eyes. Then he grinned even as his cheeks flushed, and it felt like she was on a roller coaster, her stomach twisting and turning.

Damn that smile of his. It told her there was fun to be had, even if they were just in the middle of the grocery store. It said that he had the perfect plan to cause some mischief. It told her to leave her worries behind and just trust him.

But that path was frivolous. No matter how hot he was or how her hand always tingled when he touched it, she refused to be a romantic again. Her heart couldn't take another beating.

She'd told herself that so often over the past two years since she'd moved here. It was practically part of her daily affirmations now.

Today will be a good day. You will laugh, find peace, and be happy in your work because the pain isn't worth trying to find

The Songwriter Gets His Girl

someone to share life with. This is your life now, and it is wonderful. You have friends who love you, and that's enough. You are enough.

She may or may not have written that on a note on her bathroom mirror to read every morning.

Oh God, he was walking her way. Her heart raced, and she glanced from side to side looking for an escape. No escape. No hiding. She forced her feet to remain still.

"Need a hand with your melons?"

His voice made the hair on the back of her neck stand up. It was deep and smooth, like the best whiskey. If she took a sip, would he leave her choking or craving more of that smooth burn?

She giggled, then felt her cheeks heat even more. Oh God, what's with the giggling? Turn it off, turn it off!

"I'll handle my own melons, thank you very much."

Sweet Jesus, what was wrong with her? Why was she acting such a fool?

He tilted his head, making the blond streaks of his hair shine like spun gold in the bright lights as he laughed. He slid around his cart, stepping into her space and jerking her out of whatever spell he'd cast on her.

She glanced away and dropped to her knees to pick up the cantaloupes.

He cleared his throat, then knelt beside her and reached for a melon. "I know you can handle yourself, but if it's all the same to you, I'll still help pick these up. You okay?"

His dirty, calloused hand picked up a melon so gently. Would his hands be rough on her skin? Shit, he'd asked something. What was it?

"Oh yeah, I'm fine. Sorry, I was just thinking of what I could make Maryanne for dinner tonight."

"It's not a tofu something, is it? Because you know that

didn't go over well at the last get together, even though it was delicious."

She'd taken a tofu casserole to a potluck at his parent's house a few months ago, when everyone was there to celebrate his mom's birthday. Only she and Landry had eaten it, but he'd had such a pained look on his face while he swallowed every bite.

She giggled at the horrified expression on his face as he knelt and picked up the last of the melons, placing them back on the display. When his fingers brushed hers, she pulled away to tuck her hair behind her ear, avoiding his eyes.

"Your face that day said it was definitely not delicious."

He propped a hand on his hip and tipped his chin up. "Tofu is apparently an acquired taste, but give a guy a break, will ya? It was the first time I'd tried it." He laughed, drawing her gaze to his twinkling eyes.

She grinned, relaxing slightly. "Don't worry, it's not tofu. I was thinking macaroni, cornbread, and beans. I know Maryanne wanted Southern comfort food. Think that's alright?"

He leaned on the handle of his cart and nodded. "Yeah, only thing that'd be better would be to add some fried chicken and maybe a pie."

Holly rolled her eyes. "I'm not making fried chicken."

"Hey, not everyone can handle being a vegetarian. Personally, I can last about half a week before I give in."

"Wait, you've tried being a vegetarian?"

He nodded. "Still trying. I call it being a half-a-week vegetarian."

She laughed. "When did you start that?"

He shrugged and glanced away, a tinge of pink on his whiskered cheeks. "A year or two. Don't remember exactly,

The Songwriter Gets His Girl

but it suits me. You have nothing in your basket yet. What do you need to grab?"

He grabbed her basket and put it in his cart, moving his food out of the way.

She grinned and mouthed off. "I just said macaroni, cornbread, and beans. Geez, Lan, do you need to clean your ears?"

He threw his head back and laughed, making her breath hitch in her throat. He was taller than her, beefy because he had to do so much heavy lifting at his handyman jobs. His chest was broader than it'd been five years ago when they'd first met.

She wanted to look away but was captivated. Her palms began to sweat at being close to him again, like they did when they'd practically dry humped on the bathroom floor.

They walked to the canned goods, his laughter fading into an awkward silence. "So, how have you been since the incident?"

"Great. Everything's great. You played great at the Fourth of July celebration." She winced, reaching for the beans on the shelf. What the hell was wrong with her? One kiss and she suddenly forgot how to speak like a semi-intelligent woman.

He cleared his throat, placing a hand on her forearm. Tingles shot up her arm, and she dropped the can into the basket, her fingers no longer able to hold on to it.

"Seriously, Holly. That night was terrifying. How have you really been?"

She avoiding his eyes and shrugged. "I'm fine. I've been slowly moving a box a day to the apartment over the studio."

His hand fell away, and a part of her missed it. "Did you burn the sheets, after what we saw in December?"

She laughed and shook her head. "Not yet, but I've thought about it. Has Kendall said anything to you about it at poker night?"

He snorted. "Yeah, guys don't kiss and tell like that. Has Lola said anything to you?" She shook her head, and he continued. "What's the hold-up been on moving in? I figured after what you saw of Kendall that night you would have moved in the next day. Then maybe he'd have sex in his own damn house."

She laughed, surprised by the saying. "Yeah, he's always been more of a father figure, which makes it doubly awkward. He was thirteen when I was born and babysat me while our mom worked. But he hasn't mentioned what he and Lola got up to that night, and neither has she."

They reached the baked goods section, and she grabbed cornbread mix and pie shells before holding up two different boxes for pie filling and looking to Landry for a choice.

He pointed to one. "The chocolate. It was Maryanne's favorite growing up. Speaking of growing up, where was your dad, if Kendall was your father figure?"

She put back the other box. "Oh, he took off a few months after I was born. Kendall's dad died in combat, and my mom remarried. But Kendall always said my dad was a bit of a jerk."

There were no memories of her dad, and her mom hadn't talked about him much. It was only Kendall who'd had anything to say about him, about how he didn't deserve to be in their family and that's why he'd left. It was one of her earliest memories, arguing with him about her dad. As an adult, she'd let the argument go, since he was obviously right.

"Well, good riddance, then. Maybe you're better off without him."

She breathed deeply of his leathery scent. It helped clear her head, but her stomach was rolling. This was the first time since moving to town that she'd opened up to someone other than her friends Maryanne and Lola. Why him and why now? Surely it wasn't because of those damn kisses.

This was something she needed to talk to her new therapist about. Probably needed to tell her about the kisses and make-out sessions too.

She shifted on her feet, ignoring the butterflies in her stomach. "Maybe. Probably. This is all I need for now, I think. What projects are you working on this week?"

He raised a brow at the subject change but launched into a description of his work this week while they walked to the checkout.

The cashier was a freckle-faced pimply girl and couldn't stop stealing glances at him, but he seemed oblivious as he loaded the conveyor belt with their food, adding a divider to separate them.

"So, when are you going to be fully moved into the apartment?"

She frowned at him, wondering why he kept asking. "Not really sure. Kendall has been working nights at the hospital and Lola's mom isn't doing well. And since I'm still not ready to drive—"

"Ah, you need some muscles and a truck? I'm your man."

Her heart tripped a beat at his words, her eyes widening as she glanced away. She didn't trust herself to be alone with him. Every time they'd been alone in the past few months, they broke the rules.

Then he cleared his throat and asked quietly, "You like the apartment? You're happy with my work?"

The uncertainty in his voice melted her heart. He was the best handyman for two towns in any direction, surely he knew that. Maybe this was why he kept asking about the apartment, because he thought she wasn't happy with the space?

She laid her hand on his arm, feeling the hair on hers stand up from the contact. "I'm thrilled with the remodel. I'm more than ready to be on my own for a while, and the apartment is everything I dreamed it'd be."

His face lit up like a boy coming downstairs on Christmas morning.

"Oh yeah? Why don't I load up your bike and take you home in my truck? Then I can help you move whatever you need moved?"

Holly laughed as she paid for her groceries, his excitement infectious and calming her fears of being alone with him. They've been friends for years. Surely it would be fine. They could still hang out. They wouldn't cross that line again.

"Sure, we can do that. But at least let me make you dinner or something, a thank you for the help."

They walked out into the sticky humid breeze, Landry pushing the cart with all their groceries to his old powder blue Ford truck. She grabbed her bicycle, rolled it over to him, and he put it in the back. His muscles rippled at the motion, but she glanced away and hopped into the passenger side, shoving aside the way her body hummed to have him near.

The radio started playing Michael Buble's *Just Haven't Met You Yet* when he started up the truck, making her smile as he started singing softly under his breath.

The Songwriter Gets His Girl

His voice was smooth as honey and just as sweet, even though he normally sang country with a bit of rock. When it was over, she said, "I miss hearing you sing in the studio while working on the remodel."

He grinned and met her eyes before winking. "Well, maybe you can go with me to some of my gigs in Dallas to hear me play on the weekends."

"How's that going? Did you ever go to Nashville to record the song your manager talked about?"

Landry shrugged. "Dallas is going good, but no, I haven't made it to Nashville yet. Supposed to go in three weeks, though."

"Oh Landry, that's so exciting."

Another song came on, and he started to sing it too, his voice louder and filling the cab. Several times when he was working on the studio, she'd walk in the back door to find him already upstairs, singing to the radio. She knew it was going to be a good day when she heard him.

Chapter Sixteen

You make me so mad I could cry, the way you bite your lip and try not to fight. But I want the fight, I want the real you. Tell me what's on your mind, baby. Tell me what's on your mind.

A few hours later, Holly and Landry had moved the last of her things from Kendall's and into the apartment.

Landry had gotten her heavy dresser from her room, her kitchen supplies out of the garage, and the rest of her stuff all into his truck. He was now putting up hanging rods in her walk-in closet while she washed her face and hands before starting dinner.

That kiss from the remodel in March was fresh on her mind with him back in the space, his leathery scent filling her nostrils. She was working very hard to keep her hands to herself and physically stay away from him.

Three make-out sessions were three too many. A fourth would be—well, she didn't want to think of what it would mean for her carefully laid plans of having a baby. *Focus on the baby.*

Holly washed her hands in the bathroom as Kendall's voice rang out.

"Holly, are you here?"

She cleared her throat and her tumultuous thoughts, opened the door, and peered over the railing down the stairs.

"Yeah, I'm here. Are you on your way to work? Where have you been all day?"

He tromped up the steps, and she turned into the kitchen to pull out dinner makings from her large, standing freezer.

She kept talking when he didn't answer her. "Decided it was time to move in officially, get out on my own. I'm making cornbread, beans, and pie for Maryanne, but there's plenty for us tonight too. Want to eat before you go to work?"

He nodded, then tipped his head when he saw Landry step out of the walk-in closet, drill in hand.

"Landry, what are you doing here?"

Holly took a deep breath, practicing her meditative breathing techniques to slow her racing heart.

"Just helping Holly get settled. I didn't have a job this afternoon, so we got the last of her stuff moved out of your house."

Kendall's gaze burned into her nape, but she ignored it. She wasn't about to have another fight with him about moving out and how she was too vulnerable after the kidnapping.

"You want to help me with the closet?" Landry's voice was soothing, and Kendall grunted in response.

She distracted herself by reading the boxed directions for dinner. Maybe when she was a mom, she could prepare from scratch nutritious meals for them. She smiled, thinking of a little dirty blond-haired boy running through the apartment with hazel eyes.

She stilled, her finger hovering over the oven start button as she realized who that little boy reminded her of. No, no, absolutely not. She would go to the sperm bank and request a donor with black hair, or her own blond.

After the food was ready, she turned to set the dishes on the table. Kendall and Landry were sitting on the floor, putting the couch together, talking quietly.

Had Eric and Kendall ever gotten along? Even after they'd married, neither of them had hung out in the same room together. Family dinners were non-existent, even before they were stationed away from Kendall.

She squared her shoulders and took a deep breath. "All right, boys, dinner's ready."

They washed their hands as she packed up Maryanne's, having made a double batch of everything. Dinner just the three of them reminded her of that Mother's Day weekend, after the shower incident. Her cheeks heated as she sat down, and they passed around each dish.

She let the guys lead the conversation, mostly about their friends and people in town. Landry had a way of talking with her brother that set her at ease. A nice, quiet dinner with her two favorite men was just what her heart needed to reset itself after the chaos of the past week.

She pulled out the tub of ice cream and spooned it into three bowls while Kendall and Landry tested out the couch.

"I think it works fine." Landry kicked up his feet onto the coffee table, disturbing some magazines and notebooks she had strewn on the surface weeks ago.

She glanced over to see Kendall picking up something from the floor, then grabbed the spoons.

"What's this?" Kendall's voice was sharp, making her shoulders tense. She hated that tone of voice.

She carried the three bowls over to them, her fingers brushing Landry's in the transfer. His eyes met hers, and he winked.

Her cheeks overheated, and she glanced away, handing Kendall his bowl. He held up the pamphlet she'd ordered from the in vitro fertilization place.

He shook it toward her. "What is this, Holly?"

She backed away to sit on the floor next to the coffee table and sighed. It was bound to come out eventually. "I've decided to have a baby."

"Through a sperm donor?" Kendall's voice lifted an octave, making her wince.

She shrugged, spooning a bite of the creamy goodness into her mouth. She closed her eyes, letting it dissolve. When she opened them, Landry was staring at her, his eyes flared with passion. It was the look he got right before he kissed her.

She glanced away, her spoon clattering into the bowl.

"Well, I think that's my cue to leave." Landry jumped up, turning away from the couch and walking behind it to adjust himself while he went to the kitchen. He rinsed out his bowl and turned to face them. "I'll see y'all around. Holly, let me know if there's anything else to move or if you need help setting up the apartment."

"Sure, I'll let you know." She took her bowl to the kitchen, needing some space from Kendall, her heart leaping at the thought that Landry was leaving. She walked him to the stairs and said, "Thanks for helping with all the big stuff today. I couldn't have done it without you."

He looked up at her from three steps down, his hazel eyes sparkling forest green in the light. He smiled, and her lips tingled to remember them on hers.

"Anything for you, angel. If you need anything else, you know where to find me. And I do mean anything."

He winked, then turned on his heel to descend the stairs. Certainly, he didn't mean what she thought he meant. That was innuendo, wasn't it?

It'd been so long, she wasn't sure anymore. Kendall's footsteps were already pacing a path in the apartment, and she rubbed her forehead and walked back to the living room.

"Don't you have to be at work or something?"

He scowled, standing now with arms crossed, his stance wide. "What are you doing, Holly? Are you seriously considering a baby?"

She gathered his forgotten bowl of ice cream and took it to the sink, needing to keep busy.

"Yes, I'm serious, and artificial insemination is the most logical step. It's partly why I moved into the apartment today. I need to prove that I could handle living on my own, because if I can, then I can handle being a mom."

She walked around him, ignoring his dropped jaw. It wasn't often that she got the jump on her brother, but it felt damn good. She settled on the couch and faced him as he paced again.

"Being a single mom is hard. Don't you remember how Mom struggled when we were growing up? The tiny apartment, the lack of food. There was never enough of anything."

She rubbed her temple, arm propped onto the back of the couch. "I remember Mom fighting tooth and nail to make sure we always did all the things. Field trip and needed money for it? She made it happen."

He held up his hands while he continued ranting and pacing.

"I'm not saying she wasn't a good mom. She was the best. All I'm saying is have you really thought this through? Because being a single mom is hard. I can't support this irrational decision on some crazy whim. You were just kidnapped, and I understand—"

She pulled up her knee to turn and face him. "This isn't an impulsive trauma response to the kidnapping, Kendall. I've researched it, thought about it over and over since May. Even decided on the company to use."

He crossed his arms and frowned. "For months? You're not doing this because of the shootout?"

She shook her head. "Not really. It may have been the catalyst for me to take action, but I'd already decided to do it."

She reached to the coffee table and grabbed the brochure he'd tossed down and offered it back to him. He reluctantly took it and leafed through it.

"I know you don't like change, Kendall, but this is my life and I'm going to do what I want, what I need, to be happy."

He sighed dramatically, and she raised a brow as he whined, "But like this? Holly, come on."

She chuckled. "Would you rather I find some guy in town to have a baby with? Would any guy ever be good enough for you?"

He tossed the packet on the coffee table and settled onto the couch, tilting his head to the ceiling.

"It's not about them being good enough for me. It's that they're not good enough for you."

She shook her head and patted his hand on the couch.

"You're the best brother any girl could ask for. But I need to do this, Kendall. I think it's the only way I'll be able to move on. Don't you want me to be happy?"

He turned his hand over and entwined their fingers as he looked at her. "Of course I do. That's all I want for you, all I've ever wanted."

She smiled and leaned on his shoulder, holding his hand. "That's what makes you the best brother ever. It's going to be okay. I can do this."

He kissed the top of her head and sighed. "I know you can, that's not what I'm worried about."

She sighed and leaned back to look at him. "It's the lack of control, isn't it? You know, you really need to go talk to Tasha about it. She's a great therapist."

He frowned and hopped up, looking around the living room and kitchen. "Where did all this stuff come from? We only brought a small moving truck of your stuff when you moved here, and most of it is still in boxes in the garage."

She smiled and hopped up to show him the stuff she'd had delivered to the apartment over the past few weeks.

When he finally left for work, she turned to the office desk along the wall and woke up her laptop. The in vitro website was still open to the Get More Info page, so she quickly filled it out and clicked submit before she talked herself out of it yet again.

She'd already called and made the appointment to go see them in two weeks, but this made it official. This would start the paperwork process. Talking to Kendall had been the final step. Now that he knew, she could talk to Lola and Maryanne and tell them.

Exploring the pages for the hundredth time, she could practically quote them now. This felt right, like she could have her cake and eat it too. Like she could move on but on her own terms. She could preserve the memory of her love with Eric and have a baby to love forever.

She grinned, excited for the first time in a long time. She was really going to do it. She was going to have a baby with artificial insemination using a sperm bank.

Chapter Seventeen

It feels so good it hurts. It hurts so much, I have to go. It hurts to go, and it hurts to stay. When I'm with you, babe, it's more than pain.

A few nights later, Landry had music blaring in his speakers as he grilled some chicken outside. He sang along softly, his mind wandering until Parker opened the sliding glass door to the back deck.

Landry glanced over his shoulder. "What are you doing home so early? I thought you had a hot date?"

Parker shrugged and fell onto one of the reclining lawn chairs. "It was a complete bust. Got a kiss, but it wasn't anything to write home about."

"So, no true love there, huh?" Landry smirked as he flipped the chicken and stirred the veggies simmering on the cast iron skillet. He felt Parker's gaze on him but kept cooking.

Parker groaned. "When are you going to understand that not all of us are out looking for Ms. Right and true love? And now that we're not playing at the Electric Cowboy anymore, my opportunities for getting laid have dwindled."

Landry glanced at him and shook his head. "Well, you're always welcome to come with me on the weekends down in Dallas when I play. Lots of groupies there and you're welcome to them."

Parker shifted on his seat and perked up. "Really? Thanks, man. Hey, why haven't I heard of you hooking up with any of those groupies?"

Landry shrugged. "They're not really my type."

"I don't get you, man. What the hell is your type if not a woman who loves the way you sing?"

Landry laughed and nodded his head. "Yeah, I guess you're right. I don't know, just going through a slump the past few months. No real drive to chase any of them."

"You mean no reason to let them catch you. If you just stop, they'll jump on you like a—"

"Okay, okay. I get it." Landry laughed and turned the grill off.

"Or maybe you're not hooking up with anyone else because you've got rose colored glasses about a certain yoga instructor."

Landry narrowed his eyes and frowned, holding the plate of meat out to his brother as he walked past to the door. "You hungry? Or did you get enough on your date with—hey, who did you go out with?"

Parker stood up and opened the sliding door for Landry to walk inside with the chicken now in the same skillet as the veggies.

"Ate dinner with said yoga instructor, actually."

Landry dropped the skillet onto the table and turned to glare at him. "You took Holly on a date?"

Parker rolled his eyes and went into the kitchen for plates. "Yep."

Landry's stomach bottomed out. "When did you ask her out? How did this come about?"

Parker waved his hand, eyes narrowing as he sat at the table, watching Landry like a hawk. "Oh, I asked her out a month ago or so. Tonight was a good date, but if that kiss is any sign, it was probably her first since her husband died."

"You fucking kissed her." Landry's voice was soft as he froze beside the table. His stomach was in knots, and if he tried to eat, he'd probably throw up.

Parker got up to grab forks and walked to the table, the swagger making him mad. "Yeah, it was fine, just no spark or anything."

Landry sucked in a breath and held it while counting to three. Then he blinked, spying his sneakers by the door. He took off his apron and strode to the door to slip them on.

"Uh, aren't you going to eat?"

Landry shook his head, avoiding Parker's gaze. "No, I think I'll go for a run first, then swing by the gym. I'll eat when I get back."

He pushed open the door and let it slam shut behind him, then he took off at a dead sprint down the sidewalk. What the fuck was Parker thinking? He couldn't date Holly. She wasn't ready for someone, anyone, to love her. That's why she was looking into artificial insemination, after all, instead of doing things the normal way.

She was a long-term, settling down kind of girl, and Parker was still a player. There was no way they went together. Thank God for small mercies in that Parker wasn't that impressed with her kiss.

Landry had been. Damn, the woman could kiss. Just

The Songwriter Gets His Girl

remembering it made his cock twitch, and he adjusted himself as he ran.

Think of something else quick, before you try to finish this run with a hard-on.

Landry scowled and crossed the street, almost to the gym. He stopped a block away and began to walk. Oh God, what if Holly had liked Parker's kiss? What if she wanted to keep dating him, but Parker wasn't into it anymore? What if there was a third date?

Part of him was relieved that Parker hadn't been impressed, but part of him wanted to beat his brother into accepting her if she wanted him. Hell, most of him wanted to beat up Parker just for taking her out.

He walked into the gym and immediately went to the punching bag in the corner. A few other high schoolers were in there, but it was mostly empty this time of night on a Friday. He put on the punching gloves and began to bounce on the balls of his feet.

Thump. Why would she go on a date with Parker and not him?

Thump. Maybe because she doesn't know you want to go on a date with her, Sherlock.

Thump. Hadn't he told her in May that he'd be willing to date her and put a baby in her?

Thump. Maybe you need to tell her again, make sure she knows the offer was serious.

Several minutes later, Landry's arms were shaking and sweating when Parker appeared on the other side of the punching bag. Landry frowned and hit the bag again, harder.

"What the hell was that all about?"

"What?" *Thump.* If Landry ignored him and made it

seem like not a big deal, maybe he'd leave well enough alone.

"You literally ran out of the house when you found out I'd taken Holly on a date and kissed her."

"So?" *Thump*. Go away, go away, go away.

"Talk to me, Landry. It's me, remember? We don't keep secrets, and you've been keeping this one for months, years even."

Thump. Landry growled, "It's not me, it's her. She's a forever kind of girl, a one-of-a-kind woman who should be treasured, but you're not that kind of guy. You're not the guy for her."

Parker snorted and crossed his arms. "Yeah, I know I'm not. But you know who is? You."

Landry's arm slipped, and he didn't connect with the bag. Instead, his body lurched as he grabbed the bag to keep from falling.

He met Parker's raised eyebrow and scowled. "No, I'm not, dipshit. She's already had her perfect guy. No one will ever live up to him."

Parker pushed the bag into Landry and made him stumble back. "You can't know that if you don't try. Admit it, you have feelings for her, but you're too scared to take a chance on them."

Landry shoved the bag back at Parker, making him grunt when he caught it. "You don't know what you're talking about."

Parker shoved it back. "I do so. You've been mooning over her for months, years."

"No, I haven't. You've never been the brightest brother, but you're reaching here."

Parker narrowed his eyes and grabbed the spare gloves on the shelf to slip them on. Landry shuffled his feet around the punching bag to the little open area in the middle of the room. No one else was here now, just empty workout equipment along the walls.

Parker bounced on his feet, and they circled each other. He growled, "Admit you like her."

"Nothing to admit." Landry took a swipe at his brother, but he easily blocked it and lobbed a counter blow. Landry shifted out of the way, and they circled each other.

"You want to date her." Parker threw a punch, and Landry let it hit so he could throw one at the same time into Parker's ribs.

They both grunted, and Landry wheezed out, "She's not ready to date."

Parker tried to sweep his leg, but Landry jumped out of the way. "She's not, or you're not? You've both been wallowing in grief for too long. Pops has been gone for years now, Lan, and you're still clinging to him."

Landry straightened in surprise, and Parker took advantage of it. He threw an undercut to the chin, and Landry's head snapped back.

Landry saw black spots and shook his head, then lunged at Parker, tackling him to the ground. Pain jolted through him and Landry gasped, "I'm not wallowing. I'm happy, Parker, so don't bring Pops into this. This is about Holly, and the fact that you dated her."

Parker got the upper hand and pinned him to the ground. "That I dated her or that I kissed her?"

Landry roared, bucking and turning to pin Parker beneath him. He threw a punch and it landed with a satisfying thump. "You fucking kissed her. No sparks? Well, you obviously weren't doing it right, because she kisses like the angel she is. You don't deserve her. No one deserves her."

They were exchanging punches left and right while he yelled.

Parker's voice broke through the red haze in his brain. "When the fuck did you kiss her?"

"December, March, and May, you motherfucker. I kissed her first, and you can't do this." Landry rolled off him onto his hands and knees, glaring as his brother slowly sat up.

Parker frowned, his breathing fast and shallow. "Why didn't you tell me you kissed her? I would've backed off, Lan."

Landry growled and lunged for him again, making them roll as he tried to land another punch. "The hell you would've! You've taken my toys all my life, and you can't do this again. No more, Parker."

"She's not a fucking toy, Lan, and she's not a fragile thing to put on a shelf either. You don't get to decide if she dates or not. Hell, you're just as bad as Kendall."

Parker shoved and this time was successful with his leg sweep. Landry fell onto his back while Parker stood a few feet away. "I didn't sleep with her, and we're not dating. We may flirt, but we have no chemistry."

Landry sat up, stunned and blinked rapidly. "You don't?"

"No. Tonight's date? That was an accident. I got stood up, and she was at the Diner to pick up her food. She sat down to keep me company. And for fuck's sake, I kissed her on the cheek. God, you're easy to rile up."

Landry felt the air leave his lungs. His lips tingled where it was split. Parker took off his gloves and held out a hand to pull Landry to his feet.

"But if you're this upset about one date, one kiss? Lan, you need to figure this shit out, because someone's going to take her home, and it's not going to be you if you don't tell her how you feel. She's not going to wait around forever. She wants to be a mom. She was talking about it tonight, all excited. She's the marrying type, the long-haul, the forever one. Man up and ask her out before it's too late."

Parker slammed the gloves onto the shelf, then strode out of the gym, leaving Landry swaying on his feet, his breathing as fast as his heart rate.

Parker was a little shit, and he didn't know what he was talking about. He couldn't kiss her anymore. It would ruin their friendship, and he couldn't lose her. It was better to only have her as a friend than to not have her at all.

Besides that, she simply wasn't ready to start dating. Then there was this baby thing she'd been thinking about for months. She hadn't acted on it yet but talking it over with Kendall was a step forward.

He shook his head and stood up to clean up the gym.

Two days later, Landry stumbled into his house early Sunday morning. He laid his guitar case against the back of the couch and kicked off his shoes. His head throbbed from the loud music he'd played, then all the booze. For once, he'd let the others talk him into joining them for the after party.

Parker came out of the hall bathroom with a towel around his waist. He gave Landry the side eye, then disappeared into his room. Landry went into the master bedroom at the end of the hall and pulled his shirt over his head. His muscles were still sore from his fight with Parker, and he needed a hot shower to wash away all the cheap smoke smell lingering on him.

When he came out of the bathroom in his basketball shorts, Parker was lying on his bed playing on his phone.

Landry scowled and walked to his side table to plug in his phone. "What do you want? I need a few hours of sleep before church."

Parker didn't look at him. "I wondered if you'd just stay up or not, since it's almost sunrise."

Landry just grunted and pulled his covers back to crawl into bed. "Go away. If you must be awake, go make breakfast."

Parker chuckled and turned his phone so Landry could see the open social media app. He squinted, then groaned as he saw himself refusing the advances of some girl, then a guy shoving him before the two started throwing punches.

Landry winced and turned away onto his side. "Go away."

"No can do, compadre. Mom's going to see this, you know. And Mike's going to have words too, about your image."

Landry groaned and pulled the covers up over his head. The bed dipped as Parker got up, the sound of his steps going to the door echoing in the room.

He paused. "I know you stayed out because you're avoiding those feelings for Holly, but you can't keep doing that shit. You're going to lose her."

Then Parker softly closed the door, leaving Landry alone in the dark.

Again. And if Parker was right, he'd be alone forever if he didn't talk to Holly and make her see he really did want to date her. He groaned and rolled over, not looking forward to the scolding his mom was going to give him over that video.

Chapter Eighteen

Hey, hey, what's with that look? You're glaring daggers and casting your spell. But I'm already caught, love, no need for that evil eye. Just get on over here, and let's work this match made in hell.

"Come on in, guys. Hamburgers are on the grill already. How y'all doin'?" Landry smiled as the guys came into the house for their weekly poker night. Andy and Kendall held up two six packs of beer each.

Andy set his on the kitchen island. "Hey, Landry. We brought beer."

"Sweet! My brothers are out back cooking."

Kendall's eyebrows rose as he set his beer down. "Really? Even Gunner? I figured he wouldn't let Maryanne and baby Connie out of his sight, after the shootout at the barn."

Landry laughed as he pulled out the condiments from the fridge, desperate to turn the conversation to Holly. He'd been so worried after last weekend, and he'd made a deliberate point to ask at least one person each day about her, to see how she was doing. She'd seemed fine at the grocery store and when they'd moved her stuff in, but the rumor mill could be very useful.

He still couldn't bring himself to check on her in person. What was he supposed to do, just drop by? That'd be weird, no matter how worried he was after Kendall found the in vitro paperwork. He knew they would've fought, and it would've upset her.

He set the condiments on the counter while Andy stepped outside to take a phone call. "And yet you've let Holly out of your sight."

Kendall scowled and crossed his arms. "Not by choice. She let me coddle her for like two days after the incident, then she kicked me out of the house. Apparently that wasn't enough space though, since you helped her move."

Landry snorted. "I didn't think you'd ever let her actually leave."

Kendall glanced away and ran a hand through his blond hair. "We were fine at the house together, but apparently this life-threatening experience has made her realize she wants to be a strong and independent woman. She talked my ear off about it while she was unpacking the last of her bags."

Andy slapped him on the back. "Well, good for her. Y'all fight like cats and dogs anyway, so I'm honestly surprised by how long she put up with you."

Kendall frowned. "Her moving out isn't the worst part, though. She's also decided to go to a sperm bank and have a baby."

Landry grabbed his beer and opened it, avoiding eye contact as he regulated his breathing. He'd made the spur of the moment offer, but she'd been all he could think about

The Songwriter Gets His Girl

since December. The feel of her body on top of his, plastered against him, haunted him.

Come on, Landry. Snap out of it. Time to relax with the guys.

He cleared his throat. "I'm glad she finally decided to take the plunge."

Kendall crossed his arms and stepped into Landry's path, blocking him. "What do you mean, finally?"

Landry rolled his eyes and took a sip of his beer. "She's been thinking of it for months. Don't you guys ever talk?"

"Apparently not enough. Months?"

Landry nodded. "Yeah, since Mother's Day when Dot and Cindy both announced their pregnancies. It really hit her hard. I'm assuming she's done a ton of research in the meantime before making her announcement. She wouldn't have told anyone if she wasn't sure about it."

Kendall raked a hand through his hair, his shoulders sinking as he leaned against the wall.

"But she's not ready. This is a stress response, a jealous response because everyone else is having a kid. How's she going to raise a baby on her own? And in an upstairs apartment, no less. Wasn't that the same reason Gunner used to convince Maryanne to move into a house? Think it'll work with her?"

Landry clapped a hand on Kendall's arm and stared into his green eyes, so similar to Holly's it brought a slight comfort to Landry's heart. He couldn't hang out with Holly, but it made him happy to hang with Kendall and talk about her.

"Holly's stronger than you give her credit for. If she wants to raise a kid in that apartment, it's going to be fine. She has the support of all her friends and family to help, including you... right?"

Kendall looked sheepishly at the ground. "Well, I might

have told her that I absolutely did not support this decision."

Landry shook his head, sliding around him and opening the back door. Parker was grilling while Hunter and Gunner chatted with him. There was no mistaking his brothers. Tall, dirty blond hair, and hazel eyes for all of them.

He sank into a cushioned outdoor couch and propped his feet up on the wooden coffee table.

It'd been a long week of restless nights and weird dreams. The shootout at the barn had hit him harder than he'd expected, and then there was the fight with Parker and all the feelings that had brought up.

Kendall followed him through the door and sank onto the chair beside him.

Landry cleared his throat. "You know you have to tell her you'll be there for her, protective brother bear that you are."

Kendall rubbed his forehead with a sigh. "Yeah, I know, but I'm just not happy about it."

"You can't control her or any woman. That's what makes life so fun and interesting."

Kendall nodded to him. "What's with the bruise? Is that a black eye?"

Landry winced and met Parker's smirk from where he was grilling brats for the guys. "Yeah, I might have gotten into it with Parker over the weekend."

"And that guy from Dallas. Social media is going nuts over it." Parker said loudly, making both Kendall and Landry frown.

Kendall looked between the brothers. "You beat up Parker?"

Landry nodded while Parker rolled his eyes. Then Kendall smiled approvingly. "Wonderful. That means I won't have to, since he and Holly had dinner the other day."

Parker pointed the tongs at them. "You both need to chill. I was just making her feel better for being stood up. But Landry's a pretty good back-up brother for her. He was pretty pissed about that dinner."

Landry narrowed his eyes at the tone he used on the word brother, and Parker lifted his brow in challenge. He glanced away and adjusted himself in the seat, trying not to squirm as Kendall glanced at him and then back at Parker.

"Is that true? You two fought over the fact that he dated her?" Kendall's eyes pierced into him.

Landry pursed his lips and crossed his arms. "So what if I did? She's not ready to date."

Kendall tilted his head and just stared as Andy opened the back door and walked out.

Andy sat beside them on a chaise lounge to prop up his prosthetic leg on the coffee table. "Hey, guys. How's it going? Any update on the kidnapper guy?"

Kendall took a sip of his beer and sighed. "Yeah, he died this afternoon. This is going to have major consequences for Gunner."

Gunner walked over from the grill and sat in a chair.

"We were just talking about you, man. You doing okay with the perp's death?"

Gunner's jaw practically snapped as he sat stiffly on the chair beside Landry. Landry had constantly checked on his brother this week but hadn't wanted to intrude into the house with Maryanne and the baby. He'd known Holly was there most of the time, but he wasn't sure if he could stay away from her if it was just them in a room together.

So he'd kept his distance and just focused on Gunner,

who'd been stressed to the max juggling the case and the hospitalization of the kidnapper.

Gunner ran his hand on the back of his neck and stretched it. "I'm fine, but the state is launching an investigation now, since it was my bullet that killed him. It could take a few weeks, and they're placing me on administrative leave while they look into it."

"Damn, is that good or bad?" Landry took another sip of his beer.

Gunner shrugged and sighed. "Neither, both. I don't fucking know anymore. Maryanne says to focus on the good, and this means that we won't have to worry about him causing trouble anymore, that I'll get to be home with her and Connie for the next few weeks. So I'm happy about that."

Landry finished his beer and shook his head. "Yeah, but you not working is like a fish out of water. You're going to have to take up a hobby or something."

Kendall laughed, and Gunner glared. They talked more about Maryanne and Connie. It was kind of sweet that Gunner's eyes went all dreamy when he talked about them. Landry had never seen him talk so much before, but when he started sharing about all the little baby things with Connie, he just wouldn't shut up.

Finally, Parker turned off the grill, and they all went inside to eat and play poker.

Chapter Nineteen

I can't escape, don't stop, won't stop. I can't deny, don't stop, won't stop. I can't pretend, don't stop, won't stop. You're my only friend, heart stops, heart stops.

She was trapped, and he couldn't get to her. He was running in the barn, trying to get to where the hay bales were. But the bales were churning like cement in the mixer. And she was lying on the ground, slowly being swallowed up.

"Landry, help! Why aren't you helping?"

"I'm trying, angel. Just hold on. I'm running as fast as I can."

He panted, his heart feeling like it was going to jump out of his chest as he pumped his arms, trying to make it to her side. But instead of getting closer, she seemed to get farther away as she sank into the floor like quicksand.

A loud bang rang through the air, the hay bales lighting up. Fire spread from their centers slowly licking closer to her, and fear like he'd never known slammed into him, knocking him to the ground. He tumbled and fell as both fire and quicksand consumed her.

No!

He sat up, drenched in sweat, his heart racing from the nightmare. The same damn nightmare he'd been having for weeks now, ever since the stupid barn shooting between Gunner and Maryanne's ex.

Fear still raced through his veins, and he scrambled out of bed. He threw on his basketball shorts and sneakers and was soon pounding pavement through his neighborhood.

Once again, he tried to outrun the nightmare, the sinking feeling that he was losing something precious. His feet seemed to whisper to him, *Hol-ly, Hol-ly, Hol-ly,* every step a litany in his mind. He turned onto the road that left the neighborhood, knowing from repeated use that it would take him to the center of town.

The past few months, his heart was drug through the fire, hardening him as once again he was left on the outside of happiness. Throughout high school, he'd been the third wheel, the geeky band nerd little brother.

After high school, he'd learned the business, taken handyman certification classes, and watched as friend after friend found their special person and got married. He'd slipped into a pattern of one-night stands and girlfriends who only lasted a few weeks before they realized he would never move out of his hometown or get a different job.

When Holly moved to town, he'd hoped for more with her. But it was a pipe dream meant for everyone else but him.

Some part of him still felt like that twenty-four-year-old kid, waiting in the hot tub for his dream girl to join him. Only to be slapped in the face with rejection when he realized she was already in love with someone else.

Every memory, every interaction with her from the past two years played in his brain as he ran. It was only when he

The Songwriter Gets His Girl

was across the street from the yoga studio that he slowed to a halt. He looked up at the windows of her apartment, knowing he wouldn't find movement at this time of the morning. It was after two but not quite close to dawn, the night sky still dark and twinkling overhead.

Landry stretched his arm behind his head, then the other before moving on to his legs.

He was bent over, hands on the ground when a soft voice whispered, "What are you doing out here?"

He froze. Slowly, he turned his head and saw cute little feet in a pair of flip-flops. His heart raced again, and he breathed in deliberately, trying to slow it to normal. Why was she outside at this time of night?

When he rounded up and turned to her, he blinked. Her silky tank top had lace across her breasts, her nipples perky in the cool, morning air. The matching silk shorts were cut so high they would put Daisy Dukes to shame.

The moon fell on her upturned face, her pale hair appearing white in the night. He leaned forward, drawn to her, before freezing his posture.

He cleared his throat and shrugged, standing straight. "I could ask you the same question."

"I asked first."

He grinned. "Fair enough. Nightmare woke me up, so I went for a run to clear my head. You?"

She crossed her arms, pushing those tits up. "Haven't figured out how to sleep in the apartment. I've tried all the oils and all the things, but it hasn't been working yet. So I decided to walk to the gazebo on the square and see if the quiet would settle me."

He did a lunge to stretch, but really he just wanted to hide his boner in his too thin gym shorts.

"Did it work?"

She chuckled, the sound making the hair on the nape of his neck stand up. "I haven't tried to go back to sleep yet, so I don't know."

He grinned and switched legs. "Well, go on then. I hope you sleep well, Holly."

He turned to walk down the sidewalk, afraid of staying in her vicinity this late at night, this close to her with no one else around.

The only thing to do was to remove himself from temptation.

"Landry, wait. Come get some sleeping oils to take back with you. You need to sleep too."

He paused, not turning to her, his mind working furiously as he argued with himself. This was a bad idea, to go up to her apartment, to stay near her longer.

Yeah, but what man in his right mind wouldn't take the chance here? What if this is your opportunity to get out of the friend zone?

She's not looking for anyone to get out of the friend zone with, she's looking for a baby. Not a man.

Dude, you can give her that baby. Remind her of that fact. What's the worst that could happen? You've nothing to lose here. She's already been ignoring you since that make out session in May.

The man in his head had a point. He was quite brilliant sometimes.

Landry turned and shrugged, his smile already on his face as he nodded. "Sure, I'll try anything once."

She laughed while they crossed the street. "You have to be consistent with it for a few weeks, Lan. You can't just try it once."

She pushed open the front door of the studio, then locked it behind him. The click of the latch was loud in the dark and empty room.

"I can't see anything beyond this shadow from the window. Where are you?"

Holly grabbed his hand and pulled him to the left where he knew the stairs to be. His hand tingled where they touched.

"Don't worry, it's all clear down here. It's the apartment you have to worry about."

He laughed. "Still messy, huh? How's that going to work with a baby in the apartment? Don't they start to crawl and get into stuff?"

She paused, halfway up the stairs before moving the rest of the way. "I'm working on keeping things organized, but it's a slow process."

They topped the stairs, then turned to walk past the massage room and bathroom to the open floor plan of the apartment. He'd loved restoring this beauty last summer. It was a cool mix of industrial city loft and farmhouse.

She flipped the light in the kitchen, the track lights over the island providing a soft glow. Then she went through to the long pantry he'd installed and rummaged around.

"Is anything in the apartment giving you trouble? I'm happy to come out and tighten any bolts or screws that might need it." He walked slowly through to the living room, looking at a large picture collage on the wall.

That was Holly and Eric on the beach at their wedding. He'd not seen any of these photos, and his heart flipped to see her so carefree and happy. Not for the first time, he felt the urge to put that look on her face again.

She returned from the pantry and set some little bottles on the counter.

"Everything in the apartment is great. I love it here. It's just, the night is really quiet, and as much as I love this small town living, I grew up in the city. The quiet and I don't really get along that well."

He nodded and walked to stand next to her at the island.

"Same with me. Well, not the growing up in the city part, but the quiet part. It's why I play music non-stop when I'm in the house alone."

He nodded at the bottles. "So what do we have here, and how do I use them?"

She arched a brow and leaned away from him to stare into his eyes.

"What? No snarky comment about how these voodoo oils won't work? Most guys just make fun of it and push back against using them."

Landry grinned and leaned closer to her to whisper, "I'm not most guys."

His breath tickled her ear, and he saw her shiver. He glanced down, seeing her nipples pebble, and he knew it wasn't because she was cold.

See? You turn her on.

He ignored the voice in his head when she laughed, the sound ringing out in the air and lifting his soul.

"And thank God for that. I don't think we'd be such good friends if you were."

He tilted his head, and leaned one hip on the counter, fully turning to face her. "Are we still friends, Holly? Because you've been ignoring me since May."

Her face turned an adorable, peachy color as she blushed and glanced away. "Um, yeah, we're still friends."

He let the silence stretch a little longer before he slid his fingers up her bare arm to her shoulder, gently brushing her hair back. She shuddered, but didn't move away from him, so he leaned forward and kissed her bare shoulder.

The Songwriter Gets His Girl

"My offer still stands, Holly, if you want that baby the natural way. It would probably help us both sleep too. You know, natural stress relievers like orgasms are the best medicine."

He was only partially teasing as he leaned back and trailed his fingers along her collarbone. She shivered again, and her breathing became fast and shallow.

She sucked in a deep breath, yet still didn't move, didn't meet his eyes. "That's a good idea. I might try that after you leave, by myself, thank you very much."

"Sure you can. You're an independent woman who knows what she wants. But can you honestly tell me that you've been able to have as intense of an orgasm as you had with me back in May?"

She turned her head and met his eyes, hers startled and her mouth slightly ajar, drawing his gaze to that kissable mouth. "How'd you know that?"

He arched a brow, sliding his fingers up to cup her cheek. "Because it's what I've been doing too. Every damn day, I picture you grinding on me as I stroke my hard cock. And every day that passes, I get more and more frustrated because my hand is not you."

His fingers curled around her nape, and he pulled her mouth to his in a hungry kiss. She gasped, and he didn't waste a moment before sweeping inside. With a groan, he turned to press her against the counter, her body finally flush with his.

This was what he'd been craving, for weeks, months. Hell, for years he'd wanted exactly this, with her. He wasn't such a fool that he expected her to fall in love with him. He knew she loved Eric, and no one would ever take his place. There was hella respect for that, and he wasn't even going to try.

But once he had her, once he put a baby in her, he'd be able to move on with his life. Surely he'd be able to let go of this obsession, this driving need to be near her every day.

He'd be able to finally focus on his music, his business, and finding a girl who would love him for who he really was, instead of being hung up on a girl who would always love another. That's what he ultimately wanted, a love like his grandparents had, like his parents.

She moaned, bringing him back to the present heaven on earth. His hand still on her neck, he angled her head and pulled his body away, just enough to slip his hand into those silk shorts.

When his fingers slid through the short stubble to her clit, Holly grabbed his bare shoulders and dug her nails deep. This was really happening, and her body was freaking out in anticipation.

Her mind was nowhere to be found. She might have left it outside.

He circled the nub before applying the exact pressure she needed, making her moan and pull him closer. His finger eased inside, and she pushed forward, trying to take him deeper. She wasn't surprised to find that she was already slippery and ready for him.

What did surprise her was that she wanted this. Like, really wanted it, really needed it, like a bird craves the air. There was no hesitation, no worrying about Eric—although she knew that'd come later.

She'd had months to think about this, about him. Months to wonder if it had really been that good in the bathroom or if it was just a dream.

He added a second, and she felt her toes curl with his fingers. Damn, it really had been that good. And by good, she meant mind blowing, earth shattering, change your life kind of orgasm.

And if he was that good with his hands and kisses, how good would his cock feel inside?

She moved her hands down his biceps to her hips—God, his muscles were huge from all that manual labor—and she jerked her shorts down to give him more access, letting them pool at her feet. His hand on the back of her neck made her feel secure, anchored to this rock solid oak in the middle of a hurricane.

He leaned down to go deeper, and she gasped at the sudden violence of her orgasm, her legs shaking from the effort to stand while wave after wave of pleasure crashed through her. It caught her off guard, stealing her breath.

His fingers slowly pulled out, and he grabbed her by the ass and lifted her onto the counter, never breaking the kiss. When he'd shoved his shorts down, he spread her thighs and pulled her to the edge of the counter.

She tensed, her mind starting to think again. This was a big step, and she wasn't even sure if she was ready. She doubted she ever would be, though. It was like ripping a Band-Aid, and she just needed to do it. And it'd be so worth it in the end, her body already craving another orgasm, craving him.

He slowly pushed inside, stretching her so wide that she wiggled on the counter until he grabbed her hips. Then he moved her knees over his forearms and spread her wide, his hands wrapping around her thighs. The slow assault was pure torture. She wanted him deeper, the pressure already building for another release.

He leaned back, too damn slow, then pushed in further.

She groaned into his mouth, their tongues still dueling. Although his hand no longer held her mouth to his, she couldn't break away, couldn't look at him.

But she could use her hands. She grabbed his hips when he slid out, and then pulled them to her, telling him with her hands what she wanted. And oh boy, did he listen.

He pushed in to the hilt, and she whimpered into his mouth. Before she could catch her breath, he started slamming into her, hitting her clit at just the right angle to have her gasping for air. Grunts, moans, and even squeals rang through the air, neither of them breaking the kiss.

She didn't care who was making what sound or even how good his beefy hands felt wrapped around her thighs as he held her legs open. She didn't care about anything, her mind narrowing down to the little point where his pelvis met hers.

The orgasm built as wave after wave climbed higher until the tsunami slammed into her alongside his hips, making her shake and moan as she spasmed around his thick cock. She raked her nails down his back, then held on tight as the orgasm crested. He kept pounding, his breathing ragged until he, too, stilled, pumping her full.

Their kisses slowed as her body relaxed more than she'd experienced in years. She broke the kiss and buried her head in his neck, the scent of leather filling her nose and calming her mind even more. Dear God, what had she done?

Chapter Twenty

I done messed up. I done broke out of that mold you put me in. I won't go back, you can't keep me away, locked in that prison I've been livin' in.

Holly stretched, the summer sun bright in her apartment as it fell across her bed. Her body was sore, but for once she felt well rested and—

She froze, her eyes locked on the tan, rough arm draped across her naked, pale stomach. She followed it to the biceps that popped, even relaxed in sleep, to the shoulder covered in tattoos.

Landry's blond hair was falling across his eyes, his jaw covered in that short beard that drove her crazy. He looked so sweet and innocent as he slept, but her heart was racing at the implications of what she'd done.

She'd slept with another man, one who wasn't Eric. A knot formed in her stomach and didn't go away. She'd changed a lot in the past year. Never before would she have given in to the desire that flowed through her whenever Landry was around.

She was disappointed in herself, but the part that scared her the most was that it wasn't because of Eric. It was because she'd been wanton, immediately accepting of it, jumping at the opportunity. She'd wanted it so desperately that she'd thrown aside all thoughts on why sleeping with Landry was a bad idea.

Her heart started to race, her body hot from the sun and his body heat. She slid out of the bed slowly, not wanting to wake him and confront the reality. Tiptoeing to the bathroom, she took care of business, washed her hands and face, and put on the silky pink robe that hung on the back of the door.

She reached for the door handle, then paused. Maybe she should take a shower instead, as she felt sticky. She slipped the robe off and started the water, hoping Landry would just wake up and leave. Then she'd just keep avoiding him like she'd been doing for months.

Landry awoke to the sound of running water, and it quickly caused an increase in pressure on his bladder. He opened his eyes, blinking rapidly at the bright light spilling through the floor to ceiling windows.

He groaned, realizing where he was and what he'd done last night. If she had ignored him after their make-out session, what would she do because of this? He rolled out of bed, made the bed and fluffed the pillows, then slipped his boxers and shorts back on. He walked downstairs to the public restroom for her yoga clients, then hustled back up the stairs.

The Songwriter Gets His Girl

If he gave her a chance to run away, she'd avoid him again. No, he needed to stay, talk this out, make his case for giving her a baby. Did he want to have a baby and not be there for every little moment of his kid's life? Absolutely not. When he held his niece Connie, something had shifted in his chest. He knew how precious she was, how much he wanted one just like her.

He snorted and wiped down the counters. Baby fever apparently didn't happen to just women.

But if this was the only way he could have Holly, he'd let go of his idea of being a dad. It wasn't a permanent thing, as he knew he'd find the one someday, maybe even as soon as he let go of Holly. And when he found her, then he'd go through all the traditional steps: boyfriend, fiancé, husband, dad.

She was still in the shower, so he opened the fridge and found a bottle of water. He drank while he eyed the contents, then started snooping around in her kitchen.

By the time she came out of the shower, clad only in a pale pink silky robe that showed her perky nipples and made his mouth water, he had two loaded veggie omelets on plates with orange juice and coffee. He'd also cleaned up the kitchen and done the dishes, hoping against hope that if she was fed and happy maybe she would accept his proposition.

"Good morning, or should I say good afternoon? When is your first yoga class today?" He sat in one of the seats in front of the food and picked up his fork. His hands were sweating, the apartment hot in the midday sun, and he made a mental note to call the electrician to wire a fan. He watched her walk to the walk-in closet and grab clean clothes.

She cleared her throat. "Not until two. It may be

summer, but few people want classes on weekdays. I'll be right back."

She practically ran to the bathroom to change, returning a few minutes later in black biker shorts and a purple tunic tank top. Sadly, the top was long, covering her delectable ass.

He took a sip of his coffee and nodded to hers. "I wasn't sure how you took your coffee."

She fidgeted on the chair, and he wished they were sitting across from each other so he could see her face.

She cleared her throat. "I like it with a little vanilla soy milk, but regular is fine."

He tucked the information away for future use and took a bite of the omelet. She pushed her fork around on the plate, not eating. By the time he'd finished his food, hers no longer even looked like an omelet.

He couldn't let her keep agonizing over this, especially when it was so amazing. Grabbing his plate, he walked to the sink, rinsed it off, and placed it in the dishwasher. Then he turned and leaned against the counter, crossing his arms. Time to take the bull by the horns.

He sighed. "Look Holly, I know this is weird, but it doesn't have to be."

"Yes it does," she cried vehemently, slamming her fork on the counter and making a piece of egg fly. "Eric was the only one I'd ever slept with before, and now he's only a memory. I know it's irrational, but it feels like cheating on him."

His breath caught in his throat at the surprise of it. She was the most gorgeous woman he'd ever met, and he'd only been her second.

You should be her last too.

He turned away, spying the rag he'd used on the coun-

The Songwriter Gets His Girl

ters earlier, and grabbed it to wipe up the egg on the table. His heart rate was pounding again, afraid that he was going to mess this up.

Come on, you can do this. He stepped forward and grabbed his coffee, needing more caffeine to boost his confidence.

"I'm sorry you feel that way, Holly, because it wasn't my intention. I'm not the kind of guy to steal another man's girl, and I would never want to replace him."

He paused, sipping his drink, feeling the smooth brew go down easier than this conversation. He had to get her to focus on the baby she wanted. Maybe he could slip under her defenses and into her heart if he could get her to shift from self-recrimination to determination to have that baby. *With him.*

"No one can replace him in your heart, Holly, but that's not what this is about. You wanted a baby, right? I can help with that. My mom had six boys, and I have dozens of cousins on both sides of the family. Heck, even Maryanne and Gunner got pregnant without even trying. My family is pretty fertile, so all this boils down to one question."

He took another sip, waiting until she finally met his gaze for the first time that morning. Her green eyes shone bright in the light, pain and confusion radiating out as she bit her lip.

He wanted to see her bite her lip because of him, but he shook the thought away. He rinsed his coffee cup out and set it upside down on the counter, waiting her out.

"What question?" Her voice was soft, hesitant.

He shrugged. "Do you really want a baby via artificial insemination? Or do you just want a baby, period? If I help, you'll save a ton of money, which you can then use to spoil that little kid beyond belief."

She blinked, surprise flying across her features and smoothing out the frown wrinkle on her forehead. He pressed on.

"If you choose me, you'll know what genes you're getting. With a sperm bank, you can't do that. Any medical questions about grandparents, extended family? I can answer those. What if you go to a sperm bank and something pops up later for the kid but you can't ask about it because you only have limited information from the donor? There's safety with me, angel. What you see is what you get."

She looked away, like she couldn't stand to see him for another second. The pain of rejection spread through his chest, the feeling familiar with her, but he stood his ground and waited. Arms crossed, hands holding his elbows, he was afraid to move and spook her.

Her eyes were focused on the wall, and his breath hitched in his throat as he realized she was staring at the picture collage. His heart sank, knowing there was no way she would ever choose him. There wasn't anything he could do to ever measure up. He'd never be good enough.

Chapter Twenty-One

Bonfire on a dark October night, friends gather round with laughter on my lips, beer in my hand. Come on, girl, take a sip of that bottle of love. Gimme that bottle of love.

Holly's heart was racing in her chest, and her stomach was churning with nerves. She took a deep breath and stood, pacing from wall to wall and keeping the island between them.

She stopped to stare at Eric's pictures, hoping he'd give her direction on what to do. But like always, it was just radio silence, her head only full of her own haunting thoughts.

"This is a bad idea, Landry. There's no way we could keep this a secret from our families or friends."

She felt his eyes tracking her every step, but she refused to make eye contact again. She couldn't think straight with his hazel eyes burning through the walls around her heart and making her want to say yes to anything he asked.

She saw him reach for his coffee before settling back and

crossing his bare ankles. How could he be so relaxed with this conversation? He was a typical guy, always wanting a good time, but having a baby was a major life event.

She didn't have a lot of experience with men, but she hadn't pegged him as the kind of guy who could just knock a girl up and go on his merry way. Although it wasn't a surprise that he knew his way around the bedroom. If she looked back over the last two years, she'd realize he was a ladies' man from all his time spent at the Electric Cowboy playing in the band with his brothers. He was always leaving with some girl.

His voice sent chills up her spine, smooth as silk and bringing her back to the issue at hand. "We could keep it a secret. There are lots of secrets in this town, some well-known, many not."

She snorted. "Yeah, I doubt that."

"It's true. You've only been here two years and aren't from a small town, right?"

She twisted a strand of her wet hair and paused, nodding before he continued.

"Lots of secrets here. Other than you and Parker, no one knows I've sold songs that are now on the radio. But I guess it just depends on if you want to take the risk. I mean, we could always set rules that would make it less likely for others to find out."

She tilted her head. "Like what?"

He shrugged. "Mike's still asking me to come to Nashville to record. We could go there or go down to Dallas for a weekend. Make a rule that we can't make a baby in Crimson Creek. If we're not here, there's less chance for snoopy church ladies finding out. Honestly, that's the biggest concern I have."

The Songwriter Gets His Girl

She rounded on him and waved her hands wildly. "*That's* the biggest concern? Seriously?"

He nodded, making her throw her hands in the air and look to the ceiling. "Ugh, you're such a guy. There are so many things to consider."

Holly's phone began to ring, so she scrambled to find it buried under a blanket on the couch.

"Hello?"

"Hey, Holly. It's Tasha. Are we still on for our appointment today?"

Holly glanced at the wall calendar Maryanne had forced her to install, then glanced at the clock. She rubbed her forehead and sighed. "Dang it, yes. We're still on, I just forgot. Give me a minute to brush my teeth, and I'll be right there."

"Take your time. I don't have another appointment until four, so I'm all yours. See you soon."

"Bye."

She hung up and saw Landry pulling on his sneakers. He was bent over, his shorts stretching over his tight ass and making her body warm. He was like beefy Viking, with his scruffy short whiskers and blond hair falling over his forehead but shorter in the back.

"I'll go out the back door of the studio and jog the long way home. Think about my offer, Holly. You know where to find me." His bedroom eyes pinned her in place as he stopped in front of her.

She sucked in a breath as he slid his hands on either side of her head and kissed her. Fiercely. Deeply. Actually, it was more like devouring, like he was a starving man savoring his last meal.

Her body shook with want, her core clenching as it

remembered his touch. She wanted him again, and that was dangerous.

He broke the kiss and pulled back, staring at her intently before cracking his charming smile and winking. A quick peck on the lips, and he spun on his heel and sauntered to the stairs. When she heard him going down, she could finally suck in a breath and jump into action.

Eight minutes later, she parked her bike a few streets over and leaned it against the wall of the building. The dentist, home health company, and other offices were all located together, including Tasha's counseling office.

She pushed her way through the door, her heart still pounding as she smiled at Tasha. The office was one of the smallest, with just one main room, the back wall separated between the bathroom and a little kitchenette.

Tasha sat on the couch, her feet propped up on the coffee table and her laptop on her lap. She smiled and waved Holly in.

"Sorry, I woke up really late today."

"That's okay, hun. Sit wherever you want. It's good to hear you slept in. Does that mean you're sleeping better?"

Holly felt her cheeks burn as she sat on the opposite couch and slipped her sandals off to tuck her feet under her. She fiddled with the hem of her tunic and mumbled, "Sort of."

"Hm, what does sort of mean?"

Holly buried her face in her hands and groaned. "Fine, just tell me patient confidentiality is a thing, right? Like, you can't talk to anyone about stuff I tell you?"

Tasha's delicate eyebrows rose, visible above her glasses, and she set her laptop on the coffee table before nodding slowly. "Right, no one will ever hear about any of our sessions."

The Songwriter Gets His Girl

Holly leaned her head back and closed her eyes, taking a deep breath before launching into how she kissed Landry in December in the barn, the painting mess in March, and the incident Mother's Day weekend. Then she explained last night when she couldn't sleep and how Landry helped solve that problem.

"So let me get this straight. He's offered to donate the sperm for you?"

Holly nodded with a sigh. "And no one would ever need to know that he's the father. But what if he changes his mind later, and wants to be active in the baby's life?"

Tasha scowled and pushed her glasses up on her nose. "Yeah, that's a possibility. But statistically, most guys have no problem abandoning their families or children."

Holly shook her head. "Not Landry, though. He loves his family. Of all his brothers, he's been to Gunner's house the most. You should see the way he holds baby Connie. His face lights up and goes all soft at the same time."

She smiled and leaned back, then caught Tasha's raised eyebrow and groaned. "All I'm saying is Landry's an honorable guy, and I don't see him letting a baby go."

She bit her lip. That really was it, wasn't it? The one thing holding her back from accepting his offer. Could Landry really stand to stay away from his child? From what Maryanne had told her, he was fully supportive of her and Gunner getting together because of the baby. It didn't make sense that he wouldn't think the same for his own.

"Perhaps, but isn't he a bit of a player?"

Holly frowned. "Yeah, he was always leaving the bar with a different girl every weekend when he was playing in the band. But since he's been playing weekends in Dallas or Fort Worth this year, I don't know if he still is or not."

Tasha tapped her chin. "There was a video going

around of him rejecting a woman who was hitting on him last weekend."

Holly gasped, and she sat up straight. "Oh God, what if he has an STD, and I didn't even ask? Oh God." She sank her face into her hands again.

What if he'd slept with someone last weekend and now her? It felt like a brick was pressing on her chest, and she closed her eyes to breathe deeply. In and out, she took her meditative breaths.

"You won't know if you don't ask him. I suggest you open a new note on your phone and write that down. Write out all the questions you want to ask him about how this would work."

Holly did as she asked, typing in the question. Then she looked up with a frown. "What about the sperm bank appointment?"

"Go to your appointment and write all they say too. Then you can compare the information to see which one makes the most sense. This doesn't have to be an emotional decision. Actually, it shouldn't be an emotional decision at all, but I think you need to talk more about why you want a baby now."

Holly snorted and crossed her arms. "Well, that's easy. Because all my friends are having babies, and I don't want to be left out."

Tasha rolled her eyes, making Holly laugh. "Seriously, Holly? Be real. It's me you're talking to."

Holly sighed and pursed her lips. "Fine. It's not only because of that. I feel like I need to do this to finally move on with my life. I've been stuck in this limbo grief state, missing Eric and our little girl and not being able to... I don't know, let go, I guess."

"And you think this will help finally set you free?"

The Songwriter Gets His Girl

Holly nodded, knowing a baby would be a balm to her battered soul. But a baby with Landry? She didn't want to just be another one of his flings. He'd made her feel so special. He always did, with the way he looked at her. But she wasn't ready for a relationship and didn't want to co-parent. She massaged her temples as she kept mentally debating back and forth.

Chapter Twenty-Two

I never knew until today why they say your love is like a battlefield. I had you in my arms, in my heart. But now you're gone away.

End of July

Holly slid into Lola's passenger seat with a sigh. Lola might be her best friend, but today, they'd fought the entire way down into Dallas.

"So, how'd the appointment go?" Lola asked, backing out of the parking spot.

Holly shrugged, shoving the papers and brochures into her big purse and pulling on her seatbelt. "It went well. I got some final numbers and narrowed down the sperm donors to the top five. They answered a lot of my questions too."

Lola pulled onto the highway and merged into traffic. The traffic didn't faze Holly, as she'd grown up in Dallas. It was weird to see Lola gripping the steering wheel so tightly, her lips pursed as she was hyper aware of her surroundings. They made it to Denton before Lola relaxed at the wheel.

"I need gas." Lola's voice was still tense, clipped as if she were angry. Normally it was only Kendall she was angry at, so Holly didn't know what had set her off first thing this morning. It didn't matter though. She'd get over it sooner or later.

She wrinkled her nose, knowing better than to open her mouth when Lola was in one of these moods and flipped through some of the paperwork. It was more expensive than she'd thought it'd be. She bit her lip, thinking about Landry's offer.

Lola pulled over and slammed her door closed, pumped gas, then opened Holly's door.

She held the door open and waved. "Come on. Out with you. If you're serious about this sperm bank thing, that means you're going to be a mom. Moms take their kids to soccer and doctor's and the playground. So, you're going to drive the rest of the way home."

Holly gasped, her heart racing. "What? No, that's not—"

"Yes, that's exactly how it works. Do you think that Kendall or I can take you to all the doctor's appointments while you're pregnant? Or the baby checkups?"

Holly frowned, her hands shaking as she put the papers into her purse. "I—I hadn't thought that far."

"Exactly." Lola crossed her arms and tapped her foot. "You haven't thought this through at all. But if you're going to do this you have to face your fears and get back on the horse. So come on, you're driving the rest of the way home."

Holly stumbled out of the truck, but pursed her lips.

She swallowed hard as Lola put the gas nozzle away. "The last time I drove your truck, I hit Andy. What if we wreck?"

Lola's face softened, and she reached for Holly's hand, squeezing gently. "We're not going to wreck. Both hitting Andy and your wreck were at night, right?"

Holly sucked in another breath, feeling like she was drowning and couldn't keep her head above water. She squeezed her eyes shut. "Yeah, it was night."

"And raining?"

She swallowed hard and nodded. "We were on our way home from the Army Ball. It was late, and we'd just dropped off his friend when it started raining. A car swerved into our lane, and I went off the road to avoid them. Hit a tree."

Eric slumped against the passenger door as she pushed the air bag away from her face. "Eric? Eric, are you okay?" She reached for his hand and grabbed his fingers.

He groaned. "Holly?"

"Holly?" Lola's voice brought her back, making her jerk and open her eyes. Holly's face was wet from tears as she met Lola's blue eyes. "Holly, it's fine. You don't have to drive home."

"It's not fine, Lola. It's never going to be fine."

Lola gave her a quick, tight hug. "I know, Holly, and it doesn't have to be. But if you're going to have a baby, you're going to have to get back behind the wheel."

Holly pulled out of her arms. "You think I don't know that? I'm taking baby steps. First, I moved out of Kendall's and into the apartment."

"And what's second? Your hair? Driving?"

Holly shrugged and glanced away. Lola had a point, and she'd known for months that she needed to drive again. But did it have to be today?

The Songwriter Gets His Girl

Lola squeezed her hand again and stepped back. "Being a mom is going to be harder than this. And if you can do this, you can rock this mom job."

Holly swallowed the lump in her throat and nodded, dragging her feet as she walked around the back of the truck to the driver's side. She stepped up into the high seat and adjusted the mirrors and pedals.

Holly glanced at Lola. "You do realize that the last time I drove your truck, I hit Andy at the Electric Cowboy."

Lola laughed, her bright hair bouncing light from the sun through the cab. "And that ended up okay, didn't it? It got Cindy and Andy together, so all's well that ends well."

Holly snorted. Yeah, but all didn't end well with Eric, did it? The pressure built in her chest, but Lola was right about one thing. It was time to conquer this fear.

She put the truck into drive and eased out of the parking lot, the GPS still navigating them home. Breathe in, breathe out. She focused on breathing steadily while she merged back onto the highway.

"You're doing good, Holly. See? It's like riding a bike. You can do this."

Holly barely heard Lola's soft voice over the pounding of her heart. "I know you're freaking out inside. But Maryanne said you handled driving that guy's car like a champ. A screaming baby is going to trigger some of that stress, but if you can handle that guy, you can handle this and you can handle being a mom."

The whole way home, Lola said sweet, encouraging words that Holly just barely heard. By the time she parked on Main Street in front of the Diner, her hands were numb from gripping the steering wheel.

She shut off the engine and sat back against the overly large seat with a sigh. She'd done it! She'd driven, successfully, without hitting anyone. She threw open the driver's side door, grabbed her purse, and rushed into the Diner, the bell above the door ringing loudly.

Maryanne was already seated in their normal booth, so Holly strode over and put her hands on her hips. She grinned widely as she said, "Guess what just happened."

Lola laughed behind her and slid into the empty booth seat. Maryanne glanced from one to the other, her face tired, her hair in a messy bun, her eyes curious.

"Hot rod here drove home from Denton."

Maryanne's eyes widened as she squealed, coming out of her seat to wrap Holly in a hug.

Dot arrived to take their orders. "What's going on here?"

"I drove, Dot! I drove from Denton all the way to Crimson Creek. And I didn't wreck or hit anyone."

Dot grinned and patted her on the back. "Congratulations, hun. That's a big step."

Maryanne sat back down to tease Lola. "And Lola didn't have a gun pointed at you, right?"

Holly laughed and took a seat next to Lola, who was frowning and now arguing with Maryanne.

Holly turned to Dot and nodded to her barely protruding belly. "How's the pregnancy going?"

"It's going well. I'm through most of the morning sickness. Cindy's been bringing the kids out to the ranch for horse riding lessons, so we've been comparing pregnancies. What's this I hear about you getting pregnant? How far along are you?"

Holly grinned and shook her head. "It hasn't happened yet. I just came back from the first appointment with the sperm bank."

The Songwriter Gets His Girl

"Oh, that's so cool of you. Very brave." Dot shifted on her feet as Lola elbowed Holly in the side.

"Very brave and idiotic. We all saw how hard it was for Cindy being a single mama."

Holly frowned and crossed her arms. "Yeah, but I won't have three kids. Just one, thank you. I can handle that."

"Of course you can," Dot said. "You're the strongest woman I know, with all you've gone through."

Holly shook her head. "I doubt that. It's like the pot calling the kettle black, because you've gone through some crazy stuff too, just in the few years I've been living here."

Dot laughed and waved her hand. "That's true too. While I can stand here yapping all day about that, I bet you ladies are hungry after your trip to the city, aren't you?"

They nodded, and Dot took their orders before leaving.

Maryanne sipped her drink before clearing her throat. "So, how was the appointment?"

"It went well. Do you want to help me pick out the sperm?"

When Lola and Maryanne's jaws dropped, Holly burst out laughing. Then she pulled out the papers the facility had sent with her and spread them on the table.

They each picked up one and read through it.

"Blond hair, brown eyes, six feet, and a firefighter."

"Brown hair, brown eyes, five feet eleven, and a professor."

"Blond hair, brown eyes, six feet one, and a policeman. Holly, are these guys all blond or brunettes? You don't want any tall, dark, and handsome men like Andy?"

Holly shrugged, looking at the next file and avoiding their eyes. "It's not really about that. Just, Eric had black hair."

Maryanne sat back and nodded. "Ah, and you're afraid a black haired baby would be too painful."

Holly nodded curtly and read the last files to them. "This one is a cowboy, and this one is a pilot."

Dot brought Holly and Lola their drinks before taking care of another patron.

Lola sipped her drink and tapped one of the papers. "These don't have a lot of medical information. What if they have family with cancer or diabetes?"

Holly leaned an arm around Lola's shoulder and squeezed in a side hug. "And how's your mama feeling?"

Lola shook her head. "Not good. She's not feeling up for the road trip to the family reunion in Virginia this summer. It's the first summer she's missed since she married my dad and moved out here forty years ago. We didn't even miss it after my dad left."

"I'm sorry, Lola. Is there anything we can do to help?" Maryanne reached across the table and squeezed Lola's fingers.

"Nope. Nothing we can do at this point. I actually asked your brother to come out and see her once a week. Did he tell you?" Lola glanced at Holly, but Holly just shook her head.

She hoped her brother wasn't causing Lola's blood pressure to go up, because those two always fought like cats and dogs. It was like watching lions circle the same kill on the discovery channel. One of them was going to take down the other, but it was anyone's guess on who would pounce first.

One of them had snapped at the wedding back in December, but neither had ever said anything about it. And Holly wasn't going to be the one to let the cat out of the bag.

The Songwriter Gets His Girl

Secretly, Holly hoped they'd fall in love. Then Lola would be the sister she'd always wanted. She'd always wanted a big family to make up for the loneliness that was her childhood. But if she could only have this one baby, it'd be worth it.

Their food arrived, and Holly put the papers back in her purse.

"So which one are you leaning toward, Holly?" Lola asked before biting into her burger.

Holly mixed her salad to get every piece covered in dressing. "I'm not sure yet. I assume that the pilot and cowboy would make a baby who was a bit of a daredevil, don't you think?"

Maryanne shook her head. "No, the policeman and firefighter would be a bit more of a daredevil type of personality."

Lola tilted her head and looked at Maryanne quizzically. "But Gunner's not a daredevil. He's a protector."

Maryanne nodded her head. "True, true. But if the cowboy is like Gunner's parents, then the kid would be pretty laid back and chill."

"Does it say what kind of cowboy? Because there's a difference between a rodeo cowboy and a ranching cowboy," Lola asked.

Holly shook her head. "No, it doesn't say. Maybe I should just go for the professor. Can't go wrong with a smart kid, right?"

Maryanne snorted. "Do you want a kid that's smarter than you?"

Holly thought about it and smiled while she chewed her food. "I don't care, honestly. As long as it's a healthy, happy baby."

They finished their meals and kept debating the different guys on her list until Lola asked, "What about the cost? As your bookkeeper for the studio, I recommend that being a big factor in this decision."

Holly nodded. "Yeah, I know. It's a bit more than I expected, but I'm paying to get as much info as possible and for the best qualified donor possible."

Maryanne stared at her, making her squirm in her seat. "How much, Holly."

Holly sighed, glancing away. "Forty thousand."

Lola choked on her drink, and Holly slapped her on the back.

Maryanne sputtered, "You can't be serious. Holly, that's more than most cars. Oh, and about that. You're going to need a car, if you're going to be driving again and hauling a baby around and going back and forth from the doctor's. Oh my God, the doctors are going to cost so much money too. What's your insurance like?"

Lola wiped her mouth and half turned in her seat with a frown. "Holly, you can't spend that much on this baby thing. Yes, the yoga studio is turning a nice profit, and you can actually afford to hire someone to help you now, but forty thousand?"

Holly crossed her arms. "I have the money, Lola. I saved and invested Eric's life insurance payout. And I have survivor benefits, so I don't have to worry about insurance for the doctor's appointments. That's covered for as long as I'm single and unmarried."

"But Holly—"

Holly hit the table with her fist. "No buts. This is my life, and I'm going to fucking live it how I want to live it. You're my best friends, and I need your support on this. So, I suggest you find it before this baby comes along."

She stood up and threw down a twenty to cover her meal, then grabbed her purse and strode out. They couldn't do this to her and still call themselves friends. Besides, she was late for an appointment, and thank God for it. She was about to lose her cool.

Chapter Twenty-Three

My bubble gum angel, guides me day and night. My bubble gum angel, always holds me tight

When Holly was a few doors down the street, she slowed her pace. She regulated her breathing and matched her steps.

Yes, her friends made some excellent points, but she knew what she was doing. Yes, it was going to cost a lot of money, but this was what she wanted. Her phone alarm went off, and she glanced at it while she walked.

Not three minutes later, she walked into Tasha's office and collapsed onto the couch.

"Long day?" Tasha sat her computer onto the side table and pushed an unopened water bottle across the coffee table to Holly.

Holly huffed out a breath and swiped it up, chugging it. After she'd wiped her mouth, she took three deep breaths and nodded.

"Yeah, you could say that." Then she explained everything that had happened to Tasha.

"So, you're hurt that your friends aren't supporting you in this."

Holly nodded, pointing her finger. "Exactly. If this was a traditional relationship like what happened with Maryanne, and I was telling them about the baby after the fact, they'd be all lovey dovey and helpful."

"Ah, so there's a little jealousy still there. Do you hear it this time, Holly?"

Holly took a breath and held it for three seconds. Then nodded and released it, leaning back against the couch.

"Yeah, I'm still jealous of Maryanne. I mean, she's got her husband and her baby girl. That was supposed to be me, Tasha. Can you really blame me that it's taking this long to process?"

Tasha shook her head. "Don't blame you at all. Just want to make sure you're aware of it, because identifying is the first step in learning to cope, process, and let go. But I do find it interesting that you're jealous not just of Maryanne having her baby girl but of also being in love with her husband. Are you sure you want to do this baby thing alone? What about a relationship, love, and the support of a loving husband?"

Holly snorted and crossed her arms. "Yeah, I had that too, remember? You only get one great love in your life, and I've had mine."

Tasha's lips curled just barely on the edges, making the hair on Holly's neck stand up. "Are you sure about that? That palm reading showed you have two great loves of your life. What about Landry? You slept with him, Holly. And while you told me the facts, you didn't tell me how that made you feel."

Holly glanced away and sucked in another breath, her heart beating too fast and her palms sweating as she thought of him.

Tasha tapped a pen against her lips as she observed. "Your cheeks are flushed, and you're fidgeting in your chair. Why is that?"

Holly blew out her breath in a huff, then jumped to her feet to pace behind the couch. "Because Landry is... Because it was... I don't know, Tasha. I don't know how I feel about him."

"Was the sex good?"

Holly stumbled to a stop and gaped at Tasha. "Are you serious? That's like asking if a banana is yellow or if the sky is blue."

"Ah, but a banana could be green, and the sky could be gray."

Holly rubbed her temples and started pacing again. "It was fantastic, okay? It was the best sex of my life."

She whispered the last statement, facing the front door away from Tasha, wishing she could just keep walking and not admit any of this.

"Including Eric?" Holly nodded, her throat closing as Tasha continued. "Is that why you're so upset about it? Why don't you want to start a relationship with him or take him up on the offer to be your sperm donor? Because you're afraid of your feelings for him?"

Holly slowly turned to face her, her face blank and cold. Her whole body was cold, regardless of it being the end of July. Her sun dress fluttered around her knees as she thought.

Did she have feelings for Landry? She reared her head back. "No, I don't have feelings for Landry. It was just great sex, okay?"

Tasha tilted her head and pushed up her glasses on her nose. "So, if it was just great sex, why not get more of it? Two birds with one stone kind of thing, since you want the baby. Then you could save all that money and have fun in the baby making process. You haven't really had a lot of fun in the past year, and you're going to have to learn to let go, laugh, and enjoy the little things if you're going to be a mom."

Why does everyone keep saying that? *If she's going to be a mom.* She'd already told them she was going to be, so why did they keep saying that?

"I've gotta go." She shook her head, turned on her heel and walked out.

"Make your pros and cons list and write questions for Landry." Tasha called just before the door closed.

The week after sleeping with Holly and not hearing from her, Landry stepped out of the Uber onto the sidewalk. He knew from Maryanne that she was going to the sperm bank today, and he just didn't want to be in town to hear about it.

"I can't believe you're actually here. It's good to see you, man. It's been too long." Mike's grin stretched ear to ear as he hugged Landry in front of the recording studio in Nashville.

"It's nice to get out of town, actually. I needed the escape, and now that I'm here, I'm not sure why I put off coming to see you."

Landry grinned as Mike led him deeper into the building. Shoving his hands into his pockets, he glanced around. It was a lie, but Mike didn't need to know that Landry hadn't wanted to leave Crimson Creek since Holly moved to town.

Being back in Nashville was a stark reminder of five years before when he'd first met Holly. He stopped at the window, his thoughts on her once more.

Mike rounded his desk and said, "Make yourself at home. We can get into the studio in about ten minutes, when the people in there now clear out."

Mike went to a mini-fridge behind his desk and pulled out two beers. Landry took one, then spied a framed piece of paper beside a window. He looked closer, and his jaw dropped.

"Mike, what's this?"

Mike chuckled. "That's the first song you wrote for me. Remember that one? Luke recorded it, and it went Platinum."

"Yeah, but this is the rough draft. The one I wrote on the plane ride home five years ago." The one he'd poured his heart and soul into because Holly had gotten engaged to another man.

"Man, that was an epic weekend. I still can't believe you went to see your Army buddy instead of partying with us."

Landry laughed. "Yeah, Parker still brags about all the stars he met. And the autographed picture of Willy Nelson is one of Dad's most prized possessions."

He looked at the little scrap of notebook paper, remembering the day after the party. Andy had taken him fishing, and while sitting on the dock waiting for a bite, he'd not been able to stop thinking about his bubble gum angel slipping through his fingers. He'd written dozens of lines that day.

Then the next day when he'd gotten up on the plane to go to the bathroom, Mike had rifled through the little notebook he'd left in his seat. One thing had led to another, and Mike had coached him through taking the best parts of what he'd written and forming a song.

"This was the beginning of it all, wasn't it?" Landry's voice was softer than he'd expected it to be.

"The beginning for both of us. It's what made my parents realize I was serious about joining the family business."

"And thank God for that. You're fantastic at it." Landry swept a hand at all the trophies on the shelf and albums framed on the wall.

Mike just shrugged and took a sip of his beer. "These two new songs you've sent me are a different direction for you, more family oriented and less small-town vibe. I know Gunner having a kid was the push for the change, right?"

Landry smiled, nodding. "Yeah, she's the cutest little thing, Mike. Holding her is like the purest form of joy. It's softened Gunner up a lot."

A knock sounded on the door and a little brunette with glasses poked her head inside. "Mr. Malone, the studio is open now."

Landry's palms began to sweat, and the fear and dread started to creep up his neck and into his head. *You're not good enough. I can't believe you're going to record your own songs. What was wrong with letting others record your words? This is way too risky.*

Mike clapped a hand on his shoulder before walking to the door and dropping his now empty beer into the trash can. Yeah, that was a good idea. Landry downed the last of his beer to relax his nerves.

He imagined all the negative thoughts filling the beer bottle as he walked to the door and tossed it away. He could do this.

"You think this will work, Mike?"

Landry followed him down the hall, shoving his hands in his pockets once more as his stomach roiled.

"Of course. Even if none of the songs hit it big, it's going to make a great Christmas present for your family. And who knows? Maybe it'll knock Willy Nelson down a peg or two in your dad's eyes."

Mike winked and Landry chuckled, feeling his shoulders relax slightly as they entered the recording room.

Landry walked to the guitar leaning against the wall and picked it up, turned to the music stand and set his notebook down. Then he sat on the stool and pulled the microphone down before slipping on the big headphones hanging on the stand.

Mike spoke through the headphones in the other room, visible through the window. "How you feeling? Temperature okay?"

Landry cleared his throat and nodded. "Yeah, I'm good. Can I just play around for a bit before we start?"

"Sure, warm up however you need to."

Landry strummed his guitar and adjusted the knobs while he hummed one of his grandpa's favorite songs, *Everybody Loves Somebody* by Dean Martin.

Then he transitioned into his new song, First Love.

There she was, her fingers wrapped around mine,
Was I ready for this? I lost myself with that first kiss.
She's more precious than diamonds, more real than the sea,
She's got my whole heart, and I'm laying it at her feet.
I'll protect her with my dyin' breath,
until there's nothin' left, because she's my angel, my

He broke off and hummed a little more while he played the guitar. No, he couldn't mention angel in this song. It was for his new niece, Connie. Wasn't it?

The Songwriter Gets His Girl

When he ended, Mike came through the head-set.

"Great warm-up, Landry. You ready to get started? I'm overflowing with ideas on this one, and it's gonna rock to do this live with you instead of over the phone."

Landry grinned and nodded, ready to get down to business and channel all his feelings of inadequacy and being left out into the song. These songs were about Connie and watching his brother fall in love with Maryanne. That's all this was and why the emotions were thicker in his throat than normal. At least, that's what he was telling himself.

Chapter Twenty-Four

Watching and waiting, biding my time. Aiming and Aching, my heart on the line

A few days later, Landry's breath caught in his throat as he froze at the end of the aisle close to the produce. What the hell? Why was he always running into Holly at the grocery store?

Damn, she was gorgeous. Her soft little hand felt the tomatoes, and he groaned, imagining her squeezing him like that.

It had been three weeks since he'd wrapped her up in his arms. He'd escaped to Nashville for a few days when it became apparent she was avoiding him.

Part of him hoped she'd gotten what she wanted that night, and she was already pregnant. His eyes traveled down her tight pink yoga top to her flat stomach, picturing her round with his baby.

His mouth watered, but it took a few tries to swallow

and snap himself out of the fantasy. She placed her tomatoes into the bag and looked around, catching him staring.

He plastered on his smile and nodded. Her eyes widened, and she looked around like a deer caught in the headlights, looking for a way out. But they couldn't avoid each other forever, as they both had to live here. He cleared his throat as he walked the few feet to her side, careful to keep his cart between them.

"Hey, how's it going?"

Holly glanced around, noticing the two other customers nearby and nodded. "It's going good. How have you been?"

"Good, good. Can't complain."

Ask her if she's pregnant. Ask her if she's thought about your offer.

Shut up, now was not the time. They were in a public place with people around.

Silence fell, and she refused to make eye contact, shifting on her feet. But he couldn't look away and couldn't move. His eyes just soaked up her pert little nose and luscious lips. His nose breathed deeply of her lavender scent, calming him even as his heart raced. His fingers twitched with the need to touch her.

She turned to the peppers and picked out a few. "Have you heard anything about the investigation into Barry's death? Is Gunner in trouble?"

He jerked out of his trance and shook his head. "No, I haven't heard, but I'm sure Gunner is going to be fine. He did what he had to do, and I would've done the same in his shoes. No news is good news, right? And no one in town has mentioned anything. I've been working on an update at the Clip-&-Curl this week. You know how gossipy they can be."

Holly clapped her hands and finally met his eyes, hers sparkling with excitement and taking his breath away once more. "Oh, are they finally getting the manicure and pedicure station put in? I've been waiting for Kate to install that and find someone to come in and work it."

"They are and have already hired someone. I met the new girl, and actually, you should talk to her. She's dual certified in yoga. Might be helpful, if you ever need to take a sick day or when you go on maternity leave."

Her eyes widened and her jaw dropped before she glanced away and walked a few steps to the fruit. Landry followed her, knowing he looked like a lost puppy following his owner and not caring.

He cleared his throat. "Having a new girl would make managing the studio better too. Weren't there a lot of things you wanted to do with it but didn't have enough hands?"

She nodded, still avoiding his gaze as she picked up some bananas. "Yeah, I want to organize a monthly get together, like a fun workout for families or couples going on dates or something."

"Maybe this girl will be interested."

"I'll talk to Kate about it and see if she can set up a meeting. Heck, maybe I can be the new girl's first mani-pedi client. What's she look like?" Holly finally met his eyes, her own narrowed.

He shrugged. "Taller than you, brown hair. She laughed a lot while I was there."

Holly took a deep breath, and it drew his eyes to her breasts, hidden under her sports bra and yoga shirt. His mouth watered as he wanted to taste of those juicy peaches. And her other peach, as he'd not been able to do either on his one night with her. God, there were so many things he wanted to do with her.

"Did you ask her out?"

His brows rose before he grinned, meeting her eyes

again. "Does it matter if I did? I mean, no one has accepted a different offer."

She glanced around, and he realized they were now alone in the produce aisle. Then she leaned in and whispered, "This is not the time nor the place. But yes, we need to discuss it, so text me later."

He leaned in and winked before whispering back, "Why don't I just give you a ride home again, and we can discuss it in the truck?"

She sniffed, turning her cute little nose in the air before nodding regally. "Fine. I'll meet you out front when I'm done."

"As you wish, princess."

Her startled look was worth it and made him grin even wider. Then he turned his cart around and finished his shopping.

Twenty minutes later, he was sitting in his truck as she came out the front door with her bags. He pulled up to the front where her bike was resting against the building, hopped out, and loaded it into his truck while she got in.

She closed the door and buckled up, then he pulled out of the parking lot.

"So, did you ask her out?"

He glanced at her, then back at the road with a frown. "Who?"

She waved her hands. "The new girl at the Clip-&-Curl. Or anyone else. I don't want you to have a secret girlfriend in Dallas that you see on the weekends while you're up here in the week knocking me up."

His heart nearly burst out of his chest, and his foot slipped off the gas causing the truck to lurch. He swallowed hard and corrected his driving, taking a few deep breaths as he processed what she was saying.

It sounds like she's going to take you up on it, dude.

Hush. Don't count your chickens before they hatch.

"I don't have a girlfriend or anything like that."

"When was the last time you were with someone else?" She crossed her arms, and he clenched his jaw to keep from glancing at her boobs pushed up against the fabric of her shirt.

Eyes on the road, eyes on the road.

"November, I think."

She gasped. "But that was like eight months ago."

He shrugged. "The gigs down in Dallas have groupies, but I'm too busy on the weekends to mess with them. It's just too exhausting to juggle chasing a girl and getting home for church and all the back and forth."

She uncrossed her arms and turned to face him. "Wait, so it's only been me in eight months?"

He nodded, stealing a glance at her stunned expression and smirking. He knew what his reputation was around town, that he was always going home with some girl from the Electric Cowboy on the weekends. But honestly, those times weren't that often in the past few years.

"What about STDs and diseases? When were you tested last?"

He chuckled. "I get tested every six months, so I'm good there. And no, I don't have any diseases or disorders. Neither do my brothers, but my mom has high blood pressure, my grandmother had a heart defect and needed a pacemaker, and my other grandmother died of cancer. The doctors say it wasn't a hereditary type, though. Anything else?"

"What about your grandfathers? Aunts and uncles?"

He shifted in his seat and clenched his jaw as he pulled up behind the yoga studio near the back door. He parked and then turned the engine off, staring at a blank spot on the exterior wall without blinking.

"One grandfather died from pneumonia after checking on the herd too much in a blizzard. The other died of a broken heart a few years after my grandmother died. He's the one who gave me the handyman business and trained me to run it. This is his truck too."

Silence fell, and he didn't move. Then she whispered, "When did he pass? I remember you talking about him at that party all those years ago."

"Almost four years now."

"Time doesn't really help us miss them less, does it?" Her soft whisper nearly broke his heart, but when she put her hand on his arm, he jerked out of the trance and turned to face her with a forced smile.

"That it doesn't. But let's get your groceries inside, shall we? Can I bring my milk in and put it in your fridge while we talk?"

"Sure."

He opened the door and hopped out, grabbing her bike and leaning it against her bike rack. He took some bags from her so she could unlock the back door, then he followed her inside where they both slipped their shoes off. It looked like her entire shoe collection was down here by the back door.

He went upstairs and set the bags on the counter while she started to put the groceries away. The place hadn't changed in three weeks. It was still messy, with just a few things out of place. His hands itched to pick it all up, but he forced himself to the couch instead.

After folding the throw blanket and fixing the pillows in the right spot, he sat down and waited for her to finish. Nervously, he picked at the dirt under his nails, one of the frustrating parts of his job being that they were always dirty.

She came over and handed him a bottle of water, then pulled out a legal pad from the stack of papers on the coffee table. It had a list of some sort.

"I want to draw up a contract, and this is what I have so far. I don't want to get lawyers or anyone involved though, because I don't want this to get around town."

"So, this is a contract just between us? Let me see." He rubbed his jaw and leaned to read the legal pad. But she pulled away and held it to her chest.

"Just—hold on while we go over this stuff. I want to go one by one, not have a cursory glance."

He frowned and slid one arm along the armrest and the other along the back of the couch so he could semi-turn and face her. He propped his ankle on his knee and arched a brow.

"Wait, do we even know if this is necessary? What if the first night was all it took? You could be pregnant now, and we wouldn't need this contract."

She shook her head, her cheeks turning an adorable shade of pink that reminded him of the color of her nipples. He shifted in his seat, trying to adjust his hard-on without her noticing.

"I had my period last week, so no, I'm not pregnant. I expect it might take a few months to actually work, which is why I went to the in vitro clinic. Their success rates on the first try are pretty good. Eric and I spent months before he deployed trying to conceive. It was almost a year before we finally got pregnant. Hopefully, we won't have the same problem, as I'm tracking my ovulation cycles and know when the most fertile window is."

He was getting excited about this, but he was afraid to hope. "How many items are on this list?"

"Ten so far, but you might want to add your own."

He groaned and leaned his head back on the couch. With an overly dramatic sigh, he met her eyes and whined, "Fine, let's hear them."

It made her chuckle, which was all he wanted in life. His goal was to make her happy, and it looked like his job was about to become much more involved for the foreseeable future. It made his own heart race with excitement.

Chapter Twenty-Five

Your kiss is better than champagne, more intoxicating. It sweeps me under. My head is spinning, and I hold on tight to you, my sunshine so bright.

Holly looked at Landry, suspicious of his laid-back attitude about this whole thing. But maybe he'd change his mind once he heard the list. She ignored the stab of disappointment at the idea and cleared her throat.

"Number one, no more kissing. Number two, no lights on. We can only do it in the dark. Number three, no cuddling afterwards. Number four, no messing around in town. I liked your idea that we could avoid all the busybodies if we go out of town."

He was frowning now, his jaw clenched, but she continued. "Number five, no flirting. This is a business arrangement, and we need to still be friends after. We'll still have to see each other in town and at friend events. Which leads us

The Songwriter Gets His Girl

to number six, no telling anyone else. It must remain secret."

She glanced at him, her palms sweating. For once, she couldn't see what he was thinking because he was just sitting there waiting for her to finish.

"Number seven, no getting involved with the kid's life, since everyone will think this is a sperm bank donation. I was fine without a dad, and my kid will be too. Number eight, no spending money on the baby or the pregnancy outside of normal friend status. You are allowed one gift at the baby shower, but that's it."

He arched a brow, and she tilted her nose up to continue.

"Number nine, no more messing around once I'm pregnant. Once the mission is a success, we go back to being just friends. And finally, number ten, no falling in love. That's too much of a complication, and I love Eric."

Her words sounded hollow, but it had to be said. Silence filled the air as Landry rubbed his jaw. Her own fingers tingled to touch that short stubble.

"I want veto power." His hazel eyes burned into hers with their intensity.

She frowned and shook her head. "No, you said I was the princess earlier, and I rule this kingdom. These are my terms."

His eyes narrowed, then he slowly started to smile. "I guess that makes me the court jester, huh? Fine, I agree to your terms."

The way he ended that sentence made her think he was silently saying *for now*, but she couldn't be sure. Maybe if she prodded.

"I hear a but in there."

He wiggled his eyebrows. "Not yet, but there will be soon."

Her eyes widened, and she laughed, slapping him on the leg. "Landry, no, I meant do you really agree to the terms or are you going to add any or suggest any counter arguments to it?"

He rubbed his jaw again. "Just one or two, I suppose. No dating anyone else, for either of us, until we win the game and get pregnant. You went out with Parker and Nick, but no more."

She snorted. "Yeah, that's not going to be a problem. I'm good with that. Any others?"

"One more. For every night we spend together, we have to do something fun, a non-sex activity together."

She tilted her head and frowned. "What, like a date?"

He raised a brow and crossed his arms. "If that's what you want to call it, sure. But if I'm going to be on my best behavior—you know, follow your rules and give you my best swimmers—I'm going to need to de-stress from the pressure and just let loose a little. Plus, you're long overdue for some fun. Do we have a deal?"

She looked at her list, then back at him, her stomach clenching as the nerves set in. This was such a crazy idea, but was it so crazy that it might actually work? She looked behind the couch at the photo collage and sucked in a ragged breath.

She silently pleaded for answers, for guidance, but none came. When she looked at Landry, his hazel eyes were clear as he waited. He didn't rush her, didn't look impatient or bored. Just watched her with curious and open eyes, eyes that had always accepted her even from that first night all those years ago.

Then he smiled slightly, his lips just tipping up on the

corners as he raised a brow, and her shoulders relaxed in response. Her nerves were still jumping around in her stomach, but it was going to be alright because Landry was going to be there every step of the way.

She nodded, sticking out her hand. "It's a deal. Shake on it?"

He glanced at her hand, then back into her eyes. His eyes had gotten darker, and he reached for her hand to shake it. But instead of shaking it, he brought it to his lips and kissed the back of her hand. Her breath caught in her throat as he kissed her knuckles, then her finger tips. Finally, he took the tip of her pointer finger into his mouth and sucked on it.

She gasped, her jaw going slack, and pulled her hand back. "I—I thought we agreed no kissing."

He grinned wickedly, and her core clenched in response. "Oh, all kisses? I thought you were just talking about kissing on the mouth."

He shifted closer on the couch, and she felt like he was sucking all the air out of the room. She jumped up and hopped around the coffee table to keep something between them other than these crazy sparks. The notebook fell on the floor, and he picked it up, scribbling his additions to the bottom.

She pointed to the calendar on the wall. "I—I'm ovulating next weekend. I plan on telling everyone that I'm going to Dallas for the procedure, and I'll be there all weekend. Do you—can you—"

He chuckled and stood, tossing the notebook onto the coffee table and pushing his hands into his pockets. "Am I free next weekend?"

She nodded, her throat nearly closed as she breathed heavily through her nose.

He shrugged and glanced away. "Sure, I need to go back to Nashville. While I wasn't planning on next weekend, I can move my trip up if you'd like to come with me."

She searched his face and frowned. He was shifting on his feet and avoiding her gaze. "This thing in Nashville. What is it? It is to meet with your music producer? What was his name?"

His cheeks turned pink, and he rubbed his jaw again. "I'm working on a Christmas present for my family, so you can't tell anyone about it, okay?"

She nodded and crossed her arms. What kind of Christmas present required going out of state and starting on it in July?

"But yes, I'm meeting with Mike. It's a record, professionally made in a studio. This way he gets me singing a few of my own songs, and I get a badass present."

Her brows rose in surprise. "Landry, that's amazing. It sounds like a lot of fun. Is there anything I can do to help?"

He seemed to relax as his shoulders sagged and his smile returned. "Just keep me company, if you'd like to join me."

"I'd love to. We can leave Thursday night and come back Monday? That'll be better rates for flights."

He bounced slightly on the balls of his feet, his grin eager. "Sounds great. I'll make all the arrangements."

He walked around the coffee table and swept her up in a hug, spinning her in a circle and making her laugh. Her heart soared, happy that he was so happy. This was going to work out well. They were good friends who supported each other, had good communication... it was going to work out.

He set her down and leaned forward to kiss her before catching himself. With a rueful, self-deprecating smile, he shrugged. "Well, I'll text you to work out the details. See you later, Holly."

Holy shit, she said yes. *She said yes.* Landry hopped in his truck and drove home, barely remembering to grab his groceries and bring them inside. He felt like the Joker because his smile was hurting his face, and he couldn't turn it off.

Maybe if you whistle, it'll make your face return to normal.

He laughed at himself as he opened the front door and set the groceries on the counter. He tried to whistle, but it was no use. Instead, he turned on the vintage looking radio in the kitchen's corner and began to dance as he chopped veggies for dinner.

When Parker walked in the door, Landry was singing into the wooden spoon as he stirred the spaghetti. Landry danced over to Parker and held out the fake microphone, making his brother laugh before singing the chorus with him to Journey's *Don't Stop Believin'*.

When the next verse hit, Landry turned to stir the pot while singing. Parker disappeared only to return with both of their guitars. Landry grinned, turned off the stove, and slipped the guitar strap over his shoulder. Parker turned the radio up as loud as it would go as they started playing in the kitchen, Landry dancing around with his guitar. Parker laughed and sat on a chair as he played bass.

When the guitar solo came on, Landry felt his heart soar with every note. The next chorus, he sang as loud as he could with Parker singing the backup vocals.

The song ended and both of them were panting. They looked at each other and burst out laughing.

Parker wiped his eyes with one hand. "Damn, it's been forever since we've done that."

"Since high school. Remember how it used to drive

Mom crazy?" Landry turned the radio down and stood his guitar against the cabinets in the corner. He spooned up the spaghetti and set a plate in front of Parker.

He glanced at his brother, who was just resting his hands on his guitar and watching him. It wasn't like Parker not to answer a question, but Landry hoped he wasn't thinking of questions of his own to ask.

"So what's with this great attitude? What's got you singing and grinning so wide?"

Landry groaned and turned to grab forks and drinks. "Nothing much, except I'm going back to Nashville next weekend."

Parker's brows rose, and he set his guitar on a spare chair next to him. "Oh yeah? That's great, man. Maybe I'll come with you since I don't go back to school until the second week of August."

"No!" Landry spit out the word and choked on his pasta. Parker slapped him on the back, but he waved him away and took a drink of his water. It was several minutes later before he'd cleared his throat enough to return to eating.

Only Parker wouldn't let him. He just sat there, leaning back in his chair with his arms crossed. "Just no? Come on, you gotta tell me why not."

Landry shook his head and shoved in a bite of noodles. He chewed slowly, which made Parker roll his eyes.

Quick, think of something that will keep him away.

I'm trying, genius. Need to stick as close to the truth as possible though.

He swallowed and cleared his throat. "Holly's going to her sperm bank appointment, and I'm going to drive her down on my way to the airport."

"Ah, finally you're getting some alone time with her.

That's over an hour in close quarters. Way to go, man. I'm proud of you."

"Shut up." Landry grumbled, forking another bite into his mouth.

"I guess if she's actually going through with the in vitro baby, you can't really start things up with her though, huh?"

Landry shrugged, ignoring Parker.

"Unless you wanted to be an instant dad like Andy. Can you imagine?" Parker chuckled, then picked up his fork to eat.

Landry's mind raced as he thought about Andy. He'd said Cindy's boys had been really excited about having a dad. Would his kid be okay without him being there for all the dad things? What if Holly ended up falling in love in ten years? Then his son or daughter would have a step-dad.

The pressure built in his chest, threatening to push him under. He couldn't finish his pasta, the taste turning to ash in his mouth and making him want to gag.

Would it be worth the pain of missing out to spend this time with her? He pictured her face that first day she bought the studio, tears pouring down her cheeks as she hyperventilated.

He breathed a deep sigh of relief. No, she wouldn't fall for anyone else. She'd loved Eric with her whole being. It was true love, and she wouldn't fall for anyone, not tomorrow, next year, or ten years from now. He didn't have to worry about someone else raising his kid.

It would be okay. His son or daughter would have the best mom in the world, and the whole town would love that kid. And Kendall would be the best uncle and a great father figure. He could do this, could love her and give her the baby she needed.

Love her?

His fork fell to the plate, the sound jarring him from his thoughts. He shoved the chair back and carried his half-eaten plate to the sink. He set it down and walked away, his mind on Holly and not even caring that he was leaving the kitchen uncleaned.

Chapter Twenty-Six

You've got my back in times of need. What'd I do without you? I hope I never have to find out.

August

Holly packed up her toiletries while Lola fumed on her bed. When she came out of the bathroom, she tossed her little bag on the counter. "Did you really come over just to give me the silent treatment?"

She swung by the pantry where she kept her essential oils. She wanted to pack the ones that'd help her manage the stress of the trip and of this huge life step. Not just having a baby but having it the natural way.

Her mind shied away from that as she went back through the kitchen, grabbing her toiletry bag on the way to her bed. She shoved it in the corner of her pink carry on.

Lola crossed her arms and raised a brow. Somehow, she

looked just as regal laying on the bed as she did standing with her hands on her hips.

Fed up with Lola's attitude, Holly pursed her lips. "If you use my bed while I'm gone, make sure the sheets and blankets and everything get washed this time, okay?"

Lola narrowed her eyes. "What the hell are you talking about?"

Holly widened her eyes and tilted her head in that innocent look she'd perfected when she was younger. "Don't you remember the wedding reception last December? I had to wash my bedding twice just to make sure it was properly sanitized."

Lola gasped and jerked up on the bed, nearly causing the bag to fall on the floor. Her face drained of all color and her jaw dropped.

"You—you—"

"Saw you boning my brother? Yeah. Been waiting for you to say something but you never did." Holly rolled her dress up and put it in her bag. Lola just threw her face in her hands and fell back onto the bed.

Holly sighed, not enjoying being this upfront with her best friend, but if it was a means to an end, she could do it. She took a deep breath and patted Lola's hand.

"Look, I'm not going to give you grief, and you can bet your ass I haven't mentioned it to Kendall. Can you need to back off on judging me for this in vitro thing though? This is what I need to do right now. I know you're worried, and I love you for it, but can you accept this? Accept me?"

Lola groaned and turned onto her side to face Holly. The sun from the windows fell across her face, highlighting her freckles and blue eyes. "Okay, okay. You know I love you and just worry about you. There are so many things that can go wrong—"

"But they won't." Holly squeezed her hand, then stood up to finish packing. She pulled out a drawer and bit her lip, debating on which pajama set. All of them were silky tank tops and shorts, so it wasn't like it mattered. She grabbed the lilac-colored ones and tossed them into her bag.

She smiled as she opened her underwear drawer, then grabbed the bright pink set that he'd seen when he'd inspected the bathrooms last winter. She froze, frowning as she stared down at it. What was she doing? He wasn't going to be seeing any of it, since they had the rules.

She turned to toss them into the bag and saw Lola rifling through the magazines on her coffee table. She zipped up her bag and moved it to the floor to hear Lola gasp.

Holly glanced up and froze. Lola's eyes were round as she held up the legal pad and waved it around. "What the fuck is this?"

Holly lunged for it, but Lola was an Amazon of a woman and easily held it above her head.

"Lola, no, give that back. It's nothing important."

"Nothing important? Then why are you trying to climb me like a monkey, short stuff?"

Holly gritted her teeth and jumped onto the couch, then launched herself onto Lola's back. Lola grunted under the extra weight and almost fell onto the coffee table.

"Holly, get off."

"No, give me my notebook."

She'd almost reached the legal pad when Landry's voice came up the stairs.

"Holly, are you up there? I'm coming up to help with your bag. I texted but you didn't respond."

Holly scrambled down, and Lola moved the legal pad under the back of her shirt. Landry strode down the little hall that led to the stairs, his smile making Holly's heart stop in her chest.

"Hey Lola, how's it going?"

Lola glanced at Holly and raised a brow before smiling at Landry and answering. "Going good. Just came to make sure she had everything she needed for the weekend. Thanks for dropping her off at the clinic, Landry. We're swamped at the farm this time of year, and I couldn't get away."

"No problem. I do have to catch my flight though, so we need to get going. Holly, is that your only bag?"

Holly nodded, unable to talk past the lump in her throat. Her heart was still pounding too fast from panicking over Lola finding the notebook, but she followed Landry, grabbing her large purse from the coat rack.

When Landry took her bag down the stairs, she spun on her heel to face Lola.

"Lola, I can explain."

"Sure you can." Lola smirked and crossed her arms. "And I expect you to, but for now you have to go. We will resume this conversation when you get back."

Holly grabbed a light sweater and frowned. "Just lock up downstairs when you go home."

She spun on her heel and raced down the stairs, stopping only long enough to slip on her sneakers that were by the back door. When she hopped into Landry's truck, her hands were sweaty and shaking.

He backed up and drove them out of town, the song on the radio playing softly in the background.

"It'll take about an hour to get to the airport. Do you want to listen to any specific type of music?"

She shook her head and watched the fields roll past her window. "No, whatever you want to listen to is fine."

The Songwriter Gets His Girl

"You okay? Having second thoughts?"

She sighed and rubbed her forehead. "No, once I decide to do something, there's no turning back. Even if I am nervous."

"There's no reason to be nervous. We're just two friends who are traveling together for a weekend of fun. Relax. It's going to be great. Just think of the fun stuff we're going to do and not all the mind-blowing sex."

She burst out laughing and caught his twinkling gaze before he looked back at the road. "Alright, what fun stuff do you have planned? You'll need to tell me if I'm going to take my mind off the sex."

They talked about their weekend plans, which led into a conversation about food and restaurants they wanted to try. Landry wanted to go to a comedy club and had to spend a few hours in the studio.

Once they'd parked, gone through security, and found their gate, they sat waiting to board. Holly's knee started to bounce as Landry wrote something in the little notebook he kept in his back pocket.

She glanced over. "What are you writing?"

He looked up and met her eyes, then looked back down at his notebook. He leaned toward her to show her the paper, and his leather scent filled her nostrils. Her leg stopped bouncing as she relaxed, but now there were gymnasts doing somersaults in her stomach at having him nearby.

"See that family across from us? The one with the little dark-haired boy with the robot backpack? I'm writing a song about their family."

We know exactly what we have,
Family more precious than gold
I love our house, our little world,

Because family binds us and holds,
Against all the storms of life, and all the fear and pain,
The family binds us, family keeps me sane.

She read what he'd written so far and raised her brows. "Landry, that's beautiful. I can't wait to hear what it sounds like."

He shrugged and returned to sitting normal. She could breathe easier but leaned toward him, following him, before she realized it and jerked back.

"When did you start writing songs? I never asked."

"I didn't used to write songs. I started writing poems in high school after my other grandpa passed away. It really helped me process the pain. Writing helped me keep my head on straight when all I wanted to do was skip class and throw things."

She nodded, feeling the pain and loss start to creep up her chest and into her throat. She cleared it, but it remained heavy on her shoulders. "I can understand that. It's why I got into yoga actually. The grief can pull you under and losing my mom and aunt within a year of each other was hard. I was a bit of a mess when I moved in with Kendall right after I graduated."

"I'm sorry about your mom and aunt. What about other family?"

She shook her head and picked at the hem of her jean shorts. "Don't remember any of my grandparents. They died a long time ago. My aunt wasn't married and didn't have kids, so now it's just Kendall and me."

The silence stretched, and her leg started to bounce again. He reached over and grabbed the hand still picking at her shorts, lifting it to his mouth. Her eyes watched as he kissed her hand and set their joined hands on the armrest between them.

The Songwriter Gets His Girl

When her eyes met his, he smiled. "You have me too."

His deep voice sent shivers up her spine. Did he mean what she thought he meant? No, he couldn't. Her eyes widened, and she tried to pull away. But he sighed and kept their hands right where they were.

"And Maryanne and Lola, and Cindy, all the girls night yoga crew, and all your yoga students. The whole town loves you, Holly. We're family by choice, not by blood, so never think you're alone in all this."

The gate agent called the first group to board and Landry glanced at their tickets, confirming their group. She was finally successful in pulling her hand out of his, but it left her feeling empty and nervous again. She pulled out her Stress Away oil and applied it under her ears and on her chest.

They made their way down the ramp and to their seats. Landry put both their bags in the overhead compartment and ushered her to the window seat. She felt herself start to sweat when the safety brief began, and her heart raced.

She wiped her palms on her shorts and looked out the window. A hand settled on her bouncing knee, stilling it as he stroked it softly, back and forth. She turned to see him with one brow raised, his hazel eyes bright.

"You okay, angel?"

She shrugged. "Yeah, just not a fan of flying. Also, I'm pretty sure that counts as flirting, and it's against the rules." She pointed to his hand on her leg, but he just squeezed it and winked.

"Hey, I see a girl in need, and I'm gonna help her. Is it the whole flight that makes you nervous or just the takeoff and landing?"

She sucked in a breath and thought about it. "No one's ever asked, but I guess it's just the taking off and landing.

I'm not a fan of roller coasters either, if that makes a difference."

He nodded and turned in his seat to face her as the captain came on the PA to announce time for takeoff. She reached for his hand and squeezed, leaning her head back on the seat and closing her eyes.

She felt the pressure building in her chest, her stomach in knots. She was fine, she could do this. Not that bad, just a little nerves. She wasn't going to throw up or hyperventilate or anything.

They started to roll away from the gate, and she focused on regulating her breathing. She kept hers closed, but she could feel him looking at her, his gaze burning into her and making her hot.

Their plane lined up for takeoff and she squeezed his hand. When he pulled it out of her grasp, she opened her eyes and turned to him, only to have him grab her head with both hands and kiss her.

Her breath stopped, and he pushed his tongue inside, sweeping into her mouth and scattering her thoughts, worries, and fears. The smell of leather and mint filled her nostrils as she breathed him in, absorbing his peace, his calm, his essence.

He pulled back and gave little kisses on her lips, her cheeks. Still holding her face in his hands, he looked at her, searching her eyes for what she didn't know. Her mind was still scattered on the wind from that kiss.

Then he nodded to the window behind her. "We've leveled out now. Feel better?" His voice was rough as sandpaper and made goosebumps break out on her arms.

She glanced out the window and saw nothing but clouds. She hadn't felt the rush of the engines or the acceleration. She'd been so focused on him and their kiss that she'd miss the entire thing.

Her leg wasn't bouncing anymore and her muscles were relaxed. Except for her core, which was randomly spasming in anticipation of later tonight.

She cleared her throat and nodded. "Yeah, I'm good now. Thanks. But also, stop breaking the rules. No kissing."

He chuckled and pulled out his notebook. "Like I said, I'm going to help when you need it. Even if it breaks the rules."

Her heart raced at the thought. What other rules would he break? He'd agreed to them, so hopefully that was the only one. Except, that thought didn't seem to make its way to her pussy, because it was throbbing at the thought of breaking the kissing rule again.

Chapter Twenty-Seven

When you're scared and hurt, just call out and I'll be there. When you're alone and shaking, just call out and I'll be there.

A few hours later, they walked through the Nashville airport to the car rental desk. There were a lot of people around, and Landry had grabbed her hand to stop her from being run over by an airport cart. Then he'd kept hold of it as they'd walked.

It was another rule broken, but she ignored that voice in the back of her head that reminded her about it. Instead, she drew strength from him, leading them through the crowd. He took her breath away, not from walking too fast but because he was so confident, calm, and collected as they went.

He'd been like that the entire trip. He'd not rushed her through security or to their gate. He'd turned to her when they'd begun their descent and kissed her again. No asking or coaxing, he'd just gone for it and it was one of the hottest things she'd ever experienced.

He'd not rushed or stressed about getting off the plane either. It was like he was just normal Landry, relaxed and smiling, but also this confident man with a purpose who knew exactly where he was going and what he was doing. He'd always been confident but traveling with him was so different than what traveling with Eric had been like.

Maybe she liked this laid back go with the flow way of traveling a little too much.

She frowned as he let go of her hand to sign for the rental and grab the keys. They walked to a little blue Hyundai Sonata. He popped the trunk and slung his carry-on inside.

She pushed hers to him. "I had a car like this."

He winked and carefully put her bag inside. "I know. It was white, though."

Her jaw dropped as he closed the trunk and turned to her. "I heard from Maryanne that you drove home the other day—in Lola's big ass truck, no less, which is quite a feat—but I wondered if you'd like to give driving something familiar a try?"

She opened and closed her mouth, tears pooling in the corner of her eyes. She sucked in a shuddering breath and tried to hold back the overwhelming realization that he *saw* her. He enveloped her in a tight embrace, bringing a sense of safety and protection. A warmth bloomed in her chest, and the tears cascaded down onto his blue t-shirt.

He just held her as she cried, her arms wrapped around his waist. It didn't last long this time, but she stayed in his arms as her mind whirled, moving past the pain of the loss and car accident and to this man in her arms. He'd remembered what kind of car she drove from *one night* five years ago. What did that mean? How did he remember that?

"It's okay, angel. There's no pressure to drive, okay? But this is the car we'll use all weekend, so if you feel like it, you can. Either way will be fine."

She nodded, the scratch of his shirt against her cheek and the smell of leather helping to calm her nerves. She pulled back and avoided his eyes by looking at the car. "Not right now, if that's alright? Maybe tomorrow."

He reached out a finger and tilted her chin up so she'd look at him. His eyes were open and clear. The laugh lines at the corners made her wonder what he'd look like in fifty years when they'd set deeper from experience, laughter, and love.

"As you wish, princess. Want to grab dinner somewhere or eat room service at the hotel?"

Her fingers gripped his shirt at his waist before letting go. She could feel the heat spreading on her cheeks as she walked to the passenger side of the car. Finally, taking a deep breath without his scent lingering, the fog on her brain cleared only to become muddied again when they both got into the car and shut their doors.

His scent enveloped her, and her body hummed. The hotel would lead to baby-making, and that was the whole point they were here. Her stomach twisted with nerves. This was more than just a heat of the moment like that time in her apartment. She gulped and looked out the passenger window, staring at anything but him.

"Room service is fine, or we can just see what's around the hotel when we get there. Maybe we should walk a little, after being cooped up on the plane." She bit her lip and wiped her sweaty hands on her thighs.

"Sounds like a plan to me." He plugged in their destination on the GPS before adjusting the radio and backing up.

The closer they got to the hotel, the more nervous Landry became. This weekend had to go right, because if it didn't, it would scar her for life. He might be the only one besides her husband she'd ever sleep with, and he needed to make it so good for her that the memories would last him a lifetime.

The way those fucking rules were laid out, she obviously didn't want to make this a special time, but it would be for him. He turned into the parking lot of the hotel and took a fortifying breath. Her lavender scent calmed him, but he'd had a semi hard-on since that first touch of her leg on the plane.

But first, he needed to wine and dine her.

He smiled at her and shut off the engine. "Here we are. Let's check in and take our bags up first."

He got out and rounded the front of the car to open her door, but she was already stepping out. He smiled, proud of her for being so strong and independent. He was the kind of guy to always open doors for ladies, always be a gentleman and respectful. While he wanted to do that for Holly, she wasn't the lost and broken woman she was when she'd first moved to town.

They walked into the hotel, the golds and reds popping under the chandeliers and making him feel underdressed in his t-shirt, jeans, and boots. They might have been clean and pressed, but this was a fancier place than he'd expected.

He tilted his chin at the manager behind the counter and smiled. "Hello, checking in please, under Landry Williams."

The man smiled and typed on his computer. Landry watched Holly out of the corner of his eye as she took in the lobby and fidgeted with the strap on her purse. Her eyes were big as saucers and her pretty little pink mouth beckoned him.

The manager cleared his throat. "Ah, here you are, Mr. Williams. You're on the ninth floor. Continental breakfast is included, there's room service available until one in the morning, and the pool is down the hall to the left just past the elevators to your room. Do you have any questions?"

Landry looked at the man and asked, "Yes, just one. Do you know of any good vegetarian restaurants around here?"

The man wrote several down on a post-it and explained his recommendations, then Landry grabbed it and the keys.

"Thank you. Ready, angel?"

She glanced at him and then looked away nervously. It made his heart jump, and he rolled both their bags down the hall. The elevator ride was tense, and she shifted from foot to foot while staring at the floor. He was going to have to get her out of her head and to stop worrying about what they'd do in this hotel room.

His hand shook as he swiped the key card though and pushed open the door. She walked ahead of him, her hips swaying and drawing his eyes more than the large hotel room. She spun in a slow circle while taking in the gold and white striped wallpaper and the gold and green patterned carpet.

He moved their bags to the closet. The king sized bed looked comfortable with its giant fluffy pillows and pristine white bedspread. There was a red wingback chair in the corner with a matching footstool. He took a few steps to check out the bathroom and grinned. It included a large Jacuzzi tub just as he'd requested.

The Songwriter Gets His Girl

Holly walked to the floor to ceiling window and drew back the white curtain. He walked up behind her and traced his fingers from hers up her arms to rest at her shoulders. She tensed under his hands until he started to rub her shoulders. Then she moaned, the sound going straight to his cock and driving him crazy.

"You're nervous, and that's making you tense up. Relax, Holly. It's just me."

His voice sounded rougher than normal, but he couldn't help it. When he wanted to fuck her, which was almost every moment of the day, his fought to maintain his casual, guy next door demeanor.

Slowly, she relaxed under his hands, and he leaned forward and kissed the spot on her neck where it met her shoulder. She tensed and spun out of his arms, dancing away and making him feel empty and cold.

She eyed him wearily and shook her head. "No, we talked about this, Lan. No kissing. Remember? You agreed."

He nodded slowly and clenched his jaw. "I did, and that's fine. Let's do it your way, then we'll go eat. Unless you want to eat now?"

He arched a brow and waited. Based on the rapid rise and fall of her breathing, the pink tinge in her cheeks, he had more than a fifty-fifty shot that she'd want to find some relief from those plane kisses and the massage.

She pursed her lips and waved a hand. "Fine. We can have sex now, then find food. Just close those red blackout curtains while I hit the lights."

He grinned, "As you wish, angel."

Chapter Twenty-Eight

Your laugh tinkles in the air, your eyes sparkle in the light. When we're together, there's no stormy weather, because I love you with all my might.

Landry turned and closed the curtains. When he spun around, he could barely see the light shining from under the bathroom door. Apparently, expensive hotels did a pretty damn good job of making rooms dark even in the day.

When his eyes had adjusted all, they could, he called softly, "Holly?"

"I'm over here. Are you joining me or not?"

He grinned and pulled his t-shirt over his head, dropping it to the floor while he kicked off his boots. He pushed down his jeans and underwear, then wrenched off his socks. But when he walked to the bed, he stubbed his toe on the wingback chair.

"Damn it." He hopped on one foot.

Holly's voice echoed with laughter. "Are you okay?"

He found the bed and placed one hand on it as he flexed his toes. "Fine, just stubbed my toe in the dark. I found the bed, though."

He crawled onto it and found a warm lump under the covers. If she wanted to do this in the dark under the covers, he was going to damn well do it. He licked his lips and pulled the blankets back to join her.

He stuck a handout and hit something.

"Ouch, what was that?" came her muffled voice.

"Um, my hand. Why, what'd I hit?"

"That was my eye."

He chuckled, then felt a hand slap the blanket beside him. "Sorry, sorry. Not laughing at you, just the situation. Are you okay?"

"Yeah." She huffed out a breath, which just made him grin wider. Maybe she'd get so frustrated with her way of doing things they could renegotiate the terms of the rules.

He slid closer and found her thigh with his hand, making her jump. Then she spread her legs, and he moved over her. He rested on his elbows, his chest just slightly touching her breasts, and shifted his hips to line himself up with her sweet heat.

He pushed forward, but she placed a hand on his chest. "Wait, Lan, wrong hole."

"Well, where's the right one?"

"Hold on." She reached down and grabbed his dick, making him groan at the touch even as he chuckled at the awkwardness. She had to see that this was more than a business transaction. She lined him up where he was supposed to go, and he pushed forward, her hand guiding him slowly until she hissed. "Stop, stop. You're too big, and I'm not wet enough."

He paused at her opening, gritting his teeth as she

wiggled beneath him. "I'm not too big. You took it last time. Just be still."

She slapped his bicep playfully and growled, "That was different."

He pressed his forehead to hers, caging her in his arms as he held himself still on his knees. "Holly, as much as you want this to be a business transaction, neither of us are the stick it in, wham bam thank you ma'am, kind of person. If this is going to work, we need to bend those rules a little."

She searched and found his hand, then intertwined their fingers. He prayed that she saw it his way because he wanted to be so much closer to her than this.

"Landry, I don't know how to do this if we don't have the rules. It makes me scared to not have them."

He held his body weight on one elbow and pulled their joined hands to his face, kissing her knuckles. She cupped his cheek and even though it was dark and neither of them could see, he could feel her softening to him, could imagine the look in her eyes.

He kissed her palm. "I know it's scary, but some of the best things in life happen because we face our fears. If I'd stopped being a handyman the first time I hit my thumb with a hammer, I'd have never found the joy in seeing a remodel come together or my favorite client's face when she saw her new yoga studio finally completed. If I hadn't pushed past the fear of a power saw, I never would've spent all that time with Pops. This could just be something that you need to push past, if you actually want a baby. Rules have their place, yes, but if we're going to do this, we might need to adjust a bit. If you don't want to do this, that's okay too. I'll still be here, and we'll figure it out together."

He pushed his fingers into her hair and pulled her into

his arms, turning onto his side and holding her tight. They laid there, giving her time to think and hopefully feel their naked bodies warm to each other. Slowly, she relaxed, the tension melting from her.

When she tilted her head to his and kissed his chin, he groaned and rolled onto his back to bring her on top of him. She gasped, her hands coming up to his shoulders and pressing him into the bed while her legs automatically fell to either side.

Her knees clutched his hips and her warm center settled over his stomach. He flexed his fingers in her hair and rose to meet her lips. Their kiss was explosive as she opened immediately. Their tongues dueled as she angled her head to take the kiss deeper.

His other hand came up over her stomach, and it quivered at his touch. His heart soared at her responsiveness. Surely it was more than just physical for her too. It had to be.

When his hand reached the gentle curve of her breast, he cupped it, feeling the perfect weight, the softness that was the exact opposite of his rough fingers. This was paradise, heaven on earth, nirvana. He rolled her nipple between his fingers, and she shifted on him. It made the tip of his cock graze her ass, and he groaned, thrusting up.

She shifted again and slid lower, not breaking their kiss as his hand moved to her other breast. Now the head was in the heat of her as she ground up and down on him. She ground on him, raking her clit up and down his dick. Her breathing grew shallow, matching his as he kept getting closer and closer to the goal but was kept just out of reach.

He let go of her hair and breast and moved his hands to her hips. He lifted her up and held her off him as he teased her entrance. Then he slowly let gravity do its job and bring them fully together.

God, she was so wet now. How had she gotten so wet in such a short amount of time? She broke the kiss in a gasp and arched her back, causing him to go even deeper. He rose slightly to capture a perky nipple in his mouth, and she grabbed him by the back of the head to hold him to her.

He sucked and raised her hips before slamming her back down on him. Then he flicked her nipple and grazed it with his teeth before easing her up slowly, then down fast and hard. Over and over, he pulled out almost all the way, only to plunge so deep into heaven he could see the planets and stars behind his eyelids.

Her muscles gripped him tighter when he moved to the other breast. Her whimpers were soft music to his ears, driving the crescendo higher and higher until she pushed on his chest and made her nipple pop from his mouth.

Then she rode him, hard and fast, grinding as she clawed his chest and pressed him into the bed. It was glorious, the feel of her rotating her hips as he plunged into her wet heat. He held onto her hips and pulled her down, harder and harder, keeping the tempo steady when she started to buck wild.

He felt more than saw her throw her head back and gasp, then she clenched on him like a vise, spasming once, twice, three times before he couldn't hold back any longer. He came in a rush, shuddering as he poured himself into her, mind, body, and soul.

He panted as it seemed like she milked him of every drop, her muscles clenching on him over and over. As his heart rate slowed, so did their aftershocks, until she slumped onto his chest with a sigh.

He wrapped his arms around her and kissed the top of

her head, the lavender of her shampoo engulfing him in the darkness. If he hugged her closer, perhaps he could draw out this perfect moment and hold on to it for eternity. He stayed silent, afraid if he opened his mouth he'd tell her how much he never wanted to let her go.

Chapter Twenty-Nine

Life is full of surprises. They throw us a curve ball no one can hit. But together, we'll face the stadium. Together, we'll stand through all the shit.

Holy mother of pearl. What had she just done?

She'd slept with him, again, and—and... She sighed, feeling his hands stroke her back, her body still feeling like jello. Damn, he was a good fuck. Eric had been good, but that had almost always been making love.

With Landry, it was more primal, more intense, more off-script. Just more. She felt a stab of guilt at that thought and bit her lip as he slipped out. She rolled onto her back and bent her knees, feet flat, to keep his swimmers from escaping. She'd read somewhere that it helped.

His hand found hers in the darkness, interlocking their fingers. She tried to pull away, but he held firm.

"Lan, the rules—"

The Songwriter Gets His Girl

"Said nothing about holding hands. This is allowed. Besides, didn't we just decide to bend the rules a little?"

She sighed, frowning and closing her eyes. "Yeah, but we can't keep doing that. Outside of the bed, we're just friends, Lan. Do you get that?"

"Oh, I get it." He released her hand, the bitterness in his voice clear when she couldn't see him. Her heart skipped a beat at the sound. Didn't he want to be friends? Did he want something more?

She felt and heard him shuffling around, then light filled part of the room as he pushed open the bathroom door. The shower turned on, then he strode out and opened the closet. He messed with his bag, but her eyes were riveted to his ass, his back.

Those thighs as thick as tree trunks and made her mouth water. What would it feel like to trace her hand down his spine? Would he be soft there or rough like his hands? And those tattoos that stretched almost over his entire upper back.

She swallowed hard and clenched her thighs together. She must have made a sound because he glanced over his shoulder, then turned to look at her. Her jaw dropped as she caught sight of him. She'd been spellbound by the back but damn.

If a Renaissance sculpture and a lumberjack had a baby, that would be Landry, all rippling muscles, soft short hair, and piercing eyes that chipped away at the wall around her heart.

"You alright, angel?"

His cock jumped as her eyes fell to it, and she gasped. "That fit in me?"

He chuckled and moved his clean clothes to one hand.

With the other, he gripped himself and stroked slowly. Her eyes widened as he got wider and longer. Her fingers twitched. She had doubts that her hand would fit around it, and her breath quickened when she realized she wanted to try.

"Are you complaining?"

She licked her lips and saw him suck in a breath, standing taller somehow. She cleared her throat and glanced away, pulling the covers up over her nakedness as she shook her head.

He sighed and turned on his heel, walking to the bathroom. "I'm going to shower, then we can go out for dinner if you'd like."

"It's the middle of the day. Why are you showering?"

He shrugged and paused in the doorway to look at her. "We just had sex, and I don't like to be sticky and sweaty. Sometimes I take two showers just because work is dirty. What can I say? I like to be clean." He paused and arched a brow. "If you'd like to join me, you can."

Her breath caught, and he winked before turning to go into the bathroom, leaving the door wide open. She was conflicted, her heart racing. If she went in there, she'd be breaking another rule because the light would be on.

But kissing had definitely helped them move past the awkwardness. So breaking that rule had had good consequences. Maybe this one would be okay too?

She tried to think of what the negative consequences could be, but her brain was still scrambled from that amazing orgasm. The bottom line was, she wanted to join him.

So why don't you?

The voice echoed in her mind, sounding a little like her mother and a little like Eric. She scoffed because that was crazy.

There was no one stopping her but herself. And it was going to be fine. This was going to turn out exactly as she'd planned, and before she knew it, she'd be pregnant and on her way to living out her dream.

Well, half of it anyway.

Her mind shied away from the missing piece as she rolled out of the bed and padded across the carpet to the bathroom. She took a shaky breath and stepped through the door.

The shower didn't have a door, just an opening, and Landry stood under the ceiling rain shower head, his eyes closed and face tipped back as the water ran down his magnificent body. He ran a hand through his hair, slicking it down.

She stepped inside and reached out a hand, tracing the compass tattoo over his heart. He froze, then opened those penetrating hazel eyes to peer into her soul. She glanced down, breaking eye contact as she ran her fingers over another tattoo.

"You didn't have any of these five years ago. Which one was your first?"

He touched the inside of his shoulder. There was a triangle with pine trees and a bird flying inside. "Andy and I got matching ones."

She raised her brows and traced it. "When? Why?" She couldn't seem to make her fingers stop touching him.

He clenched his jaw. "Five years ago, two days after that party where we met. As for why?" He shrugged and reached for the soap, breaking eye contact. She grabbed it before he did and lathered her hands, then kneaded them into his chest. A slight scattering of blond hair stretched across it, barely visible against the tattoos that covered almost every inch.

"I guess you liked getting them, huh, since you have so many now."

He shook his head. "Not really."

She raised her brows and rubbed down his stomach, tracing an outdoor scene that included a buck, horse, and turkey in front of a lake with a fish jumping out of it. "Why did you get so many if you don't like them?"

He reached for the soap and lathered his hands while hers traced around to his other side, which was a long line of words, quotes about love and pain.

"I got them every few months to remind myself to feel, to not give in to the pain of loss and heartache. I was numb for a long time because I couldn't handle it crashing down on me."

He ran his hands down her back, washing her but only their hands were touching each other's bodies. His hands distracted her, and she shuddered, her breathing shallow and ragged. What were they talking about again?

"Because you lost your grandparents?"

He paused, then bent his lips toward her ear. He was so close, her nipples had pebbled in anticipation as she slid her hands up his ribs. His voice was a low whisper barely heard over the water.

"Because I lost you." She gasped, and he nipped at her ear. "How do you think I felt to see you get engaged to him that night? This gorgeous, sweet, fiery woman of my dreams just slipped through my fingers, and there was nothing I could do about it. It broke me for a long time."

He kissed and bit the side of her neck softly, making her moan. His hands ran over her ass, the soap making them slippery when he pulled them roughly together. Her body was hot, a bonfire of lust that threatened to consume her.

It confused her in its intensity because it had never

The Songwriter Gets His Girl

been like this before. The closer they became, the more they had sex, the more intense her need for him. His words reverberated in her mind with every touch of his lips on her body. He'd gotten all this ink because she had made the pain so unbearable that he'd gone numb. This wasn't possible.

His lips made their way to her breasts, nipping softly and making her squirm. When he flicked her nipple with his tongue, she reached her hands up and grabbed his head to pull him closer. She needed him, but he pulled his head back, just kissing her softly, gently.

"Tell me what you want, angel." His voice sent a shiver down her spine, flooding her core with an ache for more.

She shifted her legs together, but there wasn't enough friction. She pulled him back to her breast and gasped, "Suck it. Please, Lan."

Then he did, and her heart stopped. He made her hunger with raw, wild need inside as he sucked and nipped at her pebbled flesh. When he broke contact, she cried out, arching her back to bring him closer, but he just moved to her other breast and feasted again.

She sighed in relief, but soon was squirming in his arms again. The feel of his short stubble of a beard on her skin drove her need forward until he lifted her, and she could only wrap her legs around him. He pressed her against the wall, gripped her ass and pushed his way inside so fast that she cried out in surprise.

The pleasure made her eyes flutter closed because her pussy was finally getting what it craved. She followed him into the throes of passion and consequences be damned, rules be damned. He pulled back and slammed into her repeatedly. Her head settled on his shoulder, and she bit and clawed him. She held on as wave after wave of raw need swept over her. She was so close, but she didn't want it to end.

He growled, dipped his head, and bit her where her neck met her shoulder, that tender spot she never knew could feel so good. She cried out, her breathing ragged. His mouth pushed her over the cliff, and she fell into ecstasy, shuddering around him as he pistoned out of her.

Her orgasm kept going because he kept going. It could have been moments but it felt like an hour before his tempo changed and his breathing became erratic, the whole time her body clenching him over and over.

Then he exploded inside, filling her with his heat. It was violent and virile, leaving her gasping as her orgasm finally slowed with his. She had never felt so good, so filled and replete. She panted, marveling at the power he had as he held her, at the peace she felt in his arms, at the feeling of love and safety that spread through her veins.

She couldn't believe it had been years since she'd felt this cherished. She questioned if she had ever truly felt this at peace before. Perhaps it was a temporary high that would eventually fade once she got her baby and he went back to just being her friend. Her stomach twisted at how they would go back to the way they used to be. Her mind and heart were at war as she struggled to make sense of her emotions.

Her stomach growled, and Landry chuckled, slowly lowering her feet to the ground. "Sounds like someone's hungry. Let's get washed up and find some food."

When her legs threatened to buckle, he held her up and kissed the side of her head. She whimpered, then found the strength to stand even though her legs still felt like jello. He pushed her beyond what limits she'd placed on them and on herself, but he never poked and prodded too much. He

The Songwriter Gets His Girl

always left the decision up to her, never tried to persuade or manipulate her into anything.

Everything with Eric had been explosive. He'd loved hard and deep, and they'd argued but had made-up just as fiercely. Landry watched, waited patiently, and accepted her decisions when she made them.

He reached for the shampoo and lathered up his hair while she collected herself, standing on her own feet and—now that his hands weren't distracting her—some of her thoughts settled.

"You knew all along the rules weren't going to work out, didn't you?"

He paused, glanced at her and winked. "Perhaps. But you needed them that safety net, and they served their purpose, didn't they? They allowed you to seize what you really wanted?"

She sniffed and tipped her head in the air, reaching for the shampoo and lathering up. "We're not ditching all of them, Landry. Just one and two."

"For now." She swung a startled gaze at him, only to catch him wink and grin. "Whatever you say, princess."

She groaned and rinsed out her hair. "Landry, I'm serious. The rest of the rules stay, okay?"

He shrugged and stepped out while she finished washing. When she turned off the water, Landry had a towel wrapped around his waist and was holding up another for her to step into.

He toweled her off, his hands running it up and down her arms, her legs, even her hair as he hummed some song. She felt her heart melt as he took care of her, wrapping her up in the towel and kissing the tip of her nose.

"How are you feeling? Do you still want to go find some food?"

She shook her head and felt her cheeks heat. "No, let's just order room service."

"All right. We can watch tv and talk like the good friends we are."

She followed him to the room, ignoring the way mentioning being friends frustrated her. He picked up the hotel's folder to find the menu. By the time their food came, she'd brushed and braided her hair and slipped on her pajamas. They sat with the food between them, leaning against the headboard, and watched America's Funniest Home Videos on TV.

The sound was turned down low so they could talk, and boy did they. He must have been in a talkative mood because they played twenty questions. He teased and flirted as they bantered back and forth, talking about their favorite shows and foods, their dislikes and likes.

When her sandwich and soup were all gone, they split the fruit cup for dessert. It was still early, but she was sleepy from traveling. He cleaned off the bed while she brushed her teeth and crawled under the covers. He turned the TV down even more and turned off all the lights except the bathroom before joining her.

She faced him, hugging a pillow to her chest to keep herself from trying to scoot into his arms. She'd been fine sleeping alone the past almost three years and one night with him wasn't going to change that.

He chuckled at the TV, and her eyes fluttered.

She closed them but her mind was still on a loop, his words from earlier now roaring in her mind. *I'd lost you, this gorgeous, sweet, fiery woman of my dreams had slipped through my fingers. It broke me. I was numb from the pain and heartache of losing you.*

It made no sense because they'd only met that night.

They'd talked for a few hours before Eric showed up. But her engagement was the catalyst for all those tattoos?

"Hey, Landry," she whispered into the semi-darkness.

"Yeah, Holly?"

She didn't know what to say, what to ask. Her head spun with the possibilities and shied away from most of them. They didn't need to talk about this heavy stuff on their first night together. It would probably ruin it, and then where would she be?

He'd probably back out of their deal. Her heart skipped a beat because she didn't want that to happen. She wanted it to be him. She wanted her baby's daddy to be him.

She sighed. "Thanks for doing this."

He chuckled. "Get some rest. I'm a night owl, and I might wake you up for another round before I get tired."

The bed shifted and she felt him kiss her head, then he went back to watching TV. She smiled, ready to go to sleep now that she wasn't so alone. This was going to be a great weekend.

Chapter Thirty

Rules were meant to be broken. No kissing? I can't stand it. Your lips draw me in like a bear to honey. My sweet bee, don't sting, just sing.

Holly came back from the hotel breakfast buffet with an extra plate and a carton of juice. She didn't know how long Landry had stayed up, only that he'd woken her up around two. Her cheeks heated at the memory, and she sat the food and drink down on the dresser.

She glanced at the clock and kicked off her sneakers. Then she sat on the bed and pulled the covers away from Landry's face. He was on his stomach, his arms under his pillow making his biceps bulge.

She traced her fingers over his wide shoulders. "Landry, are you going to wake up? What time did you say we needed to be at the studio?"

He groaned and shifted away from her, turning his head to face the other direction. She chuckled and pushed the sheet down to his hips. Then she straddled the tops of his thighs and massaged his shoulders.

He groaned again as she made her way down his back, then she leaned forward and kissed her way down his spine. When she'd made it halfway down, she sat up and rubbed her hands over his back.

"Wakey wakey, eggs and bakey. I brought you a plate up from breakfast if you're hungry."

She tried to swing her leg off him, but he turned onto his side and pulled her flush. She gasped, and he took advantage of it to kiss her with abandon. It was a deep, soul-stirring kiss, reminding her of the morning they'd woken up at the barn.

He broke the kiss and nipped his way along her jaw to her ear. "The only breakfast I want is you, angel."

She melted into his arms and pulled him closer. Her clothes seemed to melt off and soon he was sliding home. She sighed, feeling sore, yet her mind fractured around that feeling of rightness. With him, it felt like home, and she hadn't had a home in a very long time.

Neither of them lasted long, perhaps because he kept her body in a perpetual state of arousal. It felt like just a few minutes of savoring him before her body exploded, and she clenched on him, triggering him to fill her up as he bit the side of her neck.

He came back to her mouth and kissed her again, slow and sweet. The kiss held promises she wasn't sure she was quite ready for. When he pulled away, he padded into the bathroom to clean up.

She watched him walk away and laid there a few moments to catch her breath. It felt like her head was still spinning, but if she were honest with herself, she'd admit her mind had been spinning since the shootout at the barn.

Her entire life was off kilter, but whether that was a good thing or not was still up for debate.

She sat up to put her clothes back on, her hands shaky and her legs weak. She adjusted her black yoga pants and glanced at her scoop neck short sleeve shirt that hung off one shoulder.

He came out of the bathroom to catch her frowning, but he just chuckled and nodded at her shirt as she removed it once again. "Something wrong with your shirt there?"

She glared at him. "Shut up. It's not my fault I put the stupid thing on backward."

He laughed softly, the sound making her relax and fight a smile. His laugh always made her want to smile. "I guess I just screwed your brains out, huh?"

She giggled as he came near, sliding her arms around him as he pulled her close and kissed the top of her head. They hugged, a simple embrace, yet her mind searched for the last time someone had just hugged her for the hell of it. Maybe it was him when he comforted her after Maryanne delivered Connie.

A heaviness settled in her chest because if that was the last time someone had hugged her, it was an incredibly lonely thought. Maybe the spinning, off kilter world was more like a snow globe. Maybe she just needed her life shaken up a little before it settled into peace and tranquility and happiness.

He kissed the top of her head and let her go, spinning to find the plate. Her body leaned forward to follow him, but she spread her legs to stay rooted to the spot.

"Thanks for the food and for waking me up. We'll leave for the studio in half an hour, but pack whatever you need for a day out. I plan on taking you out for a date."

"What kind of date do you have planned? Am I dressed

right or do I need something else?" She slipped her sneakers back on and glanced in the mirror, adjusting a few stray hairs from the braid she'd redone this morning.

He swallowed his juice before replying. "You're fine. We'll come back to the hotel tonight before our dinner reservations at the comedy club."

Her eyes widened, and she saw the excitement in them in her reflection. "A comedy club? I've never been to one before."

"I've only been once, the last time I came here. Mike took me out; you'll meet him today. It was so much fun, and I want that for you, Holly. You need more fun in your life."

Her stomach was in knots already though, so she hopped up and made sure all her calming oils were in her big purse. She hoped the studio trip would go well for Landry. She practiced her breathing techniques while he finished eating and got ready.

When they arrived at the studio, Landry's stomach threatened to rebel from breakfast. Sweat beaded on his neck as they walked in and entered the elevator.

He bounced back and forth from one foot to the other and shoved his hands in his pockets.

"You seem nervous."

He glanced at Holly to see her curious green eyes looking at him. He jerked his head in a nod and took a deep breath to relax. She dug in her purse and pulled out a little roller bottle, opened it, and handed it to him.

"What am I supposed to do with this?"

She rolled her eyes and took it back, then rolled it under his ears and down the sides of his neck. "See? Easy peasy, lemon squeezy. It's just lavender and some stuff to help you relax. Why are you nervous?"

He shrugged and glanced away as she put the bottle back in her purse. He had to tell her, but it would make her the third person to know after Mike and Parker.

The elevator dinged, and they stepped out to walk down the hall. Mike met them, and the moment to tell her vanished. Mike was tall but built like a brick house, solid everywhere, with brown hair that fell in waves around his neck. He grinned and held out a hand to Holly.

"So this is the girl. It's nice to finally meet you. I'm Mike, Landry's manager."

Holly frowned and glanced between them. "I thought your manager was in Texas and getting you those shows in Dallas on the weekends."

Landry shrugged but Mike laughed and led them back to his office. "I do that too, but from Nashville. Been trying to convince him for years to join me here, but the stubborn ass won't do it."

He saw Holly's surprised face before she followed him into the office.

"I told you, Mike, I can't leave the business behind. The town needs me."

Holly looked around the office while he and Mike sat down. Holly and Mike made small talk about the trophies on the wall.

"See this framed piece of paper? That was Landry's first song he ever wrote for me."

Holly smiled and leaned forward to read it, her brows raising. "When was this? It's beautiful. I think I've heard a version of this on the radio."

Mike nodded. "Yeah, Luke recorded it almost five years ago. Landry flew to Nashville with me and his brother, then ditched us for his friend who lived on the military base. This original version was written on the plane ride back to Texas."

Holly looked at him, her eyes glittering before she looked back at the picture and continued talking with Mike.

He sat down, avoiding her gaze. His leg bounced, and he wiped his sweaty hands on the arm rest. Then he pulled out the well-worn notebook from his back pocket and a pen. He needed to distract himself from all the crap building up and winding him tight.

He flipped through his notes on the two originals he planned on recording today, songs about true love lasting forever to honor his grandparents and his parents. He still wanted that, knew it was meant for him too. His grandpa used to tell him when a Williams falls in love, it's forever.

The waiting for it sucked, though. He'd thought it was Holly, all those years ago, but he was still working hard to let her go. She wouldn't ever love him back, and he'd been fine with it until this weekend.

But now he wasn't so sure.

Spending all this time with her made his head and heart spin with possibilities, and every time he tried to shut it down, she did something sweet and thoughtful. Those little actions made him feel like he was slowly falling through quicksand like in the dream he kept having.

The door opened and the assistant stuck her head in to let them know the studio was ready.

When they walked down the hall following Mike, Holly leaned to him and whispered, "You alright? Still nervous?"

Landry tilted his head and thought about it, then felt his brows raise as he met her eyes. "Actually, no, I'm not nervous at all. Thanks for the oils, because they helped."

Or maybe it was just her support and presence. Either

way, the tension was gone from his shoulders, and while he was nervous about her hearing him sing like this, it wasn't as big of a deal as it had seemed half an hour ago. He was more concerned about all these fucking emotions from being constantly with her.

She smiled that self-satisfied smile, similar to the one she wore after they had sex, and it made his cock twitch. He grabbed her hand and locked their fingers for the rest of the walk, loving how it made her cheeks flush.

They parted ways when Landry entered the recording room. He watched Mike and the sound tech do their thing, showing Holly how different things worked, while he slipped on the headphones and pulled out his notebook. He picked up the guitar in the room and tuned it, running through a few practice rounds and humming.

"Ready when you are Landry." Mike gave him a thumbs up through the window that divided them.

He sang three songs to put on the Christmas album for his parents, two of them the originals. He watched Holly bobbing her head as she listened through the headphones, and it made him smile as he sang. He couldn't sit on the stool for these, instead moving his body with the music as he played and had fun with it, putting on a concert just for her.

A few hours later, he sat the guitar down and took off his headphones with a grin. Mike and the sound tech were more excited than normal and the energy was high. Landry went through the connecting door just as Holly slipped out down the hall.

He felt a twinge in his heart and his smile fell before Mike slapped him on the back.

"Don't worry, Landry, she just went to the bathroom. But this session was pure gold, baby. I've never heard you sound this good, with so much raw emotion."

The Songwriter Gets His Girl

Landry laughed and shook his head. "Gee, thanks, Mike. I really appreciate that."

Mike placed both hands on his shoulders and shook him slightly. "I'm serious. If she's the reason you're sounding so smooth and writing all these new songs, then keep going. It's obviously working."

He searched his friend's eyes, but only saw open curiosity and joy. Perhaps he could talk to Mike about her since everyone back home was off-limits to talk to.

Landry sighed. "You know the paper you have in your office? That first song we worked on five years ago on that plane ride back to Dallas?"

Mike nodded and let his hands fall.

Landry squared his shoulders and pushed his chin forward. "It was about her."

Mike's eyes widened as Holly came back in. Landry glanced at her, then back at Mike and shook his head, eyes wide and probably sad, pleading with his friend not to say anything.

Mike cleared his throat and clapped him on the back. "Like I said, I really want you to sign a release before you go, because some of these I want to send out to the local radio stations, okay?"

Landry rolled his eyes, and Mike winked before turning back to the sound tech. He was a good friend, but always looked for a way to turn a situation to his advantage.

Landry's heart skipped as he smelled her lavender scent. When she stepped up beside him, he saw the joy in her eyes. It caused his heart to beat twice as fast, her smile making him reciprocate.

He turned back to his friend. "Mike, I don't think the local radio stations need another love song. These are just Christmas presents with a lot of holiday songs."

"No, it's more than that. It's a love letter to—" He paused long enough to give Landry's heart a few too many quick beats before he smirked and said, "your family, and it's beautiful. Please, Lan, just do it. Stop thinking about it, and just let it happen."

Landry rubbed his forehead and sighed deeply. Mike hadn't ever steered him wrong in this business, and Landry doubted he'd start now. But this was a new direction for him, as normally he just sent the songs and rough cuts of the melodies and harmonies to Mike for someone else to sing.

This time, it was him singing, and it had been nerve-wracking enough when it was just Holly listening.

As he started to breathe too fast and sweat started to bead on his forehead again, her hand slipped into his, their fingers interlocking. He looked over, and she tilted her head, giving him a small smile and an even smaller nod.

He frowned. "You think I should?"

She shrugged, her skin begging him to kiss it where her shirt hung off her bare shoulder. "What do you have to lose?"

He took a deep, slow breath. He could lose her, but he didn't really have her. He could lose his family, the town, his business. But if they heard him singing on the radio, they'd probably be happy. Right?

He sighed. "Fine, same cut as normal or is it different if I'm the one singing them?"

Mike nodded and picked up the headphones. "You'll get five percent more."

Holly crossed her arms, letting his hand go. "Fifteen percent. His songs, him singing and doing the work."

Mike burst out laughing, the sound tech's eyes were wide as he watched the exchange. Landry just stood there, because it had been a long time since someone had stuck up for him like that.

Mike held out a hand to Holly. "Seven percent."

"Twelve."

"Ten."

She glanced at Landry, but he shrugged, letting her handle it. She was smart, strong, and damn, was he proud of her. Was it any wonder he was in love? His heart hurt, wanting to tell her the truth. After the past twenty-four hours, he couldn't deny his feelings for her anymore.

She grinned and shook Mike's hand. "Deal."

"Tell Linda at the front desk to amend it to ten. She'll find the file for you to sign. Then we'll get it notarized and be good to go. Can you come back this afternoon for another session?"

Landry frowned and glanced at his watch. It was almost noon, and he had plans with Holly that didn't include another round here but in the bedroom. Then there was the comedy club later.

He felt her hand on his arm and turned to peer into her emerald eyes, so bright with hope and shining with some emotion he was afraid to identify. "Can we, Landry? It was so fun, and you said you wanted to have fun, right?"

"But our plans—"

"Can we do whatever it is tomorrow instead?"

He reached a hand out and cupped her cheek, her soft skin smooth on his rough palm. How did he get so lucky that this woman wanted to spend time in a studio just listening and hanging out?

He leaned forward and kissed her forehead. "If that's really what you want, then yes. We can come back after lunch."

She whooped and pumped her fist in the air, making

him laugh. He completed the plans with Mike and then took his girl to lunch. His hands started to sweat at that thought. His girl.

It's what you want.

But not what I can have forever. Give up that pipe dream, dude.

They walked hand in hand down the street to the restaurant, his head warring with his heart as she talked.

Chapter Thirty-One

Is this real or is it just fun? I want to hold you forever. It's real to me, but will you break my heart and throw the pieces in the river?

The next day, they headed out right after breakfast for a full day of fun.

"But where are we going, Lan?" Holly fidgeted in the car's seat as he drove out of Nashville. It was cute, but he just wanted her to relax and have fun.

"We're going on a picnic, but we have to hike there first. We'll be gone all day, but it's just over an hour to get where we're going."

"Hiking? I've never been hiking."

He felt his eyes bug out and his jaw drop. "Are you serious?"

She nodded and picked at her sweater, turning to face the window and away from him.

"Yeah, we grew up in Dallas so there weren't a lot of hiking places."

"What about when your mom died? Going outdoors and hiking is one of the most cathartic ways I dealt with the loss of my grandparents. What did you do?"

She shrugged. "Yoga, mostly. Then when my aunt died, and I moved in with Kendall, I got into the essential oils and holistic medicine. It started out as rebellion, with him just finishing med school then. But it ended up helping me a lot."

"Do they still help?"

"Yep, I think it's the only way I could function for a long time. Months, maybe. Hey, let's play a game. I'll tell you one thing I want to do for a bucket list and then you tell me one of yours. I'll go first because I've just added going hiking to my bucket list."

He laughed and relaxed into the drive as they played the game. Turned out she wanted to travel a lot and see the things she'd never gotten to see as a kid. When they stopped for gas and to order their lunch to go from a local restaurant, he waited for Holly to come out of the bathroom.

She frowned as she walked toward him. "How much farther do we have to go?"

"About twenty minutes down this road. You want to drive yet?"

She bit her lip and glanced away, then nodded as she tucked a stray hair behind her ear. "I think so, yeah."

He hugged her, feeling her body pressed against his. It made his own breathing catch in his throat. "I'm so proud of you, angel. You can totally do it, and I'll be with you the whole time."

They loaded up, and she fiddled with the mirrors and seat, adjusting every little thing. He gave her time, watching out of the side of his peripheral vision while she fiddled with the GPS.

The Songwriter Gets His Girl

When she was ready, she took a deep breath and pulled out of the parking lot. She drove slowly and cautiously, but never fell below the speed limit. She was hyper vigilant, constantly checking the mirrors.

He sang softly with the radio. By the second song, she was relaxing. By the third, she was softly singing with him, and he grinned.

"You're doing so good, princess," he whispered in between songs. She gave that satisfied smile that made him feel tingly inside.

Soon, they parked in the back of the partially full parking lot for Rock Island and got out. He pulled a backpack from the trunk and slid their picnic food and water bottles into it.

"Ready?"

He watched her look around in awe while he closed the trunk and set the bag on top. He pulled out the bug spray and sprayed his legs, bare in his cargo shorts. Then he leaned down and sprayed hers from the hem of her yoga shorts down to her cute little ankle socks and sneakers.

"Are there a lot of bugs out here? I don't like bugs." She looked around at the ground, as if afraid a cockroach would jump out at her.

"Nah, just mosquitoes, mostly. Most of the trail is shaded, but we'll need sunscreen too. Hold your breath." She looked at him when he held up the spray can then closed her eyes and held her breath.

She looked so cute it took him a second to spray her down. Then she released her breath and stepped away to breathe cleaner air. He sprayed himself, then tossed it back into the bag with the bug spray.

"Now I think we're ready. Do you want to hit the bathrooms here before we hike to our picnic spot?"

Her eyes said she was happy before she shook her head and put on her sunglasses. He grabbed her hand and walked to the trailhead. He hoped this date was good, because not all the girls he'd dated had been outdoorsy people.

Except you're not dating her. You're just having a baby together. Even though you love her and want her to have all your babies.

They walked hand in hand for most of the hike, unless Holly stopped to take pictures. When they reached the waterfall, her eyes lit up, and she practically skipped to the railing to get closer.

"Oh, Landry, this is beautiful."

Her smile glowed in the morning summer sun, her pale hair reflecting the golden rays. It seemed like the trees, grass, flowers—everything around her—shone with extra vibrant life, brighter and more majestic because it was in her presence.

"You're right. You take my breath away every day."

She turned to face him, her eyes soft at the words but sad. "Lan... you can't say things like that."

He stepped closer and tipped her chin up, running a finger down the side of her neck and making her shiver.

His voice dropped to a near whisper when he said, "I can't seem to stop them around you, angel. You just bring it out in me."

She sucked in a breath and stepped out of his reach, glancing around at the others on the trail around them. She wrapped her arms around her waist.

He sighed. "Come on, we're almost to our picnic spot. Just a few minutes further."

He took the lead and didn't push her to hold his hand or even offer it to her. His hand twitched from wanting to

The Songwriter Gets His Girl

touch her, but he couldn't. Not right now. She clearly didn't want him to and that hurt.

He took the path down to the water and found an unoccupied picnic table. Holly stopped beside him, and he offered the hand sanitizer before pulling out their food.

"I'm pleasantly surprised that most of it is still warm, so dig in."

They sat in silence next to each other, side by side so they could both enjoy the view of the waterfall. It was a peaceful silence broken only by the birds in the trees and the sound of rushing water. Not even the people swimming below or the kids running around seemed to intrude on their commune with nature.

"You're right about this being therapeutic. It's very peaceful." She finally broke the silence when she finished the last of her fried rice and spring rolls. He finished his water while she collected their trash and took it to the bin a few yards away.

"Now for the swimming."

"Swimming? But I didn't bring my suit. Why didn't you tell me?"

He wiggled his eyebrows and glanced at her white yoga tank top. "Probably because I've been picturing that top being wet all summer."

She blushed and frowned, putting her hands on her hips where she stood beside him. "Landry!"

He loved when she got onto him with that tone of voice. It made him feel naughty and playful. He laughed and held up his hands.

"It's okay, Holly. Our suits are in the backpack. I went through your bag and found yours this morning when you were in the shower."

Her face looked taken aback, then her hands fell from her hips, and she smiled. He fished out their suits, and they went to the separate showers to change. His mind raced with ways to sneak into the women's showers to help her, but she'd pulled away on the hike.

Sometimes it seemed like she was having fun, enjoyed being with him, and other times she seemed to remember this was a business arrangement and threw up walls between them.

He much preferred the first, when they were open and honest and just acted in ways that felt natural. Not holding her hand while hiking had definitely felt unnatural and wrong.

He put his clothes in the bag and waited for her. When she came out holding her clothes in one hand, his mouth went dry. It wasn't the same bright pink bikini from five years ago, but it was close. Same color, but with polka dots this time.

She dropped the clothes on the picnic table and held out her hand. His mind shorted, and he just glanced at it until she smiled and lifted a brow.

"The sunscreen? We need to reapply now that we're less clothed."

"Oh, right. Good idea." He cleared his throat and pulled out the can, handing it to her while he put her clothes in the bag. Then he stood up and held his breath while she sprayed him. Why hadn't he gotten the kind that needed to be rubbed into her beautiful skin? This was a wasted opportunity.

Maybe next time, dude.

There might not be a next time. This could be it because they could be pregnant right now. This might be all he'd ever get of her.

The Songwriter Gets His Girl

He shuddered a breath as she tucked the sunscreen back into the bag. Maybe he could turn swimming into something else. Maybe it would help convince her to love him.

Chapter Thirty-Two

She walks down to the river, her hips swaying in the sun. Her hair glimmers, shimmers, and shines, and I want her to always be mine.

Landry took her hand and led her down to the swimming spot under the falls. The terrain was rougher, and he wanted to keep her safe. She frowned but took his hand, climbing next to him like a champ.

"So, tell me about the songwriting. How long have you been doing that?"

He cleared his throat and avoided looking at her in her bikini, unable to think with her so close and nearly nude. Then he told her of their trip five years ago, Mike being Parker's roommate, and how they ended up working on that first song on the plane ride home.

"Wow, it was good fortune that you sat next to him on the way home."

"Yeah, but only Parker knows that I write songs for him. No one else in town knows, so don't tell anyone, okay?"

The Songwriter Gets His Girl

She tugged him to a halt and turned her curious eyes to him. "You said that back when we painted the apartment. Why keep it from them?"

He shrugged and glanced at their feet. "I don't know, just don't want the attention I guess."

"Bullshit."

His head jerked up, and he looked at her. "What?"

"You heard me. I call bullshit on that. You get up and perform every weekend and have for years. You can't tell me you don't want the attention or are bothered by it. So, what is it really?"

He blinked and turned to face the water, staring at the waterfall and letting it soothe him as they stood on a small ledge halfway down to the water.

"I guess it's different when I sing covers from other artists versus what I do here with Mike. Here, we record songs I write or that we write together. It's more like exposing your beating heart to someone and hoping they don't accidentally give you a fatal paper cut by saying some offhand comment about it. That's how I feel about these songs."

The sounds of water washed over him as he pulled out his notebook and wrote that down. Who knew, it might come in handy later and turn into a song.

"How big are your songs?"

He nodded and took a deep breath. If he was going to tell her this much, he might as well tell her all of it.

"Three have been pretty big and two others are semi-successful so far."

"What counts as semi-successful?"

He shrugged and met her eyes. "Well, the three that hit it big have made me about a hundred grand a year for three years now. Each. The two semi-successful ones are still rather new, so the royalties on it haven't paid out as much yet but are on trend to break the previous three successes."

The longer he talked the bigger her eyes got until she mouthed, "Wow. That's some serious money."

"Yeah, I paid off my house and my parent's ranch mortgages. But don't tell them, because they think they won an anonymous rodeo lottery which paid their mortgage."

"Does Lola know? She manages the finances for the yoga studio and was a big help in the bookkeeping aspect."

He shook his head. "Actually, you've heard that my other brother, Chase, is still in prison? He's the one that helps me manage it all. He was always the whiz, and for his help I've invested some of it for when he gets out. It was hard for him to get computer time at first, but the past few years he's been able to have regular access."

They talked about his brother as they finished their walk down to the water. Then he set down their bag, and they walked in.

She squealed, "It's so cold."

He laughed, holding her hand and tugging her deeper. "What'd you expect? Wait, is this your first time swimming in a lake or river?"

She frowned and tipped her nose up. "You don't have to say it like that and make me sound so snobbish."

He laughed and picked her up, making her squeal again. She was light in his arms as he strode deeper, and she held onto his neck protesting as they got further out.

"No, Landry, this is not the best idea. Don't go too deep. Did you forget I'm shorter than you? And I can't see the bottom. Lan, where's the bottom?"

He shushed her with a kiss on the mouth. Their tongues dueled, and he held her tighter, not wanting to let her go. It

The Songwriter Gets His Girl

had been hours since he'd last kissed her, and he felt like a drowning man finally gasping for air.

He broke the kiss and panted, then lowered himself slowly into the water, squatting and holding her tight to him.

The water took away her breath when it hit her skin. "Lan—"

"Sh, I'll keep you warm, angel. It's going to be okay. I'll never let anything hurt you. I won't drop you or anything. Just hold on because I've got you."

She shuddered a breath as they finally were submerged, everything but their shoulders and heads. "I—I didn't know that. When I used to go to the pool with Eric, he and his friends would throw me in. They were always pulling pranks on each other, and I'd get caught in the crossfire sometimes. We'd play chicken and have fun, but I always felt out of place with them."

His heart lurched, and he cursed himself for wanting to beat up a dead guy. Her husband should have been protecting her, not rough housing with her. She was a delicate flower who needed nurturing.

"I'm sorry, angel. They shouldn't have done that." He spun in slow circles, her body now almost floating in his arms. Her breasts pushing against the bikini top right under his face was a distraction he did not want to miss. He watched as they bobbed in the water.

"I was just along for the ride most of the time, and it led to some anxiety. Most of the military guys were tall, but I'm short. They wore uniforms, acted the same, ate the same, but I was the odd one out. It was pretty intimidating to be different."

"Makes sense. I remember going to the rodeo as a kid

and getting lost, running through the crowd and being overwhelmed by all the adults bigger than me."

"Exactly. It was scary, right? That's how it was sometimes. Not all the time, but enough that I don't miss the military parties, balls, and barbecues at all."

"Do you miss meat from those barbecues?"

Her eyes were closed now, and she only held onto his shoulders with one arm, leaning back into the water. His arm moved from her back to her neck to let her relax and keep her head above water for her.

"Sometimes. Can I tell you a secret?"

"Of course, that's what friends are for." It hurt to say that because he wanted to be so much more.

"I was rebelling against Kendall, yeah, but the secret about going vegetarian? I just hate touching raw meat. It's so gross, and it was just easier to go vegetarian after my aunt died so I wouldn't have to figure out how to cook with meat."

He kept spinning them slowly, but inside his mind whirled.

"That's a pretty smart way to get out of cooking it." He chuckled, getting an idea. "But if you ever want to learn how to cook meat, let me know. If you start to crave any meat or anything when you get pregnant, I can secretly bring it to you, so no one realizes."

She pulled her legs down and wrapped them around his waist, then leaned back with both arms out to her sides. They were only touching where her legs were wrapped around him, but his cock stood up and took notice of how close she was, separated by just two flimsy pieces of cloth.

He looked around, seeing that the other patrons swimming were further upstream, closer to the waterfall. No one else was swimming in this still little side pool where the current was almost non-existent.

He slid one hand under her ass and the other he stroked slowly up her bikini line to where her leg met her torso, that little bend of flesh that was always so sensitive.

She gasped and stuttered, "I—I'll keep that in mind for when the time comes."

"Speaking of coming..."

He slid the fabric to the side and rubbed a thumb over her clit, making her gasp.

"Landry, we can't—this is a public place. There are people about."

"Sh, no one is watching. I'll keep an eye out, princess."

"The rules—"

"Say nothing about this. It just says no flirting in public. I'd hardly call this flirting, would you?"

She gasped as he slid a finger inside. The warmth wrapped around him, and his heart raced.

"If it makes you more comfortable, I think there's a more secluded spot over here." As he talked, he slowly walked them around a little rock outcropping until they were completely hidden from view of those swimming and those on the trail above.

Then he moved his hand from her ass and pulled his shorts down, lined up, pulled his fingers out, and slid inside. "There, is that better, angel?"

"God, yes," she gasped and jerked, so he grabbed her by the lower back and pulled her upright until she wrapped her arms around his shoulders. He crashed his mouth to hers and kissed as he pumped in and out. His fingers dug into her bikini covered ass as he pulled her off then slammed her back down.

It was fast and rough, just how they liked it. Her nails dug into his shoulders, and she bit his lip when she came. Her spasms set off a chain reaction in him, and he held her close, wrapping his arms tight around her as he spilled inside, kissing her cries.

She broke the kiss and buried her face in his neck. Their breathing was still fast, but she pulled away and stood. The water only came to her breasts but she kept her shoulders under water as she looked around nervously.

His chest tightened as he paused, still breathing heavily. There was no way he'd misread her; she'd wanted that as much as he had. He adjusted his shorts, then reached for her. "Are you alright, angel?"

She moved away, frowning and avoiding his eyes. "No, Landry, this was pointless. It may be the least effective method of getting pregnant. It's all immediately washing away so there can't be any fertilization. And we could've been caught. How embarrassing that would've been."

Pain ripped through his chest. He was just a stud horse in the grand scheme of things. She looked around with embarrassment. He'd thought they wouldn't have to deal with that if they were out-of-town away from people they knew, but the joke was on him.

He pasted on a brittle smile and adjusted his shorts again. "Well, we didn't get caught and those swimmers are all water under the bridge now. Literally." He laughed, hearing the bitterness in it but not caring as he strode around their little alcove and through the water to the main swimming hole.

"Landry, this is no laughing matter."

He turned to face her, water at his hips. "I get that you're embarrassed, and I'm sorry, Holly. If you don't want to hang out, that's fine. I'm going to go explore the waterfall, then we can head back for our dinner reservations."

He fell back, splashing under the water and letting the quiet of the water settle his body.

Chapter Thirty-Three

When she walked by, popping that bubble gum, hair swinging and eyes sparkling, I was a goner. She's a slayer. She's a slayer. She's slayed my heart all over the walk.

Holly leaned her head against the window of Landry's truck as they left the airport parking lot. It was mid-morning, but they'd been up early to pack and head to the Nashville airport. She was tired, exhausted from all the fun things they'd done this weekend, and the last nights of passion in his arms.

She frowned, remembering that the only way she could get Landry up so early this morning was to cover him in kisses. But he'd pulled back, as he had since their fight by the waterfall yesterday. The intimacy had been missing when he'd flipped her onto her hands and knees for a fast and furious quickie. He'd then taken a shower while she'd finished packing.

She glanced at him, not able to see his eyes behind his

The Songwriter Gets His Girl

sunglasses. Yesterday, Holly had been the one to drive the entire almost two hours back to the hotel. Landry sang for a while with the radio, then he pulled out his notebook and wrote while humming.

That had been the beginning of him pulling away from her. He hadn't been as talkative after their trip to the waterfall. The look on his face when she'd said their swimming sex was pointless had haunted her last night, making it hard to fall asleep.

When they had talked, it had been the smiling, joking Landry that she'd known the past few years, but that was just a mask he wore, not the real him. It felt forced and today the silences between them kept stretching. On the plane, he kissed her to distract her from the takeoff and landing, but there wasn't much talking to speak of.

Holly sat up as Landry pulled his truck into a car dealership outside the Dallas airport.

"What are we doing?" she asked.

Landry turned the engine off and turned to her, his eyes still hidden by the sunglasses. "I did some research last week and found a little four door car like the one we rented this weekend. If you like it, it's yours. It's ready for a twenty-four-hour test drive now. We just have to go in and give them a copy of your driver's license."

Her jaw dropped, and surprise drained the color from her face. Even with their fight, he was still trying to take care of her. Before she could say anything, he opened the door and stepped out into the hot still air. She shoved her door open, and he caught her around the waist, pulling her to the side and shutting the door behind her.

She looked up at him, gripping his t-shirt and taking a deep breath. "Landry, I can't just buy a car." This was like at the waterfall all over again. He just kept making her do things outside her comfort zone.

With his arm around her waist, though, she felt like she could take on the world. The thought of the car wasn't as scary as she expected.

He released her arm and shrugged, stepping back and giving her space she no longer wanted. She took a hesitant step forward, but he just turned and walked to the front door of the office.

"It's just a twenty-four hour test drive, Holly, not rocket science. No harm in looking at it or taking it home tonight."

She rushed to join him. "No harm? This is the middle of DFW. What if I can't handle the traffic? What if I wreck again?"

She'd almost caught him when he stopped so suddenly, she bumped into his back. He spun and held her elbow, literally holding her at arm's length. "You're not going to wreck. You did a great job driving around Nashville this weekend, didn't you?"

He dropped his hands and stepped away. She stomped after him. "Damn it, Landry, why won't you just hold me? Stop freezing me out, because I need—"

She broke off and took a shuddering breath, wiping the corner of her eye. He stepped closer and swept his sunglasses off, his eyes intense.

"Holly, this is in a public place, and that's against the rules, remember? Do you want the rules or do you want us—"

"I don't know!" She frowned as the frustration mounted, her hands fisting at her side.

He rubbed his forehead and slid the sunglasses back on. "Look, you're not going to wreck again. You're an excellent driver, Holly, and the crash that took your family was just a

The Songwriter Gets His Girl

crazy, random thing because of the rainy road conditions. It could've happened to anyone."

She pressed on her eyes. "But it didn't. It happened to me, because of me."

He sighed and pulled her into a hug. "I refuse to believe that. If you actually want to have this baby, you're going to need a car of your own. You said that, not me. I'm just helping you take that next step, Holly. Of course, if you don't want this baby, then we can go home right now."

She wrapped her arms around her waist and closed her eyes, breathing hard but focusing on making it slow and even. Her stomach fluttered and her mouth was dry, but she took a deeper breath when she realized that she wasn't actually panicking at the thought of driving again or of having a car of her own.

No, she was mostly just nervous because it was a surprise. She was overwhelmed, and it was against the rules. This counted as buying gifts, right? His arms around her made some of the chaos in her mind settle.

She exhaled and opened her eyes, pulling her shoulders back and lifting her chin. When she nodded, he grinned, making her stomach flutter even more in response.

Then he whispered, "That's my girl."

He waved an arm to the front door and like magic it opened to reveal the short balding salesman. Landry reached a hand to shake and introduced them, then asked for the salesman he had been emailing with.

Two hours later, she sat behind the wheel of the little silver Hyundai Sonata while Landry shook the man's hand again. She started it, and he opened the passenger door and sat down, leaving his door open.

She fiddled with the buttons, and he set up the stereo stations and GPS to take them home.

"That's all set so you should be fine now. I put your bags in the trunk so you can go straight home."

She nodded, her throat closed as she blinked back tears. She was thankful for the sunglasses to keep him from seeing her like this. What a mess. The easy way they were together yesterday was eye opening. Since then, he'd been sticking to the rules. That's what she wanted, but it all felt wrong now.

He reached over and slid his palm across her cheek. "Hey, it's okay. I'm going to follow you, so if anything happens or you start to panic, just pull over and I'll be there, alright?"

She naturally turned her face into his hand and rubbed the rough texture, smelling the leather and myrrh that was just him.

It instantly calmed her, and she smiled, her throat no longer tight. She took a deep breath. "Yeah okay, I can do this. Thanks for a great weekend, Landry. When will I see you next?"

He dropped his hand slowly, and she ached to prolong the contact. She wanted to see him again, wanted to recapture some of the magic from this weekend.

He smiled that tight, fake smile of his and shrugged. "It'll be back to business as normal, as per our agreement. You'll let me know if the weekend was a success or if we need to plan another trip?"

She sucked in a deep breath and nodded before he reached for the door and got out. He was such a gentleman, sticking to the baby plan. So why did it make her stomach twist in knots and feel so wrong?

"Landry," she called, not wanting him to go but needing to make sure they were going to be okay when they got back. "We're good, right? Friends?"

He leaned down, one hand on the door and one on the

top of the car and smiled. It was soft around the edges, a real smile that settled some unknown fear in the pit of her stomach.

He nodded and said softly, "Yeah, I'll always be your friend, Holly, no matter what."

With that, he shut the door and strode to his truck. Her mind, body, and heart were sore and aching. Her mind was swirling with the implications of driving home, of this being her car after tomorrow. Her body was sore from their vigorous rounds of sex, yet still craved more. And her heart was beating too fast because his scent still lingered in the small space, making her want things that she couldn't have anymore.

She'd had her happy ever after with Eric, and Landry wasn't another. People didn't get two like that. It didn't matter what her heart ached for. Sticking to the baby plan was for the best.

She breathed deep and slow, then backed out of the parking lot. It was all going according to plan and was going to be fine. Maybe she was pregnant right now and just didn't know it.

That put a smile on her face as she turned up the radio and drove home, the vintage blue Ford trailing behind her.

Holly drove back to the dealership by herself the next day. A good night's rest in her own bed had done her good, and she'd woken with a renewed sense of purpose, although her mind still went back and forth over what she actually wanted, more time with Landry or to be pregnant now.

Either way, this time next year, she would be a mom and

this little car felt good. The paperwork was ready to sign, so she went in determined to get it over with.

Twenty minutes later, she was frowning and sitting up straighter in the chair in front of the salesman, Bob.

"What do you mean, it's already paid for?"

The man smiled under his oversized beard, a patronizing one that made her skin crawl. "I mean that your boyfriend yesterday took care of it. It's bought and paid for, with cash, which doesn't happen often. You just need to sign these files and the tags and title will be mailed to you in four to six weeks."

She grabbed the pen and wrote furiously, then he handed over the copies and the spare key. Before she'd even gotten out of the chair to head back to her new car, she was dialing Landry.

"Hello?"

"Landry, what the hell? You bought the car? That violates the contract. No big purchases outside of regular friend status, remember?"

She paced on the sidewalk, her sandals slapping on the concrete.

"Ah, but that rule was for purchases for the baby. The car is for you, and the contract didn't say anything about that."

She ground her teeth together and ran a hand through her long hair. "Well, I'm amending it now because that's a technicality that doesn't count. How much was the car? I'll go straight to your house and write you the check."

His sigh was world-weary on the other end, and it made her pause her pacing. His tone of voice shifted from light and playful to serious.

"Look, you need a safe, reliable vehicle for all the doctor's appointments. I need to do this, and we both know from our conversations this weekend that I'm not hurting for cash. It's not even a blip on my bank account. So save your money for the baby and all the things you won't let me help with, okay?"

The bite to his voice at the end made her wince. Her spine jerked in surprise, and she spun to walk to the driver's side door. She didn't want to offend him or make him upset, but judging by his tone, he definitely was on edge. The thought of that she was to blame for that made her skin crawl.

No one in their right mind would say no to a free, so why did it bother her so much?

She slammed the door closed and leaned her head back on the headrest. "Are you sure, Landry? It's a fucking car, for crying out loud."

He snorted. "It's not a big deal, angel. It's practical. You need a car, so here's a car, one I can trust to be reliable for you. I'd worry if you just went with whatever was cheapest or convenient to buy."

She frowned and closed her eyes. "Fine, if this is what you need to do to feel better about the situation, then so be it."

"Well, if you want me to feel better about the situation, you'll let me buy more stuff. I can't be there to take care of you during the pregnancy, as per our agreement. A car is just one step to making up for the morning sickness and whatever else you're going to go through."

She rubbed her eyes. "Yeah, but I'm putting myself through this. It's my choice, my baby, my body. There's nothing to make up for, Landry."

Silence stretched between them, and her heart felt like a brick pressed on it. She rubbed the spot.

He sighed, his voice hard and sardonic. "Trust me, I'm

well aware of the situation. I gotta get back to work, though. Later."

She closed her eyes and replayed the conversation. His tone had gone from weary and tired to bitter and annoyed. She'd never heard him sound like that before, but it just proved she was right.

A tear slipped out of the corner of her eye, and she brushed it away as she started the engine. If he was going to be this protective, thank God she had the forethought to write out that contract.

She'd known he was going to get too close. She'd known he was going to have a hard time separating this from the business transaction it was meant to be. Guilt that he'd spent so much money on her had her rubbing her chest at the tightness. It was like he was taking care of her needs without even asking. Eric hadn't even been that considerate.

Another tear slipped out, and she turned up the radio to sing at the top of her lungs, trying to dislodge the pain in her chest that threatened to suffocate her.

Chapter Thirty-Four

Berries ripe on the vine, red staining your lips, you taste extra sweet, and I can't seem to get a grip. Breathless. Restless. Obsessed.

Mid-August

Holly reached for the muscadine berries on top of the tall bush. She picked the ripe ones and tossed them into the bucket that hung on the side of her ladder.

"Why do I always get the ones on top? It's so hot up here, but y'all get the ones under the shade." She huffed out a breath and pushed the stray sweaty hair out of her face that had escaped her ponytail.

Lola's grandma laughed from the ground below, her blue bandanna waving on her head and barely holding back her unnaturally red hair. Her purple shirt had sequins in the pattern of a giant pair of lips and was tucked into her cut-off jean shorts. Not the most practical shirt for farming, but at least the purple rain boots with daisies balanced it.

"Lola and I have the tallest reach, but you're short and small and a perfect fit for the ladder job."

"I'm not that short," Holly ground out with a snort. "I'm average, I swear." Average height for a woman from two hundred years ago, maybe.

Lola spoke up from the other side of the bush. "Don't mind her, Granny. She's been temperamental for a week now, ever since she came back from that in vitro clinic."

"Ah, lots of emotions stirred up that weekend, eh? I have to say, Holly, I'm very proud of you for buying that car and doing the whole thing on your own, almost as proud as I am of you going to the clinic. You're a stronger woman than me, that's for sure."

Lola reached for another berry. "Thank God you didn't have the option to go to a clinic like that when you were our age."

Granny cackled, "Oh yes, thank God for that. I had to have my kids the natural way, but that was more fun, so I think I'm the lucky one."

"Granny!" Lola scolded, and Holly grinned, spying her freckle-faced friend turning pink in embarrassment.

"What I meant, child, is that Holly's finally facing the things that have kept her in a rut all this time. She's a strong woman for doing that."

Holly frowned and glanced down at the woman. "I'd hardly call grieving a rut."

Granny's head bobbed. "Maybe not, but you can't live there forever. The grief eats away at you and at some point, you have to dig it out before it chokes the life out of you, like a weed in the garden."

Holly shook her head and picked more berries. She

hummed, trying to capture some of the peace she'd felt the previous two years helping them with the harvest. But Lola was right; she had been rather cranky the past week.

It wasn't because of the clinic though. She hadn't seen or heard from Landry at all. Not at the grocery store, not around town. She'd even driven by his house but couldn't bring herself to stop.

What was she supposed to say? Show up on his doorstep for no reason and tell him she was missing him? No, that was against the stupid rules. She jerked a few berries off the bush, smashing them slightly in her hand before she tossed them in the bucket.

Granny merged the half-full buckets into one then hauled it over to the farm truck fifty yards away to join the other buckets. "Gonna take these to the house and wash them. I'll be back with some iced tea."

She drove it back to the house while Lola and Holly kept working.

When the sound of the engine died down and it was just the sound of cicadas in the heat, Lola cleared her throat. "This is the first time we've had a chance to talk since you left. Are you ready to dish on that list I found?"

Holly paused, then resumed her berry picking. "I don't know, are you prepared to spill the beans about December with my brother?"

Lola froze, avoiding her gaze. "I'll talk if you will. Did you really go to the in vitro clinic last weekend?"

Holly rubbed her forehead and grabbed her water bottle out of her bucket. She took a drink but couldn't think of any way to get out of telling her friend the truth. And honestly, she desperately wanted someone to talk to about this, someone who wasn't her therapist.

Even if it broke one of the rules.

It wasn't like they hadn't broken a few of them already. Besides, Lola found out on her own about the list; Holly didn't tell her. If he was going to buy her a freaking car on a technicality, she could certainly talk to Lola on one.

She cleared her throat and resumed picking. "Um, no I did not go to the in vitro clinic this weekend. I went out of town to make a baby the all-natural way."

Lola's jaw dropped, and Holly felt her own cheeks heat.

"Are you serious? With whom? Was it Landry? Is that why he drove you? That list was pretty specific, and it seemed like you know the guy really well. Plus, the last two items were written in a different handwriting. It has to be him."

"Well, as per that rule list, I'm not supposed to tell, remember? But yes, he drove. I went out of town and had sex all weekend long."

Lola laughed. "And how did that feel?"

"Well, it felt about nine inches long, if that's what you mean."

They both burst into laughter at that, and Holly shook the ladder so much she had to climb down before she fell off. She laid in the grass in the shade, staring up at the leaves above her.

Lola nudged her with her boot. "And did it feel good to get back out there?"

Holly tilted her head back and forth. "Yes, and no. The sex itself felt amazing. The man knows exactly what he's doing in that department."

"Is that why you've been cranky, because you're not getting any more now that you're home?"

Holly chuckled and tucked her hands under the back of her head. "No, not really. It's just, before we came home, he kind of pulled away emotionally. I said some stuff, and I think it hurt him. So, while the sex was awesome, it didn't feel good to deal with another's feelings like that again."

"What'd you say?"

She bit her lip and shook her head. "I can't even remember anymore. We had sex while swimming by this waterfall, and I said it was frivolous or pointless or something because the water would wash away all the sperm."

Lola snorted. "Yeah, that'll pull anyone out of the moment. Swimming by a waterfall? Let me guess, you also had a picnic, didn't you."

Holly sat up, leaning on her hands behind you. "How'd you guess?"

Lola set her now full bucket down, grabbed another, and began to pick more berries.

"The guy's a romantic. Was it his idea to add those last two items to the list of rules?"

Holly nodded her head slowly. "Yeah, no dating anyone else and for every night of passion, there will be a date."

Lola glanced at her, her brow raised as she pointed a purple stained finger. "See? He's a romantic. He's not just in it for the sex, but to get closer to you. If it's not Landry, I'll eat my hat. I can't believe you rejected his romantic gesture of the waterfall, picnic, and sex."

"It's not supposed to be romantic at all. This isn't a relationship, but a business arrangement." Her stomach twisted at the words, uncertainty filling her on whether that's what she still wanted or not.

Lola shrugged. "Maybe, but I wonder... you don't have to tell me who it is, but I'm going to assume it's Landry, since it said something about no messing around in town, right?"

Holly stood to get back to picking, staying on the

ground for now. "I refuse to confirm or deny. What's it matter?"

Lola snorted but shared her bucket as the two worked side by side. "Well, if it's Landry and he lives here, knows you, sees you every day or occasionally around town, it's going to be so awkward when you're carting around his kid to all those places. What's he going to do, ignore the fact that it's his?"

Holly shook her head. "What makes you think it's him? Just because he picked me up to take me to Dallas doesn't mean it's him."

Lola paused, and Holly felt her glare. "Holly, have you seriously never noticed how he looks at you? He's been in love with you since you moved to town. He may have agreed to a business arrangement, but if it's Landry, I guarantee he wants something more."

Her hands slowed to a halt. "Hmm," she said. Surely Lola couldn't be right. He didn't look at her any differently than he did Lola.

"I'm right, aren't I? I'm always right."

Holly laughed. "Yeah, not if you ask my brother. Speaking of—"

Lola groaned, so Holly elbowed her in the side. "Time to fess up. What happened back in December? Was that the first time you hooked up with Kendall or have there been other hook-ups? Tell me everything, except the sexy details. I don't want to know any of those."

They both chuckled at that before Lola launched into a tale that started before Holly had even moved to town. Holly was captivated by the story, but inside she was still antsy, her mind spinning to sort out whether Lola's idea about Landry held merit or not.

Chapter Thirty-Five

The only one for me. The only one I see when the night settles and I close my eyes, only for you will I arise.

The door wasn't locked at Andy and Cindy's, so Landry walked in to the sound of women's voices in the kitchen. Cindy sat at the dining table with her feet propped up in a chair.

She smiled at him when he came in. "Hey, you made it. I was getting nervous."

Landry grinned and set his present down on the dining table. "Sorry, I was setting up some obstacles in the woods between here and my parent's cabin. I've got a few hay bales and even got Hunter to drop off the tractor. It's ready to go."

She breathed a sigh of relief and nodded. "Okay, and these are the paintballs that won't hurt as much, right? I don't want any of the kids crying."

He shrugged. "They all hurt about the same, but they're teenagers. They'll be ok."

She winced, rubbing her stomach. "That's what Andy says. Do you want to help put up the rest of the decorations while Andy's gone? Kids will start arriving in about an hour."

"Sure, whatever you need."

She directed him to the ladder in the garage. When he returned, Holly stood in the doorway. They both froze, their eyes locking. Her cheeks turned pink.

If only she'd let herself fall for him, he'd be a happy man. Then he could walk up to her and kiss those pouty lips like there's no tomorrow.

Landry had wanted nothing more than to sweep her into his arms and hold her. He wasn't a selfish man. He didn't *have* to kiss her. Holding her would do.

He set the ladder down and shoved his hands in his pockets to keep from reaching for her.

Had she gotten even more gorgeous in the past two weeks since he'd seen her? His pixie-sized bubble gum angel. He sucked in a breath as she smiled slowly. Her green eyes practically sparkled, happy and hesitant.

Was she happy to see him? His heart raced in hope.

He glanced around, trying to shake himself out of the trance she constantly cast over him, and saw Lola setting food on the dining room table, watching him. Holly shut the front door.

He grinned and swept further into the room. "Well, if this isn't the prettiest group of women in town. I'm a lucky guy to have y'all to myself."

Cindy waved her hand with a laugh. "No, we're lucky to have you here so early. We have a ton of things to do. Holly

The Songwriter Gets His Girl

and I are going to finish the appetizers, but can you confirm the pizza order? Also, drinks?"

"Gunner and Maryanne are bringing the drinks. And I confirmed the pizza with Mr. Johnson last night."

Holly turned to face him, her little button nose and lush lips drawing him in like always. He'd dreamed of those lips, and they'd only gotten more vivid since Nashville.

His mouth tingled, remembering the feel of her as he'd kissed her. It was more than he'd ever thought she'd share with him. He never thought she'd sleep with him or agree to have a baby.

There was a knock at the front door, and Parker opened it with Gunner and Maryanne behind him. Gunner carried the baby in the car seat and a bag of drinks.

Parker carried the pizzas and grinned. "So this is where all the pretty girls went tonight."

Lola snorted. "Don't even start. Landry already tried that line."

Landry laughed at the look on Parker's face. The room was a flurry of activity while they set up the food.

He hung back until Maryanne came over to him holding the baby. He took her easily into his arms, careful to cradle her head. He smiled down at her and her big, beautiful brown eyes captured him.

Maryanne dug through her diaper bag. "When are you going to ask Holly out?"

Landry scoffed and crossed his arms. "Psh, I don't know what you're talking about."

"You think I haven't seen the way you look at her? Just ask her out, Lan."

His heart was racing, and he met his long-time friend's eyes.

"How long did it take you to convince Gunner to go out with you?"

She jutted out her chin, the baby beginning to cry. "Years, but you know that. You know I was asking him out every day at the bakery, but have you even asked Holly out once?"

He sighed, opened and closed his mouth before finally just shaking his head and handing her the baby. "She's not ready. She was so in love with her husband, M. You didn't see the way they looked at each other."

Maryanne turned to soothe the baby, checking her diaper. When Lola came over and caught the tail end of the conversation, her jaw dropped open.

"You saw them together? Holly and her husband? When?" Lola's voice was a low whisper as she leaned closer, the baby's noises growing louder but not quite a cry.

He sighed and rubbed the back of his neck. "Five years ago when I went to visit Andy in Kentucky. It was the night they got engaged, and the way they looked at each other... she'll love no one else the way she did him."

Maryanne tilted her head, her eyes softening even as baby Connie grew fussier. "So you're not even going to try?"

Voices rose and Maryanne turned to him, handing him the baby. "Here, can you take her? I swear, you're the only one that can get her to settle down when she's like this. She's not hungry or wet. She just doesn't want to nap."

He chuckled softly, tucking the girl against his chest and bouncing slightly from side to side. "She just likes my singing. She's got good taste."

Maryanne laughed and walked to the kitchen to help Cindy finish the appetizers. Holly still stood on the other side of the room, fidgeting and helping with the food.

"I know it's you." Lola's voice was low, and he turned to her with a frown.

"What do you mean?"

"I saw that list of rules, Landry. It's you, isn't it? You're going to be the baby daddy."

His stomach knotted up, threatening to rebel, and he sucked in a breath. He froze until baby Connie started fussing in his arms again, then he started bouncing nervously.

Lola crossed her arms and shook her head. "What the hell are you doing, Landry? Someone's going to get hurt."

He sighed and nuzzled the baby's head. "I don't want to hurt her. I want to love her for however long she'll let me. If it's only until she gets pregnant, so be it."

"Then you'll be the one hurt." Her forehead wrinkled, and she uncrossed her arms.

"I know." He turned as Maryanne and Holly came, his heart racing as she neared.

Maryanne smiled and reached for her baby. "You did it. You got her to go to sleep. And I didn't even hear you sing that time."

He chuckled, trying not to stare at Holly.

Lola cleared her throat and motioned for Maryanne to join her. "Maryanne, help me finish in the kitchen. Landry, weren't you going to put up the decorations?"

Holly nodded and held up the bag. "Cindy said to bring you this."

Lola and Maryanne left, tucking the baby into her carrier to nap, and it was just him and Holly in the living room. She looked into the decorations bag, her cheeks pink.

"Some of these need to go on the ceiling. There's a banner. Let's hang it here."

She pulled out the banner and pointed with it to where the hallway met the living room.

He grinned and saluted. "Yes ma'am. Has anyone ever told you how sexy you are when you're bossy?"

She blushed deeper, the pink making him dream of where else on her body would be that particular shade. "Sh, don't talk like that. No flirting, remember? Here, take the bag and open some of it. I have specific ideas about where all this stuff should go."

He had specific ideas about where his stuff should go too. He shook his head, trying to rid himself of the thought as he handed her the banner and the push pin. Her ass was right there in front of his face, encased in a beautiful pair of jeans, her wide hips drawing him in.

He remembered those hips riding him, holding them as she ground on him. Curvy and perfect for gripping tight, she was a little pixie, a pocket-sized imp who flew around his head while he dreamed, spreading horny dust all over him and waking him with a raging boner.

She descended the ladder, and he moved it to the next spot, starting the torturous process all over again. But this time, her foot got caught in a rung, and she slipped.

If he hadn't been eyeing her ass so closely, he might not have caught her. He wrapped an arm around her waist and spun her away from the ladder and against the wall. She was short, barely reaching his shoulder, but it was the perfect fit for him.

When her toes touched the ground, her body slid down his. He couldn't help the groan that slipped out; just like she couldn't help the widening of her emerald green eyes when she heard it.

Her hands rested on his arms, and he leaned forward.

The Songwriter Gets His Girl

He couldn't stop himself, her lips drawing him in yet again. He'd never flown so close to the sun.

He brushed her lips with his, his hands going to those hips and sliding around to her ass. It fit perfectly in his meaty palms. Her gasp wasn't wasted, and he swept inside, his tongue tangling with hers. The kiss was soft but built in intensity faster than a wildfire.

She broke it abruptly and jerked back, blinking rapidly. He let her go, feeling her take the warmth with her as she frowned and shook her head.

"No, Landry. We can't break the rules, or we risk ruining our friendship."

She tucked her hair behind her ear and glanced away, picking up another decoration nervously. He tried to shrug off the pain of rejection and reached for the ladder.

She didn't realize that their friendship was already starting to change and be affected, even with the rules. He hadn't fucking seen her in weeks and was pretty sure she'd been avoiding him.

His chest hurt as disappointment raced through him, but he pasted on his smile anyway. "Where does that decoration go?"

Chapter Thirty-Six

Don't leave, baby. I can't stand to see you cry. Let me hold you, let me make it all better. Stay with me, baby. Stay with me.

Holly let out a shuddering breath, avoiding Landry's hazel eyes that always saw too much. "This one goes on the ceiling. You're taller, so you can put it up. Can you spread these around the room and maybe the small ones down the hallway? Then we'll weave these streamers through the curtains."

Holly's voice was threadier than normal, so she cleared her throat. What was wrong with her? She'd wanted that kiss, and her lips had tingled in anticipation. His kiss was just as sweet and panty-melting as she'd been dreaming and remembering, and her stomach had flipped with nerves.

How could she let herself get that close to him, to anyone?

Eric would be so disappointed. She couldn't do that to his memory. It'd been almost three years, but she was only twenty-six. There was plenty of time to find someone and settle down again, but not yet. It was too soon. She couldn't get close to anyone yet.

This was just about the baby. It was just a business arrangement. The past few weeks without him had put it all back into perspective, but that kiss...

They finished putting up the decorations right as Andy and the kids arrived. She stepped to the side as Parker and Landry roped them all and organized the food line. The pre-teens were ravenous after their soccer practice this afternoon.

She smiled, thinking that in ten or twelve years she'd be doing this same thing with her own kid. Maybe she'd have a boy. He'd have Landry's blond hair, maybe even his strong jaw.

Maryanne walked by with Connie in her arms. The dull ache in her heart pulsed at the sight, and she fought the jealousy that came with seeing it.

Soon, the house was overflowing, and Cindy was panicking from the chaos and noise. Holly pulled her aside and offered her a drink of water, making her sit down and prop her feet up while Lola ran interference with the other parents and adults.

Landry and Parker still had the pre-teens under control, playing some sort of game in the living room while they ate.

After the presents and cake were done, Landry pulled out a bag and started handing things to the boys gathered around him. Their voices rose and Gunner leaned over to look into the bag.

Gunner frowned. "Are those paintball guns?"

Landry's lopsided grin made her heart race. Whatever he had planned, it was going to be epic.

Landry nodded. "I have a course set up from the

driveway to the cabin in the woods. Who wants to play? Let's team up!"

The teens cheered.

Parker slapped Landry on the back and grinned as he walked to the other side of the room. "I'm team captain, and Landry will be the other. Parents, there's plenty for y'all to join in too. Y'all have two minutes to pick a side before we pick for you."

Holly shuffled to Parker, her drink in hand. She didn't want to get too close to Landry again.

Gunner shook his head. "Maryanne and I are sitting this out."

Andy nodded. "Cindy is too, but I'll play. Every kid needs a buddy. I don't want anyone getting lost in the woods."

One of the teens pointed to Holly and Lola standing by Parker. "Three girls on Coach Parker's team isn't fair. Girls have cooties. I'm going to Landry's team."

Lola narrowed her eyes and crossed her arms defiantly. "I'm playing, kid. It's been a long week and shooting something is just what I need to blow off some steam. You go to Landry's team, and I'm taking you out."

Parker put an arm around Lola and the other around Holly and grinned at the kid. Holly smiled but her mind whirled because his touch did nothing to her. It was warm and friendly, but it didn't make her heart race the way Landry's did. What did that mean?

"We'll whip your butt with the girls. Don't worry."

Holly snorted her drink out of her nose, choking on a laugh as the kids started talking smack between the teams.

Lola bent and grabbed a paintball gun from the bag. Holly finished her drink and set it on the dining table, then took the gun Parker handed her.

The Songwriter Gets His Girl

"You know how to use this?"

She arched a brow and reared back. "Does a bear shit in the woods?"

Parker laughed, the lines next to his eyes growing deep. "God, you're hilarious. Why won't you give me a chance?"

She winked and blew him a kiss. "I only date winners, so let's go destroy your brother's team."

"Hell yeah! That's the spirit."

She laughed, Parker's flirting always making her feel light-hearted and carefree. She knew it didn't mean anything with Parker. He was harmless, and guys flirted all the time. Well, guys that weren't Landry.

Landry hadn't ever flirted like that, maybe because it was too real for him like Lola seemed to think. Perhaps he'd always known they could be great together. Just then, Landry looked over and smiled, his face softening just for her.

Shit, did he look at her different than he did the other girls?

Landry cleared his throat, looked away, and held up his hands to get the group's attention.

"Okay, let's go over the rules. Everyone has between fifty to seventy-five shots. We have red and green glow stick necklaces, so we know which team is which in the dim light. Parker's team gets green, mine gets red."

Holly grinned as the necklaces were passed around and the kids broke the seals to make them light up. This was gonna be fun; it'd been a long time since she'd played something like this.

Memories of paintball, putt putt, and go-kart races floated through her mind as she listened to Landry go over the rest of the rules. Maryanne was sitting on Gunner's lap on the couch, ignoring most of them. Holly remembered the last time she'd gone paintballing with Eric and his squad.

The front door opened and the guys started piling outside, so Holly followed them.

The humid night air hit her in the face, making her suck in a deep breath. It wasn't too hot at this time of day. Being the end of August in Texas meant it was barely ninety degrees in the day. It had cooled off a little as dusk approached. Her blood pumped in anticipation of the game.

Everyone walked down to the edge of the driveway, turned right, and gathered around Landry and Parker.

Landry waved dramatically.

"We're in teams, but straight through that path lies a cabin. Somewhere near the cabin is a Crimson Creek soccer banner. That's your goal. First team to take the banner wins. If you get hit, put your hands on your head and come back to the driveway here. My other brother, Hunter, is at the cabin with a whistle, which he'll blow when someone wins."

The scent of fresh cut grass floated on the breeze, mixing with the cedar and pine of the forest in front of them. Someone sneezed.

Parker pulled his soccer whistle out of his pocket and whistled twice. Then Landry yelled out, "Go!"

Holly raced to the first tree, quickly leaving everyone behind. She peered around the edge, then turned back to see a kid on her team stumble. She laughed as the kid's partner helped him, then they went in the other direction.

She listened to the sounds around her, the sneezes, giggles, and paintballs finding their mark, then peered around her tree before racing to the next. She spied Andy, saw his red necklace, glanced around, then shot him twice in the leg before ducking and weaving to the next tree.

The edges were her favorite for paintball. She found a hay bale and dove for it. She started to lean around it but heard footsteps and pulled back just as a shot whizzed past her shoulder.

She tossed her gun on top of the bale and climbed up, landing softly and silently on top thanks to her yoga flexibility. The rush of adrenaline filled her as she had a bird's eye view of the entire course. A few were on the other side, a few were in the middle, and two kids were looking around the edge for her. She saw their red glow stick and grinned.

Her gun came up, she aimed, and shot twice. Even in the darkness, lit only by the rapidly descending sun, she could see the surprise on their little faces when they looked up and saw who had gunned them down.

She laughed silently as one saluted and both jogged off with hands on their heads. She spied an old tractor, a few more bales, and then a break in the trees. She could faintly make out a cabin.

No one was between her and the target, so she hopped down and crept up to the old John Deere.

When she reached it, she felt her stomach lurch, not from normal adrenaline but from something else, awareness that only happened around one other person. Then she heard rustling footsteps on the other side of the tractor. She knelt down and looked through the grass. She saw boots but didn't have a clean shot.

She climbed up the tire of the tractor to the front and leaned over. Landry was looking around the back, but her foot got caught right before she took a shot.

For the second time that night, she fell, a silent scream stuck in her throat until big arms wrapped around her.

They fell to the ground, Landry letting out a grunt as she landed on top of him.

She pulled back, her legs naturally straddling him as she pushed her palms to the cold ground.

"Oh my God, are you okay? Did I hurt you?"

His hands gripped her hips and stilled her frantic movements to check him for injuries. She felt his bulge right at the most delicious part of her body. It was suddenly too hot as his fingers found the soft skin under her shirt, just above her jeans.

"Landry, are you ok?" Her voice was soft and warbled on the last bit. She could barely see his face in the tractor's shadow, the green and red glow sticks casting an eerie light between them. Her body betrayed her. She couldn't stop as she ground against him, gasping and eyes widening as they met his own.

His were hungry, and his fingers squeezed her waist. A twig snapped nearby.

Suddenly he rolled them, pinning her to the ground and raising his gun as a thud sounded.

She glanced up to see Landry glaring at Parker, both men now wearing paint.

Parker held up his hands in surrender and walked off the field with a smirk. Landry looked down at her, his hard face chiseled in harsh shadows.

She reached up and palmed his cheek, her hand shaky. "You good? Those paintballs hurt like hell."

Landry arched a brow. "Yes, they do. Want to kiss it and make it better?"

His voice sent a shiver up her spine, and he ground his hips into hers. When he lowered his head, she turned her face to the side and giggled as panic danced in her stomach.

The Songwriter Gets His Girl

He kissed up her jaw to her ear, then pulled the lobe into his mouth. She groaned and wiggled under him.

She couldn't let this happen. It was against the rules, no matter how much her lady bits wanted him to grind into her again. No matter how many nights she lay in bed remembering his kisses. She sucked in a deep breath and pushed slightly on his chest.

"We can't."

His eyes shone bright in the semi-darkness, and disappointment ran rampant over his features before he blinked twice. Then he winked and grinned, his charming persona back.

"Fine, but if you're not pregnant already, we can have a rain check next time."

That's right. Remember the baby. Remember the goal.

She patted his cheek again, ready to agree to anything to get him off her. Her body was going nuts, tingling in all the right places at the contact. If he didn't get up soon, she'd pull him down for more than a kiss.

"Maybe, but let me up so I can go win this thing."

He chuckled softly and rolled off her before getting to his feet. He held out a hand.

"Let me help you."

She waved him away. "It's fine. I need a minute."

He lifted a brow and shrugged, walking off the field. She laid there for a second longer, trying to rid her body of the tingles being smashed against him had brought.

A cheer echoed through the woods, then two whistles sounded to signal the end of the game. She stood up as kids began to race back toward the house, laughing and stumbling like awkward pre-teens do.

The adults followed behind, and she joined the crowd. Andy and Cindy handed out goodie bags while the kids said their goodbyes. Holly looked around. Parker was helping Landry pack up all the gear, so she went to the bathroom.

Her body was definitely revved up and ready to go. It'd been weeks since they were in Nashville and feeling him pressed up against her had been a shock to her system. She might break out her battery-operated boyfriend and relive it later.

Wait, what? No, absolutely not. She jerked her pants down to use the toilet, and her world stopped.

She gulped, blinked, and sucked in a deep, shuddering breath. So that was that. She wasn't pregnant. She looked under the sink and found a pad, her body numb as her dreams were dashed.

It shouldn't have surprised her. She'd taken two pregnancy tests this week and both were negative.

She had to be patient. It had taken a while to get pregnant with Eric too. Shit, she needed to think about Eric, his arms, his kiss. She washed her hands and went into the kitchen to help put away the food.

The littlest kids there, Mandy and Owen, ran through the kitchen and skidded to a halt in their socks. A tiny hand tugged on her shirt, and she looked down into big brown eyes. Her chest felt like a brick was pressing on it, but she pasted on a smile for the kids.

"Holly, can you get us some milk? Mama says to get ready for bed, but I need some milk first."

"Sure, go change into your pajamas and wash your face and hands while I get it. You still have mud right here." She grabbed a dish towel and rubbed a smear off Owen's cheek.

Mandy giggled. "I told you you were too dirty. Come on." They took off running down the hall, and she opened cabinets to find the sippy cups.

The Songwriter Gets His Girl

When she turned to put them on the counter, Landry was leaning against the doorjamb, ankles and arms crossed.

Voices rose softly from the living room, and it was just them in the kitchen.

"You're going to be a great mom someday." His soft, low voice made her freeze, her knuckles turning white.

Then she spun and opened the fridge with a shaky hand. She pulled out the milk and turned, only to run into his chest. His hands circled her arms, holding her steady, and she glanced up, tears pooling in her eyes. His touch caused tingles to race along her spine but his words made her want to weep.

"What is it, angel?"

She swallowed, gripping the jug of milk tightly in one hand. "Nothing. Just emotional right now, as I—I just started my period."

His eyes widened and he nodded. "Ah, so the mission wasn't a success then. I'm sorry."

He pulled her into his arms, holding her. Her head settled on his big chest, and she sighed. He was warm, safe, and didn't make a joke or brush it off. He just held her.

A laugh rang from the living room, breaking the spell. Little footsteps ran up the hall, and she pulled away just as the two kids came back for their milk. She quickly poured and screwed on the lids while they talked some kid nonsense about toothpaste.

Then they ran off. She avoided Landry's eyes and went into the living room. Cindy and Andy were sitting on the couch while Lola and Parker were taking down the decorations. Parker took the ladder out to the garage.

Holly cleared her throat and smiled. "Thanks for letting me help with the party. It was fun."

Cindy pushed awkwardly to her feet, holding her belly. Then she hugged her tight.

"I'm so glad you're here, Holly. I know it was hard for you, but I couldn't have gotten through tonight without you."

Andy stood and shook her hand. "Thanks for taking care of Cindy tonight, Holly. She was pretty overwhelmed with the party."

"No problem, Andy. Anything to help. Like I said, it was fun."

Holly grabbed her purse and headed to the door. Landry cleared his throat. "I'm going to head home too. You ready Parker?"

They followed her out the door, and she walked swiftly to her car. She felt his gaze follow her every step, but she refused to look at him. If she did, she'd break down. It was too much, too overwhelming, and all she wanted to do was go home and cry in the hot shower.

Chapter Thirty-Seven

Missing you like the sun in winter. I'm low, I'm twenty below without you in my arms.

Beginning of September

A week later, Holly went into Half Baked, the bell dinging above.

"Morning Holly, how've you been?" Zarrel asked from behind the counter. He finished ringing up a customer as he greeted her.

"I'm doing good. Can't complain. Is Maryanne here? We're going to the salon today."

The customer left and Zarrel came around the counter to push open the swinging door to the back. "Sure, she's in the back with Connie. Can you believe how big she's getting?"

Holly followed him into the back to find Maryanne

sitting on the couch in her office, feeding Connie and scrolling on her phone. She looked up when they crowded the doorway, her smile wide.

"Oh hey, is it time to go? Give me a few minutes; she's almost done."

Zarrel tilted his head. "What's the plan with the kiddo? Do you need to leave her here with me while you go?"

Maryanne shook her head, pulling a now sleeping Connie off and rearranging her shirt. "No, Gunner is doing paperwork today in the office, so I'm going to leave her with him. Joey's there to take any calls, so it'll be fine. Thanks for offering, though."

Zarrel turned to take something out of one of the ovens. "Anytime you need her godfather to babysit, just say the word. She's an easy baby compared to what my nieces and nephews were like at that age."

Holly took the precious baby and rocked slightly back to forth with her on her shoulder, smelling her dark hair as she burped her. She smiled, her heart filling with joy and peace.

Her vision blurred, and she closed her eyes. A tear slipped down her cheek, and she turned her head to wipe it on her own shirt.

"You okay, hun?" Maryanne asked as she gathered the diaper bag and car seat.

"Yeah, it's just... the in-vitro didn't take. I have to go back and try again."

Maryanne put her hand on Holly's back in a side hug. "Oh, I'm so sorry, Holly. Is there anything I can do to help?"

She met her friend's dark eyes and smiled, her heart aching. "Just let me hold this cutie anytime I want, and I'll be okay."

Maryanne chuckled, and they told Zarrel bye. Holly

The Songwriter Gets His Girl

carried Connie across the street while Maryanne talked about the two-month baby check-up appointment. When they pushed open the door to the sheriff's station, Connie still hadn't stirred in her arms.

She breathed in that baby smell of powder and pure joy before Maryanne directed her to put her in the baby carrier next to Gunner's desk. She stood with a sigh and stepped back, her arms now empty and aching even more for her own little bundle of joy.

Gunner rolled his chair over and tucked the thin blanket around his daughter, the transfer making her stir slightly and throw her hands up in a stretch. She yawned, and it nearly melted Holly's heart.

"Thanks for bringing her over. This being back at work thing has me missing her entirely too much." Gunner glanced up at Maryanne and winked.

Maryanne grinned and raised her dark eyebrows, crossing her arms. "What about me? You missing me too, G?"

He pulled back in his chair slightly and grabbed her by the belt loop, pulling her onto his lap as she chuckled. Holly stepped back into the doorway, trying not to watch as they kissed and whispered to each other.

The pressure increased on her chest, and she stepped into the main room. With a shuddering breath, she walked to the front window and stared out. Sunlight filtered through the trees in the park where they'd had the fourth of July celebration. She could see the bakery and her own yoga studio from here too.

A powder blue Ford drove by, and her heart leaped in her chest, her sadness turning to excitement like the snap of fingers. The window was rolled down, and Landry had his arm on it, making his shirt sleeve push up slightly. She saw his biceps, the scruff on his jaw. His eyes were hidden behind the sunglasses, but he didn't even look her way, keeping his eyes on the road and tapping a rhythm with his fingers on the steering wheel.

When he passed out of sight, she realized her palm was on the glass, reaching for him. She stepped back and pushed her hands into her short pockets. It was the first time she'd seen him since the party.

True to their agreement, he hadn't reached out, texted, or swung by the studio, and it made her feel like she'd just been dumped, which was ridiculous. She'd been nothing but cranky for weeks, whether from loneliness or more, she didn't know.

She sighed, pulling out her phone as a notification came through from social media. She probably should tell him about another baby making attempt, but did he even still want to participate? It was hard to tell since they hadn't seen each other, and they hadn't really discussed it at the party.

She switched to his name and opened the messenger app. Her mouth went dry as she hovered over the screen.

But it was the right thing to do, even if it did make her nervous. She took a deep breath and tapped, hoping it was easier to break the silence by text.

Hey, whatcha doing on Main Street?

Just pulled up to the hardware store.
Need supplies for a job. What are you up to?

Just saw you drive by and wanted to check in. Say hey.

God, that was stupid. She just wanted to say hey? That

was the lamest attempt at playing coy in the history of flirting. She groaned, tapping her head against the window.

And flirting was against the rules. What was she thinking? Three dots showed on the screen, and she stood up straight, holding her breath.

Lol Well hey. You okay? Car working out all right?

Yeah, it's all good. Just missing you.

She sighed, biting her lip. It took three seconds to realize that probably wasn't the wisest move to make and a clear violation of the rules. She tapped quickly, trying to recall the message.

I miss you too. Are you ready to make another attempt?

Her heart stilled as she read his words. Maybe it was alright to talk like this in text. It wasn't against the rules to be real and raw with each other, and she was tired of pretending, tired of working so hard to keep all the walls up. God, this was so confusing.

Yeah, you busy next Thur-Sun?
That's when my phone app says is best.

I have to re-do my parents' cabin next week. New floors and paint. Want to help? We can stay there.

Sure, sounds fun. I liked painting the studio with you in Mar.

Maryanne came out of the office, her lipstick smudged and her cheeks pink. Holly stood up straighter and fired off one last text.

Gotta go to the salon now. Later.

She slipped her phone into her back pocket and followed Maryanne through the door.

"Who was on the phone? Was it Lola? Is she meeting us?"

Holly shook her head. "No, she's canning with her grandma today. You and Gunner seem to be doing well. How's married life?"

Maryanne sighed and twirled a piece of bright pink hair. They normally did their hair together, but today Holly was going for a complete change.

"It's better than I thought it'd be. We're still figuring out how to talk and be open with each other, but I never thought this time last year that I'd be happily married with a baby. So weird."

Holly laughed as they crossed the street. "Hopefully this time next year, Connie will have a friend to play with."

"When do you go back for another attempt?"

"Next weekend, actually. I'll be able to drive myself this time too." She was proud of how well she'd been driving the past few weeks. It really was like riding a bicycle, easy to pick back up where she'd left off.

Maryanne linked their arms together for the last few yards to the salon. "It was good of Landry to take you last time. Did y'all have a good drive?"

Holly blushed, tucking her hair behind her ear. "Yeah, it was good. We listened to music, and he sang."

She felt Maryanne's gaze on her cheeks but she refused to make eye contact.

"I always thought you'd end up with Landry. Not gonna lie, I was kind of hoping the hour drive into Dallas would make you wake up and see how perfect you are together."

The Songwriter Gets His Girl

Holly did look at her friend that time, but only to frown because she was crazy. Her and Landry as a real couple? "What's that supposed to mean? You know I've already had my happily ever after. Eric was perfect for me, not Landry."

Maryanne sighed. "When are you going to realize that you can have another one? You're not even thirty yet, Holly. You probably have another sixty years of life to live, and you are choosing to do it alone when you don't have to."

Holly gritted her teeth and pushed the Clip-&-Curl door open, pressure on her chest increasing as thoughts of Landry swirled in her head. She pasted on a smile as Kate finished styling Cindy's hair.

"Welcome, girls. Have a seat, and I'll be right with you."

Maryanne grinned and sat in one of the four open seats near the door. "I didn't know you were coming in this morning, Cin."

"We would've gotten here earlier and chatted if we'd known." Holly sat beside Maryanne and grabbed a magazine, flipping to random pages.

"I didn't know y'all were coming in either. Don't y'all do your own hair?" Cindy frowned as Kate used the straightener on her hair.

Holly cleared her throat. "Yeah, but I decided if I was going to do this baby thing, then I should ditch the silver and go back to my natural blond. That kind of massive change needs a professional."

Kate waved the straightener at her. "And I'm so very glad you called. I've been telling Lucy to swing by the yoga studio and meet you, but I don't think she's done it yet, has she?"

Holly shook her head. "No, I haven't met her. I heard she was still settling into her apartment."

Kate nodded and they chatted about the new girl, who

was expected any minute for Maryanne's nail appointment. Cindy finished, then lumbered up out of the chair, her baby bump now prominent.

Holly nodded at her belly. "How's the pregnancy going this week? You need to swing by for a massage?"

Cindy smiled and rubbed her stomach. "It's going well. We're not doing a gender reveal until the baby's born, but I feel a lot different than I did with the boys. So I'm guessing it's a girl."

"Mandy will love that." Holly smiled, picturing Andy's three-year-old daughter.

Cindy's face lit up. "Speaking of, we're going to have her a birthday party in a few weeks. Do you want to come?"

Holly laughed. "Didn't you just have a birthday party for Cody?"

Cindy nodded and rubbed her forehead. "Yeah, these first birthday's with Andy around are driving me crazy. It can't be just a simple thing. He's nervous because they're his first birthday parties as their dad. I think he's going a bit overboard with each of them, but it's too sweet to stop him."

"Oh, how fun. I'd love to come. Do you need help?"

The door opened and a willowy little brunette came in. She had her hair up in high pigtails with sparkly scrunchies.

She waved and smiled. "Hey everyone. I'm Lucy, the nail tech. Which one of you is my appointment?"

Maryanne held up her hand, and Lucy clapped.

"Excellent. Just let me wash up, and we'll get started. Have you picked out your colors yet?"

Maryanne nodded. "Yep, I have them right here. Take your time. I'm going to say bye to my sister."

Cindy waved her hand and took Holly's seat as Holly walked to the chair that Kate had just cleaned off.

The Songwriter Gets His Girl

"Actually, I think I'll hang out a bit. I have the whole day off today, and other than a nap, I have nothing planned."

Maryanne chuckled while Holly climbed into the chair and turned to show Kate pictures of what she wanted done to her hair on her phone. The voices mingled as Lucy set up and Maryanne sat at the table.

Half an hour later, the conversation turned to men, of course.

Maryanne shook her head and laughed. "I can't believe you've been in town for months now and haven't gone on a date yet. Have you found anyone who's caught your eye?"

Lucy blushed and looked away. "Doesn't matter even if I have."

Cindy shifted on her chair. "Uh oh, that means you have found someone. Who is it?"

"Maybe we can help." Since Maryanne and Gunner had gotten married and more recently declared their love, she wanted everyone around her to have a special someone. It was one of the reasons Lola wasn't there today, because Lola just couldn't handle all the lovey dovey stuff all the time. Only in small doses.

Holly saw Kate smirk in the mirror. "I know who it is. It was plain as the color on her shirt that she liked him."

Lucy frowned and shushed her, but Kate just laughed. "Oh hun, don't worry about it. Holly's the only one who didn't grow up with him. The Martin sisters could give you the inside scoop on getting a date, though."

Kate stepped in her line of sight, so Holly couldn't see Lucy anymore. But she heard her loud sigh.

"Fine, it was Landry. He came in to help set up the table and remodel the space to make room for me when I first got here. Then he helped me move all my stuff from the moving truck up the stairs to the second-floor apartment."

"Oh, he's a good one. You can't do any better than Landry. He's Andy's best friend." Cindy's voice echoed through the narrow room while Holly stared at the red and black checkered floor, the comb pulling through her hair. Her hands started to sweat under the apron, and she rubbed them on her shorts.

"Did you ask him out?" Maryanne asked. Holly's ears started beating like a drum, her heart racing.

"Of course not. I would never."

Maryanne snorted. "Well, you'll not get many dates if you wait around for someone to ask, especially someone like Landry. He normally picks girls up at the Electric Cowboy, but now he's down in Dallas on most weekends. If you want a date, you'll have to ask him."

Holly's blood ran cold, and she fisted her hands under the apron. She'd need to give Landry a heads up about Lucy, because it was part of their contract that he couldn't date until after she got pregnant.

You sure it's not because you're jealous?

She frowned as Kate wrapped her hair in a cap to cure. This time the voice definitely sounded like Eric. The ladies continued talking about their past dating history, but Holly kept quiet, her stomach roiling as she thought about Landry dating.

Chapter Thirty-Eight

Corn stalks blowing in the wind, cicadas chirping and tractors running. Sweet tea in my hand, the only thing missing is you.

After Kate washed her hair out and Maryanne settled in the pedicure chair for Lucy to do her toes, the conversation turned again.

"Lucy, you do realize that quiet little Holly here is the owner of the yoga studio next door, right?"

Kate brushed her hair while Lucy blushed again.

"I had heard that, yes. I've been meaning to stop by but wasn't sure when a good time was."

"Our classes are posted on the website, so stop by anytime and join a session." Holly winced at her flat tone and gave a tense smile to counteract it. She couldn't see Maryanne's face, but her friend would definitely pick up on her attitude if she wasn't careful.

Kate trimmed her hair. "Lucy has some yoga certifications too."

Holly sighed. Apparently, she really did need to have this conversation right now. And it was petty of her to put it off just because she didn't like the idea of Lucy dating Landry.

The goal of having a baby was more important, and for that to happen, she'd need a back-up instructor. She gritted her teeth and clenched her fists.

"What certifications do you have? I'm sure you heard, but I'll be having a baby sometime next year and will need a back-up instructor to take over my classes while I'm out on maternity leave."

"Congratulations. That's so exciting. I have a standard certification, then was getting additional ones in hot yoga and aerial yoga before I moved. I need about ten more hours in each for those certifications."

They chatted with Holly asking more questions. By the time her hair was done, she was feeling more relaxed about Lucy and less like she wanted to punch her in the face. In the back of her mind, she kept picturing Landry and Lucy walking together through the grocery store. Her stomach twisted at the thought, and she drank water as Kate brought her the card swipe machine.

When she finished paying, Holly gave Lucy her number. "Text me anytime and we can figure out when you can finish those hours for your additional certifications. You can come in once a week for class to get to know our residents, if you'd like. Check out the class list and let me know when to expect you, okay?"

Lucy nodded, her eyes bright and her pigtails bouncing. Holly smiled, her shoulders relaxing even more. There was no way Landry would like such a young woman. He was an old soul, probably a result of how much time he'd spent with his grandparents.

Maryanne followed her out of the door and linked their arms again. "Well, that was interesting."

"Why, does my hair look okay?" Holly shook her hair over her shoulder, running a hand through the now light honey gold locks.

"Of course, it does. It looks good on you too. The silver worked, but this is just... you, I guess. But that's not what I was talking about. I was talking about how your tone of voice changed when Lucy was talking about Landry."

Holly stumbled on the sidewalk before they turned to cross the street. "I—I don't know what you're talking about."

"Uh huh, I bet you were jealous, weren't you? I bet it made you so—"

"Hey girls, how's it going?" Lola called from down the street before she closed the door to her truck. They adjusted their stride to head her direction, and Holly breathed a sigh of relief at the interruption. "Holly, your hair looks so good! Is this your natural color?"

Holly nodded, flicking her head from side to side to show off her hair. "It feels good to be me again."

"It's fabulous, just like you." Lola gave her a little hug, then stepped back.

Maryanne nodded at her. "What are you doing in town? I thought you were canning today."

Lola shrugged. "Granny sent me to town for more sugar. Figured I'd find y'all and see how the salon visit turned out. Want to run to the Diner with me?"

Maryanne showed off her nails and toes as they walked down the street and into the restaurant. They took the booth at the back, and Lola slid in next to Maryanne. The waitress took their order as they chatted about Lucy and the salon, Kate and Kate's niece who owned the Electric Cowboy.

Maryanne raised an eyebrow. "It was interesting at the salon, though, because I could have sworn Holly was jealous that Lucy was talking about asking Landry out on a date."

"I wasn't jealous." Holly's voice was shrill and waspish even to her own ears. She winced and glanced away to sip her water.

Lola cleared her throat and Holly's gaze shot to her bright blue one, pleading with her not to say anything. Lola's brow lifted as she said, "Well, actually—"

Holly interrupted. "How long until you have to pick Connie up from Gunner? Will she be getting hungry soon?"

Maryanne shrugged and crossed her arms. "Yeah, I felt my milk drop on the walk here, but Gunner has a spare bottle available if she needs it."

Lola pursed her lips and slapped the table, leaning forward and staring at Holly with narrowed eyes. "I know you don't want to talk about this, but we're going to, with or without Maryanne. You better prepare yourself right now, chica."

Maryanne's eyes went wide as she glanced from Lola to Holly and back again. "What am I missing here?"

Lola leaned closer to Maryanne and Holly barely heard her whisper, "She's not doing in vitro. She's made a contract with Landry for him to be her sperm donor. And they're doing it the all-natural way." Lola made air quotes around the "all-natural" part.

Holly groaned and rubbed her temples. She really did not want to have this conversation with them either. Ever since Nashville, she'd been blowing hot and cold, back and forth on what she wanted. One minute, she'd want more with Landry, then the next she'd want to keep this strictly a

The Songwriter Gets His Girl

professional arrangement. One minute, she was devastated that she wasn't already pregnant, and the next, she was excited to have more sex with Landry.

Maryanne gasped and leaned forward. "Are you fucking kidding me? You've been lying to me all month? What the hell, Holly?"

Holly fidgeted with her shirt and shifted on the bench seat. The waitress brought their food, and the silence stretched between the three of them as they began to eat.

When the waitress walked away, Holly lowered her voice and frowned. "Look, you didn't tell us about Gunner for a few months either, so just back off."

Lola chewed her food, and Maryanne mouthed back. "But you just told me today that the in vitro didn't take, and you were going to try again next weekend. Does that mean you're actually meeting Landry?"

Holly nodded once and ate a bite of her food. It tasted like ash in her mouth, and her stomach rebelled as she tried to swallow. She didn't like lying to her friends, but the scrutiny was getting to her. Her hands were shaking as she tried to take a drink.

Lola put her drink down. "The contract is all kinds of bullshit, Maryanne. You should've seen it."

Holly slammed her drink down hard. "It's not bullshit. It's necessary to keep this a professional relationship."

Maryanne snorted and rolled her eyes. "Yeah right, you're sleeping with Landry. There's no way this will be a purely professional business arrangement by the end."

Holly leaned forward, her food forgotten as she gripped the edge of the table. She'd had niggling doubts about that exact thing, but for them to say it out loud made her break out in a cold-sweat. "It has to be. I'll have my baby, and he'll move on with life, go on a fucking date with Lucy, and marry her for all I care. I'll have my baby, and that's all that matters."

Even to her own ears, it sounded like she was trying to convince herself.

Maryanne's eyes softened as she reached across the table and grabbed Holly's hand. "I'll say it again, over and over until you truly listen. You deserve happiness, Holly, and you can have another happily ever after if you just open yourself up to it."

Lola pushed her now empty plate away and leaned back in the booth. "The contract is her way to control the situation so she won't let herself open up. It says stuff like no kissing, no cuddling, no flirting, and no lights on. What's up with that?"

Maryanne put her chin in her hand and leaned on the table. "What's Tasha say about this arrangement and the contract?"

Holly tilted her head up. "That's between me and Tasha, isn't it?"

Maryanne rolled her eyes, and Lola continued. "What's interesting is that Landry added two rules to the bottom of the contract. What were they again? I can't quite remember."

Holly glared at Lola's twinkling eyes and crossed her arms. "He said we have to have a date for each night spent together. And no dating anyone else, which is why I'm not jealous of Lucy. He's bound by our contract to turn her down."

Holly felt some of the tension leave her stomach until Lola's words twisted her up in knots again.

"But that's only until you get pregnant, right? Then he's a free agent and can date her, even marry her like you said. How's that going to work out if they get married and have kids? You'll have to see him around town, holding hands, kissing her—"

Holly jumped up and grabbed her purse. "I gotta go. I'll talk to y'all later." She threw a twenty on the table and spun on her heels while Maryanne was trying to grab her hand to get her to stay.

"Damn it, Holly, stop running away from lunch," Lola growled, but she didn't stop walking through the Diner.

This was bullshit, and she didn't have to put up with this crap from her so-called friends. She had groceries to buy for the week, classes to plan, a studio to clean... plenty to keep her busy before next weekend.

Chapter Thirty-Nine

She's the one who lights my fire. I can't escape and I can't hide. Running through quicksand never works and neither does staying away from my boo.

Landry stood on the front porch of the one room hunting cabin on the far corner of his parent's land. They had the largest horse ranch in Texas, specializing in rodeo ready horses. The cabin was a ten-minute drive over a dirt road, and he'd cautioned Holly against driving her car out here, but she was stubborn and proud to finally be driving again. It made his own heart swell to know that she loved it and was comfortable in it, but it was almost dark, and she still wasn't here. She'd be nervous about driving in the dark.

All the lights were on so she could see the place. He had dinner waiting inside, had cleaned and remade the bed with fresh sheets. There was nothing left to do. Instead of pacing he sat on the rocking chair next to the front door, thinking.

He and his grandpa used to come out here about this

The Songwriter Gets His Girl

time of year, preparing for the hunting season. They'd scope out the trails, find the nesting grounds, and watch the deer every morning and night.

Headlights shone in the low hanging sun, and he breathed a sigh of relief. Except for the birthday party, he'd only seen her in passing this past month, and it'd been one of the hardest things he'd ever had to do. He hadn't wanted to stay away from her. Far from it, he wanted to spend every single day and night with her.

He'd thought helping her with this baby problem would finally get her out of his system. He hadn't thought about anyone else since that first kiss in December, but instead of expunging her, he just craved her more. The lights of her car appeared on the dirt road, and he sucked in a breath, his stomach twisting with nerves and excitement.

He'd stayed away partly because of that contract, but partly because it scared him how much he missed her. If he found it this hard after only a weekend with her, how much harder would it be when she was pregnant or had the baby, and he couldn't be there for them?

It worried him, but those thoughts fled as she opened her door and stepped into the light. Her blond hair shone in the setting sun, and he stood on shaky legs as she took his breath away. His heart stopped, then felt like it was racing straight to her.

Something snapped in his mind and a whisper on the breeze said *It's her. She's the one.*

No, it couldn't be. He just needed to get her out of his system.

Bullshit. You love her, boy. Man up and stop denying it.

His grandpa's voice rang through his head as Holly walked through the grass he'd mowed just this week around the cabin. Time seemed to stand still as the sun settled on her like a halo. She was his angel, and his gut said she was the one.

The scent of earth and pasture wrapped around him, and he stepped down to the ground and pulled her flush. His arms wrapped around her, and his mouth crashed to hers. She gasped, and he swept his tongue inside like a starving man. Then her arms wrapped around his neck, and he lifted her by the ass until she wrapped her legs around him. He stumbled back onto the porch and through the front door, kicking it shut behind him.

They tumbled onto the bed along the far wall, dislodging their kiss. He trailed his fingers under her tank top, the touch of her skin burning him like a brand.

Who was he kidding? She'd been branded onto his soul years ago. There was no denying it any longer. He swept her shirt off and tossed it aside. She reached behind her to unhook her bra, and he sat up on his knees to take his own t-shirt off. He slipped the shoes off his feet, and their shorts were thrown to the floor. Her sandals had fallen off somewhere, but when he glanced at her lying there naked, he paused with his heart on his sleeve.

"You're the most beautiful woman I've ever met, angel." The awe echoed in his raspy voice, and he had to swallow past the lump in his throat. He knelt between her legs and kissed her gently on the lips, their softness drawing him in and making him want to just plunge into her silken heat.

But he needed to slow down, make this count. He kissed her jaw, so strong and delicate. Nipped at her ear and made her squirm under him. Trailed his lips down her neck to her breasts that called to him. Licked and sucked on each until she was gasping and gripping his hair and holding him close.

Then he moved down to her navel, dipping his tongue

The Songwriter Gets His Girl

in while he spread her thighs with his rough hands. He sat back and kissed the inside of her knee, then met her eyes.

"Lan, wh-what are you—"

"Sh," he whispered, taking in her dazed expression, her hair spread on the pale blue pillow. He wanted to capture this memory forever and never let it go. It was something to remember when all this was over, and he was truly alone again.

He loved her. There'd be no one else for him, and he needed to make these memories now. It was her or nothing. It always had been. She'd drawn him in five years ago, but now he was held captive by his love.

"Let me love you, angel." He saw her eyes widen at the word, but before she could protest, he knelt and licked at her wet center.

Her hips bucked, but he held them wide and narrowed in on the little bundle of nerves that drove her wild. He swirled his tongue, kissed and sucked until she was moaning and pushing her hips up rhythmically.

She gripped his hair again, fucking his face, and he loved every minute. The sweet taste of her was addicting. The scent of her arousal filled his nostrils, making him drunk on her until he saw stars behind his closed eyes.

Then he pulled back. She cried out, but then groaned with him as he slid his cock inside her tight, wet pussy. He held himself still, afraid that if he moved too soon, he'd explode before he could make her come all over him.

Her hands fluttered around his shoulders, and she pulled him down onto her, pressing her breasts to his chest. He buried his head in her neck, eased out, then plunged back into heaven. Her nails dug into his back, and he set up a steady rhythm that had them both panting.

He arched his back, moving his hand to her clit to rub

while sucking on a nipple. She thrust up to meet him, grinding against his thumb. A few thrusts were all it took before she gasped and clenched around him, squeezing and causing a chain reaction.

His balls tightened up, and he groaned, thrusting deep and burying his neck in her shoulder again as he spilled inside. Their breathing was ragged, and he sank onto his elbows to keep most of his weight from crushing her.

Her voice was soft in his ear. "Wow, if I'd known that was what awaited me, I would've gotten here sooner."

He chuckled, "I didn't expect it to go that way, but I'm not complaining. Are you?" He kissed her softly on the cheek, slipping out and rolling off the bed to walk the few feet to the bathroom to clean himself off.

His hands were shaky, but when he'd cleaned himself off, he returned to her side with a warm washcloth. He handed it to her.

She smiled up at him and the cabin seemed to grow brighter. "Not complaining one bit."

She didn't say anything about trying to keep the swimmers in there, and he wasn't going to remind her of their fight at the swimming hole last month. When they were both dressed, he asked, "You hungry? I made dinner."

"I'm starving, thanks. Just let me go grab my bag from the car."

"No, make yourself comfortable. I'll go get it." He slipped on his shoes and bounded into the now dark evening. The smell of rain was in the air, but the stars were shining bright and clear.

When he came back inside, she was pulling a hard seltzer and a beer out of the fridge. The kitchen area was just three cabinets with a sink, a microwave, a stove and oven combo, and a fridge. A small square table was pushed up against the front window that looked over the porch.

The old red velvet couch sat before the fireplace, and the bed was all the way along the far wall, directly across from the front door. The bathroom door was beside the bed.

She set the drinks on the table by the two plates he'd laid out, then sat in one of the old wooden dining chairs. He pulled a small casserole dish from the oven and set it on the table.

"Hm, this smells delicious. What is it?" She leaned forward, and her blond hair fell forward over one shoulder, reminding him of the night they'd met all those years ago.

"Your hair is gorgeous. I've missed the blond. Reminds me of the night we met."

She blushed and ran her fingers through her hair to tame the stray waves. "Thanks, it feels good to have it back to normal. I thought it'd be harder to let go of the silver, but it wasn't."

He smiled and spooned up a serving for each of them. "I'm glad. And this casserole is an experiment. You said you didn't mind meat but couldn't stand the idea of touching it raw or cooking it. So I made a chicken rice casserole. It has ranch, broccoli, cheese, and bacon too. But if you don't want to try it, I made some without the chicken and bacon. Do you want me to get it?"

He started to stand up to turn back to the oven, but her hand shot out and rubbed his forearm. Her eyes were soft green in the dim lights of the cabin, and her eyes were watery as she smiled.

"You remembered and went to so much effort. I'll definitely try it because it sounds like something my mom used to make."

He settled back into his chair and picked up his fork, but

he couldn't bring himself to eat until he saw she was going to like it. He watched as the fork went between her soft lips. Her eyes widened, and she breathed through her nose as she chewed.

"Is it okay?" He shifted side to side on the chair, spinning his fork in his hand.

She nodded and swallowed. "Oh my God, Landry, this is exactly like my mom's! How did you know that?"

He shrugged and winked. "I might or might not have asked Kendall a few discreet questions at poker night this past week."

Her back straightened, and she frowned. "How discreet? The reason I got here late tonight was because I didn't want anyone to see me on the road out here."

He arched a brow and tilted his head. "Exactly why I wanted to pick you up, but it was hard to explain that in text."

She shrugged and took another bite, so he continued.

"Anyway, we were all talking about our favorite dishes growing up, so Kendall told us his. Then I asked what yours was. Then I asked Andy and Gunner what Cindy and Maryanne's was. We ribbed them for not knowing the answer."

Holly nodded and smiled, making his heart settle. This was what he wanted, sitting across a table from her at the end of a long day, chatting and just hanging out.

But how was he to convince her to take that chance with him? She might not ever love him the way she loved Eric, and that was okay, but it was going to be a long road to walk to show her that they could still be happy together if she'd just let him love her.

Chapter Forty

Living the life with you in my arms, sun's coming up, and so am I. Kiss me awake, angel, prove it's more than just a dream.

Holly stretched and felt the weight of an arm around her torso. She glanced behind her to see Landry still asleep. The watch said seven but that was sleeping in for her. Now she was wide awake.

She slid out from under his arm, causing him to turn over onto his other side. Then she went to the bathroom, slipped on her shoes, and tiptoed out the front door. The sun was peaking over the horizon, the air was crisp, and the dew was shining in the pale light. It was going to be a fantastic day.

She just wanted to run for the joy of it, but an uneven field probably wasn't the best idea. Instead, she stood in front of her car on the cut grass and stretched. She'd been cranky and frustrated for the past few weeks. Today she'd woken up on the right side of the bed, though.

Maybe because Landry was in it.

She froze, then frowned as she went into several yoga poses, breathing deeply of the hay, cedar, and pine. She worked to clear her mind and shake off the little voice in her head that still sounded like Eric. The cabin butted against a small forest, which was unusual for this part of Texas.

The sound of laughter filled the air, and she followed it behind the cabin to the trail in the forest. She walked for what seemed like a long time but might have only been a few minutes. The trees and underbrush began to thin out as she spied another cabin, this one familiar.

She frowned, slowing down and ducking behind a large tree. That was Cindy and Andy's house. She peered around the tree and saw Andy and the kids out front, playing soccer.

Ah, so the cabin was the same one that had held the flag during the paintball game, the one she'd never gotten to before the game was over. She'd thought the road here was familiar.

Cody was already in his soccer uniform, ready for the first game of the season. Andy was laughing as they all played. Even Mandy and Owen were outside, running after the ball and screaming in delight as they ganged up on Cody. Owen acted as goalkeeper.

She watched for a few minutes, her chest growing heavy the longer she stood there. It was the picture-perfect family, but it was more than that too. She knew how happy they all were together, even when the cameras weren't snapping memories. This kind of thing would never happen for her unless she did what Maryanne said and opened herself up to another happiness.

The Songwriter Gets His Girl

She immediately thought of Landry, but was that something he'd want? And if he did want it, did he want it with her or someone else? He deserved to go find someone who could love him like he deserved.

You could love him like that.

Eric's soft voice floated on the breeze, and she turned her head, expecting to see him. The sound was so vivid and real.

Her heart didn't skip a beat at the idea of seeing or hearing him, though. When she thought of him, It did nothing but feel warm with a sad sort of peace.

A door banged open, drawing her gaze back to the cabin. Cindy stood on the porch, holding her belly. "Breakfast is ready. Y'all better come eat so we can head to the game."

Andy grabbed Owen and Mandy around the waist and lifted them both into the air, spinning in a circle and making them both squeal in laughter. When he set them down, the kids raced inside, and Andy grabbed Cindy's hand before she could follow them.

They kissed, their arms wrapping around each other as the door banged shut. Holly blushed but didn't look away. When they both pulled back, Cindy patted his cheek and smiled. It was a satisfied, happy smile, the smile of a woman who is exactly where she's supposed to be in life, with the person she's supposed to be with.

They went inside, and Holly turned back onto the path to walk slowly to the Williams' cabin. What if Maryanne was right, and she could have another chance at a happily ever after? Even if she could let go of Eric long enough to convince someone—she snorted, let's be honest, she wanted to convince Landry—to have an actual relationship, there was no guarantee. It could end in happiness like Cindy and Andy, but it could fall apart.

Eric was her first real boyfriend, the first man she'd slept with. Her handful of dates this year had shown her that she wasn't attracted to just anyone. Landry was different. It was so natural with him once, she'd let go of some of their rules and just went with the flow. It was only after she'd tried to stick to the rules that it had been weird.

Like last night when she'd arrived, she hadn't stopped to list all the rules they were breaking. He'd just swept her up in his arms and made love to her. She stumbled to a halt, seeing the cabin just ahead.

Had that been making love? It had been full of their normal hot and fiery, curl her toes passion. But he'd said... he'd said...

"Let me love you, angel." It bounced around her head, growing bigger and bigger until it felt like her whole body would explode.

It sounded like he was developing feelings for her, but that couldn't be it. He'd just missed her and wanted to show it physically, right? Right.

She resumed her walk and opened the door to the cabin, kicking her shoes off. He was still sprawled on his back asleep, even though he'd not stayed up late last night. She chuckled and crawled into bed with him, curling into his side as he wrapped an arm around her. She kissed his chest where her head lay, then flicked his nipple with her tongue.

He groaned, stirring slightly as she trailed her fingers across his chest and down his stomach. He'd tasted her last night, and she wanted to reciprocate. She leaned up, licking her lips and easing down the bed. He was still naked and in his semi-consciousness he already had an erection.

The Songwriter Gets His Girl

She rubbed the head then slid her hand down the shaft before leaning forward and licking the tip. She felt more than saw him suck in a breath, then she took it into her mouth.

It was musky but not unpleasant, and he swelled even more as she went down and back up so slowly. She nearly let it out of her mouth before sliding deep again, over and over. She felt his leg tense beside her, and she ran a hand up his thigh while the other worked him in time with her mouth.

His breath caught, and his hand fisted her ponytail. "Holly."

His gasp sent a shiver up her spine. There was such raw need behind that single word. He jerked on her hair, pulling her off his dick with a pop.

She glanced up into his hooded hazel eyes and followed as he slowly pulled her up his body. Together, they pulled her shorts down, and she sank onto his thick cock with a groan.

It was the best feeling in the world, to have him inside her. Her hips began to move, and he curled his big hands into them. She clenched at the feel of his hands and opened her eyes as she leaned over him.

Their eyes met as she panted. He thrust, never breaking eye contact. Their noises grew louder and louder until she jerked on top of him. Her orgasm took her by surprise, the convulsive waves gripping her tightly. When she spasmed around him, he groaned as he flooded her with his warmth.

It was like lightning inside her, touching every hidden recess as he pumped, gripping her hips before his muscles relaxed under her. He smiled a sleepy, satisfied smile, and it made the warmth spread through her core to her heart. She loved that she could make him happy like this.

They might not find a relationship or a happily ever after, but they had this. For now, that was all they needed.

"Good morning, princess. I've missed waking up to you like this." His gravelly voice made goosebumps pop up on her arms. It was soothing and exciting all at the same time.

She smiled and rolled onto her side, tucking her legs to keep some of his seed inside. He didn't turn to face her, instead hopping up to go to the bathroom. The shower turned on, and she sighed.

Maybe tonight they'd be able to cuddle after. She frowned, wondering when she'd thrown that rule out. She hopped out of bed and glanced at the floor with a frown, remembering why he was here this weekend. They were well-worn but didn't look bad.

She padded barefoot into the bathroom and joined him in the large shower on the far wall. There was also a jacuzzi tub in the middle of the room, with a toilet tucked between the tub and the shower. The sink was directly across from the bathroom door, and extra wide with two faucets in the one long bowl.

She slid the shower door to the side and joined him with a smile. He was already shampooing his hair.

"What's the plan for the day with the floors and the paint?" She needed to talk to take her mind off his glorious ass as he turned into the water. She trailed her fingers along the tattoos on his back, tracing an eagle and the flag.

"We need to paint today, then tomorrow we'll sand the floors. Should be ready to stain on Sunday before we leave. You might need to help me move some of the heavy furniture out of the way."

She nodded as they switched places under the spray of water, his hands circling her waist and sending sparks through her before he let go. Her body wanted to lean into him, but she reached her hands up and washed her hair instead.

"I can help lift stuff, but it's starting to look like rain outside. Where are we going to move it to?"

Landry shrugged. "We can load up my truck today with the couch, table, and chairs and move them to the barn. The bed will stay though, and we'll just have to do the best we can."

His hands settled on her hips again, and she rinsed out the last of the conditioner. Opening her eyes and wiping the water away, she met his hazel ones. They were light, the laugh lines prominent today. She cupped his cheek in her palm, and he turned to kiss it, the move reminding her of Cindy and Andy earlier. Could he grow to love her? Did the pounding of her heart mean she wanted him to?

He cleared his throat. "Thanks for helping with this project, angel. You're the best."

She smiled, then reached up on tip toe and kissed him. It was a sweet kiss, deep and long. It spoke more of promises than passion. He broke the kiss and bit her lower lip, making her pussy clench as she smiled.

With a quick kiss, he pulled back and stepped out of the shower, leaving her alone and suddenly cold without his arms around her. She turned the water hotter, taking her time as she soaped her body.

When she finally stepped out, he had breakfast on the table. Her brows rose as she picked up her spoon.

"Thanks for breakfast. This is my favorite."

He grinned and poured orange juice for them both. "I know, I remembered from Nashville. Coffee?"

She nodded, eating her blueberries, yogurt, and granola. He set a cup down in front of her, and she took a tentative sip of the dark brew.

She glanced at him under her lashes as he cleaned up their bowls and cups in the sink. His green t-shirt stretched over his back, pulling it tight. His khaki cargo shorts were stained and clearly his work clothes, but the way he wore them made her heart speed up.

Who knew a man's calves could be so sexy? Certainly not her. What was even sexier was how he'd remembered how she took her coffee. She saw the vanilla soy milk on the counter beside the fridge and coffee pot. He had to have brought that for her.

He remembered so many small details, things that had taken Eric and her years to learn about each other. She wasn't sure what that meant in the grand scheme of things, but she wasn't paralyzed in fear anymore. Her heart beat with need for a baby as much as with the need for him. The only question was if he wanted to see where this could go too.

Landry wiped his brow as they came back from the barn to an almost barren room. It was noon, but the air conditioner was working, and it was time to paint. They stretched out the plastic over the floors, which Holly taped down to the baseboards even as she questioned why if they were just going to re-do the floors anyway.

Landry shrugged and stretched his shoulders. "Yeah, I know we're just going to stain it tomorrow anyway, but there's no need to make a mess when we can get it done just as efficiently this way."

She laughed and threw her head back, mesmerizing him at her beauty. "You're such a stickler for messes. What are you going to do when you have kids someday?"

The Songwriter Gets His Girl

His heart raced and he gave her the side eye, but she was taping down the plastic and didn't see. In his mind, he saw half a dozen blond, green-eyed little kids running around as they tried to refinish the floors in another seven or eight years.

Sadness washed over him, as it was unlikely to happen, not unless she fell in love with him as he had with her. It'd taken him years to admit to himself he loved her. If it took her years too…

He pursed his lips and shook his head. "I'll teach them how to clean their messes up, that's what."

She laughed again, the sound soothing part of the frustration from his heart. He wanted to hear her laugh and have fun this weekend. He needed to hear it, see her joy, soak up her attention while he had it.

"Do you want kids, then?" Her voice was suddenly quiet, curious.

"Yeah, always have. I'll have half a dozen someday, I'm sure."

She sat up straight, her legs tucked under her from where she was taping the base boards. A frown marked her pretty face, making him glance away, unable to meet her confused eyes.

"Then why did you agree to this crazy scheme of mine for a baby? Why did you push to do this the all-natural way when I could've gone to the clinic?"

She sat there waiting while he climbed onto the ladder to tape the ceiling. When he finished taping that section and needed to move the ladder, he climbed down and looked at her.

"I don't know anymore," he said quietly. "All I know is that when you said you wanted a baby, the thought of you having one with anyone else curdled my stomach. If you want a baby, I'll provide. That's all I know for sure, all I know feels right."

He shrugged and moved the ladder to finish taping the ceiling. She was quiet, so he began to hum. When it was time to start painting, he turned on his phone's music app and started to sing along with it.

Chapter Forty-One

How do you make me want so much, make me live outside my normal?
How do you shake my world so much and make me think things so
carnal.

Two hours later, he'd finished the top half of the walls, and she was almost finished with the bottom half. He moved the ladder and caught her swiping a hand under her cheek.

With a frown, he knelt in front of her and reached for her chin, turning her face to him. Tears streaked her cheeks and melted his heart.

"What's wrong, angel?" He had to fix this, couldn't stand it when she cried.

She sniffed and waved to her phone sitting next to her. "I saw the date on my phone. It's the third anniversary of the car wreck today. The day I lost my baby girl and Eric. I didn't think the date would hit me this hard this year. I thought I was over most of the grief and only had to deal with this lingering emptiness. But I feel awful."

He sat on the floor and pulled her onto his lap, leaning against the wall. Her tears fell and she squeezed a fist into his shirt. He brushed her hair back, then the sobs broke. They wracked her body as she cried, asking in shuddering breaths why her baby had to leave. He just wrapped his arms around her and rocked.

A long time later, when her tears had turned to hiccups and soft, shuddering breaths, he sang softly to her with the radio as it played *Bless the Broken Road* by Rascal Flatts. It took everything in him to keep his voice steady and not cry for everything she'd lost.

When the song ended, he kissed the side of her head and cupped her face, holding her against his chest, trying to heal her with his love.

"I don't know why she couldn't stay, but I bet she's having a birthday party up in Heaven right about now. I bet your husband is taking good care of her right along with your mom and aunt."

She sniffed. "You think so?"

"Yep, did you name her?"

Her head shifted on his shirt. "Yeah, Neveah. It means heaven backward. She was so small."

"Just like you, tiny and practically perfect in every way. It's a beautiful name. Do you want to talk about that night?"

She was quiet for a few minutes before taking a deep breath. "Everything was going well with the pregnancy. There was a military ball to welcome them home from deployment. I'd gotten pregnant while Eric was home on mid-tour leave, then he went back to the Middle East. He'd been back for a month when we—"

She paused, the silence stretching as he rocked her. She took several deep, shuddering breaths before she could continue, every word making his heart break even more.

"Since I was the designated driver, I took some of his Army buddies home. We'd just dropped the last one off and were driving back. It was dark and had just started raining. Lost control and—and when I woke up, the paramedics were rolling me into the ambulance."

He kissed the side of her head, the pain in her voice ripping through him, leaving him raw.

"I—I had to deliver her at the hospital, after they told me Eric was gone. The doctors said the wreck did something, and it was the only shot I had to save her, but—but it didn't work. She had internal bleeding and only took a few breaths before she died in my arms. She was so tiny and beautiful."

Her voice trailed off, her tears soaking his shirt as more seeped out silently. His own tears fell into her hair, the knot in his throat preventing him from saying anything. And what could he say? Words would never take away the pain or help ease the burden of what she went through.

But he couldn't let her just drown in her sorrow and memories. He had to do something, anything, to help her. A few minutes later, after her tears had slowed and he just sat holding her, it hit him. He kissed her forehead.

"Come on. I have a surprise for you that I was going to save for later, but we could use a snack and a break." She pushed up from him to stand, and he joined her, his eyes going wide when he felt his shirt stick to the wall.

He stepped away and looked behind him, only to hear her giggle. The sound melted some of the tension, and he played up the problem to encourage her to smile.

"What the hell? How did this happen? Holly, is it bad or do you think the paint will wash out?" He turned to show her his back, which was completely covered in a pale blue paint.

She laughed and shook her head. "Yeah, that's not coming out at all. You should just toss it in the garbage."

He raised an eyebrow and smirked, stepping close to her and tapping her on her cute little button nose. "You just want me to finish painting shirtless, don't you?"

She grinned, tipping her head back to the perfect kissing angle. He pecked her lips gently and pulled away. It took everything in him to hold back, because she wasn't emotionally ready for another deep kiss.

"Maybe I do, maybe I don't. You won't know if you don't take that shirt off."

He chuckled, then pulled her by the hand to the fridge. "Maybe after we finish our snack. See? I brought a mini-cheesecake for dessert tonight, but we can eat it now. Grab some plates. We'll have to eat on the floor picnic style."

She laid a blanket in the middle of the room where the couch had been, then grabbed two waters, plates, and forks. He set the cake down and knelt beside it. When she joined him, he slid three candles onto the cake. Various sizes, they were emergency candles that were kept in a drawer. But hopefully it would work for the purpose.

She gasped, her hand going to her mouth, then her big green eyes met his after he lit them.

"She may be partying up in Heaven, but we can still sing happy birthday to her, right? If you want." He was suddenly nervous that it was too much, that it was insensitive or the wrong move.

But as fresh tears rolled down her cheeks she just nodded. "You sing," she rasped out.

He sang happy birthday, and when it came time to blow out the candles he said, "You make the wish and blow them out."

She did, and a tear dripped onto the cake. He ignored it

and plated a slice for each of them anyway. Their silence wasn't heavy, but peaceful, and he hoped she felt it too. He watched her as they ate and listened to the music. Her eyes were puffy, her nose was red, and she was still the most beautiful woman he'd ever met in real life.

But her shoulders weren't hunched anymore. She looked lighter and more relaxed, and some of the worry around his heart eased.

Holly washed the empty plates and forks, a sad smile on her lips as she glanced out the kitchen window above the sink. The rain had started, matching her mood as it grew overcast.

Her head knew being taken by surprise with today's date was part of moving on, but it had hurt like a swift kick to the head. Did the fact that she forgot make her a terrible mom? She frowned and scrubbed the plate harder.

The first anniversary, she'd stayed in her room, crying and watching sad movies all day. The second one, she'd tried to do the same thing, but Kendall had pushed her out to lunch, where she'd run into Lola and Maryanne. They'd all distracted her, then gone shopping.

Landry had honored her pain though, honored the loss and the heartache. Somehow, it had been a balance of solely focusing on the pain from year one and totally ignoring it in year two. Some of the pressure on her chest had eased with it.

She turned from the sink to find him holding his now ruined t-shirt up and shaking his head. She chuckled while he grumbled, barely heard over the sound of the rain outside.

"I can't believe I did that. I haven't made a mess this big since I was a kid."

She grinned and wrapped her arms around him from behind, kissing the eagle tattoo on his spine. "Oh, come on, have you forgotten the painting fiasco in my apartment? I'm honestly surprised you asked me to help."

He chuckled and squeezed her hand. "I guess I have to get messy every once in a while, just to keep life fun."

She grabbed his hand and pulled him to the front door. "Come on, I have an idea. Let's get dirty."

"I like the sound of that. I can get dirty with you all night long, angel."

She looked over her shoulder to see his eyes twinkling but when she threw the door open, he frowned and dug in his heels.

"What are we doing? It's raining. This isn't the kind of dirty I like to be."

She put her hands on her hips and shook her head. "This is part of the rules, to do something fun, right? Come play in the mud puddles with me, Lan."

She took off her shirt and tossed it on the rocking chair, not wanting to get it stained. Barefoot, she stepped down onto the grass and squealed, tipping her head up as the cold rain hit her skin. Her bra and shorts were soaked by the time she turned around to see Landry standing safely on the porch, his jaw slack and eyes wide.

She cupped her hands to catch some of the water and threatened to throw it on him, but he just waved his hands, his chest rippling with the movement.

"No, no, no. I—"

"There's that jacuzzi tub inside. We can take a long, hot bath right after this, if you just come join me."

She hoped bribing him with some naked time would

work, because this was the light-hearted fun they both needed.

The rain was coming down harder now, making her car barely visible as she spun in a slow circle, arms out wide and head tilted back. She felt hands circle her waist and pull her to a stop in front of him. He held her, only touching where his hands settled.

His eyes were green with golden flecks from the dim light, hazel with no blue anywhere. Water crested on his long lashes, and she wound her hands up his slick arms and around his neck. Her stomach clenched when it met his, the skin to skin contact burning like fire.

"How do you do this to me, angel?" His voice was raspy as they stood in the rain, blinking away water and staring into each other's eyes.

"Do what?" she whispered.

"Make me feel so much I think I might explode. Make me want so much more that it scares me. Make me..." His forehead wrinkled as he searched her eyes. Then he cracked a grin and pulled back, breaking the spell.

"Make me get out in the rain and jump in puddles." He laughed, then threw his hands wide and spun in a circle like she had.

Only the ground must have been a little wetter than before, because he slid. Arms flailing, she grabbed a hand, but it just made them both go down in the mud.

He groaned under her, and she pushed against him to sit up.

"Landry, my God, are you okay?"

He nodded, eyes closed as she climbed off him and to the side to run her hands over him.

"I'm fine. Just bruised from this rock that dug into my back, but all right other than that. Are you okay?"

She sighed and sat on her butt in the pooling water. "Yeah, I'm good." She slapped at the puddle, worried that he was hurt more than he was saying.

He pushed up to sit. "Well, this might not be jumping in puddles, but is it dirty enough for ya?"

She looked at him, smiling softly and caught his hand before he could stand up. He stopped, staring at her in the rain as they sat in the mud.

She took a deep breath, and bit her lip. "You make me want things too, Landry, things I have no right wanting."

A rough finger grazed her cheek, and he smiled. That one touch, that one look spoke to her of hope, patience, and acceptance.

"What things do you want, Holly?"

She swallowed past the lump in her throat. "I—I want a family."

He ran his thumb over her lip, making it quiver. Actually, her whole body was shaking now, whether from the rain or from the words she wasn't sure.

"You're going to get your baby, princess, don't worry about that." His eyes were sad as he dropped his hand and stood up, pulling her up carefully.

He didn't realize she meant a full family, not just a baby, but she was too chicken to clarify.

Chapter Forty-Two

Let me love you like you deserve. Let me worship you, kiss you, and provide. You're too stubborn for your own good. You won't give in to what others can't deny.

She ground her teeth to keep them from chattering as they walked up the porch and to the front door. He blocked it and lifted a brow at her.

"Strip. We're not going to drip all over the floor as much if we're naked." She grinned as he unzipped his shorts and shoved them down. His cock sprang free, drawing her gaze and making all other thoughts flee. The thought of being so bold outdoors wasn't as scary as she thought it'd be.

He chuckled, then pushed her own shorts down before wrapping his arms around her to unhook her bra. She breathed deeply, smelling the scent that was him mixing with the dirt, rain, and earth all around them. When he stepped back and they were both naked, she was even colder than before.

He grabbed her hand and went inside, straight to the bathroom where he drew a hot bath and turned on the shower too.

She frowned, rubbing her arms as she stood shifting from foot to foot. "Are you not getting in the bath with me?"

He arched a brow and opened the shower door to usher her in. "Yes, we are, but we have to wash all the mud off first. Otherwise, we're just sitting in mud and that's not going to get anyone clean."

She threw her head back and laughed, feeling tears roll down her cheeks. She laughed so hard her side hurt, while he just chuckled, grinned, and scrubbed his body. When she finally got under the warm spray, her laughter slowed.

"Only you would want to clean up before taking a bath, Landry."

He shrugged. "What can I say? I am who I am, and you'll have to take it or leave it."

They both froze, their eyes meeting before he sighed and stepped out. She scrubbed her hair yet again, trying to get all the mud out of it. Did he mean it? Did he want her to take him as he was, accept him and love him?

She turned off the water, her mind swirling with all the possibilities as she joined him in the tub. He'd somehow set up a few candles on the counter, and they flickered. She sat across from him, but he spun her around until she settled between his legs, her back to his front. He wrapped his arms around her and leaned back, bubbles frothing in the jets.

She sighed and leaned her head back onto his chest. She played with the bubbles absently, feeling the warmth spread through her as thunder boomed outside.

"Talk to me, angel. Tell me what's in that gorgeous head of yours." His voice reverberated through her body, making her nipples perk.

The Songwriter Gets His Girl

She smoothed bubbles over them. "I was thinking bad thoughts."

"Naughty bad thoughts, or bad bad thoughts?"

She shrugged. "Bad bad ones, not naughty ones. I was thinking that Eric and I never just sat and bathed together. We never showered together, either. I guess I was just shy, with him being the one and only person to ever see me naked."

"Why does thinking that make it bad?" His fingers splayed on her stomach, and she twitched, feeling his hardness digging into her back. She imagined him doing just this with her belly big with child.

Except, they wouldn't because they'd made an agreement. This wasn't a relationship.

But it could be.

She frowned. She'd much rather just turn around and ride him than have this conversation or keep thinking about him like this, but she was tired of keeping it all bottled up inside too. She felt so safe with his arms wrapped around her, like she could say what she wanted and it would be fine.

"Sometimes you do things, and it makes me feel fantastic. Not just sexual things, but sweet and thoughtful things. And I start to think Eric never did that or Eric would've never paid attention to that. It makes me feel awful because I loved him so much."

"I know you did, Holly, and he loved you too. I saw it on your faces, remember?"

She nodded. "We were good together. It was a good marriage, even if we were young and didn't communicate very well."

A peaceful silence fell, only the jets of the tub whirling. One of his hands caressed her arm slowly.

"The way you two looked at each other that night? That

was true love. My grandparents shared that look. My parents still do. Someday, I'll that for myself. I've looked and looked for someone to love—"

He cut off abruptly. She heard the silent 'but' at the end of his sentence and stilled, resting her hands on his knees in the water. She held her breath but had to release it slowly when he didn't continue.

The lights went out and the jets stopped churning. She moved forward as he stood up and grabbed a towel.

"Power went out. Must be the storm. You stay here while I go flip the breaker."

He walked naked into the main room, leaving her feeling more alone than normal. She closed her eyes, her mind at war with her heart.

He came back a few minutes later and stripped down, his teeth chattering.

"It's really coming down out there. Is the water still warm?"

She nodded and moved so he could sink back into the water, but then she turned and straddled him, wrapping her arms around his neck.

"There, this will warm you up." She purred in his ear, giving it a lick. She kissed her way down his neck. His hands cupped her ass, and he stood abruptly.

She squealed, wrapping her slippery legs around him and holding on as he carefully stepped out of the tub.

"Where are we going?"

He grabbed a towel and wrapped it around her back, then cupped her ass and carried her into the main room.

"It'll be warmer by the fire I started while I was gone. Plus, you know, the tub will wash all the swimmers away, and we wouldn't want it to go to waste. Again."

The barb stung even though he said it with a grin. She

sighed as he went to his knees on the blanket they'd laid out for their cake earlier, laying her on her back.

She grabbed his face in both hands and held him still. "Landry, I'm sorry for what I said that day, but why did it bother you so much?"

He settled between her legs, teasing her opening, resting most of his weight on his elbows as he searched her eyes.

"The truth? It made me feel like a stud for hire, good to you for only one thing." With that statement, he swiftly slid his cock inside.

She gasped, throwing her head back. "You're not—a horse."

He growled. "Fucking right I'm not. I'm so much more, angel. So. Much. More." He pressed in and out with every word, pushing her back onto the hard floor. He hit deeper, harder than ever before.

Her hands fell to his biceps, and she held on for dear life, trying to keep in place, planting her feet on the ground and widening her hips. The new angle made her groan.

"I can give you so much more than just a baby, princess." He slammed in faster, panting. Her mouth went slack, and her hands shook as she clawed him.

"I can give you the world—if you just let me—love you —like you—deserve."

He bucked wildly, and she screamed, convulsing around him as he continued to nail her to the floor with his hammer cock. Her spasms went on and on, never slowing, just wave after wave of bone-tingling orgasm rushing through her with every thrust.

His body tensed, and the hot blast inside began as he plunged deeper once, twice. He stilled as he flooded her, groaning, every muscle straining. She pulsed around him, his words bouncing around in her head like an echo.

His fingers brushed the hair away from her eyes, and he sat up slightly to look into her eyes. His were darker, the green barely visible in the multiple shades of brown.

Her body was sprawled limply under him, her hands barely holding onto his as she'd lost all will to move. Deep inside, she wondered if he meant it or if it was just the heat of the moment. Was it wrong of her to want him to mean it?

Landry stared into her green eyes, the darker ring on the outside of both, but the left one with the deep green dot in the bottom outside corner drawing his eye as always. It was now or never. He couldn't hold back any longer.

He shuddered in a shaky breath and cupped her face.

"You want a family, but a family is so much more than just having a baby, Holly. A family full of love has cousins, aunts and uncles, grandparents. A family doesn't leave you lonely and aching for connection and acceptance at the end of the night. A family already has those things."

He saw tears crest her eyes, and he wiped his thumbs to sweep the moisture away into her hair. Her lip trembled.

He took another breath, feeling himself slide out but for once not caring about the cleanup, his mind totally focused on this moment.

"You want a family, but what about a dad, husband, lover, friend? I've looked for someone to love, but what I didn't realize until yesterday was I'd already found her."

Her eyes widened, more tears spilling out.

"I want to be with you, Holly. I want to wake up with your kisses every morning. I want to be there to feel the baby kick, to be there to welcome him into the world. I want to see you smile, hear you talk and laugh every day. The past month without seeing you? Angel, it nearly killed me. I've not felt that lost since my grandpa died."

She licked her lips and whispered, "What are you saying?"

"I'm saying I want to have a real relationship with you. I want to be by your side every day and hold you every night. I want to be your family, angel. Now and forever."

She pushed against his chest, and he sat up. He grabbed a napkin leftover from their snack earlier and handed it to her. She ignored it and jumped up, pacing before the fireplace in all her naked glory.

He cleaned himself off and watched her, a weight descending on his chest with every step she made. When a man declared himself to a woman, she wasn't supposed to think it over. She was supposed to know how she felt and love him back. A sense of dread settled through him.

He'd known she wouldn't love him though, hadn't he? He'd known she wasn't ready, would never be ready. His stomach roiled, and a sour taste filled his mouth.

She waved her hands wide as she spun on her heel to walk the other direction.

"This—we can't—Landry, what happens if we start a relationship, and it doesn't work out? If we spend months or even years raising a baby, only to drift apart or for something to—to happen. There's no guarantee that this would work out."

He stood up and crossed his arms, frowning. "So you're not even going to try? Just because something happened with Eric doesn't mean it would with me. We could spend the next sixty years together, happy and healthy."

"Or you could leave me like everyone else."

His heart softened, and he reached out to grab her

hand, pulling her into a hug before the roaring fire. Her body was stiff in his arms, unrelenting, scared. "The only way I'd leave you, angel, is if you made me. I want to be with you, but the only one keeping us apart is you."

She jerked back, leaving his arms feeling bereft and empty. She stopped and stared at the fire, crossing her arms and cocking one succulent hip.

"I'm so scared, Lan. If we start a relationship, and it doesn't work out later, it would be you, me, and the baby getting hurt. Your family would hate me, our friends would have to pick sides… No, this way is better so less people get hurt."

He tipped his chin up and clenched his fists, staring at her rigid back. "You're not even going to try? Take a chance on us? On love?"

Her shoulders hunched, and she shook her head side to side. He sighed, raking a hand down his face.

Maybe some food would settle the gnawing pit in his stomach. He spun on his heel, grabbed his shorts and jerked them on. If that's how she wanted it, then that's how it would be. He couldn't force her to love him, accept him.

A cold numbness washed through him as he turned to the kitchen and pulled out something that could be cooked over the open fire.

"Well, we can heat the vegetarian casserole in the fire. Have you ever cooked over an open flame? If it's on your bucket list, tonight's the night we'll cross it off."

He kept up a steady stream of chatter while he moved around the space, pulling the grate down from the side of the fireplace and placing the glass dish on top. He talked about how he and his grandpa had finished the floors four years ago, how they added on the bathroom when he was in high school. He talked about each of his brothers, his parents.

When he plated up the food, she was clothed, and they sat in silence on opposite sides of the blanket. His head felt like it was spinning, and all energy had been sapped from his body.

He stood on shaky legs and took his plate to the sink. It clattered into the bin, and he turned to see Holly's green gaze staring at him. He rubbed the back of his neck, his hand coming away wet and clammy.

"I—I think I'll brush my teeth and lay down. If the power's not back on tomorrow, we might not do the floors."

He felt like he was talking around a cotton ball, so he grabbed some water and drank while he walked to the bathroom. Looking at his reflection in the mirror, his eyes glassy and already hollow looking. He felt like shit, like he had right after he'd lost his grandparents.

He had been wrong. The past month without her hadn't felt this horrible. This was so much worse.

Chapter Forty-Three

My body burns for you. Your touch lights a wildfire that nothing can quench but your love, your love, your love.

The storm eased in the early morning hours. Holly knew because she was still awake. This time, she was the one who'd stayed up late, her mind not turning off long enough to find deep sleep.

Actually, her mind was at war with her heart. Part of her jumped at the idea of starting a relationship with Landry, but the other side was scared. Scared of being left, abandoned, and alone.

A distant boom of thunder sounded, and she turned over to snuggle up to Landry's side. She put her hand on his chest and frowned. Sitting up, she ran her hand over his forehead. He was burning up, most of the covers wrapped around his legs.

She scrambled out of bed and raced to the bathroom, but the lights were still not working. She went back to the

The Songwriter Gets His Girl

bed and grabbed her phone, turning on the flashlight to look under the bathroom and kitchen sinks. She finally found a forehead thermometer and sat back on the bed beside him.

She winced as she stood up and went to her purse. Over 101. She rummaged around and found her peppermint oil roller, hoping it would break his fever like she'd always done. She rolled it under his ears, causing him to roll over and hug a pillow. She pulled the blankets up over him, then stoked up the fire.

Some packets of oatmeal were in the lone cabinet that doubled as a pantry. She ate the last of the blueberries while the water heated on the fire. Landry turned back over on the bed, but she knew he'd sleep for another few hours. Hopefully, his fever would break by then.

A few hours later, she had cleaned up her breakfast, set out food for him, and completely painted the second coat on all the walls. She took his temperature again, but it was holding steady with no change. The sun was peeking through the clouds and the rain finally stopped, but the power was still out.

A groan sounded from the bed as she was finishing the second coat with the brush on the corners. She knelt beside the bed and felt his forehead again, then took his temperature and rolled on the peppermint.

He rolled onto his side, and his hazel eyes blinked open.

"Good morning, sleepy head. How are you feeling?"

"Like death warmed over." His raspy voice caused her to jump up and grab a bottle of water. He propped up on one elbow and drank almost half before handing it to her and falling onto his back.

"I bet you do, since you've had a fever all morning. Now

that you're awake, let's get you in the shower to break the fever, okay?"

He moaned, and she pulled back the covers while he got up. He walked stiffly to the shower, and she used her phone flashlight to light the way. While he turned on the water, she lit the candles from last night. When she turned back, he was sitting on the shower floor with the water washing over him.

She felt the water and almost burned her hand, then turned it cooler.

"What, no, turn it back. I'm cold."

She shook her head. "No, we have to break the fever. I'm going to go stoke the fire and heat your breakfast. I'll be right back."

"I don't want to eat. I'm not hungry."

"We'll see." She walked back into the main room and warmed his breakfast in the fire. When he stumbled into the room, she eased him back onto the bed and covered him up. He was shaking now, and she set a bottle of water and warm bowl of oatmeal next to him while she took his temperature.

She frowned. It'd gone up, not down. "How are you feeling?"

"Whole body hurts. Joints are stiff. Tired, hot and cold at the same time."

She nodded, then glanced at her phone to call Kendall, but it was dead now. She hadn't been able to charge it overnight. She picked up the spoon and fed him a bite of oatmeal.

He crossed his arms and leaned back against the headboard. "I have a fever. I'm not an invalid. I can feed myself, woman."

She chuckled and handed him the bowl, then stood up

The Songwriter Gets His Girl

to gather the paint brushes and rinse them out in the kitchen sink.

"You finished the second coat on all the walls?" She nodded and kept washing. "It looks good. Thank you. Did the power come back on?"

She shook her head and washed the roller brush.

"I think we'll call it a day then and head home early. Can't do the floors without the power, and I feel like shit. We'll clean up what we can, then leave. What time is it?"

She glanced at the clock above the front door. "Almost noon."

His phone rang. He reached under the bed to where it lay and answered it.

"Hello... oh hey, how's it going... you're kidding, right... I don't know... yes, I know it's a big opportunity, but I have things to sort out." His eyes met hers, then he glanced away. "Yeah, something like that. Can I call you back tomorrow with my answer... okay, talk to you then. Bye."

He stood and brought the empty bowl to the sink. His gait was shaky but solid. He leaned against the cabinet and crossed his arms and ankles while she finished washing his bowl.

"Who was that?"

"Mike, from Nashville. He says hi, by the way."

"What'd he want? You said there was a big opportunity?"

Landry shrugged and turned to his bag, throwing his stuff back into it haphazardly. She frowned, knowing how he'd packed in Nashville so meticulously, everything neat and folded. He must really be feeling crummy today, for him to not even look at his bag while stuffing it.

"He said there was a cancellation with Carter Kennedy's tour. The pre-show needs a new act, and after a few weeks of my two new songs climbing the charts, Mike's negotiated to get me the spot."

"Wait, what does that mean?"

He sat on the bed and shook his head, his eyes raised. "I don't know for sure, other than the tour starts next week and goes almost through the end of the year. It'll be more publicity, playing concerts a few nights a week."

"And you'll be on the road the whole time? What's your mom going to say about you missing the annual Halloween party, Thanksgiving, and Christmas?"

He frowned and nodded. "Yeah, that's a good point. I'll have to ask Mike about that, if I take it."

"If you take it?" She walked over and knelt in front of him, taking his hot hands in her own and rubbing them. She stared up at his hazel eyes, brighter than normal with the fever.

"Landry, you have to take it. Mike's right, this is a great opportunity. Life is throwing a good thing at you, and you need to take it."

He blinked, pulled his hand out and cupped her cheek. "But the only good thing I want is you, angel."

She felt her heart stutter, and she kissed his hand before smiling softly. "I know, but I'm scared, Lan. I don't know if I can do what you want, be who you want."

His hand dropped and he shrugged. "You already are, angel. You just won't admit it. Now come on. Let's get packed up and headed home."

He stood and weaved, putting one hand on his head and the other going straight out to help find his balance. She hopped up from the floor and grabbed his waist to steady him.

"Landry, I think you're getting worse. Just lay down for a

The Songwriter Gets His Girl

little while longer, and I'll get everything cleaned up, alright?"

He nodded, his eyes distant as he climbed back under the covers. His whole body was shaking, and she put his duffel bag over his feet to warm them. She raced out to his truck and found the extra blanket he had stored under the seat.

After he was tucked in and she'd added more wood to the fire, she glanced around. There wasn't really anything left to clean up but her own stuff. That barely took five minutes, so she checked his temperature again.

He was sound asleep now, his body still shaking. Her heart skipped a beat when she saw his temperature was almost to 104. She bit her lip, leaned down and kissed his cheek.

She grabbed his phone but couldn't get it unlocked to call anyone. She wanted to call her brother, but if she couldn't, Cindy was right next door. Surely, Cindy and Andy would keep the news that she was here with him a secret. And they'd help, since Cindy was a nurse, and Andy was his best friend.

So she slipped on her shoes and strode out the door and through the forest. Her stomach was twisted in knots, and a headache was forming behind her eyes. When she came to Cindy and Andy's house, she twisted her hands.

This was what Landry needed, and it didn't really matter that letting them into their arrangement could make the whole farce blow up in her face.

With a solid knock on the door, the noise inside quieted down. Then the door opened to Andy's surprised face.

"Holly? What are you doing here?" He glanced behind her and frowned. "How did you get here?"

Cindy peered behind Andy, and she put a hand on his

arm. "Holly, what a pleasant surprise. Would you like some lunch? We just sat down but there's plenty."

Holly shook her head and thrust her hands into her pockets as she shifted on her feet. "No, thank you. I was wondering if you had anything to bring down a fever?"

Cindy frowned, grabbed Holly's hand and pulled her into the house. The kids were eating, watching intently as the adults talked. Cindy felt Holly's cheek but Holly just pulled away.

"No, not me. It—it's Landry. He's at his parents' cabin, and he had a fever early this morning after we were caught in the rain last night. It stayed steady at 101, then climbed to 104 after he got up, showered, and ate brunch. He's shaky, weak, and just fell back to sleep for a nap, but I'm worried. Do you have anything to help?"

Cindy's eyes had widened with every word until she looked like a cartoon character. Holly shifted on her feet and glanced between her and Andy, who was scowling. Then he spun on his heels and went to the kitchen, coming back with Pedialyte.

"We have this. It helps with fever and we keep it on hand for the kids just in case."

Cindy seemed to snap out of her surprise, and she raced down the hall as quickly as she could with her pregnant belly. Holly wiped her sweaty hands on her pants, then took the jug of juice from Andy.

"Thanks, I appreciate it."

"No problem. You'll be lucky if you leave without Cindy going with you."

Cindy came back down the hall, her arms full of a first aid kit. Andy took it from her as she arched a brow. "Of course I'm going with her. It'll help her worry less if I do. Heck, it'll help me worry less too."

The Songwriter Gets His Girl

Andy simply nodded, then turned back to the kids at the table. "Cody, you're in charge. Y'all finish eating, then put on that new movie Mandy and Owen wanted to watch while you and James do the dishes. If we're not back in half an hour, I'll call Aunt Suzie to come over. Sound good?"

All the kids nodded in unison, then Mandy and Owen began to whisper about their movie.

Cindy pointed a finger at them. "If you don't listen to Cody or if something happens that shouldn't, there will be no fall camp out this year, do you understand?"

"Yes ma'am," James and Cody said while the littler ones' eyes widened. They shook their heads again, and Andy and Cindy slipped on their shoes.

Holly held the jug of juice and tried to walk as slowly as Cindy needed to go, but she wanted to bound through the forest and get back to his side.

They had barely stepped off the porch and past their vehicles when Cindy said, "Okay, now tell me the rest of the story. What are you doing at the cabin with Landry? Maryanne said you were going to the in vitro place this weekend."

Holly sighed and hunched her shoulders. "Yeah, I haven't been going to the in vitro place. I've been meeting with Landry."

"Are you guys together? I haven't heard anything." Andy took Cindy's elbow and helped her over the wet and muddy ground.

"No, we're not together. And you can't tell anyone. Well, Lola and Maryanne know, but other than that, keep it quiet. Landry volunteered to help me get pregnant, and that's all. We're not together."

Even though you want to be.

She rubbed her forehead. "It's complicated."

Chapter Forty-Four

Family is stronger than steel. Our love holds through all life's sorrows. With you by my side, I'm not lost in the big ole family back home

Holly slowed her steps again to match Cindy's waddling ones. They broke through the trees and rounded the back of the cabin. Holly stumbled to a halt to see another truck behind her car.

"Ah, the pieces are falling into place," Ava, Landry's mom, said from the front porch, her hands on her hips and her hair pulled up in a fancy bun on her head.

Holly gulped and blinked, her feet continuing to take her to the front door. "What—what are you doing here?"

Ava shrugged. "When Landry didn't show up for church this morning, I decided to come check on him. Hunter tried to stop me, but I wouldn't listen."

Hunter stood leaning against the wall, his arms and ankles crossed much like Landry had this morning. The two looked so similar it was almost spooky, and her brows rose as she met his eyes.

"Sorry, Holly. I saw your car driving down the path a few days ago. I was checking some fences, so I rode over, saw you get out of your car and how Lan met you. But Ma wouldn't listen when I told her to leave him alone today."

Ava waved at Hunter. "You hush. I'm glad I came over to read him the riot act, or I wouldn't have known he was sick."

Holly blinked as Ava glared at her. "I—my phone died because the storm knocked the power out. So I went to get Cindy to see if she could help."

Cindy pushed past them all and through the door of the cabin. Landry snored softly on the bed, the covers twisted around his waist once more as he hugged a pillow on his side, thankfully in his silk basketball shorts. Holly followed behind her, ignoring the others as they came inside. Cindy touched his forehead, then pulled out her own thermometer. Holly wrung her hands until Cindy tried to put the thermometer under his tongue.

He groaned and rolled onto his other side, away from her. Holly walked around to the other side of the bed and sat down, running her hand over his shoulder and pulling the blanket up. "Sh, it's alright, Lan, we just need to take your temperature."

Cindy handed her the thermometer. "Here, you put this under his tongue, and I'll take his blood pressure."

She took the thermometer and ignored the gazes of everyone staring at her. All that mattered right now was figuring out how to help Landry. The rest could wait. She'd delay facing the truth with his mom for as long as possible.

"You hear me, Lan? Open your mouth." She teased his lips with the tip of the thermometer, and he gave a delirious grin, his eyes opening and catching her gaze, his glassy with fever.

"Only if you open up for me, angel."

She rolled her eyes and eased the thermometer under his tongue, while Hunter and Andy chuckled behind her.

"Aw, he calls her angel. Isn't that adorable?" Ava sighed, the excitement clear in her voice.

Hunter snorted. "Ma, don't get your hopes up. This might not be what you want."

Holly felt her cheeks burn as the thermometer beeped.

Landry frowned, turning onto his back and sitting up on an elbow. "Mom? What are you doing here?"

Ava arched a brow and came closer to the bed, standing behind Holly. "You didn't show up for church this morning, so I got worried."

He groaned and fell back onto the bed. "This is not how I like waking up from a nap."

Cindy chuckled, pulling the blood pressure cuff off and taking the thermometer from Holly. "Well, it's a good thing we're here, because Holly was right. Your fever is way too high. It's 103 now, so it might be going down. You got caught in the rain last night?"

Holly felt her cheeks burn again as he looked at her out of the side of his eyes and smirked. "Yeah, something like that. I slipped in the mud and fell onto my back."

Cindy frowned and nodded. "Alright, roll to your side, and let me see."

He rolled toward Holly and wrapped an arm around her waist where she sat on the bed. She pushed the sweaty hair off his forehead, and he glanced up at her. She wanted to take care of him, protect him, make sure he didn't get sick like this again. It was nerve-wracking, to see him so miserable and not be able to do anything about it.

The Songwriter Gets His Girl

"Hm, there's a big bruise, but I don't think you punctured it or got any parasites from the mud. I think this is just a case of getting chilled from being in the rain. It should be a twenty-four hour thing, but you can go to the hospital or call Kendall if you'd like."

Holly's eyes widened while Landry rolled onto his back and sat up to look around at everyone. "You're kidding, right? It's just a fever. I'll be fine with some water, rest, soup, and maybe some Tylenol or Ibuprofen or something."

Cindy nodded. "I agree, but I had to ask anyway. I brought some meds, if you'd like them. We have to get back to the kids, since they're at the house by themselves. Do you need anything else?"

Landry shook his head, and Holly smiled at her.

"Thanks for coming to look him over, Cindy. I appreciate it. Swing by the studio this week, and I'll give you a free massage, okay?"

Cindy perked up and nodded with a smile. "Sounds good to me. Drink all this Pedialyte too, alright?" She handed him the drink along with some cold medicine.

"Will do. Thanks for stopping by, guys." Landry raised the drink in a half toast, then downed the medicine and drink.

Andy arched a brow and put his hand on Cindy's back as they turned to the door. "I'll text you, Landry. We'll get together sometime this week to catch up."

Landry sighed and rolled his eyes. "Fine, see you later."

When they left, Hunter cleared his throat. "I'm sorry to say this, but when we drove out this way, we almost got stuck a few times. There's no way Holly's car will make it back to town in all this mud. It'll need to stay here until it dries up a bit."

Landry ran a hand over his face and groaned. "I hadn't

thought of that, but it'll be alright. I'll bring her back to get her car when it's dry. Thanks, Hunter."

Hunter nodded, then glanced at their mom. "Ma? You coming?"

Ava crossed her arms and shook her head. "Nope, I want to hear what this is all about."

Holly's shoulders fell, and she met Landry's gaze.

Landry leaned back against the headboard and crossed his arms. His head was pounding, and he was both hot and cold at the same time. With a foggy brain, he couldn't think, but he had to do damage control with his mom before she railroaded Holly into something Holly didn't want.

He clenched his jaw. "Mom, not now. We can discuss it later, but all you need to know is Holly had a problem and I volunteered to solve it."

Ava snorted. "A problem? You call wanting to get pregnant a problem?"

Holly started to stand, but he reached over and grabbed her hand, keeping her on the bed beside him. He locked their fingers together, but she opened her mouth and met his gaze with a worried one of her own. He didn't give Holly a chance to argue.

"No, it wasn't a problem. She wants a family, and I'm going to give her one. This is between her and me, Mom."

"No, it's not, because if y'all are going to have a baby, that's going to be *my* grandchild. Maybe even grandchildren if she has twins. Are you going to keep grandkids from me?"

Holly threw off his hand and stood, her hands held palms up to placate his mom. "No, of course not. Well, actually I didn't think about it affecting you at all, but that's

The Songwriter Gets His Girl

just because Landry and I had a contract. It clearly stated that once I got pregnant, he was free to go back to his regular life, doing whatever he wanted to. No one else was supposed to know."

"But we know now." His mom said, crossing her arms and tapping a boot-covered foot. "Amend that contract if you must, but you're not keeping my grand baby from me. He's going to be at Christmases and family holidays, reunions and monthly Sunday dinners. And if he's going to be there, I assume you will too. So you two need to work on what story you're going to tell everyone, because I guarantee they're going to have questions when I'm there at the birth and helping at home when you're discharged from the hospital and—"

"I'm not giving birth in the hospital." Holly interjected, tilting her head. "This is my baby, and I'm going to use a midwife and deliver at home."

"In your tiny apartment?" His mom frowned, as Hunter placed his hands on her shoulders from behind, his eyes meeting Landry's.

Hunter smiled and leaned to the side. "Come on, Ma. Let's leave these two to iron out the details on all that. It sounds like they were trying to keep it a secret, and now the cat's out of the bag, they need time to redefine their relationship and figure out all those details."

The word echoed in Landry's head, causing his heart to race because he wanted a relationship with her. He wiped his hands on the blankets. "Maybe give us a few days, if you don't mind, so I can get over this fever and think more clearly."

His mom turned her fierce gaze on him, her brown eyes meeting his own. He knew she was worried, but there was nothing she could do right now. She pursed her lips and nodded curtly, relaxing slightly as Hunter kneaded her shoulders.

"I need more than a few days. This is my entire life's plan changing." Holly sounded panicked as she crossed her arms around her stomach and hunched her shoulders. She turned to stare out the window.

"Fine, I can be reasonable. When you announce your pregnancy, you both come tell me first, along with your plan on how to raise this baby and let me love him the way a grandmother wants. Deal?"

Landry nodded. "Fine with me, as long as you both keep quiet in the meantime. Holly?"

He stared at Holly's back, and she nodded without turning around. Then he looked at his mom, and her eyes turned questioningly.

He shook his head, and she mouthed, "Later." He nodded and turned in Hunter's arms to leave.

"I'll check on you later tonight to see if your fever has broken." His mom waved and went through the door.

Hunter grabbed the door but said, "I'll flip the breakers out here and see if the power will come back on before we leave. Later." He shut the door behind them, leaving him with Holly in the now silent and still room.

Chapter Forty-Five

*Butterflies in my stomach bricks on my chest. With you, I'm not myself,
I'm better, better than all the rest*

He sighed a huge breath of relief and leaned his head back with his eyes closed. "Sorry, angel, I didn't expect any of that to happen."

"It's not your fault, Landry." Her voice was small and defeated, the sound making his heart ache along with his head. "I was worried, so I went for Cindy's help. I—I knew there could be consequences to that."

"I'm sorry about my mom. It was one thing to keep the baby from her when she didn't know, but it might break her heart if you keep her from him now."

Holly spun around and slapped her hands on her hips, her face pinched and angry. "I'm not keeping her from my baby."

"Then why are you angry?"

He didn't understand women. He'd expected her to be

worried about gossip but wasn't sure how to interpret her anger. She started to pace from the window to the end of the bed and back again.

"I'm angry because this should be a simple thing. I'm angry because my plans aren't working out. I'm angry because I didn't get pregnant in Nashville which could've avoided this entire disaster of a weekend. I'm angry because your mom has so much love that even when she was surprised and pushing us, I could still hear the excitement in her voice. I'm angry because my own mom isn't here to help me with all this. I'm angry because it's easier than being scared."

He rubbed his forehead. "Wait, why are you scared?"

She stopped by the bed and stared at him, her eyes narrowed. "I'm scared because this was going to be easier to do on my own. Now all these people know and are going to be involved. It's no longer just me and my baby against the world."

Landry reached forward and grabbed her hand, his thumb running over the back of it.

"You were never going to be alone. The whole town stands behind you, even in this, because they love you. Now my family becomes yours. Even if you won't let me love you, take care of you, be there when all the pregnancy stuff happens, you'll still have the support and love of my family and friends on top of your own."

She shook her head, pulling her hand out and making his heart hurt. "And I appreciate it, but it's just—"

"Just what, Holly?"

She shrugged and turned away. "Love leaves. People die, and the only one you can rely on is yourself. While it'll be nice to have all that support, but I can't depend on it."

His stomach lurched and he breathed deeply through his nose. "You're still going to do this on your own, then?"

She nodded, turning once more to the window. The faint light from the sun shone down on her golden honey hair, calling out to him. He shuffled off the bed, feeling every joint in his body ache as he walked toward her. He wrapped his arms around her waist and pulled her back against him, and they both looked outside at the hay field.

She sighed. "I have to do this on my own, Landry."

He kissed the top of her forehead and closed his eyes, his heart breaking at the rejection. He needed to get home to his own bed, where he could curl up and feel miserable with no one else messing with his life.

He stepped away and sighed, reaching for the bedding on the mattress to strip it. It'd need to be washed, and he'd bring it back later this week when he came to do the floors.

"Fine, if that's what you want, then we tell people the truth. You wanted a baby, I volunteered. The only thing that needs to change is that now I'll get to be a dad. Oh shit, now I get to be a dad."

He sat down hard on the bed, the pile of blankets and sheets next to him in a big ball. His heart sped up and the light from the window shone on him, picking him up and giving him a ray of hope.

This baby may be the only one he'd ever get, because he wouldn't be able to find another love like her. He'd tried to replace her in his mind and heart for five years since he'd first met her, but no one had ever measured up. It had been lust and the idea of missing out, but now that he knew her, the real her?

He loved her and there was no one else in the world who could ever take her place. He knew how she felt about Eric because that's how he felt about her. He might never have her love in return, but they could share this baby together.

He'd be able to take his baby to church and see him in the Christmas program, teach him how to play baseball and ride a horse and swim. He'd be able to do all the things he'd always imagined doing with his brood of kids. Only, this would be his only one, his only child.

"He's going to be more loved than George Strait at a country festival." Landry chuckled, then laughed, the action making his head hurt even worse. He put his head in his hands and pressed on it, but it didn't help.

"What do you mean, you get to be a dad?"

He glanced at Holly and slipped on his shoes and a t-shirt before gathering the blankets to take them to his truck outside. "Do you agree that the baby will be at all the places my mom rattled off earlier?"

She followed him with her bag. He opened the door and eased the blankets under the seat while she tossed her bag into the bed of the truck.

"Yes, I already agreed to that with her, and I won't go back on my word. Unless it's that stupid contract we made and broke."

He grinned, then went back inside to pack the groceries and dishes he'd brought back into the box he'd slid behind the fridge.

"Well, in that case I'll get to spend time with him. He'll call my parents Memaw and Papa, and I'll be Dad." He grinned and met her eyes. "Isn't that fantastic? I'll get to take him fishing and teach him how to play the guitar."

He finished packing the stuff up and turned to find her standing with her arms crossed, legs spread. He wanted to ease the frown on her face, so he gathered her into his arms and slowly danced her around the space.

The Songwriter Gets His Girl

"Landry, this is going to be so much harder."

"I'm already so much harder, angel," he growled in her ear, pressing his groin to hers as they danced.

She pulled her head back and gave him that look that women seem to master from a special age, but it just made him grin and wiggle his eyebrows.

"We need to meet to go over a new contract on how we're going to raise this kid, Landry."

He sighed and released her to pick up his bag and the box of food. She opened the door for him to go through as he said, "I know we do, but right now, my head is killing me, and I just want to get home, okay?"

She opened the truck door, and he placed the food in the middle of the bench seat.

"Fine, but I'll drive. Let me take your temperature before we leave. I want to see if those pills are helping or not."

She slapped something onto his forehead and held him still. Her eyes were emerald green in the light, that darker ring around the edges drawing him in. He leaned forward and kissed her cheek, changing directions at the last minute. He didn't want to get sick germs on her by kissing on the mouth, even if her lips called to him.

"It's only 100 now. It's going down." The relief in her voice made him smile, and he released her waist to go look through the cabin one more time before they left. When he came out, he found her in the driver's seat with the truck running.

His brows raised as he got into the passenger side. "You know how to drive a stick shift?"

She nodded and frowned. "Yeah, my aunt had a stick shift. It wasn't a truck but this one is still smaller than Lola's. I can handle it."

He buckled up and they slid a little in the field before getting onto the muddy dirt road, but that was to be expected. When they got to his house, he frowned and looked around. He might have dozed off on the ride but would never admit it.

"Holly, we need to take you home first."

She shook her head. "No, I'm going to stay until your fever breaks, then I'll go home. Come on, Lan. Let's get you inside."

He opened his door, forgetting about the buckle until he went to get out and it caught him. He frowned, feeling like he was moving through molasses as he unbuckled and practically fell out of the truck.

She was there to catch him, and he wrapped an arm around her shoulders. Her hand around his waist, her tiny fingers dug into his t-shirt and made him feel loved. It was like they were walking into their future together, side by side.

But he knew it wouldn't last.

She opened the door, finding it unlocked as Parker watched football in the living room. He glanced behind him, his eyes widening as he took in the two of them.

"Well, I didn't believe Hunter when he called but it looks like it's true. Is he really sick?"

Holly nodded, and Landry frowned. "I'm right here. You don't have to talk about me like I'm not."

Parker and Holly shared a smile that made Landry's eyes narrow. Parker stood up and waved down the hall as they walked.

"His royal pain in the ass can show you where his room is. I'll get the stuff out of the truck."

"Thanks, Parker." Holly's voice was singsong sweet, making Landry clench his jaw as they walked to his room.

As always, it was spotless. He pulled back the cool sheets, and he kicked off his shoes, frowning because he didn't kick them off by the door.

He shoved his shorts down and tossed his t-shirt off, then climbed into bed in just his boxer briefs. Holly went to the window and drew the curtains, then grabbed his spare blanket off the back of the bed frame.

She tucked him in, and he sighed. Mumbling he said, "I like you taking care of me. I'd put up with a pounding headache every day if you'd take care of me just like this."

"Shh, just rest while I make some soup. I'll be right back."

She grabbed the clothes he'd tossed off and left the room, closing the door softly behind her. Parker had dropped all their things into the living room floor, and he was back in front of the TV.

She found the hall door that opened to the washer and dryer, then started a load of his dirty clothes and the sheets before exploring the kitchen. The pantry was organized almost as much as Kendall's, which made her smile. It felt a little like home to see it, and she quickly found the cans of soup and box of crackers.

She set them on the stove, then found her phone charger and set her phone to charge in the kitchen while she waited for the soup to heat. She moved their bags into Landry's room, catching him snoring softly as she tiptoed in.

When the soup was done, she set it to warm, grabbed some water, and joined Parker in the living room. He glanced up at her as she sat in a recliner.

"So." He arched a brow.

She sighed, shaking her head. "Don't you start too."

He grinned, the same quirky tilt to his lips as Landry, but he didn't make her heart speed up at all.

"I didn't say anything yet. But you know, this makes an odd sort of sense."

She tilted her head and curled up in the chair. "How so?"

"You and I had no chemistry. Sure, we flirted, but that kiss we shared was like kissing my sister. And now you will be!"

She choked on her water, spewing it all over her shirt. She burped, choked some more, then finally took another drink to clear it all out. When she finally got herself together, she rasped out, "What the hell is that supposed to mean?"

He grinned and wiggled his eyebrows. "Hunter says Mom already has you two married with a dozen babies in her head. Is that not where this is headed?"

She waved her hands furiously. "No, absolutely not. I was already married once before, remember? To the—"

"Love of your life, yeah, I remember. But Holly, what if you get two loves? Or hell, even three? When I was growing up, there was a widow in our church who'd been married five times, and she always said she'd loved them all equally."

She sucked in a breath and took another drink of her water. Maryanne had said much the same thing, but that didn't mean that she could just choose to love Landry. Love wasn't a choice. It either was there or it wasn't.

Like with her and Parker. She loved him like a friend, but definitely not how she loved Landry.

She froze. Blinked. Slowly lowered her water. Blinked.

She loved Landry? But how did this happen? She couldn't. She loved Eric.

The washer dinged, and she got up to start another load, putting the first one in the dryer. She checked on Landry and brushed his sweaty hair off his forehead. He felt cooler, but still warm. She pulled the thermometer out of her pocket and took his temperature. Still 100, but lower than before they'd left the cabin.

She breathed a sigh of relief because it was just a twenty-four-hour bug, a fluke. It had to be. He was going to be alright.

But would she?

Was loving Landry the betrayal of Eric she'd thought it'd be? Now that she was here, staring at him, caring for him, admitting she loved him... it didn't seem so. She was nostalgic and sad about Eric, but he would want her to be happy for however long she had left in this world.

Landry made her happy. He made her laugh, try new things, and accepted her the way she was, flaws and all. He pushed her beyond her comfort zone but always accepted if she said she couldn't take that step out of the zone right now.

She went back to the living room and sank into the recliner. The soft sound of football on the giant television was soothing, but she needed to talk to *someone* about this, and Parker was here.

"I can't do this, Parker. I can't be this person again, someone who loves so completely that she loses sight of who she is when the other person is gone. What if I lose him? What if—"

"Life is full of what ifs, Holly. You can't control that. But if you don't take a chance with Landry, are you going to regret it?"

She looked at him and bit her lip. She set the chair to rocking, afraid of the answer.

Chapter Forty-Six

When love knocks, will you answer or will you set the lock? Let love in, let love in, let love in.

When Landry woke up, he felt like he'd swallowed cotton balls. He needed water, so he stumbled out of bed, found a pair of basketball shorts, and slipped them on before padding down the hall to the kitchen.

It was dark outside, and his stomach rumbled for the soup that he smelled in the kitchen. He grabbed a bottle of water from the fridge and drank as he tested the soup on the stove. It was cold, and he was too exhausted to turn it on and heat it up. He walked to the living room and stopped abruptly when he spied Holly asleep in his recliner as Parker watched football.

His brother glanced at him and tilted his head up. "Hey, feeling better?"

Landry nodded, then set down his water and adjusted Holly's head. He popped the recliner's seat out and pushed

The Songwriter Gets His Girl

it back so she could lay more comfortably. Then he sat on the couch and propped his feet up, his eyes on her sleeping form instead of the tv.

"You look better than when you came in."

"Yeah, I think my fever broke. I feel gross but normal. Not hot or cold anymore."

"That's good. Mom was worried, so you better call her."

He sighed and ran a hand over his face. "Yeah, I'll do that right after I shower. Heat the soup while I'm in there?"

"Sure thing."

They both hopped up and went their separate ways. Landry's back felt better under the hot water, the strong stream helping ease his tense muscles. When he came out, clothed in shorts and a t-shirt, he felt almost back to normal except for his head. He took some more medicine to help with the headache, then went to find a bowl of soup.

Holly was still asleep on the recliner as he walked past, so he tucked the throw blanket around her as a knock sounded at the door. He strode quickly to it, throwing it open and whispering, "Oh, hi Mom. Come on in but be quiet. Holly's asleep. I was just about to call you."

Ava entered, carrying a bowl of something. She glanced at Holly asleep in the living room, nodded, and walked briskly to the kitchen.

"I brought you some chicken and dumplings to help you feel better. Evening church service just let out, so I thought I'd swing by. You look better. How's your fever?"

She felt his forehead, making him smile.

"I'm fine, Mom. It was just a little fever. I shouldn't have played in the rain with Holly." His mom's brows rose, and he winced. "Um, I guess I didn't mention that part earlier, did I?"

She turned and pulled down bowls, giving Parker a side hug as he stirred the soup on the stove and turned it off.

"No, you didn't mention that. She got you to go play in the rain? In the mud?"

Landry shrugged his shoulders uncomfortably. "It's not a big deal, Mom."

Her hand stopped him as he was about to ladle dumplings into his bowl, and he met her brown eyes. "It is a big deal, Landry. All your life, you've been a clean kid. As soon as you started school, you wanted to be clean. Would take several showers a day. We had to push you to ride horses with us, help in the barns."

She laughed, letting his arm go as she lifted her own bowl for him to fill. "In fact, you're the only person on the ranch who had to wear gloves to muck out the stalls. It was hilarious. But for you to simply play in the rain and mud? I don't think you ever did that, even as a child."

Parker snorted. "Yeah, he definitely did not."

They sat at the kitchen table to eat, but Landry put his bowl on the table and turned to the living room. "Let me wake Holly up to eat."

His mom's hand on his arm stopped him again. "Let the poor child sleep. She's been worrying about you all day. I could see it on her face."

He sat down slowly and twirled his spoon as he looked in the bowl. "You think she was worried about me?"

"Hm-hm. She went through the woods to get help, Landry, even though it's just a simple cold. That woman was anxious. She obviously cares for you a lot. I can't believe I never saw it before."

Parker shook his head. "Don't beat yourself up, Mom. I went on a date with her, remember? And she didn't say anything."

"You knew how I felt about her, but that didn't stop you." Landry kicked Parker under the table, making him smirk.

"What do you mean?" Ava put down her spoon and narrowed her eyes. "Stop you from going on a date?"

Parker rolled his eyes. "It was an accidental date, Ma. It barely qualifies as a date."

Landry glared at Parker. "You kissed her. That makes it a real date."

Parker just smirked and crossed his arms. "One peck on the lips, bro. It barely qualifies as a kiss, but I bet that's not how you kissed her last December, is it?"

Ma gasped. "You kissed her in December?"

Her voice was high and Landry hushed her. Parker smirked, "And again in May. That black eye I got from him wasn't from arguing about his neat freak house rules, but because I kissed Holly on that date."

"Oh Landry." The disappointment in her voice made him cringe, but Parker still wasn't done.

"When he came back from Nashville, it was obvious he got laid. It's no coincidence that Holly was gone that same weekend. He's been half-in love with her for years, Ma, and it's about fucking time something like this happened between them."

Ava's brows rose with every sentence until they almost met her hairline, and Landry sunk lower in his chair until he was almost reclining.

"Is that true, Landry?" His mom's voice was soft in the kitchen, their meals forgotten.

"I—yes, I suppose so. When I first met her, it took my breath away."

"When she moved to town?"

Landry shook his head and rubbed his temple. "No, five

years ago, the night she got engaged to her husband, I was visiting Andy in Kentucky. I saw the way she looked at him, Mom. It was true love, the kind that Pops and Grandma had. She's never going to look at me like that, no matter how hard I try."

"But you are trying, right?"

Landry sighed and raked a hand down his face. "Yes, I'm trying. I volunteered to give her a baby because the idea of her carrying someone else's terrified me. She wanted to make a contract to keep it professional, but I added some stipulations like we had to go on dates and couldn't see anyone else."

He took a drink of his water, and his mom put down her spoon.

"Why did you add those stipulations, Landry?"

He shook his head, sitting up straight and leaning toward her to whisper furiously. "Because I wanted her to see how good we could be together. Is that so much to ask? Yesterday, I laid my heart on the line, and she didn't want it."

"She said no? But why?" His mom's incredulous voice made him snort.

"Why wouldn't she? If she loved her husband even a fraction of how much I love her, of course she'd say no. What I feel? It's all-consuming. I've tried to find someone else for five years, ever since I met her, but it's no use. She's the only one for me, Mom, and there's nothing more I can do to show her we belong together."

Her eyes were bright with unshed tears, and he shuddered in a breath. He pressed on his head, his headache returning as footsteps echoed from the other room. He turned just as Holly walked in the doorway, wiping the sleep from her eyes.

The Songwriter Gets His Girl

He jumped up, wrapping his arms around her. She frowned, blinking as she reached up to feel his forehead.

"You're normal." She pulled back to look at him.

Parker snorted. "That's still up for debate."

Holly glanced around him to spy Parker and his mom at the table, then her cheeks turned pink and she stepped out of his arms. She glanced down, shifting on her feet.

He grabbed her hand and led her to the counter, thrusting a bowl into her hands.

"We have the soup on the stove and Mom's chicken and dumplings. Which would you like?"

She bit her lip, glancing between the two. He leaned down to whisper, "It's okay to take the chicken and dumplings if that's what you want."

She gave a small smile and nodded softly, so he spooned some up.

"What are y'all talking about?" Holly asked as she slid into the chair beside his own at the table.

He panicked and met Parker's eyes across the table, begging silently for help.

Parker blinked, then smiled mischievously. "Oh, we were just talking about Mike in Nashville and Landry's music."

"Oh, splendid. Did he tell you about the call yesterday? It's so exciting, and you have to help me convince him to take it."

Landry felt the bottom drop out of his stomach, and he shifted on his chair.

His mom frowned and leaned forward. "What are you talking about? Mike is Parker's college roommate. What does he have to do with Landry? Did Mike call you yesterday? Whatever for?"

Holly's spoon clattered into her bowl, and she turned stricken eyes to him. "I'm sorry. I must not have been fully awake yet, because I—I promised I wouldn't say anything, and now I've ruined it, and—"

He leaned forward and kissed her swiftly on the lips, tasting the warmth and surprise. He pulled back and winked. "It's okay, angel. It's going to get out if I take this gig, right?"

She nodded, biting the corner of her lip, and he turned to face his mom. His stomach was in knots, but it seemed like this was a day for all secrets to be revealed, whether he was ready or not.

"You know those gigs in Dallas I've been playing at this year?" His mom nodded so he continued.

"Well, Mike's been the one getting them for me, and they've been getting bigger and bigger. I've been working with him for about five years now, writing songs he has other artists sing. The past few months, he's been pushing for me to record some of these songs myself. That's what I went to Nashville for last month."

His mom's jaw dropped and tears pooled in the corners of her eyes.

"Oh, Landry, your grandpa would be so proud. That's amazing." The awe in his mom's voice nearly brought a tear to his own eye, but he just smiled.

"Thanks. Mike thinks the new direction my songs are going is the sweet spot. He's partnered with the studio who's signed Carter Kennedy. Carter's tour is starting next week and going through Christmas, and they want me to be the pre-show before Carter goes on stage."

Parker's jaw dropped and Landry found great satisfaction in it. His mom squealed and threw her arms around his neck, nearly tipping him over in his chair.

"Whoa, Mom, I didn't know you'd be this excited." He

The Songwriter Gets His Girl

hugged her, standing to his feet to gather her closer. She sniffed, then pulled back and held him by the arms.

"I didn't know I would be, but this is a once in a lifetime opportunity. You have to take it."

He frowned and shook his head. "What about the holidays? I don't know how this will impact the holidays."

She tapped her finger to her chin, then tilted her head. "Well, find out the tour schedule. See if you can have the holidays off and fly home for them. It'll be Connie's first Christmas, so that's not optional. In fact, call Mike now and let me talk to him. I'll talk to his mama if I need to, too."

Parker laughed and stood, pulling their mom off Landry. "I don't think it'll come to that, Mom. Landry will iron out the details and let us know. But how cool would it be if he did this, and could come home for the Halloween party? It would be even bigger than ever."

Mom covered her mouth with her hand, her eyes big as she gasped. "Oh Lord, you're right. I need to get home and go through all the details, make sure we have more food and drinks than last year. Oh Landry, this is going to be so much fun. What an adventure you're going to have."

She pulled him into a hug and patted him on the back. When she stepped back, she wiped her eyes. "Oh, this is just so exciting. You're going to travel all over, singing that beautiful voice of yours, and next year you'll have a baby. Life is so amazing, boys. It really is."

Landry saw Holly's head snap up at the mention of their baby, and she smiled a tight smile as his mom said her goodbyes. Parker closed the door behind her, then turned and grabbed his empty bowl to place in the sink.

"I had no idea, Landry. Congrats on the gig. I agree with Mom, though; you should go call him now and ask."

Holly nodded, so he went into his room to make the call.

Holly grabbed her bowl and took it to the sink. "I'll do the dishes, Parker. It's the least I can do for the delicious food."

"Mom brought it by after church. It's one of Landry's favorites."

She nodded, and he turned to put the leftover soup on the stove into a container. She asked about his school year, and he kept up a steady stream of chatter about his soccer team and coworkers. She was laughing about something one of the kids had done in class when Landry came back.

He frowned, glancing between them. "Good news is, I can come home for all three holidays. Bad news, I'll only have two or three days home for each."

Holly nodded, feeling pressure increase on her chest as she thought of him being gone for so long.

Parker looked between them and raised his brows. "I'll leave you two alone to figure out what this means for Operation Baby Maker. Goodnight, guys."

Landry grabbed her hand and led her to the living room, where they sat on the couch, his arm around her. He grabbed the remote and flipped channels as she bit her lip and bounced her leg.

He found America's Funniest Home Videos again, then muted it, just like he had in Nashville. She took a deep breath, comforted by the familiarity of it.

"Tell me what you're thinking, angel." His voice was soft and low, his hand stroking her shoulder.

She laid her head on his chest and sighed. "If we weren't successful this weekend with getting pregnant, then

I doubt we'll be able to when you're home for those holidays. I don't think my fertility window will fall at the same time you're home."

He kissed the top of her head. "You could join me on the road during the time you're fertile."

"Maybe. I guess we'll see how it goes, won't we?"

The silence stretched as they watched tv. It was so peaceful in his arms. She always felt like they could figure anything out. No problem was too big for them to tackle, as long as they were together.

He'd said he was excited to be a dad, but where did that leave them as a couple? Her love for him was too new to just blurt out. It'd take a while to navigate, to see if this was puppy love or the real deal. It felt different than what she remembered with Eric.

Her lids started to droop, and he turned off the tv and scooped her up in his arms. She thought he'd be too weak from the fever, but he acted like she weighed nothing at all. She threw her arms around his neck as he walked down the hall.

"What—"

"Sh, we're both tired, angel. Let's get some sleep, okay?" He laid her in bed, then slid in behind her, wrapping her up in his arms. He was the big spoon, and she was safe as long as he was there. She sighed a deep breath. Maybe it wouldn't be so bad, loving him.

Chapter Forty-Seven

I'm too old for this game, that the world calls love, love, love. It shouldn't be this way, this hard when we're destined from the Big Guy above

A few days later, Landry took a break from the busiest week of his life for poker night. He had to wrap up a few jobs before he could fly to LA to meet Mike and the tour group on Friday. He worked from almost sunup to past sundown for two days straight on a bathroom remodel.

He hadn't seen Holly since he'd taken her to the yoga studio Monday, but he'd texted her each morning. Little things like jokes, memes, and funny pictures.

The front door opened and Andy came in, catching him as he was carrying a plate of burgers out to the back patio.

Andy grinned and nodded. "Hey, glad I came early so we could talk. What's this I hear about you leaving town for a few months?"

Landry opened the back door and set the burgers down

The Songwriter Gets His Girl

by the grill while Andy pulled up a chair and propped his feet up. Landry launched into the explanation of his songwriting career and how it was changing.

"So now that I've recorded and released two of my own songs, it's all kind of blowing up on me. They're still climbing the charts each week, and I'll be going on tour for the next three months with Carter Kennedy."

"Wow, that's amazing. And to think, if you hadn't come to see me five years ago, you never would've written that first song."

Landry nodded, his friend's words truer than he knew.

"So now tell me what exactly is going on with Holly."

Landry laughed and set the burgers on the grill. "Damned if I know, dude. I have no clue. Basically, I volunteered to be her sperm donor, and now the whole town knows because of that stupid fever last weekend."

Andy threw his hands up. "Hey, it wasn't me that blabbed. But it might have been Aunt Suzie. She was at the house when Cindy and I got back from the cabin, and the kids had filled her in on what was going on. She filled in the blanks from there, then talked to your mom at church that night."

Landry shrugged, the burden of keeping so many secrets lifted and making him feel freer, even if he was still sad about the rejection.

"It's all right. I don't mind, really, although Holly does. She wants to be a single mom and raise this kid all by herself. Personally, I'm glad it all came out because now I get to be a dad and spend more time with the kid than I would if I was just a regular friend."

Andy frowned and the back patio door slid open. "And you were okay with that original arrangement?"

Landry shook his head, poking at the burgers. "Of

course I'm not, but it was what I needed to agree to, so I could then get close and convince her we belonged together."

Landry glanced over and froze, spying Kendall standing in the doorway. His scowl was etched on his face, his fists were clenched at his sides, his shoulders drawn up.

"Um, hey Kendall. We were just—"

"Talking about Holly. I figured that part out. What I can't figure out is how you could do this behind my back. With my own sister."

Kendall took a deliberate step toward him, and Landry backed away from the grill with hands up in surrender.

"It's not what you think."

Kendall took another step for everyone that Landry took down the steps to the grassy backyard. His hands waved wildly. "Not what I think? What I think is that you're sleeping with my sister."

Landry didn't have a response to that, but he reached the flat ground of the back yard and stopped. Kendall stepped closer, then closer again, but Landry didn't move, didn't dare to even breathe. He waited for the clenched fists to fly.

"Well? What do you have to say for yourself?"

Landry blinked, not expecting Kendall to have sense enough to demand an explanation.

"All I can say is I was trying to make her happy. She wants a baby, and I couldn't stand the thought of her having one with another man."

Kendall blinked, his green eyes so similar to Holly's it made Landry realize that a little boy with her eyes would grow up to look like Kendall.

"Why?"

Landry blinked. "Why what?"

"Why could you not stand it? Why were you trying to make her happy? Why did you need to get close and convince her you belong together?"

Landry tilted his chin up. If the whole town knew about their baby plan, Kendall at least deserved to know the truth.

"Because I love her. The same way she loved Eric. The same way my grandparents loved each other. The same way my parents love each other. I love her so much that if the only way she can be with me is one weekend a month to have a baby, then I'll jump at the chance."

Kendall's jaw snapped, and Landry heard his teeth grinding together. His nostrils pinched as he breathed deep. He exhaled, blinked, and lunged.

Landry flinched, but Kendall just wrapped Landry in a hug. All the air in Landry's lungs escaped when Kendall slapped him on the back. He met Andy's surprised gaze on the patio, then slapped Kendall on the back in a standard bro hug.

They let go and stepped away, then Kendall reached out a hand to shake. Landry shook, his eyes narrowed.

"Thanks for loving her. Don't give up. She might come around."

Landry's brows rose as Kendall let go of his hand and spun on his heel to go back up to the deck. Landry trailed behind in shock, feeling like he was floating, waiting for the shoe to drop.

"You're not angry? Why aren't you angry?"

Kendall sat on a chair next to Andy and cradled the back of his head in his hands. "I was yesterday. Then Andy and I had lunch today and talked. He pointed out all the times you'd watched over her these past few years, all the times you'd asked questions about her at poker night only to then ask questions about other ladies in our lives."

Landry laughed awkwardly and flipped the burgers. "And I thought I was so slick with those questions too."

Andy laughed. "I also pointed out how you acted five years ago when she got engaged, how you were so grief stricken the next day but had been fine at the party. Am I right? Did you fall in love with her that night?"

Landry shook his head, turning to face them. "No, it wasn't love at first sight. I knew I could fall in love with her though, if given enough time. I knew I had lost out on something spectacular, and I spent the past few years trying to find someone who made me feel that same thing. But I never did, probably because no one compares to her."

Kendall groaned. "God, now he's going to start waxing poetic over my sister. Where's his notebook? He needs to write that shit down, not say it out loud."

Landry laughed as the back door slid open and more guys filed outside.

Landry had been working non-stop on three separate jobs he had committed to do around town, trying to finish before he went on tour. She'd dropped lunch off with him yesterday. He'd been at City Hall repairing a bathroom. They'd sat in the hallway and eaten sandwiches and chips. Fifteen minutes and a quick kiss later, he was back in the bathroom.

She'd wanted to help, but it was a tight fit, and she didn't know what to do. It had been a little awkward, so she'd left. And today, after having Cindy take her to their house and walking over to the cabin to pick up her car, she was driving Landry down to Dallas to catch his flight.

She parked in his driveway and pushed the trunk button, popping it open. Landry walked out with one carry-on, a backpack, and his guitar. She opened her door, watching him swagger up the walk with a nervous smile on his face.

"That's all you're taking?"

He nodded and frowned, then shifted on his feet. "I thought this was too much. Do you think I should take more?"

She chuckled as he tossed his bags into the trunk, then opened the back seat of the car to slide his guitar safely inside. He shut the door, and she fidgeted with her shirt, wanting to wrap her arms around his waist. His hazel eyes were worried and she wanted to clear the frown. On impulse, she reached up and kissed him.

She meant it to be encouraging, a distraction from his worry, but it quickly escalated. He turned and pressed her against the car, making her moan into his mouth. He smelled of leather and myrrh, making her senses whirl just from breathing him in. She wanted to memorize his scent, his taste, the feel of him against her.

She'd never taken the time to memorize Eric before he left. She wouldn't make that same mistake twice.

Landry kissed his way down her jaw to her ear. "You could turn off your car and come inside for a while."

She sucked in a breath, feeling the heat pool between her legs as he ground up against her. His scruffy chin raked against her cheek, the sensation making her gasp.

"Landry, we can't. You'll miss your flight if we don't leave in the next ten minutes."

"Ten minutes is all we need. Come on, angel. Give me one last memory to tide me over."

She shuddered in his arms. She had to remain strong. If she gave in now, she'd give in again and again, and who knew where that would lead?

She struggled to keep the rules in place, but every day it grew harder and harder. Her mind went to war with her heart. Her heart wanted to savor him, but her mind was still scared.

No matter how desperately she wanted to hold him, feel him, she couldn't. She might want to memorize everything about him, but she had to do it within the boundaries she'd set up for herself. Otherwise, chaos would reign and that route led to heartbreak.

Remember the plan. Focus on the baby.

"We can't, Lan. It's not a fertile window."

He paused his kisses on her neck, then he sighed and leaned back. She couldn't see his eyes in the sun, but he gave her a quick kiss on the lips and stepped over to open the passenger door.

When his hands left her body, she felt adrift at sea. Her heart broke as he slid into the seat, but there was nothing else she could do. Having sex would just delay the inevitable and make it harder to say goodbye.

She rounded the car and sank into her driver's seat, buckled up, and headed to the airport. The trip was uneventful. Landry told her all the places they were scheduled to stop on tour and filled her in on his busy week at work. He'd apparently set up his apprentice to run the business, with Hunter supervising every few days.

Before she was ready, they were standing in front of the airport in the departures line, pulling his luggage out of her trunk. Her heart was pounding too fast and her stomach was twisting.

"Well, I guess this is it. I'll text you when I board, but you text me when you get home and let me know you made it safe, okay?" He frowned, his eyes earnest and sincere.

How had she been so lucky to find a man as honorable

The Songwriter Gets His Girl

as he, who genuinely cared? She nodded, unable to say anything around the lump in her throat. The urge swept over her, and she couldn't resist anymore. She launched herself at him.

"Oof." He took a step back from the force of her hug. She clung to him, drawing in the scent on his shirt, memorizing the feel of his chest pressed against hers. Tears pooled in her eyes and her breath caught in her chest.

"Hey, it's okay, angel. I'll be back in a few short weeks. This isn't forever, but you know what is forever?"

He pulled away from her and crouched down to catch her gaze, using a finger to tip up her chin. When her eyes met his hazel ones, the emotion in his choked her up, making the tears spill down her cheeks.

"The way I feel about you? That's forever. This tour is just a bump in the road, okay?"

She nodded, reaching up to kiss him. It was sweet, full of promise and hope and maybe a tad of desperation. She wanted to hold on to what they had when they were alone, away from the prying eyes of the world.

His words echoed in her head the entire way home They weren't declarations of love, but he did care for her. She just needed to figure out if that's what she wanted or not.

Chapter Forty-Eight

Deep fried corn dog on a stick, Big Tex waving above, cotton candy in your hand, all that's missing is love

October

"Damn it, Holly, you know we can't stretch like that. Ease up, will ya?" Lola barked from the front of the young adult yoga class. Typically, this class could stretch and do more than the older group, but as Holly looked around, she noted that Lola was right.

She spied Lucy in the background. "Lucy, would you like to take over for a few minutes? I believe Lola is right, and a different teacher might be best."

Lucy bounced up to the front, her bright pink tights reflecting sparkles in the early afternoon sun. Landry had been gone for less than a week, and she was miserable.

Holly grabbed her phone and moved to the side of the

The Songwriter Gets His Girl

room, following Lucy's directions. She was such a peppy girl; her and Landry would have a lot of laughs if they got together. But the idea made her heart race and sweat break out on her forehead.

She moved into tree pose and focused on her breathing. When class was over, Lucy told everyone bye, speaking to each by name, before coming over to where Holly was stretching with her friends.

Lucy's big brown eyes shone bright under her wrinkled forehead, a frown marring her cute little face. "Did I do alright, Holly? I really wasn't expecting to teach, since it's only my third class."

Holly smiled, reached out a hand and patted her arm. "You did great. My head's been kind of out of it this week, so I truly appreciate it."

Lucy nodded. "I heard about you and Landry. I didn't know you were seeing him, or I wouldn't have said anything at the salon last week."

Holly shook her head. "I don't know that we'd classify it as seeing each other, which is why I didn't say anything either. The fact is, we're trying to have a baby. The original arrangement was after I get pregnant, he's free to see whoever he wants and go back to his regular life. So, you might ask him out after he comes home New Year's."

Her throat closed up and her eyes watered, so she blinked furiously, glancing away. When she looked back, Lucy was exchanging a smirk with Maryanne.

Lucy shrugged her yoga bag onto her shoulder. "Yeah, I doubt that'll happen, but it's okay."

Maryanne grinned and raised a pointed finger. "You know, Parker's single and closer in age to you. Have you seen him lately?"

Lola just groaned at Maryanne's matchmaking attempts.

Maryanne walked with Lucy to the front, talking about the men in town.

Holly sat down and reached for her toes. Lola and Cindy joined her, half-heartedly stretching with her.

"Was that true? Once you're pregnant, he's going back to his life and you're going back to yours?" Cindy rubbed her belly.

Holly sighed and nodded, tired and not really wanting to get into the details. But as Maryanne joined them, completing their little half-circle, her eyes teared up. The weight on her chest was pressing in, and her throat closed up.

Lola raised a brow. "But you said that was the *original* plan. What's the plan now that the whole town knows?"

Cindy winced. "Yeah, sorry about Aunt Suzie blabbing."

Holly just shook her head. "Between her and Ava, there was no stopping it. And it's fine, I shouldn't have tried to keep a baby to myself. Landry said a family is more than just a mom and kid, which kind of surprised me."

Maryanne wrinkled her brow. "Why was that surprising?"

"I didn't grow up like he did, with tons of brothers, aunts, uncles, cousins, grandparents. It was just Kendall, Mom, and me. Then Kendall moved out, and for over ten years, it was just the two of us. We were fine, and that's what I thought was going to happen with me. I was going to have a baby and it was just going to be the two of us."

Cindy shook her head and leaned back on her hands. "Yeah, I don't recommend the single mom route if you can avoid it. If Landry's wanting to help, then let him."

Holly put her head in her hands and groaned. "It's more than that, though. If we try to make this work, as a

The Songwriter Gets His Girl

real relationship... well, there's no guarantee. What if we break up later? Then it's not just me who ends up heartbroken but our kid and Landry too."

Lola waved her hand and sat crisscross, tucking her knees in. "Hold up, let's get the facts straight first. One, there was a contract between the two of you that included no kissing, cuddling, lights on, and stuff like that."

Holly nodded. "Yeah, but we broke almost everything on the contract that first weekend together in Nashville."

"You went to Nashville with him!" Cindy's jaw dropped, making Holly wince. So she backed up and told the story from the beginning, starting with five years ago when they met, then sleeping in the barn at New Year's, then making out in May, then the late-night insomnia night they both had that resulted in their first time together.

Lola tilted her head. "But that first night with him wasn't part of the baby making plan. It was just a spur of the moment thing?"

Holly nodded, her fingers playing with the end of her ponytail. Maryanne winked and grinned, making Holly dread what she was going to say next.

"And how was it? That first time, and then your weekend booty call in Nashville?"

Cindy tilted her chin up. "And don't forget last weekend at the cabin before he got sick. How was that?"

Holly felt her face blush and glanced away. "It was amazing. He's amazing, in every sense of the word. He remembers little things like how I take my coffee and what I like to eat for breakfast. I've only ever been with Eric before, but Landry..."

Cindy placed her hand on Holly's knee. "It's okay, you can say it."

Holly felt tears roll down her cheeks as she met Cindy's

gaze. "Landry's so much more than Eric, and that's the whole problem."

Maryanne placed her hand on her other knee. "They're two different men, Holly. Different doesn't mean one is better than the other. Take Cindy and I for example. We're sisters, but neither of us is better than the other."

Cindy nodded. "But each of us are better at different things. I'm a better nurse, but Maryanne is a better baker, obviously. Maryanne is more fun, and I'm more serious."

Maryanne smiled, and Holly wiped her tears, hope blooming in her chest. "Cindy was married before, and it didn't work out. We've all been in relationships before, some good and some not. No one knows if it'll work out, but you have to ask yourself if the risk is worth the rewards."

Lola waved her hands, drawing their attention. "Okay, y'all need to go back to the facts. They had a contract, but that original plan doesn't work anymore. Have y'all made a new contract?"

Holly shook her head, her shoulders sinking.

"Have you told him you love him?"

Holly jerked her head up and met Maryanne's brown eyes. She felt her heart racing, and she swallowed, shaking her head.

"Do you love him?"

Holly glanced down, watching as a tear dropped onto her yoga sock when she nodded.

Lola cleared her throat. "So facts. You need a new contract, or at a minimum need to define your relationship."

Holly swallowed past the lump in her throat. "I promised his mom we would have that figured out by the time we announce a pregnancy. By the time I get pregnant, anyway. Last weekend might not have been successful, so we might not get a chance again until the new year, with him being gone through Christmas."

Cindy nodded. "So you have time to figure it out, but you're not going to do that alone. Have you been talking to him since he's been gone?"

Holly nodded. "We've texted."

Maryanne scowled. "No, you need to FaceTime. He needs to see your face, and you need to see his. You'll avoid a lot of miscommunication that way."

Lola put up a second finger. "Fact two, you love him. Does he love you?"

Holly shrugged, glancing away again. "Not sure."

Just let me love you. Landry's voice echoed in her head.

Cindy patted her leg and let go. "I'll talk to Andy, see if they talked this week and if he knows anything."

Lola glanced around to each of them. "And the counter-arguments?"

Holly frowned, picking at a spot on her sock. "I don't know if it'll work out, if he feels the same. I don't—want him to die like Eric did because it'd be too hard. I don't think I could take that kind of loss again."

Maryanne's voice was soft. "Well, if he's gone for the next few months, this will show you how it feels to be without him."

Holly felt a gnawing pit in her stomach. It already sucked to have him gone. She was crankier than she'd even been after coming back from Nashville. Perhaps they were right, and FaceTime would help.

Chapter Forty-Nine

Lay it all on the table, put it out there, don't be shy. Wear your heart on your sleeve and feel everything when love dies.

The day before Halloween

Holly froze as Ava walked in the Diner, the bell ringing in her ears and drowning out the voices of Maryanne and Lola. She glanced out the window, tucking her head to the side. Maybe if she didn't make eye contact, Ava wouldn't come over.

Lola stood up, her tall form drawing several eyes, including Ava's. "Well, I best get back to Mom. She's not doing well, and Granny said to be back by noon. I'll see you later or tomorrow at the party?"

Holly nodded, watching out of the corner of her eye as Ava approached.

"Oh hello, Mrs. Williams. Do you need any help with

the party tomorrow night?" Lola turned and asked as she spied the tall brunette. She was already in costume, a cute little Minnie Mouse dress with a big, oversized bow in her hair.

Maryanne laughed when she saw it. "Oh Ava, only you can get away with wearing a costume for multiple days in a row."

"Well, it's a great costume, so why not wear it?"

Maryanne grinned and nodded. "It's the perfect costume. Connie's going to love it."

Ava curtsied, pulling her polka dotted dress to the side. "Thank you. Bill is Mickey, and we did it for her. You'll bring her by before the party tomorrow, right?"

Maryanne nodded, sliding out of the booth. "Of course. I have to go but I'll see you later." She kissed her mother-in-law on the cheek and walked out behind Lola, who waved.

Holly wiped her sweaty hands on her jeans when Ava met her gaze, then slid into the booth opposite her. Dot hustled over, wearing a skeleton shirt with a baby skeleton over her pregnant belly, and a black tulle skirt.

"Hey Mrs. Williams. Looking forward to your annual Halloween party this year, since it'll be my last year free. What can I get you today?" Dot rubbed her stomach, drawing Holly's eye and making her swallow. She didn't even hear what Ava said over the roaring in her ears.

When Dot waddled away, Ava turned her sharp eyes to Holly, pinning her in place.

"Hello dear. Haven't seen you all month. Have you been avoiding me?"

Holly's jaw dropped, and she glanced away, unable to meet her eyes. They saw too much, like Landry. He was always seeing things in their video calls, the dark circles under her eyes, the scattered thoughts when he called while she was getting ready for work.

She shifted on her seat and sighed. "I wouldn't call it avoiding you exactly. Just been busy."

"Hm, I think it's definitely avoiding. You sent Lucy to do the once a week yoga at church sessions. Couldn't handle all the questions from my friends?"

Holly scowled and crossed her arms. "Not when I don't know the answers."

Ava chuckled and shook her head, thanking Dot as she set the food on the table. When she walked away, Holly's eyes followed, her heart beating fast as she started to sweat again.

"What questions do you not know the answers to?"

Holly turned back to Ava and leaned on the table. "We've been doing video calls every few days, but I still don't know what this is. I don't know what he wants or if this is going to last. He said what we have is forever, but how can he know that?"

Ava laughed, a tinkling sound that made Holly purse her lips. "Life doesn't come with money back guarantee, hun. Do you love him?"

Holly nodded. She'd gotten good at admitting that to people over the past month, but the thought of doing so with Landry made her stomach twist in knots.

Ava nodded and ate a bite of her burger. "Have you told him?"

Holly shook her head and bit her lip. "No, I haven't but he hasn't told me either. I want to talk to him when he gets in today, but his flight is already delayed, and I need to run to Denton for my costume. I think Andy's going to pick him up later."

Ava chewed. "Yeah, he just texted that they're finally

moving on the tarmac. You know I'm excited about the baby. Knowing Landry, if he's decided to have one it's only a matter of time. I'm assuming you're not pregnant or you would have said something?"

Ava's brown eyes narrowed as Holly wiped her sweaty hands on her pants again. "I—I honestly don't know. I'm not just going to Denton for my costume. I'm going for a midwife's appointment too, so we'll see. The test I took was inconclusive, but I haven't had a period this month."

Ava's eyes widened with each sentence, then she grinned, reminding Holly of Landry. He got it from his mom. She imagined a little brown-haired boy with that smile running around and felt the tension in her shoulders release.

"Well, that's exciting."

Holly leaned forward, her hands on the table. "Don't say anything. Landry needs to know first, and he doesn't even know I'm going to the midwife."

Ava smiled and nodded. Holly sighed, leaning back and feeling her shirt stick to her back from sweat.

Landry walked through the airport door and to a bench. "Yeah, I'm here," he said into the phone. "I don't see you."

A truck honked and he spun around, seeing Andy hop out of the driver's side and wave. Landry grinned, rolling his bag up. Andy wrapped him in a hug, slapping his back a few times before releasing him.

"It's good to see you, rockstar. How's it been going?"

"Oh, don't you start too. Mom has been over the moon about all this touring stuff." Landry laughed and tossed his bag into the back of the truck, then set his guitar on top, followed by his backpack.

Andy laughed and turned to the couple trailing behind Landry.

"Andy, this is Carter and Sydney. Carter is the headliner for the tour. Guys, this is my best friend."

They shook hands, then Andy helped them with their carry-ons. When they were all settled into the truck, Andy pulled out and turned the radio down.

"I can't believe you're bringing Carter Kennedy home. Have you told your mom yet? Or your brothers? Are you going to play at the Halloween party tomorrow night?"

They all laughed at Andy's questions.

"Calm down. One question at a time. You've been hanging out with your boys too much, to be asking a million questions all at once like that."

"You have kids?" Sydney asked from the backseat. She was gorgeous, a former model and now author. Of course, she didn't hold a candle to Holly, his little pixie princess. Just thinking of her made him excited, his stomach a bundle of nerves at the idea of seeing her in just a few hours.

Andy's voice broke through his thoughts. "Landry, earth to Landry. You there, buddy?"

"Hm, what? What'd I miss?"

Andy shook his head and grinned while he drove. "I was asking what the sleeping arrangements are. Where's Carter and Sydney staying?"

"They're staying at the Old Mill. Parker talked to the owner, since she just recently shut down the bed and breakfast. She's making an exception and letting them hang for the weekend."

Carter nodded. "I'm looking forward to it. I love exploring new places, and this is going to be so fun."

The Songwriter Gets His Girl

Landry pulled out his phone and texted Holly.

On the road heading home. I have a surprise for everyone.

The three dots appeared, making his heart race. He stared at it until her message appeared.

I have a surprise for you too.
Do you have a Halloween costume?
I'm at the store getting mine now.

I have my pirate one from last year.

He interrupted the conversation in the cab. "Hey, Holly's at the costume shop. Does anyone need anything?"

"We're good. I brought ours." Carter pulled Sydney closer, making her giggle in the backseat as he nuzzled her hair. Landry sighed, used to the pang of jealousy that constantly gnawed at him around the couple. The past month on the road had been fun, but he hung more with the crew, since being a third wheel sucked.

He was so tired of being the third wheel.

"I'm going as Cat in the Hat and Cindy's going as Thing 1 and Thing 2, the baby being Thing 2."

Landry pursed his lips. Stupid jealousy needed to get a grip. He was happy for his friend, but Holly hadn't said anything about being pregnant and he hadn't asked. It was understood that they would revisit the conversation after he came back from the tour.

If you want to match me, ask Andy if you can borrow his gladiator costume from last year.
If you don't want to, I'll understand though.

His heart skipped a beat and he grinned, his shoulders relaxing on the seat. "Hey, do you still have your gladiator costume from last year?"

Andy nodded, the grin on his face dopey. "Oh yeah, I kept that one. It comes in handy, with Cindy."

Landry laughed and shook his hand. "Nope, don't need to know about that. Is it clean?"

"Of course it is. Cindy has entered her nesting phase and deep cleaned everything, so I know for a fact she's cleaned it recently too."

"Okay, great. I can borrow it for tomorrow?"

"Sure thing."

Landry shifted in the seat and fired off a text to Holly.

Andy said I can borrow it.
I'll probably spray it down with cleaner though.
Apparently, he and Cindy like to dress up.

> *LOL well, not gonna lie. I'm looking at the costume here, And I can't wait to get you out of it.*

Aw, you missed me?

> *Like you wouldn't believe.*

He put his phone down and smiled. He might only have two days home, but this was going to be the best trip. Maybe he and Holly would actually figure out where they stood on their relationship this weekend. His heart raced, speeding like their vehicle down the road.

A few hours later, Landry stood in the field by the cabin, a bonfire blazing and beer in hand. The sky was clear, the stars were bright, and the night was just a tad cool, just enough for a long-sleeve shirt. The scent of pine and cedar filled the air. Cars and trucks lined up behind him.

Nick was back in town and already drunk. Gunner was monitoring the keg and all his friends and brothers were just hanging out on camp chairs or blankets.

But he couldn't sit still. He was waiting for Holly to show up. He was getting frustrated from not seeing her and knew she'd made it back to town shortly after he did. His phone buzzed in his pocket, and he pulled it out.

> *At Lola's. Her mom just passed.*
> *Going to stay here tonight.*

His face drained of color, and he looked around. Spying Maryanne, he walked over while typing his reply.

Shit, that's rough. What can I do to help?
I'm telling Maryanne now.

> *Thanks. Once I know, I'll let you know.*

He threw his arm around Maryanne's shoulders and pulled her close to whisper in her ear.

"Holly texted that Lola's mom just died."

Maryanne gasped and jerked her head back, glancing from him to Gunner. Gunner was several feet away but must have heard her because his head whipped around. When he saw her face, he rushed over.

"What? What's happened?"

Maryanne buried her head in his shirt. "Lola's mom died. I—I need to go to her. Can you handle this and get Connie on your way home?"

He nodded and kissed the top of her head. Landry

yearned for that kind of love. Part of him hoped Holly would still come around but being apart sucked. He wanted to talk to her, touch her, see her face as she talked about everything and nothing.

Carter and Sydney came over while Gunner walked Maryanne to their vehicle.

"Ya'll having fun?" He pasted on a smile and slapped his friend on the back.

Carter grinned, wrapping his arm around Sydney's waist. "Hell yeah, we are. It's a great change of pace from the city. You were right. This is exactly the break from the tour that we all needed."

Landry crossed his arms, smirking. "See? I'm always right. Just remember that, in the future."

They all laughed, and Sydney looked around. "Where's your girl? I thought we were going to meet her tonight."

"Lord knows we've heard about her enough." Carter's mumbled words had Sydney elbowing him in the ribs.

Landry shrugged. "One of our friend's just lost her mom tonight, so she's staying with her and trying to help. Hopefully, she can meet us for breakfast or something in the morning and we can hang out all day tomorrow."

Sydney nodded. "That's hard. Losing someone. But I look forward to meeting her."

He just hoped being around Lola while grieving didn't make her second-guess their relationship again. It could remind her of losing Eric, and the fear of loving and losing someone again had kept her out of dataing for so long.

Chapter Fifty

Flying around the world, jet setting and partying it up; that's not me, babe, that's not what I need. When you're the only thing in my dreams.

Halloween

The next morning Landry woke to a stiff neck from sleeping on the floor. He looked around. Why was he on the floor and so cold?

He saw the fireplace beside him, embers glowing in the morning light. There were boots sticking off the couch, and lumps under the covers on the bed.

He was in the cabin, snores echoing off the walls. He sat up and looked around again, spying Hunter on the couch, Nick beside him in front of the fire, Parker curled up under the table, Carter and Sydney in the bed, and... he blinked, rubbed his eyes and frowned.

Tasha, Lucy, and Mayor Ruby? Their heads were

sticking out from under the bed, jackets curled up into pillows.

He tiptoed into the bathroom, easing the door shut as he took care of business. A phone rang, and he winced, hoping it wasn't his. When he came back out, a sleepy Lucy was standing by the coffee pot as it percolated, talking softly on the phone.

"Hello?" She saw him and yawned, giving him a sleepy wave. "Oh yes, he's right here. He's coming out of the bathroom now. Just a minute."

He walked carefully around bodies on the floor to reach her, but she frowned into the phone before he could get there. She wiped sleep out of her eyes, making her mascara smudge even more.

"This is Lucy. Who's this?"

She looked at the phone, then up at Landry as he stopped in front of her. She handed him the phone, then shrugged, turning back to get a coffee cup.

"She hung up."

He frowned, stepping outside and pulling up his recent calls. Holly. He clicked on her name and sat in the rocking chair on the front porch while it rang. It went to voicemail, so he hung up and called again.

After the third time, he actually left a message. "Holly, it's me. Missed you at the bonfire last night. A bunch of us crashed at the cabin. Lucy, Hunter, Nick, a bunch. Call me back, angel. I need to see you today."

He sighed, then saw a text.

> *I'm not answering, dipshit.*
> *Go back to Lucy. She's a great girl.*

He clenched his jaw and raked a hand over his face. It

was too early for this crap. Why was he even awake at—he glanced at his phone and groaned—eight in the morning. He needed coffee.

Like magic, a cup appeared next to his head. He looked up and took it from Lucy, the brew helping wake up his senses. She sat next to him in another chair and pushed the rocker into motion.

"Sorry about answering. I was afraid it'd wake everyone up. Was that Holly?"

He sighed and rubbed his forehead. "Yeah, and she's not answering me now. I think she thinks we were here together or something."

Lucy winced. "Yeah, probably because she knows I wanted to ask you out. But that was before I knew you two were an item."

"I'm not even sure we are. We haven't exactly defined our relationship."

She tipped her head. "Is that why you said what you said in that interview? The one that aired last night?"

He groaned and leaned back, thinking of the interview he'd recorded last week. "Yeah, it's complicated. You're a sweet girl, and Holly says you're great. But you're not Holly. It's her I want. Only her."

Lucy hummed. "Yep, I figured. You were a little tipsy last night and kept singing songs about her to anyone who'd listen. I think Carter even recorded a few of them to post on social media."

Landry winced and drank his coffee, trying to think of some way to get out of this crapfest he'd fallen into. He felt like it was the start of the end, like something big was going to happen and destroy everything he'd set in place with Holly. Their relationship was on rocky ground, always had been, but this might be the tipping point that pushed her away.

Landry knocked on his parents' house early that Halloween morning and opened the front door. It was never locked, with as far out of town as they were. The smell of sausage tickled his nose.

"Mom, I'm home." Landry walked through to the kitchen as his mom flew at him, wrapping him in a hug and getting flour all over his clothes.

"Oh, my baby. I know I told you to go do this, but it's been so hard. Not even having Parker gone for college was this hard."

"Oh, come on, Mom. You've handled Chase being gone. You can handle this for a few months. Besides, I brought someone to meet you."

He released his mom and stepped to the side, grinning at the look on her face when she caught sight of Carter and Sydney. Her jaw dropped and she squeaked. His mom, the tough as nails horse rancher, squeaked.

He laughed and side hugged her. "Mom, this is Carter Kennedy and his girlfriend, Sydney. Y'all, this is my mom, Ava."

His mom held out her hand, then jerked it back when she saw it was covered in flour.

"Oh my, forgive me. I'm in the middle of breakfast. Let me get these biscuits in the oven."

She spun on her heel, Sydney following her. "Can I help?"

His mom beamed, then set her to work.

"Landry, take Carter out to the barn. Your father is

hoping a foal arrives this morning so we can focus on the party tonight. Oh my God, are you going to play? At my party?"

The spatula fell into the gravy as her jaw dropped again as she spun to face Carter. He grinned and wiggled his eyebrows.

"I guess we'll find out when we get there, won't we?"

Landry led Carter outside while his mom started shouting and cussing, making Sydney laugh.

"She's not going to have a heart attack or anything if we sing together, is she?"

Landry shook his head. "Nah, she's as healthy as a horse."

"Speaking of, I didn't know they were horse ranchers. This is a nice spread. You grew up here?"

They went to the barn while Landry showed him around his childhood home. After they'd met his dad and the new foal, they all tromped back into the house for breakfast.

"Landry, you didn't tell me you were on tv! Sydney shared the link to your interview. You should have told me, and I would have recorded it last night and told all my friends. Instead, I had to text them all the link to it a few minutes ago."

He grinned and shrugged his shoulders. "It's not a big deal, Mom. Just an interview."

"Just an interview? You told the entire world you loved Holly. You're such a damn fool, just like your brother."

"Hey," Hunter said as he came out from down the hall. "I'm right here."

Ava patted his hand. "Not you, dear. I was talking about Gunner, and how he lost his mind with Maryanne there for a while. Landry's done the same."

Landry plated up his food and shook his head, trying to ignore them.

Sydney elbowed him in the ribs, making him grunt. "I asked your mom about her. Turns out you haven't told her you love her."

He frowned, then glanced at his mom. "I have so."

She arched a brow and sat down at the table. "No, you haven't. I ate lunch with her yesterday at the Diner, and she clearly said that you haven't talked about love at all. Yet you went and broadcast it to the world."

Hunter snorted as their dad came inside. "Yeah, that does make him as dumb as Gunner."

Landry shrugged. "Not sure it matters anymore. She's ignoring my calls at the moment. Not sure she's even going to see me today, and we leave first thing tomorrow morning."

Sydney caught Carter's gaze and snorted. "Yeah, she'll see you. She bought a costume yesterday, right? If she's anything like me, she'll be at the party tonight, whether she's mad at you or not."

Ava frowned. "Bill, say the blessing, please. Then Landry can explain himself."

His dad stopped plating his food and turned to the group sitting around the table. "Lord, thank you for these new friends and our family. Thank you for this food and thank you for letting Holly and Landry work this shit out so we can all be one big happy family for Christmas. Amen."

"Bill." His mom chastised, but his dad just winked. She sighed, then waved her hand at Landry. "Anyway, just tell me why she's mad."

He told her about the bonfire at the cabin and how everyone had crashed there last night, then how Holly called and Lucy answered.

The Songwriter Gets His Girl

His mom rolled her eyes and chewed her food. "Yeah, you're going to have to find her today and explain. You two keep going back and forth on your phone, but to sort this out you have to be face to face."

"I would, but I don't want to intrude. She's at Lola's helping Granny with the funeral arrangements for her mom."

His mom's fork clattered to the plate. "What?"

He blinked. "You didn't hear? Lola's mom passed away last night. I thought you knew everything, or I would have mentioned it earlier."

She jumped up, abandoning her plate to rush to the pantry. She started pulling out various items, mumbling about getting freezer meals together for the family. The rest of them turned back to their breakfast and kept eating, chatting about the party tonight and when the funeral would be.

Holly turned her phone on silent to ignore Landry's messages and went back to making breakfast for Maryanne, Lola, and her Granny. The funeral director hadn't left until after dark last night, and none of them had eaten.

She whipped the eggs while the butter melted on the pan. Lola had been stoic until midnight. Then, in the quiet of the night, after Maryanne's snores could be heard between them on the bed, Lola choked back sobs.

Holly had slipped out of the bed, rounded to Lola's side, and crawled in, wrapping her arms around her friend. They'd fallen asleep like that, but Holly had woken up before dawn, nauseous.

The midwife yesterday confirmed her suspicions, but

the nausea this week was a major clue. All of her hopes and dreams were coming true.

And it was bittersweet. This was what she'd wanted, so why did it feel so weird and off?

Because I'm not there, angel.

Landry's voice reverberated through her mind as she tossed the mixed veggies into the pan. She shuddered in a breath, her eyes puffy already from crying with Lola last night. She didn't need more of that today.

And she needed to keep the pregnancy quiet for now too because her friend came first. Her hands began to sweat as she thought of telling Landry. It was supposed to be a happy, excited moment, but instead it was going to be the end of their time together.

He was already moving on with Lucy, and her heart ached as she imagined the two of them together. She'd known about the bonfire at the cabin, had been planning on joining them.

If she'd known all it took was her being out of the way for Landry to find someone else, she'd have done it long ago.

Maryanne padded into the kitchen as she added eggs to the veggies, making a scramble.

"Morning, Holly. Did you see Landry's interview on TMZ? Ava just sent me a link to it."

Holly wiped her hands on the towel and clenched her jaw. Before she could say anything, Maryanne was standing next to her, hitting play on her phone.

"Hello, we're here with Landry Williams, rising music star whose style is a cross between Michael Buble and traditional country music artists such as George Strait and Blake Shelton. Mr. Williams, you've been singing for a while now, right?"

"That's right, Becca. I've been singing since I could talk and

The Songwriter Gets His Girl

playing the guitar for as long as I can remember. My grandpa taught me."

"You have two songs that are still climbing the charts after being released for weeks. How does that feel?"

"It's pretty surreal, but I'm used to it. I've written songs for years now, several of them successful with other wonderful artists recording them."

"Oh, that's right. I'd heard you were a songwriter first. Is it different now because these new songs are sung by you and not someone else?"

"Absolutely, yes. It's terrifying because I keep waiting for the world to reject them, me."

The woman laughed, placing her hand on Landry's forearm. Holly felt her teeth snap together as she watched Landry smile at his hostess.

"Who in their right mind would reject you? You're fantastic. I hear even before the tour started, you had quite an entourage and women falling all over themselves to be near you."

He shifted on his chair, dislodging her hand. "I wouldn't say that. I'm a one-woman kind of man. If I had women falling all over me, I didn't see them. I only have eyes for the woman I love."

"Oh, how sweet. What's her name? Why haven't we seen you two together?"

He gave a self-deprecating smile and shook his head. "She's rejected me. I'm still trying to convince her to take a chance on us."

"Well, like I said before, she'd have to be out of her mind to reject you. I stand by that statement." The woman laughed, and Holly clenched her fist at the annoying sound.

"Now let's talk about your opening act for Carter Kennedy. How's it been working with Carter?"

"It's been fun. He's a great guy, easy to get along with, and always up for an adventure. Reminds me of my brothers, actually."

"Sounds like you have a strong family back home. How many brothers do you have and are they taken like you are or single?"

He laughed, the sound soothing her frustrated soul. "One is happily married, the other three are single. And yes, my family is the best. We're loud and opinionated, but I wouldn't have it any other way. I'm looking forward to seeing them for Halloween. My mom always throws a big party, and my brothers and I play and sing."

"You all play?" The woman blinked her big blue eyes in surprise, making Landry grin.

"Yep, we used to play at a local honky-tonk bar for years. Only stopped this year when my older brother had his first kid. I guess if it wasn't because of that, I wouldn't have played on my own."

"Well, congratulations to your brother. And to you on such a successful year. I can't wait to see how high your songs go on the charts, and of course I'm looking forward to the concert on November 2nd right here in Atlanta."

The recording ended, and Holly blinked, thankful that Maryanne had taken over the eggs. They would've burnt if she hadn't removed them.

Her cheeks were hot, and her stomach roiled. She glanced at Maryanne and handed her phone back.

Maryanne grinned. "Did you hear that? He declared on public television that he loves you."

Holly scowled and set the table as she heard footsteps upstairs. "Yeah, but this morning Lucy answered his phone."

Maryanne gasped. "What?"

"Yeah, apparently they'd stayed the night at the cabin. Our cabin, where we spent such a romantic weekend only to have it come crashing down on us when he got that stupid fever. That's not love."

She scoffed, angrily shoving the dirty dishes from prepping breakfast into the sink. They clattered as Lola stumbled down the stairs, her red hair sticking up on one side.

"Morning," she yawned. Holly took a deep breath and smiled, ignoring all the emotions rolling inside.

She grabbed a cup of coffee and handed it over. "Morning, how you feeling, hun? Are you hungry? We made breakfast."

Now wasn't the time to think about Landry. She had to help Lola through the toughest part of losing her mom.

Chapter Fifty-One

I smile for the camera, my eyebrow game is on fleek. My clothes are bougie as hell, but it's only you that I seek.

The party started like every other Halloween party, but Landry quickly realized it was more crowded than normal. By nine o'clock, there were dozens of people hanging around outside, trying to make their way in. But the doors wouldn't open for another half hour.

Landry drove around to the back and parked, pointing out the outdoor games they had already set up.

"Y'all ready for this? We'll play for the first hour, then you have an hour. We end exactly at twelve, and the last song will be *Forever and Ever, Amen*. It's Mom and Dad's song and tradition."

Carter laughed. "Yeah, this is so cool. I've played in a lot of little bars and places before, but a barn?"

Sydney pushed him as they piled out of the truck. Her Daisy Duke shorts were so short, Carter had already tried to pull them down a few times. Her pink plaid shirt was tied up under her breasts and a matching pink cowgirl hat sat on her head. Cowboy boots rounded out the look and matched Carter's. His green plaid pearl snap shirt was pretty standard for this part of Texas, but Landry wasn't used to seeing him in the Wranglers.

He adjusted his gladiator costume, pulling his black boxer briefs into place.

"How's that costume working out for you?" Carter smirked and wiggled his brows.

Landry rolled his eyes. "I'm just thankful Andy told me about the underwear trick. It makes it a bit more decent."

"At least it's not cold." Sydney said as they walked into the building through the side door. "Oh, look at all this. It's gorgeous."

His mom walked past, carrying a box of cups. "Thank you, dear. It takes a lot of work every year but it's worth it."

Landry kissed his mom and took the box from her, handing his guitar case to Carter. "Here, let me help you with that, Mom. Carter, can you put this on the stage?"

He glanced around, unable to find Holly in the thin, pre-party crowd. Most of them were the waiters and catering staff his mom hired.

"She's not here yet." His mom arched a brow and pointed him to put the box behind the makeshift bar. "I hope we have enough booze."

"It's only a two-hour party, Mom."

"I know, but I'm so worried about running out. With Carter here, I'm not sure what to expect and ordered twice as much food and drink, but—"

He grabbed his mom by the hands and brought them to his chest. "But it's going to be fine. Relax, Mom. You're not the one who's got to convince a girl to love you tonight."

Her eyes softened in the dim lights. Orange Halloween lights twinkled overhead, helping offset the fluorescent lights that normally showed overhead. Fake cobwebs were in the corners of the rafters, for once being put there without his help.

"It's going to be fine, Lan. She loves you, and you love her. Y'all just need to talk it out. Promise you won't leave tomorrow until you do?"

His chest felt tight hearing his mom say that, but he couldn't quite let the hope take root in his heart.

He nodded anyway and leaned down to kiss her cheek. She hustled off to her next task, and he turned, spying Andy in the corner where the sound system was set up. He walked over, grinning to see his friend in the cat costume.

"Hey man, thanks for the gladiator outfit. I think it fits me so much better than you."

Andy glanced up and laughed. "Yeah, I bet Cindy would argue that point, but at least I'm more clothed this year compared to last."

Landry glanced down, his chest and stomach slick with baby oil. His cape at least was warm, but he knew it'd get tossed aside by the end. All the people packed inside would drive up the heat.

"You're working the sound system this year?"

Andy shrugged. "Just helping. Your mom called me this morning to see what I could do to hook up some outside speakers. It looks like it was a good call because I think the people outside could already fill this place. That's not even counting the others who will show late."

Landry nodded, pulling his phone out of his little leather pouch on his hip.

The Songwriter Gets His Girl

Can we talk tonight?

I have to play for the first hour, but then I'm free.
Save me a dance?

Nothing appeared, so he put it back and sighed.

"Trouble in paradise?" Andy asked as he worked with the sound tech guy to connect the inside and outside systems.

Landry shrugged. "You could say that. I'm frustrated because I haven't seen her since being home. I haven't really talked to her in a few days either and thought... well, I thought we'd get to spend some time together."

He was worried he wouldn't see her at all, at this point. They had this one night together, then he had to leave again. He wouldn't be back home until Thanksgiving.

Andy came out from behind the sound booth. "It can't be all that bad."

Landry launched into an explanation of the bonfire, passing out, and how he woke up. "And no matter how many times I've called, it just goes straight to voicemail. I've left three more, but she hasn't answered my texts or returned my calls. I just hope she shows up so I can try to fix this in person."

Andy clapped him on the back. "She will. Cindy said Holly was with Maryanne at Lola's all day, but they're both coming tonight. She bought a costume yesterday, right? She'll want to wear it."

Landry grinned. "That's basically what Sydney said."

His brothers started warming up on the stage. "Looks like that's my cue. I'll catch you later. If you see Holly, will you send her to me? Even if I'm on stage."

Andy nodded and went back to the booth while Landry strode to the stage.

When Holly got out of Maryanne's SUV, her nerves started to get the better of her. The barn was crowded and intimidating, completely different from when she'd been here at gunpoint with Maryanne.

"Have you been back here since the bastard kidnapped us?"

Holly nodded and cleared her throat so she could talk past the lump that had lodged there. "Yeah, when Landry and I remodeled the cabin, we brought the furniture here. It wasn't at night, so it didn't have the same feel. But seeing it here..."

"I know, same here. What am I going to tell Connie when she's older? See this spot? This is where you were born."

Holly and Maryanne chuckled as she parked, and they got out. She adjusted the white strips of mummy wraps around her white dress that flared at the hips.

Music spilled out of the barn, filling the field.

Maryanne's head spun side to side. "Is it just me or are there way more cars here than most years?"

Holly nodded, realizing she couldn't see far in the dark as they wove between the cars. She followed Maryanne from the parking lot to the double door that was thrown open.

"Definitely. I heard there's a special performer for the second half of the night. The town was talking about how it was the guy Landry's been opening for, but surely not. That guy's famous."

The Songwriter Gets His Girl

Maryanne adjusted her pirate costume, pulling the bust to cover more. Holly had no idea how she walked around in heels almost every day, but those were the same black boots she'd worn last year with her witch's costume.

Holly wore white ballet flats, her white dress falling to her knees. Some strips of fabric Lola's grandma had sewn on today tickled the back of her knees as she walked.

She had been nervous about getting ready, and Granny said she'd needed a distraction. So Holly had let her change the dress however she wanted. After Holly explained what she wanted to do, Granny had taken the dress to her room and closed the door.

Holly had taken over answering the door to all the callers from church who'd brought over casseroles. Ava had stopped by, and while Holly had hugged her and chatted, she'd made sure not to have a moment alone with her. The woman would've asked questions she wasn't ready to spill yet regarding the midwife's appointment yesterday.

They pushed their way in the door, then shuffled along the edges to the drinks. Maryanne grabbed them both waters, then they moved along the wall again.

"Andy! What are you doing back here in the corner?" Maryanne asked, raising her voice to be heard over the music.

Andy's Cat in the Hat costume made Holly grin, and she looked around for Cindy, spying her dancing a few feet away on the edge of the dance floor, her blue wig bouncing around wildly.

"Glad y'all made it in time. Landry and Gunner's set is almost over. They're going to switch to the next band in two songs."

Holly tried to see the stage, but she wasn't tall enough. Lola would've been, but she was still home with her Granny.

Both had wanted a few hours alone together, so Maryanne and Holly had left them to it.

Andy pointed beside him. "If you go this way, you can get to the stage. Are you going to put Landry out of his misery, Holly?"

She blinked and frowned. "What are you talking about?"

Andy raised a brow. "He loves you. Nothing happened at the bonfire last night. Didn't you listen to his voicemail at all?"

She shook her head. "No, I was too mad."

Maryanne frowned. "You didn't talk to him today? I thought you did. Gunner said that Hunter and Parker both woke with hangovers. But Gunner was happy because he made them all stay in the cabin instead of driving home. Apparently, there were a dozen in there because Gunner couldn't take them all home."

Holly felt her blood run cold. Surely she hadn't made such a mistake. If she had, it would've meant missing out on seeing him today. Someone from the crowd bumped into her, and she glanced over her shoulder.

Lucy reached out a hand, her mouth open in surprise. "Oh, Holly, I'm so sorry. Are you okay? This place is so crowded." Lucy's brown hair was sprayed pink to match her pink sparkly leggings. She wore a leotard over it, with an off-shoulder sweater, her pink hair teased in an 80's style.

"It's okay. I was just trying to get out of the crowd."

Lucy grinned. "Yeah, but it's so fun. Oh, before I forget. Nothing happened with Landry last night. I woke up under the bed between the Mayor and the therapist."

Holly's brows rose. "Under the bed? With Tasha?"

"Yeah, that's her. All the guys were in front of the fireplace, but somehow we girls decided our virtue would be

The Songwriter Gets His Girl

safer under the bed. I don't know why, but it made sense when we were drunk. Landry was a mess without you. He sang songs about you all night. In fact, I'm pretty sure this song is about you too."

Lucy laughed again, her body swaying to the music as she spun back into the crowd. Holly felt the last grip on her heart ease, and she started to ease along the wall to the stage as she listened.

Chapter Fifty-Two

His voice echoed through the microphone, filling the room even above the noise of the crowd.

Look at you, girl, you light up the night,
The brightest star shining, so pure, so bright.
Every glance, every smile, pulls me in,
You're the spark where my dreams begin.

I adore you, girl, you're my guiding light,
Your smile makes my heart take flight.
When the pieces fall, like shooting stars do,
You're the brightest star, always leading me through.

Some dreams are meant to be chased,
Some loves can never be replaced.
When the world feels like it's falling apart,
I find my way to you, my burning heart.

I adore you, girl, you're my guiding light,

The Songwriter Gets His Girl

Your smile makes my heart take flight.
When the pieces fall, like shooting stars do,
You're the brightest star, always leading me through.

Tears were running down her cheeks as she reached the side of the stage. Parker saw her and reached out. She grabbed his hand and stepped up, not even thinking about all the people in the crowd. Her eyes only locked on Landry as he faced them, singing and smiling a sad, bittersweet smile.

Her heart ached, and she knew this was it. She couldn't keep holding back from him. She couldn't stand that sad smile on his face and just wanted to make him happy. Deep down, she'd always known he would make her happy too.

And she was finally ready for that happiness, finally ready to let go of all the pain and heartache that'd come before. It didn't lessen what she had with Eric. The two were totally separate and very different. Somehow the past month alone, without the distraction of him, had made her realize that truth.

She took a tentative step in front of Parker, easing closer to Landry. He turned his head, and his eyes went wide.

Look at you, girl, my heart, my bliss,
Forever yours, let me hold you like this.
You're the brightest star in my universe,
My girl, my angel, my love, my pixie princess.

He stopped singing as the band continued to the end, and she stepped up to face him. He absently stroking his guitar as the last notes of the song died away. Her hands were shaking as all eyes stared at them, but his hazel ones captivated her, drawing her in and making her heart pound.

"You wrote that for me?"

He nodded, his eyes hesitant. She hated that she'd put that look on his face. She fiddled with some of the stray white strips of cloth that clung to her dress.

"Did you mean what you said in that interview?"

He nodded again. "Every word. I don't have eyes for anyone but you, angel."

Her heart pounded in her chest. "Why?"

The crowd seemed to hold its breath along with her.

"Because I love you."

She sucked in a quick breath, her eyes tearing up and her lip quivering.

"I—I love you too."

His eyebrows rose, and he blinked. "You do?"

She nodded, and he started to move his guitar behind him, the strap holding on his shoulder. She held up a hand when he stepped toward her. With the other, she pulled down part of the white strips of cloth covering her stomach to reveal the rest of her costume.

Two pairs of eyes were painted onto her dress, one with a pink hair bow over it. The crowd gasped, and one of the drum sticks fell to the ground behind her.

"Surprise. We're pregnant. With twins." She whispered, the microphone in front of him picking up her words and echoing them through the room.

He launched himself at her, scooping her up in a hug and spinning her around. She laughed, then screamed. His foot caught the edge of the platform, and they tumbled into the crowd.

But the people were packed so tightly, they just pushed the two of them back onto the stage. She blinked, looking from Landry to the crowd and back again as everyone cheered.

Good Lord, she'd almost fallen. The babies could've been hurt.

His hand cupped her cheek, and he kissed her softly, making her panic ease and her bones melt at his touch. A cheer rose from the room, deafening her as someone else stepped onto the stage.

"Well, I don't know that I can top that performance, but I suppose I can try. How y'all doing tonight?" Carter Kennedy said to the crowd.

Holly gasped, breaking the kiss and glancing over Landry's shoulder.

"He came?"

Landry grinned. "Yep, I wanted you to get to know his girlfriend, Sydney. She's a vegan, and y'all have a lot in common. Come on, I can introduce you now that it's his turn to play."

She gawked at the man as Landry led her to the edge of the stage. He hopped down next to the wall, then wrapped his rough hands around her waist. He captured her attention as he lowered her slowly to the ground.

Then he pulled her to him and kissed her like his life depended on it. Her entire world fell away, and it was only the two of them in this little alcove in time and space. She wrapped her arms around his neck as joy spread through her body, warming her from the inside.

When they broke apart, his face was practically glowing. His smile was wide, his eyes bright. He whisper shouted into her ear. "Come on. We're getting out of here. You can meet Sydney tomorrow."

He tugged her along the wall, waved at Andy, and then headed outside. He opened the door to his truck parked behind the barn, and she slid along the bench seat to the middle.

He started the truck, then put his arm around her shoulders while he backed up.

"Where are we going?" Her voice was breathless and shaky with excitement. This was what happiness felt like, this joy and peace in her heart. She didn't really care where they were going, as long as they were together.

"To the cabin. I cleaned it up today after breakfast when everyone finally woke up and left. I'm sorry about Lucy answering my phone, but I slept on the floor between Nick and Hunter. Nothing happened, and there were like six other people in the room. I would never cheat on you, angel."

He was so serious, his tone grave, and it made her sigh and lean into him.

"I know that now, but I was emotional this morning. I was freaking out because I didn't know what we were doing. We hadn't talked about our future now that everyone in town knew about our baby making plans. I don't know where you see this going or if we were sticking to the rules or had completely thrown them out."

He snorted. "Well, we threw your rules out a long time ago. The only ones we haven't broken were my additions."

He parked and opened his door, grabbing her hand so she would exit behind him.

She squeezed his hand and shut the truck's door. "Yeah, next time I need to make rules, you're going to be in charge."

They laughed and walked to the cabin hand in hand.

Chapter Fifty-Three

Going down the road, Wind blowing your hair, pink lips grinning as I sing of your glorious derrière

He pushed open the door and flipped the light switch, making her gasp. Flower petals were strewn over the floor, and the table was set with a tablecloth, fancy plates, and unlit candles beside a vase of flowers. The bed was covered in flower petals, and a small fire was dying in the fireplace.

"Landry, did you do all this? When—how?"

He shut the door and knelt by the fire to add more wood, finally releasing her hand. "I did more than just clean it earlier. I wanted to bring you back here and tell you how I feel."

He sat on the couch, patting the seat beside him. She turned to face him, her hands sweating even as she couldn't stop smiling.

"I think we said all that on stage. God, I can't believe I did that in front of everybody."

He grinned, rubbing his thumb across the back of her hand. "I'm glad you did. I've been looking for you all night, to apologize and clear things up. Holly, you're it for me. You can stick to the rules and choose to raise this baby—"

"Babies," she interrupted. He gulped, glancing down at her stomach with his jaw slack. It took several moments for him to finally reply.

"Babies. Fuck yeah, that's amazing." His eyes teared up, and he pulled her onto his lap, turning her legs to rest on the couch beside him. He placed a rough hand over her stomach, his thumb rubbing over the eyes of the two little "mummies" peeking out from the stitched-on wraps.

He grinned at her, his eyes bright in the firelight. "Did you know I was a twin? My brother died in utero from a heart defect. We'll have to monitor these mummies closely, but I'm pretty sure the technology and care is better now. They'll be okay, right?"

His voice drifted off, as if he was reassuring himself more than her. She bit her lip, not letting herself get sidetracked and worried about that.

"The midwife said both heartbeats are strong and normal, so they're going to be fine."

He nodded absently, still staring at her stomach. She palmed his cheek and made him look at her.

"Landry, I love you. When I went to the midwife yesterday, and we found the babies, do you know what I wanted to do?"

He shook his head, his scruffy chin scratching her palm and making her shiver.

"I wanted to immediately call you and tell you. I wanted you beside me at the appointment. I wanted to run home and share this with you. I—I don't want to live life scared anymore. I want to enjoy it, and these babies, with you."

The Songwriter Gets His Girl

He grinned, tears glistening on his long lashes. "Angel, I have only ever wanted you. Since that first kiss last winter, I haven't been able to even look at another woman. One kiss, and I was done for. I fell hard, and while I fought it, I didn't fight it as much as you did. I was so scared you were going to reject me forever. A man can only take so much of a beating before he gives up, you know?"

She nodded, frowning as she kissed his cheek. "I know, and I'm sorry it took me so long to come to my senses. I'm here now, and I'm not going anywhere."

He turned, his soft lips finding hers, his tongue diving inside and making her heart race. Goosebumps broke out on her skin, but he pulled back and looked at her.

"Do you mean that? I'm going to lay it all on the table, angel. When I say you're it for me, I mean it. If you won't marry me, then I won't ever get married or have more kids."

She tilted her head and blinked, her heart stopping then racing to catch up to what her ears heard.

"You—are you asking?"

He grinned and wiggled his eyebrows. "Maybe. Think you'll say yes if I do?"

She laughed and hugged him close, burying her head in his shoulder. "Only one way to find out, Lan."

It was his turn to palm her cheek and tip her face to his. He kissed her gently on one corner of her mouth, then the other.

"Holly, my bubble gum angel, my pixie princess, will you make an honest man out of me? Will you marry me and live out our days raising tons of babies with me? Will you bring me lunch at jobs and maybe stay and help sometimes because painting with you is fun? Will you let me spoil you and mark off all the things on our bucket lists together?"

Tears ran down her cheeks, and she grabbed a fistful of the cape on his costume as her jaw went slack.

"Landry, I didn't think I could ever love anyone as much as I did Eric. When he died, I thought I had buried my heart with him. But you brought sunshine to my life, joy and laughter. Things don't seem so dark and dreary when you're around, and I think that if we're together, we can handle anything."

She kissed the corners of his mouth and leaned back. "And you know what? I realize now that I don't love Eric any less because I love you now. My love for you is completely different, but just as deep, just as real, just as scary and exciting and—and I hope you're prepared for forever with me, because I don't think I can go through all this falling in love crap again. You're it for me too."

He laughed and wiped the tears from her cheeks. "So, is that a yes?"

She nodded, her smile shaky. "Yeah, let's get married and be a real family."

He crushed her to him, kissing her so deep she nearly ran out of breath. She saw stars behind her eyelids and heard the fire crackle in the fireplace. The scent of leather and myrrh mixed with the baby oil and all the love that made up Landry's unique scent filled her nostrils as she breathed deeply.

Her stomach growled, and he chuckled, breaking the kiss and rubbing her tummy.

"Looks like these kiddos are already making their opinions known. How have you been feeling? Tell me everything."

The Songwriter Gets His Girl

He led her to the table by the window, lit the candles, and uncovered the sealed container between them.

She groaned and shook her head. "Spaghetti on a white dress? No, absolutely not. That's a disaster waiting to happen."

He wiggled his eyebrows. "Well, you could always eat in your underwear. That would save the dress. Then we'd be matched since this gladiator costume is practically underwear. Why did you want me to wear this and say we were going to match? I expected you to be a Cleopatra like Cindy last year or something."

She laughed, then stood and presented her back to him. With a glance over her shoulder, she winked. "Help me with the zipper?"

His eyes widened and he reached for her dress. Every inch that was uncovered, his knuckle grazed, sending shivers up and down her body. Her core clenched, remembering him, wanting him, needing him to fill the aching void within.

Her voice was shaky as she answered. "I was going to borrow Cindy's Cleopatra costume, but then I saw the mummy dress and fell in love with it. I figured I could be a dead, mummy version of Cleopatra, but then I got carried away with the mummy aspect."

She stepped away and shimmied out of the dress, tossing it on the back of the couch, his chuckle sending a shiver up her spine. She turned, standing in her matching white lace bra and thong set. His eyes roamed her body, spending a few extra minutes on her slightly rounded stomach. "Damn," he said. "I'm brilliant sometimes."

She grinned and sat on the chair across from him with an arched brow. "You're pretty smart, that's for sure. I don't mind eating in my underwear, if you keep looking at me like that."

"Like I want to devour you?"

She grinned, holding her plate up for him to spoon spaghetti and batting her eyes. "Yes, please, can you fill me up?"

His eyes twinkled, even as they darkened with desire. "I am going to fill you up, angel. Just you wait."

She pouted, setting her now full plate down on the table and picking up her fork. "Waiting is so hard."

"I'll give you something hard," he muttered under his breath before he shook his head and made his own plate. "Now, tell me about the doctor's appointment."

"The midwife did an ultrasound and guess what? I'm fourteen weeks along. Fourteen!"

He frowned, tilting his head as he thought. "But that means—"

She grinned. "That very first night when we both couldn't sleep, all the way back in July. Yep, that's the one."

He laughed, his head thrown back, the sound filling the cabin and her heart with joy.

She grinned. "I know, right? We could've avoided this whole fiasco if we would've known. I had no idea because I kept having periods, though light. And I took four tests in August that were negative and another four in September that were inconclusive. This month they were hard to read, just super faint lines. I was afraid to get my hopes up but I went to the midwife anyway. And she found both babies, with strong, regular heart beats."

He breathed a sigh of relief and spun his fork onto his plate. "I'm so happy, angel, and not just about the babies. I'm happy we're finally together."

The Songwriter Gets His Girl

Her face softened at the look in his eye. "Me too," she said softly. "Did you really have a twin?"

He nodded, his mouth full of noodles. "I'm sorry about your brother."

He shrugged, taking a drink of water. "It's okay. Mom doesn't talk about it often, but you should ask her about it. She's going to be so excited about these babies. Probably overprotective and worried too, based on her experience with carrying twins." He shook his head. "Twins. I still can't believe it."

She grabbed her purse from by the door. When she pulled her phone out, she swiped and stood next to him, explaining the pictures of the sonogram. He was practically bouncing in his chair in excitement even as his hand wrapped around her back and rubbed small circles.

"You have to text those to me, so I can send them to the group chat with my brothers and parents. This is amazing. And the engagement! We have to tell them about our engagement."

She laughed as he pulled her onto his lap, hugging her tight. She sighed, her head on his naked oily shoulder, her hands stroking his back and bicep.

This was exactly where she wanted to be with the man she wanted to be with. He kissed the side of her head.

"I believe I asked you to save me a dance, angel. I'm going to collect now, if you don't mind."

She hummed her consent, and they stood, enjoying the feel of his body moving against hers. The belt on his costume dug into her stomach, but it was his hard cock pressing against her that made her squirm in his arms.

His voice lowered to a near growl. "Come with me tomorrow."

She froze in his arms, then continued swaying with him to an imaginary tune only he heard.

"On tour? I can't, not with Lola just losing her mom. I need to be here for her, help with the funeral. I might stay with them a few more days next week too. She was really rough last night, Lan. When my mom died, I wish I'd had someone stay with me during those first few days."

He sighed, his breath warm on her cheek as she'd tilted her head into the crook of his arm. "I get it. This is just one reason I love you so, because you're a good friend. I knew when we first met that you were special and someone that I could fall in love with. But it wasn't until we were friends, and I got to know you, your kind heart, your—"

"*Your eyes, your smile, your kiss?*" She sang the tune and lyrics to the song from tonight, her lips smiling as she kissed his chest.

"Yep, exactly. You better get used to having sonnets and songs written about you, because I'm head over heels in love with you, angel. Now and forever."

The warm glow of his love spread through her, warming her from head to toe. As the candles on the table died, they danced into their future, one full of love, joy, and happiness.

Epilogue

A thousand shooting stars fall around us, love, But you're the one I'm always dreaming of. No matter how far, no matter the fight, You're my star, you're my guiding light.

Middle of July

Landry sang softly as he finished changing his son's diaper and cradled his sleepy body against his chest. He bounced gently from side to side and caught his reflection in the mirror.

He needed a haircut and his facial hair was longer than he normally kept it, but his eyes were happy and relaxed.

When Holly had moved in at Christmas, they'd decided to remodel Parker's room and turn it into the nursery. Parker had gladly moved into Holly's apartment over the studio. They'd decided to knock down a double door width of wall between the gym and her studio to encourage more people to use both. Parker being on site helped with the transition.

They'd also knocked down a wall in the house to fit two cribs and rockers, combining two small rooms into one bigger one. They'd had a lot of fun painting, and Holly had learned pretty quickly how to handle the nail gun and put up drywall.

It was one of the best days, because it was the day they'd decided on the names for the babies. It was Valentine's weekend. He'd set up a picnic in the nursery and had fed her while she'd sat in the rocker with her swollen feet on the footstool.

Light filtered through the window, landing on her golden hair and giving her an angelic glow. He fed her a chocolate-covered strawberry, and she moaned.

"Oh my God, this is the best chocolate covered strawberry I've ever had in my entire life. We need more of these."

He chuckled. "They're specially delivered from Dallas, but I'll set up an auto-delivery for every week if that's what you want, angel. Anything for you."

She beamed at him, her eyes going soft as she laid her head back on the seat. "I feel like I've won the lottery. You're so good to me. I didn't know I could be this happy."

"You? I'm the winner here, because there's no one on earth as wonderful as you, princess."

She stopped rocking, sitting up sharply with her hands on her stomach. He dropped the next strawberry, his heart racing. "What? What is it? Is it the babies?"

She shook her head slowly and a smile spread on her face bigger than he'd ever seen. "No, we're fine. That's what we should name them, though."

He frowned and shook his head. "Sorry, angel, but you're going to have to explain this to me."

The Songwriter Gets His Girl

He'd heard about women with pregnancy brain, but no one had mentioned dad pregnancy brain. It was getting harder and harder to understand her leaps in thinking sometimes. She was brilliant and being pregnant made her even more creative than normal. She had thought of some pretty fantastic stuff lately, like how to do a speed dating event at the yoga studio for Valentine's day.

She was tired and napped all the time, but there was nothing wrong with her brain. He, however, barely kept pace with her.

She grabbed his forearm and leaned forward, her eyes shining with excitement. "The babies. We should name them something to do with winning. Like Edwin and Winifred."

His eyes widened and he nodded. "Because we both won in love."

She nodded, practically bouncing in her seat. "Yeah, and we are winning in the kid department too. They're going to be such great kids."

He leaned forward, kissing her softly on her berry flavored mouth. The excited energy in her melted as she sank into the kiss, her tongue dancing with his slowly as they both savored the other.

A kick pressed on his chest where it touched her stomach, and he pulled back with a laugh. With a hand on her stomach, he felt another kick.

Holly giggled. "I think they like their names. But let's call them Eddie and Winnie for short."

Landry shook his head. "Oh no, we can't call her Winnie. She'll get teased in school and be called Winnie the Pooh. No, we'll call her Freddie. She'll get more opportunities for job interviews with a boy name too. She'll conquer whatever world she wants to with a strong name like Freddie."

Holly rolled her eyes. "Fine, we can call her Freddie. I kind of like it. It balances things between the two of them. But I'm still dressing her in all the cute outfits and pink bows."

He grinned, then kissed her nose before lifting another strawberry to her lips. "You got it, angel."

A cry pierced the dimly lit room, startling Eddie in his arms and pulling him out of the memory of that day.

He glanced at the clock and sighed. It was barely six in the morning, but Winifred was already awake. She was just like her mother, bright and chipper as soon as the sun rose. Eddie was more his kind of kid, as they often slept in together.

"I got her. Don't worry." Holly's voice called as she rushed into the room. She scooped up the little girl, and he stepped aside so she could change her.

Eddie's bright green eyes looked up at him as he blinked and yawned. Landry chuckled and sat in the rocking chair in the corner.

"Yeah, I know, little man. She's loud, but it's something you'll just have to get used to. She's your sister."

Holly glanced over her shoulder, then finished changing Freddie. "Looks like he's awake early this morning. You sleep alright?"

Landry yawned and nodded. "Yep, I guess he's just excited about his cousin's first birthday party. What time do we have to be there?"

"Ten. It's early, but it was the best time with all the babies' nap schedules. Ours are on two a day, but the birthday girl is only on one. Then there's Cindy's baby, who can't decide how many she wants."

He chuckled. "Yeah, Andy was grumbling about that the other day."

Holly sat in the rocker in the other corner. "The flower shop called yesterday. I forgot to tell you, but we're not going to have enough daffodils for the wedding. They're going to pick some other yellow flower to go with the oranges and reds for the country chic theme."

He nodded and rocked. "You sure you're okay with

having it in the barn this fall? We can rent any place you want. Money's not an issue."

She smiled tiredly and nodded as she fed their little girl. It was one of the few ways she would stop crying this early in the morning.

"Yeah, I'm sure. It's where we had our first kiss, where I first slept in your arms. It's where we declared our love in front of everyone. It should be where we make everything official, don't you think?"

Happiness and contentment spread through him, and he nodded. This was everything he'd ever wanted in his life. The woman of his dreams, children in his arms.

"Did you hear from Mike?" Her voice was soft as the room brightened with the rising sun. Her messy bun was falling out, and there were dark circles under her eyes from the late night feedings, but she'd never looked so beautiful.

It took a few extra seconds for his brain to register what she'd asked.

"Actually, he called last night. I need to record a new song this weekend. Can you take the kids to the park or to my mom's for a few hours? I know the studio is sound proofed, but if you're around, my mind will be completely focused on the three of you."

They'd added a studio in the backyard after they'd finished the nursery. It was just a sturdy shed with good acoustics. Mike had even come to town to help him set the equipment up.

She looked away from Freddie and met his gaze, her eyes soft with her smile.

"Yeah, I can take them to see Kendall, since he's going on that road trip with Lola the following week."

Landry snorted. "I still can't believe he's going cross-country with her and her granny. I kind of wish I was a bug on the wall to hear and see what kind of trouble they get into."

Holly winced and shook her head. "Yeah, not me. I never want to accidentally see what we did on Cindy's wedding night."

Landry chuckled, remembering that night a year and a half ago.

"That night, I was just so happy to just hold you while we slept in the barn. I had no idea it'd start us on this life-long journey together."

She smiled and adjusted Freddie to burp her. "I'm glad we're doing life together, Lan. I wouldn't change a thing. I'm so happy."

Freddie burped loudly, and they both chuckled. Then he stood and handed her Eddie before taking Freddie. His daughter's eyes were a softer shade of green, but her lashes were thick.

"Good morning, beautiful. Who's the happiest, prettiest baby in the entire world? That's right, it's you."

He caught Holly grinning at his baby talk to their daughter, but he just looked up, winked, and went right back to talking to her.

"We're going to go to a birthday party today. Are you ready to show your cousins how you can hold your head up now? You're such a strong girl."

She farted in his hand, as loud as her burp earlier, and it made both of them laugh again. He bounced her in his arms, helping her get some of the gas out.

"Yes, yes, I know. You're a loud girl too, and I wouldn't have it any other way. You're going to have to be loud to wrangle your brothers and sisters someday."

He heard Holly's breath catch, so he looked up at her.

The Songwriter Gets His Girl

She scowled. "I told you, we're waiting until they're at least a year, maybe two, before we try again."

He winked. "I know, angel. I'm happy with just the four of us, if that's the way it stays too. You're my everything, Holly."

She smiled and sang one of his songs softly as she fed Eddie, her eyes never leaving his.

> *Your eyes, deeper than the ocean's embrace,*
> *Show me worlds beyond this place.*
> *Your kiss is heaven, lifting me high,*
> *In your arms, I touch the sky.*

He swayed side to side, his baby girl in his arms, as he picked up the song and sang to his soon-to-be wife.

> *I adore you, girl, you're my guiding light,*
> *Your smile makes my heart take flight.*
> *When the pieces fall, like shooting stars do,*
> *You're the brightest star, always leading me through.*

> *Look at you, girl, my angel, my muse,*
> *The pixie princess I never want to lose.*
> *Forever burning, my compass, my truth,*
> *The brightest star leading me back to you.*

It was going to be a great day full of his babies, his love, and their friends and family. If someone would have told him two years ago he'd be sitting here with Holly holding their children, he would've laughed. He thanked his lucky stars every day that he was wrong when he thought she'd never love again. Now they were together forever with more love than he ever dreamed possible.

"Hey, what are you thinking so intensely about over there?" Holly asked him, bringing him out of his thoughts.

"Just thankful for you and our little miracles here," he said, detaching a tiny hand from his finger to hold hers. "I love you and them so much. Thank you for letting me be part of their lives, for taking a chance with me."

Holly blushed a cute shade of pink that made her look even more radiant than usual. "I love you too, and I'm so glad we get to do this parenting thing together." She stood, moving Eddie to burp him, and leaned in to kiss him softly. A chorus of coos and gurgles erupted around them, the two babies talking to one another.

They both laughed, and he wrapped his arm around Holly, his heart near to bursting with love and joy.

Next in the Crimson Creek Series

vinci-books.com/surgeon-gets-his-girl

She's his worst nightmare—and his hottest fantasy.

Fiery Lola's forced into a fake relationship with Kendall, her best friend's irritatingly sexy brother. An accidental engagement and family chaos blur the lines fast. Can enemies with sizzling chemistry become lovers—or will pride burn it all down first?

Turn the page for a free preview…

The Surgeon Gets His Girl: Chapter One

REAPING THE CONSEQUENCES

June

"Kendall? Kendall." Dr. Jensen clapped him on the shoulder, and Kendall gave a start. The hospital was bustling, particularly the cafeteria where he was seated in the corner.

But Kendall hadn't noticed. He was just so tired. He glanced at the cup of coffee in his hand and sipped. He almost gagged, but forced himself to swallow the cold, weak drink. Hadn't he just gotten the coffee not even five minutes before?

"You fell asleep, didn't you?" Dr. Jensen sat heavily in the chair across from him and pulled the glasses off his face. He grabbed a tissue and cleaned them, his big jowls growing bigger as he looked down with a frown.

Kendall cleared his throat and shook his head. "Of course not. Why would I do that?"

Dr. Jensen narrowed his eyes and glanced at the clock

on the wall across the cafeteria. "Well, what else have you been doing for the past forty-five minutes?"

Kendall blinked and looked at his watch. Twisting it, he groaned, then rubbed his eyes. "Yeah, alright. I might have nodded off."

Jensen sighed and put his glasses back on. "It's not your fault, not really. We haven't been enforcing the days off policy."

"What are you talking about?"

"You've been here for just over three years, and in that time you have taken no vacation days. Zero. Nada. None."

Kendall crossed his arms, pulling his white jacket tight. "I have too. I took off for Holly when she was kidnapped last summer and when she had the babies in March."

He rolled his eyes. "Three days in three years, Kendall."

Kendall ran a hand over his face and sighed. "Yeah, ok. Message received. I'll take an extra day off in a few weeks."

Jensen leaned on the table with a sigh, arms crossing. "No, I'm sorry to be the one to break it to you, but apparently you need to hear it now."

"Hear what?" The man could talk circles around a cow, and Kendall didn't have time for this. He had missed almost an hour of work, and now he needed to catch up.

"The board has planned for you to take a month off work. We're already working on re-scheduling your surgeries to either be before you leave or after you return."

Dread settled in his stomach like a lead weight. An entire month off work? What the hell was he supposed to do for a month without work?

"But—you can't do that."

"We can, and we have. The board is concerned that you're too exhausted. Exhausted doctors make mistakes.

Mistakes lead to lawsuits and safety hazards. You're a liability in this state, Kendall."

Anger boiled in his chest, and he clenched his fist. "I am not a damn liability. I'm a damn good surgeon, and the damn board can take the vacation and—"

"I'm going to stop you right there, son. Look, you need a break. There's nothing wrong with that. It's going to happen. Take a few moments to compose yourself, and if you're too tired or angry for the final surgery today, let me know, and I'll head it up. I might be old, and you might have been the best surgeon in Dallas for a while, but I still know my way around a surgery table."

Kendall jumped to his feet, throwing his coffee into the trash and making it splatter on the inside as he stormed down the hall. Dr. Jensen hauled himself to his feet and caught up.

His meaty hand locked on Kendall's forearm, pulling him to a halt. The man was flushing from the movement, but his eyes were clear and firm.

"I know it's not what you want to hear, but this is happening, Kendall. You need a break, before you make a mistake that you'll regret. Is that what you want? To get so tired that something irreparable happens?"

Kendall sucked in a breath and narrowed his eyes. "No, of course not. I haven't made any mistakes—"

Dr. Jensen slapped his hand on Kendall's shoulder to interrupt.

"Exactly, and you won't, if you take the break. This is going to be a good thing for you, trust me. You've been looking more and more haggard this year, and we're all worried about you."

Kendall's anger deflated. He couldn't fault his coworkers for being worried. Holly had been hounding him too, begging him to be more involved in the babies' lives. His niece and nephew had been born on his fortieth birthday, but he'd only spent about an hour a week with them, and that was probably a generous estimate.

"When is this forced vacation happening?"

Jensen smiled and his shoulders relaxed, clearly relieved that Kendall wasn't putting up more of a fight. "August. There's only a few surgeries going on with back to school. I'll cover all the school physicals, and Jacobs will cover what he needs to, so that's not a problem."

His mind might still be fuzzy from the nap because he couldn't think of another argument against this forced time off.

Kendall shoved his hands in his pockets and shook his head. "But I'm already taking four days off in September for Holly's wedding. Can't I just take that whole week and call it good?"

Jensen nodded and clapped him on the shoulder again. "You need more than a week to reset. Those days in September will help you see that you need to develop that habit of taking a few days off a month. I know our hours as doctors can be inconsistent, but you have to balance work with a personal life. If you don't, you're going to drop dead from exhaustion. Trust me. I've seen it too many times to think about."

He walked off down the hall, leaving Kendall's stomach roiling. A personal life? Hell, he didn't even know what that was anymore. He went to poker night with the guys on Tuesdays when he wasn't working, and he hung out with his sister and her family on Mondays. Other than that, he worked.

He'd thought moving to Crimson Creek three years ago would bring a slower pace of life. So far, he'd just kept doing the same things he'd done in Dallas and in the Army. Work, work, work. Sleep, sleep, sleep.

What the hell was he supposed to do for an entire month off?

Lola wiped the sweat from her brow and fixed her ponytail holder. It was over ninety-four degrees today, but it felt more like a hundred and ten. Much too hot to be outside, working like a dog for Granny's orchard.

An AC/DC song blasted from her phone. Thank God, she needed a break. She strode over to the truck, trying to reach her phone before it stopped ringing.

This was her life now. Lola had quit her city job at the bookkeeping firm and moved back home to take over when Gramps got sick. He'd died right after she'd moved back, then her mom had died last October, and Lord knows Granny couldn't handle the orchard on her own.

Three years down, and they were finally in the black financially. Making a small profit too, enough to keep Granny fed and the lights on. Lola's bookkeeping clients paid for the rest.

She never thought she'd actually be happy living at home at thirty-three, but it provided a certain sense of peace to be outside much of the day. It calmed her when she was anxious or angry. If she were honest, she'd admit to having one of those emotions most of the time in the past few years.

She grabbed the phone, breathlessly answering. "Hello?"

"Lola, did I catch you at a bad time?"

"Gracie! Not at all, hun. What's up?"

Gracie chuckled. "Still no chit chat, huh? Very well. I

need to ask a favor, and I can't really afford for you to say no. So just say yes, and that'll be that."

It was Lola's turn to laugh. "No, sorry. Gotta know the score first, you know that."

Gracie sighed. Her cousin was just a year younger, and they'd spent a lot of summers together at their family reunions. "So I'm getting married."

Lola's heart jumped, and she sat in the truck, turning it on to get some air conditioning going. "I think I'm overheated with this Texas sun. It sounded like you said you're getting married."

"Yep. We met last year at the family reunion—"

"What?" Lola sat up, her mouth hanging open.

"No, no. Not like that. He's not a cousin or anything. Their family was renting the beach house next door."

Lola rubbed her forehead and drank some water. "Oh, alright. Go on then."

"I need you to be my matron of honor."

Lola groaned and banged her head on the steering wheel. "Gracie, you know I don't do the girly shit. I'd be a horrible maid of honor."

"Seriously, I already have everything planned. I just need someone level-headed that I trust in my corner, ready if anything goes wrong."

Lola sighed. She was already helping with Holly's wedding, so she might as well help with her cousin's too. "I'm always in your corner, babe. I got you. Now, what exactly do you need me to do?"

Gracie squealed. "Hallelujah! Okay, for starters, get your butt to the family reunion this year. I know you missed last year because your mom was sick, but you'll be there this year, right?"

Lola's throat closed up, realizing this would be the first

reunion trip without her mom. Those were some of their best memories, some of the only times they hadn't argued. Well, had argued less anyway, once they got to the beach.

She nodded, then cleared her throat. "Yeah, yeah, I'll be there. Second week in August?"

"Yes, and the wedding will be Friday. So we'll spend the whole week hanging by the beach and getting ready for the wedding."

"And kicking butt in the Familympics, right?"

Gracie laughed. "Yes, we're going to invite his family to join us too. They're renting the house next door again, so we'll have the run of both houses. You should be able to have a room for you and your doctor boyfriend too. No more staying in the loft with the singles."

Lola froze, the air blowing in her face. "Say what now?"

"Your boyfriend. Your mom said last summer that she wasn't feeling up to it, and your doctor boyfriend encouraged her to stay home. Plus, he couldn't get off work, and she didn't want to come to the reunion without him, as sick as she was. You are still with him, right? Your Granny said you two were still together when I called a few months ago. Did you break up?"

Lola's blood boiled, and she gripped the steering wheel hard, her knuckles turning white. "Um, no, not exactly."

"Good, because I already got you a sash that says matron of honor. If you were single, I'd have to go get a maid of honor one."

Gracie covered the phone, her words muffled. Then she laughed.

"Mom says hi. She's bugging me to tell her you're coming. We all look forward to meeting him, but Mom is particularly excited. You know how she can get."

Gracie chuckled, but Lola was still frozen in her seat. Her hands were wet with sweat.

She shook it off, pushed the door open, and choked out, "I gotta finish hauling these berries to the house now. Email or text me the details of the wedding and reunion week. Then we can talk whenever about the plans."

"You're the best, cuz. I appreciate you so much, it's not even funny. Love you."

"Love you too. Bye-bye."

She hung up, slipped the phone into her pocket, and methodically placed the buckets of berries into the back of the farm truck. Granny had some explaining to do.

Grab your copy…
vinci-books.com/surgeon-gets-his-girl

About the Author

Jane Poller always wanted to write romance. After years of back and forth, she finally took the plunge and never looked back. She still teaches online and homeschools her teenagers full-time. But with a commercial pilot and Army veteran for a hubby, she has a lot of free time in between his trips to write whatever stories the characters demand of her. She lives in Texas in a small town on four acres with her family of four, plus their two dogs. When she's not doing all the family things, she's reading in the hammock by the pond, writing in the treehouse, quilting and crafting, or arguing with her characters who refuse to do what she wants.

Acknowledgments

I'd like to acknowledge my editors, beta and ARC readers. Your support knows no bounds. Thanks for my girls at Critique Match, those in the Romance Writers Workshops, the Clitiques, and Jenni and Amy. Thanks to the many Discord servers for the friendships, laughs, and tips. Without your support and extra eyes, I'm not sure this would be anywhere near the work of art it is. Thanks to J. Preston for letting me incorporate Carter and Sydney into this story too.